TAKING WHAT'S *Mine*

USA TODAY & WSJ BESTSELLING AUTHOR

SIOBHAN DAVIS

This paperback edition © September 2024
ISBN-13: 978-1-916651-32-6

Edited by Kelly Hartigan (XterraWeb) editing.xterraweb.com
Proofread by Imogen Wells of Final Polish Proofreading
Research and critique by The Critical Touch
Cover design by Shannon Passmore of Shanoff Design
Cover image © bigstockphoto.com
Interior imagery © depositphotos.com
Formatted by Zsuzsanna of Midnight Readers PR using Vellum

The moment I lay eyes on Valentina Ferraro, I know I have to have her.

There's just one teeny problem—her husband.

So, I do what any red-blooded, possessed made man would do and I proposition him.

Five million dollars for one weekend with his beautiful young wife.

He agrees, like I knew he would, because he needs the money and he wants his secrets kept hidden from Don D'Onofrio.

Valentina is livid, but I like my women stubborn and fiery and the more she resists, the more I crave her.

One taste of those lush lips is all it takes to seal my fate.

I'm not giving her back.

I don't care about the existing bad blood between New York and Florida or how this will start a war.

Men have gone into battle for less.

Valentina is the first woman I have wanted to keep, and no other man is ever touching her again.

She is going nowhere, consequences be damned.

I am taking what's mine.

Note From the Author

This is an interconnected stand-alone dark romance set in the *Mazzone Mafia* universe. While you don't need to read any other book to enjoy this one, I recommend reading the other interconnected stand-alones in this world in the suggested reading order for maximum enjoyment.

This book is set six months after the epilogue in *Cruel King of New York*.

This is a dark romance with mature content only intended for an adult audience, and some scenes may be triggering for readers. Please refer to the content warning list on my website: www.siobhandavis.com/triggers

MAZZONE MAFIA UNIVERSE - READING ORDER

Condemned to Love
Forbidden to Love
Scared to Love
Vengeance of a Mafia Queen
Cold King of New York
Cruel King of New York
Taking What's Mine

Prepare to meet the kinkiest, most obsessed, possessive made men of all my mafioso heroes to date. You're welcome ☺ Enjoy!

Mafia & Italian Glossary

Meanings are listed per the context of this book.

- Capo – Italian for captain. A member of a crime family who heads/leads a crew of soldiers.
- Cosa Nostra/La Cosa Nostra – A criminal organization, operating within the US, comprising Italian American crime families.
- Consigliere – Italian for adviser/counselor. A member of a crime family who advises the boss and mediates disputes.
- Don/Boss – The head of a crime family.
- La famiglia/famiglia – Italian for the family/family.
- Made man – A member of the mafia who has been officially initiated/inducted into a crime family.
- Mafioso/Mafiosi – An official member of the mafia.
- Mia amore – Italian for my love.
- Mia regina – Italian for my queen.
- Nonna – Italian for grandma.
- Omertá – The mafia code of silence. Breaking omertá usually means death.
- Signora – Italian for lady.
- Soldati – Italian for soldiers.
- Soldier – A low-ranking member of the mafia who reports to an assigned Capo.
- Tesoro – Italian for treasure.
- The Cartel – Sinaloa cartel from Mexico and a competitor for the drug supply business in Florida.

- The Commission – The governing/ruling body of Cosa Nostra, which sits in New York, the organized crime capital of the US.
- The Five Families – Five crime families who rule in New York, each headed by a boss.
- Underboss – The second in command within a crime family, and an initiated mafia member who works closely with, and reports directly to, the boss.

FIVE NEW YORK FAMILIES

GRECO	MAZZONE	DIPIETRO	ACCARDI	MALTESE
Massimo Greco Don & Commission President	**Bennett Mazzone** Current Don	**Cristian DiPietro** Current Don	**Caleb & Joshua Accardi** Current Dons	**Fiero Maltese** Current Don
Sons	Sons	Brother		Brother
Cassio Greco	**Rowan Mazzone**	**Cruz DiPietro** Deceased		**Zumo Maltese** Underboss
Armis Greco	**Rhys Mazzone**			
Rocco Greco				

ACCARDI/MESSINA FAMILY

Natalia Messina Nee Mazzone — Married — **Gino Accardi** Deceased — Married — **Juliet Accardi** Deceased

Married

Caleb Accardi — Twins — **Joshua Accardi**

Leo Messina

Married

Married

Children

Elisa Accardi Nee Salerno

Gia Accardi Nee Bianchi

Rosa Messina

Step-siblings

Leif Messina

MAZZONE FAMILY

Bennett Mazzone (Ben)	Siblings	Natalia Messina (Nee Mazzone)

Married		Married

Sierra Mazzone (Nee Lawson)	Sisters	Serena Salerno (Nee Lawson)	Leo Messina

Children

Rowan Mazzone	Joshua & Caleb Accardi (Stepsons)
Raven Mazzone	Rosa Messina
Rhys Mazzone	Leif Messina

DIPIETRO FAMILY

Josef DiPietro (Retired) — Married — **Beatrice DiPietro**

Children

Cruz DiPietro Deceased

Cristian DiPietro Current Don

Sabina DiPietro

Married

Bio Son

Adopted Son

Anais DiPietro Deceased

Elio DiPietro Deceased

Half-sisters

Cousins

Alesso Salerno

Catarina Greco nee Conti

GRECO FAMILY

Maximo Greco (Deceased) — Married — **Eleanora Greco**

Carlo Greco Deceased

Primo Greco Deceased

Gabriele Greco

Massimo Greco Current Don

Married

Catarina Greco nee Conti

Children

Cassio Greco

Armis Greco

Bella Greco

Rocco Greco

MALTESE FAMILY

Roberto Maltese Retired — Married — **Ingrid Maltese**

- **Fiero Maltese** Current Don
- **Armani Maltese** Deceased
- **Zumo Maltese**
- **Sofia Maltese**
- **Tullia Maltese**

SALERNO FAMILY

Serena Salerno (Nee Lawson) — Married — **Alesso Salerno** (Las Vegas Don)

Children

Cousins

Married

Caleb Accardi — **Elisa Salerno**

Anais Salerno (Deceased)

Romeo Salerno

Married

Will Salerno

Cruz DiPetrio (Deceased)

Aria Salerno

FLORIDA FAMILY

Vitto D'Onofrio
Current Don

Married

Diana D'Onofrio

Valentina Ferraro
Nee Baresi

Married

Dominic Ferraro
Underboss

Married

Marguerite Ferraro
Deceased

Son

Mother

Cesco Ferraro
Heir

TAKING WHAT'S
Mine

Chapter One
Fiero

"**F**uck. Me. Who is *she?*" I ask Rico, hoping my tongue isn't hanging out of my mouth like a dog in heat as I stare at the woman standing at the hotel bar. I've met my fair share of beautiful women in my forty-three years on this planet. Fucked my fair share too.

But this woman.

This woman is in a league of her own.

Glossy jet-black hair falls in sleek sheets over her shoulders and down her exposed back, brushing her narrow waist and stopping just short of a peach of an ass. Shapely hips lead to long legs encased in a pair of skyscraper heels. One tan leg peeks out from the risqué slit in the left side of her body-hugging red silk dress, and I'm frothing at the mouth. My dick jerks behind the zipper of my dress pants as I imagine that leg wrapped around my neck while I thrust deep inside her.

She grabs her glass of champagne and turns around to face the room, offering me a full-frontal view that almost takes my legs out from under me. All the air is knocked out of my lungs as I stare at her like I've never encountered a woman before.

Is she even mortal? No female could possibly be this stunning. Though stunning doesn't even come close to describing the vision in red silk across the room. Words don't exist in any language to describe her or the potent need flowing through my veins, demanding I charge over there, throw her over my shoulder, and run away with her.

Mine.

My chest heaves as my greedy gaze rakes her from head to foot, lingering over her sumptuous curves and juicy rack. Her dress is unadorned, and on anyone else it might look plain, but it's complete perfection on her, clinging possessively to her womanly curves and winding around her neck. The urge to grab hold of it and rip it from her body is riding me hard. I want to storm over there, strip her bare, and bury myself so deep inside her she'll never get me out.

Mine.

My thoughts shock me because I don't do this.

I don't get attached.

I certainly don't get instantly infatuated the second I lock eyes on a gorgeous woman.

But this woman is an enchantress, and she put a spell on me the moment I spotted her alone at the bar.

I'm aware I'm staring at her in a none too subtle fashion and I'm virtually panting, but I couldn't give a flying fuck.

Mine.

That voice whispers in my ear again, and I couldn't agree more. This glorious creature can only have been made for me, and I'm taking what's clearly mine.

Right fucking now.

Before I move a muscle in her direction, a hand lands on my elbow and a loud throat clearing attempts to claim my attention. "Trouble," Rico says, answering my question. His lips pull tight as he studies the woman who has caught my eye with a puzzled expression.

I wasn't expecting an actual answer. My *consigliere* is as much of a fish out of water here tonight as I am. Although I've been traveling between Miami and New York weekly for three months now, I'm here to work, not party, and I spend most of my time with Don Vitto D'Onofrio and his *soldati*. My job is to mentor the newly crowned Florida don and to spy on him and his men to see if they are loyal to our cause or traitors.

The only females I've crossed paths with are his staff and his vacuous wife Diana. This woman is not someone I've met before. I'd never have forgotten a face like that. It's as if she's been carefully carved from the most precious porcelain and every line, dip and curve is testament to master craftsmanship. Exquisite high cheekbones reside underneath flawless olive skin. Piercing green eyes, framed by thick black lashes, roam the room in pursuit of something. Her plump red lips part infinitesimally, and my eyes are glued to her stunning face as I watch the carefully constructed façade slip for a split second.

"I know that look, and you can't afford that here, Fiero," my *consigliere* warns, pulling me back into the conversation. "The gala is swarming with made men, and I'm betting she belongs to one. No woman who looks like her could possibly be single."

His words are like a knife straight through my heart, but I won't be deterred. "I don't care." I smooth a hand down the front of my tuxedo jacket, preparing to go to her when an unfortunately familiar face lands in front of her. "No fucking way," I hiss, shooting daggers at D'Onofrio's number two as he slides his arm around the beauty in red.

"She's wearing a ring. I'm guessing she's Dominic's wife," Rico muses, scrubbing a hand along his clean-shaven jaw. "Valentina. I think that's her name."

Valentina.

I look over at her with greater appreciation. It's a beautiful name for an even more beautiful woman. It truly suits her, and I love how it rolls fluidly off my tongue. "He's never mentioned her to me."

It's not that surprising. There is little love lost between Dominic Ferraro and me. D'Onofrio's underboss is an imbecile and a lazy one at that. He's also hiding secrets. Secrets that could get him killed. I haven't disclosed my recent discovery to Vitto as I'm still unsure he's trustworthy. Although I haven't found evidence confirming foul play or linking him to the deceased Vegas don in ways other than a shared love of partying, there is a reason Cruz DiPietro was flying to Florida weekly in the months leading up to his disappearance, and I'm determined to find out what he was up to.

I haven't divulged my discovery to The Commission either. The Commission is the centralized governing body for all Italian American *mafioso* in the US, and it was re-established by Bennett Mazzone sixteen years ago to restore order to *La Cosa Nostra* across all states. We enjoyed relative peace and prosperity until recently when a few bad eggs attempted a takeover. It ended badly for Cruz and his wife, and we took the rest of the players out before they could destroy everything we've built. Now we're in damage-control mode. Florida and Vegas are far from settled, and we're attempting to restore order. Hence why I'm spending so much time here.

My fellow board members receive an update at our weekly meetings. I appraise them of developments in Florida and the newly promoted Don Alessandro Salerno ensures they're informed of the situation on the ground in Vegas.

"She was overseas until recently," Rico informs me. "Visiting her ailing grandmother in Sicily, I believe."

"Someone's done their homework."

"It's what you pay me to do."

I keep my eyes trained on that asshole Dominic and the woman in red while I converse with my trusted *consigliere*.

Enrico Bianchi is one in a million, and I'm never letting him retire. The Maltese *famiglia* would not run as smoothly without him. I inherited my underboss from my father, and he was a useless piece of shit. The only favor he ever did me was dying two months ago and finally ridding me of the last of my father's toxic legacy. Rico and I have run the show effortlessly for years, but now we are making way for my younger brother. Zumo was officially sworn in as my underboss the day after the funeral, and Rico and I are committed to showing him the ropes and getting him up to speed as quickly as possible.

But I'm digressing. I don't want to talk about made men or politics. Not unless we're discussing the imminent demise of the asshole currently squeezing my goddess's curvy ass.

A low growl rips from my lips as I glare at him.

A deep chuckle rumbles from Rico's chest. "Easy, tiger. You look like you're ready to rip his head from his shoulders."

"Reading minds now, Bianchi?" I arch a brow and glance at my friend and adviser out of the corner of my eye.

"Whatever you're planning, don't do it."

"Who says I'm planning anything?" I lie as ideas churn through my head.

"Like I said, I know that look. It's been a while since I've seen it."

"Don Maltese, it's so lovely to meet you," a female with a high-pitched voice says as she steps in front of me.

I don't even give her a passing look, uncaring who she is, what she looks like, or what she wants. She's not the first woman to approach me tonight, and she most likely won't be the last. There are not many bachelor dons of my age and caliber knocking about, and they all want to be the one to tie me down. "You're blocking my view," I snap, sidestepping her so I keep the lady in red in my sights.

"My father is—"

I tune her out and walk away, knowing Rico will smooth things over as I stride with purpose toward the object of my affection now that a plan has formed in my mind.

Ignoring outstretched hands and calls of my name, I keep walking with dogged determination as I mentally formalize the finer details.

Valentina's head snaps to the left, and her gaze ensnares mine as if she heard me silently calling to her.

The world spins on its axis the second our eyes meet, and the room quickly fades out of existence. Sound is instantly muted. All I hear is my heart pounding against my rib cage and my lust-heavy breaths. My mouth turns dry, and my tongue darts out, wetting my hungry lips. A surge of electricity ignites the space between us, flexing and writhing like an uncontrollable bolt of lightning slamming into both of us at full force. Her eyes widen for a fraction in shocked surprise, and I'm thrilled my presence seems to affect her as much as hers does me.

Up close, she is much younger than my first impression. I had put her at late twenties, but I think she's younger. Her skin has a radiant glowing appearance, and there isn't a line or a blemish on her almost translucent flesh. She is incredible. Intoxicating. Mesmerizing. Easily the most oxygen-stealing beauty I have ever laid my eyes upon.

I've got to have her.

There is no question or hesitation.

She's *mine*.

Vibrant emerald eyes skim me from head to toe as she drinks me in, and I detect a faint blush crawling up her neck and onto her cheeks. In a flash, that same fake pleasant look appears on her face as if she's just pulled a mask over her features.

6

Taking What's Mine

I slam to a halt in front of her, ignoring whatever outraged expression is no doubt on Dominic's face. Taking her free hand, I lift it to my lips and brush my mouth across her silky skin, inwardly fist-pumping the air when she shivers. "Who are you, and where have you been all my life?" I'm usually smoother than this, but I'm genuinely awestruck in her presence. My words are thick with desire, and I'm staring at her in a way that is blatantly obvious.

I want her, and she knows it.

Her husband knows it too.

I have never been the kind of man to disrespect other made men. Massimo—my best friend and current president of The Commission—and I were no saints in our youth, racking up considerable notches on our bed posts, but the one hard and fast rule we never broke was not messing with any *mafioso* wives.

Right now, I couldn't give two shits if she's married or who she's married to.

It no longer matters because she belongs *to me*. With me.

I'll annihilate anyone who stands in my way.

Mine. Mine. Mine.

She tries to withdraw her hand, but I hold on to it tight, smirking as my eyes lower to her tempting mouth, and I wonder what she'd do if I slammed my lips onto hers and devoured her like I want to.

"Don Maltese! This is the height of disrespect to me." An annoying gnat tugs on my arm, attempting to pull me away from the immortal beauty staring at me with a slight frown.

The feel of her small, warm, soft hand in mine sends a flood of heat scorching through my veins. If I'd get away with hand-cuffing her to me so she'd never leave my side, I'd do it in a heartbeat.

"Fiero." Rico's gravelly voice drags me kicking and screaming back into the land of the living. Noise returns like a thousand bongos hammering on my skull. "What are you doing?" he whispers in my ear.

"Let go of my wife," Dominic Ferraro says, shoving his fat head all up in my personal space.

"You're too old for her," I blurt because I seem to have lost all control over my vocal cords.

"And you're not? Is that the implication?" Shock mixes with disbelief and anger in his tone.

"I'm not implying anything," I retort without looking at him. I'm merely stating facts even if few in our world would agree. It's not that unusual to see an older made man with a much younger woman even if forced marriages are more a thing of the past now.

"You're not that much younger than me," he scoffs.

Try eight years, fuckface. Keeping a firm grip of his wife's hand, I briefly eyeball the slimy toad blocking me from the woman of my fantasies. "I look decades younger, and that's what really counts."

I work out and take care of myself. I'm in the best shape of my life, and there isn't an inch of fat anywhere on my body. Women trip over themselves to get to me whenever I show up at Club H, and I could have my pick of any woman if I wanted. I don't indulge like I did in my youth because it's lost its appeal, but I know I'm a catch. I'm fit and healthy, which is more than can be said for the whiskey-guzzling, red-faced jabroni huffing and puffing in front of me. I let my eyes purposely trail over his tight-fitting suit jacket, the button ready to pop where it's straining to contain his considerable gut. He doesn't even bother dying his hair to disguise the abundance of gray, and we won't even talk about his body odor issue. There's a reason I've kept my physical distance from the smelly fucker.

How is this woman married to him? It's a travesty. I can't imagine she leads a good life with this cretin, and it's no wonder she has to plaster false smiles on her face. I'd want to throw myself off a roof if I was chained to this old fat fuck.

"Remove your hand from my wife, or we'll have a big problem, Maltese." Dominic narrows his eyes at me.

"It's Don Maltese, and I'm quaking in my fucking boots."

"Is there an issue here?" Don D'Onofrio asks, materializing on my left. It seems we've garnered some unwanted attention.

Reluctantly, I let Valentina's hand go. I instantly feel bereft without her touch, and that should concern me, but it doesn't. All I can think about is getting my hands all over her and making her mine. She hasn't said anything, but she hasn't dragged her gaze away from me, and it's clear this chemistry is not one-sided.

"No issue." I flash Vitto a signature grin before pinning Ferraro with a warning look. "Dom and I were just discussing a proposal, but it's a private matter."

Brief excitement flares in Dominic's eyes before he conceals it. It's no wonder he's millions of dollars in debt. His poker face is shit.

Vitto looks to his underboss, and Dominic clears his throat. "It's all good, boss. I was just introducing Valentina to Don Maltese."

My gaze gravitates to hers again, and her eyes hold mine in silent challenge as we stare at one another, only breaking away when interrupted.

"Ah, yes." Vitto's soft gaze travels over Dominic's wife, lingering on her chest for a few beats too long if you ask me.

My spine stiffens, and I level a glare on Don D'Onofrio, which he either doesn't notice or he purposely ignores as he leans down and kisses Valentina on each cheek. "It's great to see you. I hope you are well. We've missed you."

"I'm well, thank you," she purrs in a voice dripping with sex.

My cock jerks behind my zipper, and tingles of desire ghost over every part of my body.

Fuck. Me.

Everything about this woman turns me on like no woman has ever before.

"You should meet Diana for coffee next week. I know she'd love to catch up."

"I'd like that." Valentina flashes a wide fake smile at her don that he wholeheartedly laps up because he's a fucking schmuck when it comes to beautiful women.

"I'll get her to call you," he adds, his eyes raking another path over Valentina's body.

Dominic doesn't call him out for it because there are clearly different rules for his don.

"I'll talk to you later about that other matter," Dominic says, nodding at his boss.

"Fiero. Rico." Vitto gestures at us before wandering away to talk to other guests.

"What proposal?" Dominic asks the second his boss is out of earshot.

"Let's take this somewhere more private," I suggest, unwilling to discuss this in front of Valentina.

Dominic curls his arm around his wife, hauling her in close to his body, and another growl escapes my lips. "Anything you want to say can be said here."

His smug grin rubs me the wrong way, and I want to riddle his body with bullets and remove the obstacle between me and heaven.

But I'm at a charity gala for victims of gun violence, surrounded by Miami's finest made men—yes, it's irony at its finest—and it would be distasteful, more than a little stupid, and an exaggeration to murder a man with an audience purely because I want to devour his young wife.

Besides, I don't need to eliminate Ferraro forever. Just for one weekend. So I can get my fix of this stunning creature who has rendered my brain and body to mush. I just need to fuck Valentina every which way from Sunday to sate this unquenchable desire for her, and then I can give her back to the oaf and return to my happy bachelor ways.

"Fiero." Rico attempts to halt whatever's about to go down again, but I'm beyond the point of reason.

This is crazy and not how I do things. I've never paid for a woman before. Never had to. I could steal her away from him for a few nights, but if he got wind of it, it'd cause untold problems within The Commission, and I don't want to cause issues for my buddy. It's better to do it like this. Transparent and with the full knowledge and approval of her husband.

"Back down, Bianchi." I slant Rico a look of caution so he knows to hold his tongue and remember his place.

A muscle clenches in his jaw, but he keeps his lips sealed, knowing me well enough to understand there is no talking me down when I set my sights on something.

"I don't have all day," Dominic adds, his smirk growing wider.

"Watch it." I step right up to him and speak in a low tone so no one outside our little circle will hear. "You don't hold any power in this situation. I hold all the cards. If you don't want me to divulge all your little secrets to D'Onofrio, you'll keep your mouth shut unless the word yes trips off your tongue."

Panic flares in his eyes for a few beats before he gets it under control.

Like I said, dude has zero game.

He tugs his wife in closer, digging his nails into her waist, and I'm reconsidering eliminating him for eternity.

We glare at one another, and I clench my fists at my side while contemplating the chances of us making it out of here alive if we start whaling on this asshole. But he doesn't matter. He's as inconsequential as the dirt under my shoe, so I force myself to calm down and stick to the agenda.

I flick my eyes to Valentina, noting the wariness in her gaze mixing with a flicker of anger that was missing until now. I arch a brow, and she narrows her eyes at me. My mouth lifts in a grin as excitement trickles through my veins. She's not as indifferent or coolly pleasant as she'd like everyone to believe, and all it does is ramp my intrigue, and my lust, to new heights.

"You're drawing attention again," Rico quietly states. "Get on with it."

Dragging my gaze from wife to husband, I fix Dominic with a haughty glare and say, "My proposal is nonnegotiable. You take it or leave it." My eyes dart to Valentina for a fleeting second. "I'll pay you five million dollars for one weekend with your wife."

Chapter Two
Valentina

My eyes pop wide in shock as I stare at Don Maltese, struggling to believe someone like him would pay money for any woman when women must be crawling all over him to willingly share his bed. His bright blue eyes vibrate with possessiveness, entitlement, and anticipation, and it shouldn't excite me, but it does. I should be outraged. I *am* outraged. I don't care how powerful he is in our world, I'm not a commodity to be traded on a whim. How dare he do this! How dare he reduce me to the sum of my looks.

He's no better than my husband or any of the other men who frequent our house.

But...the difference is the scorching-hot attraction between us.

As much as I loathe him for proposing this, I can't deny the frisson of excitement simmering under my veins at the thought of being with a man like him.

Which is a cruel dilemma, because I know my money-hungry husband will take the bait.

I finally discover a man I *want* to have sex with, and he is already treating me like a whore.

I won't submit to him. I don't care how much Fiero pays Dom. I'm not making this easy for him.

I felt Fiero's eyes on me before, the intensity of his stare so all-consuming it felt like a physical caress. My heart immediately started racing, and all the fine hairs on my arms stood at attention. I scanned the ballroom looking for him, purposely not glancing his way when I discovered the source of my strange feelings.

The gossip wasn't wrong—he is drop-dead gorgeous. His imposing figure looms over me now, clad in custom-fit Armani. Broad shoulders descend into a chest I'm sure is carved to perfection under his crisp white shirt and abs I could probably eat my dinner off. Bulging biceps struggle against the sleeves of his tux jacket, and the pants barely disguise muscular thighs. His white-blond hair tumbles in messy waves across the top of his tan brow. A strong Roman nose, full lips, and a chiseled jaw coated in an artful layer of dark hair completes the look, and he's undoubtedly the full package.

No wonder all the wives and girlfriends were talking incessantly about him when I returned home from Sicily two weeks ago. He has every female creaming their panties and giggling like schoolgirls.

I get it now though.

He has a commanding presence you can't ignore, and every time he pins me in place with those gorgeous blue eyes, I stop breathing for a few seconds. I can't believe he's unmarried and can only assume it's by choice.

Tension is rife in the air as Don Maltese waits for my husband to respond. Dom will keep him waiting because he thinks it gives him an edge. He may have decades on me, but my husband is a damn fool.

Dom's fingers dig into my hip, but I barely feel the stab of pain. My husband is internally rubbing his hands in glee at this unexpected change in his fortune. Little does Fiero know he could have secured me for way less or nothing at all in exchange for him keeping quiet about Dominic's gambling addiction. If Vitto knew the men Dom was indebted to, he'd be shitting his pants, but our don is as unobservant as he is ineffectual. Surely it can't be long before The Commission replaces him.

I hope that's not why Fiero's here even if speculation suggests that's the reason. I couldn't tolerate being around him if this is the effect he has on me.

This won't be like the others.

This is just like with *him*.

Except he never paid in cold hard cash. An icy shiver tiptoes up my spine, and I barely resist the urge to squeeze my eyes shut to ward off the slew of living nightmares playing out again in my head.

"Ten million," Dom says, and I almost choke on my own breath.

He is such a dumbass.

"Surely I don't need to explain the definition of nonnegotiable." Fiero fixes a lethal stare on my husband, and my pathetic heart thumps wildly against my chest wall.

This can't be happening. I thought my life had sunk as far as it was going to go, but this is a new low. If I thought the others ruined me, it will be nothing on the wreckage left after being with this man.

"No," I blurt, knowing I will earn my husband's wrath but uncaring in the moment. "I'm not for sale. I'm not a prostitute." Though my husband does his best to make me feel like I am even if money doesn't change hands. "I'm married," I add, flashing him the Ferraro family heirloom secured on my ring finger. "I'm off-limits."

"Quiet, Valentina." Dom embeds his jagged nails in my side, and I wince as pain shuttles through me.

Fire dances in Fiero's eyes, and his fists clench tighter at his side. "You're hurting her."

"She's *my* wife." Dom sneers at the younger, hotter, more-powerful man. "I can do what the fuck I want to her."

The man standing at Don Maltese's side straightens up, leveling Dom with a sharp look. From the description, I'm guessing he's Rico Bianchi, Fiero's *consigliere*. "Wives are to be revered and cherished. Always."

"Tell that to your boss." Dom points one stubby finger in Fiero's direction.

"It's clear I misread the situation." Don Maltese takes a step back. "Please excuse me." He moves to turn away, and my idiotic husband falls for the play, lunging forward and grabbing Fiero's arm.

"Let's not be hasty. We can discuss this in private as you suggested."

Fiero maintains a dispassionate expression while eyeballing my husband. "I don't like repeating myself, Dominic."

"Yes," Dom blurts. "We have a deal, but let's discuss the specifics."

"I don't agree." I straighten up and thrust my shoulders back. "If this happens, it won't be consensual, and I won't cooperate."

Dom is boring holes in the side of my head, and I know I'll pay for it later, but I have to at least try to stand my ground.

"Ignore her." My husband roughly grabs my elbow and spins me around. "Follow me."

"You're hurting me," I grit out as Dom manhandles me from the room.

"I want her unmarked," Don Maltese says, coming up on Dom's other side. "Or the deal is off."

"You can't tell me what to do with my own wife," Dom snarls, releasing my elbow and snatching my hand in his clammy palm.

"Five million dollars says I can."

Dom purses his lips, wisely shutting up as he leads me out of the ballroom. Eyeballs are glued to our backs, and I can only imagine the gossip doing the rounds after tonight.

Fiero hangs back with Rico, and they talk in hushed tones as we make our way along the corridor toward the back of the hotel.

Dom leads us into a small room that is empty except for stacks of chairs tucked against one wall. "Talk," he says, spinning us around to face the two New Yorkers, keeping a firm grip on my hand.

"I'll pick up Valentina at eight on Friday morning and return her to you before midnight on Sunday," Don Maltese says. "She'll come to New York with me for the weekend."

Apart from my recent trip, I have rarely left Florida since moving here at eighteen. I have always wanted to visit New York, and I'm equal parts thrilled and terrified.

Fiero fixes me with a hypnotizing stare. "I'll show you a good time and give you more pleasure than you've ever known."

I'm betting he will, but that doesn't make this right! The absolute nerve of this man to think he can just snap his fingers, buy me for the weekend, and I'll happily go along with it! "Your arrogance is not attractive, and you should know I'll fight you every step of the way. You'll have to force me."

"Shut up, Valentina." Dom yanks firmly on my hand, and he's literally vibrating with anger.

It's been a long time since I've fought him because I learned rather quickly that the easier option is to relent and do what I'm told. I would not have survived the six years of my marriage if I hadn't reached that conclusion in the first six months. But this situation is different. I don't think I can come out of this unscathed because Fiero Maltese has the power to make me feel again, and that will be my permanent ruination.

I can't go with him. I can't do it and survive.

"She's all talk. She'll do what she's told." Dom pins his cold gray eyes on me, silently cautioning me to get with the program. "She's had plenty of practice."

"What does that mean?" Fiero asks with a crease in his brow.

Dom smiles, but it doesn't reach his eyes. "It means I've trained her well, and she'll come through for you."

Embarrassment flares in my chest, but I disguise it behind my usual mask. Not for the first time, I curse my papa for forcing me to marry this uncaring bastard, and I hate my mama for failing to stop it and then abandoning me to my fate.

"When will I have the money?" Dom adds.

Fiero scrubs a hand across his jaw as he stares at me, taking a few beats to reply. "I'll deposit one million now as a gesture of good will, a second mil on Friday, and the rest when I return her on Sunday."

Dom's mouth opens to object, but he quickly closes it. He thrusts out his hand. "Deal."

Just like that. With no boundaries in place to ensure my safety. I have always known he doesn't care but having it so blatantly and publicly confirmed is the ultimate slap in the face. I work hard to school a neutral expression on my face because I refuse to give either of these men any more power over me.

A wave of disgust sweeps over Rico's face, and he does nothing to conceal it. Compassion glimmers in his eyes when he looks at me, but I present him with the dead-eyed stare I have perfected over the years, unable and unwilling to accept this stranger's silent comfort.

Don Maltese is maintaining a cool expression though his eyes flare brighter, confirming his delight. He shakes my husband's hand. "This remains strictly confidential between us four. No one else is to know."

"Of course," Dom lies, lowering his hand to his side. There's no way he won't be bragging about this to his cronies.

"Good doing business with you."

"Asshole." It slips out before I can stop it.

"Show Don Maltese some respect," Dom hisses, having changed his tune.

"I'll show him respect when he does the same for me."

Fiero moves in closer to me. "I have never paid to spend time with a woman. I don't have to. Women beg me to fuck them. It's rare I do the chasing."

Wow. He truly is an ass.

His mouth curves in a cocky smile, and I want to punch him in his smug, handsome face. At least if he keeps this up, it will be easy to hate him, and hopefully that will keep the attraction at bay.

"Five million dollars shows a hell of a lot of respect," he adds. "You'd do well to remember it."

"You're lucky he wants you unmarked," Dom barks, shoving me into the back of our Lincoln town car.

He'll be in for one hell of a surprise then.

I scoot to the far side of the seat and briefly close my eyes, wondering what I did to deserve this kind of life. Dom slams the door behind him and instructs the driver to head for home. Before I can buckle my seat belt, he lifts me by the waist and sets me up on the seat on all fours. "But you're still due a punishment for that stunt you pulled." He shoves my head down onto the ripped weathered leather seat and forces my legs apart.

Shame slams into me knowing Bruno will bear witness to this

because the privacy screen died last week, and there is no money to repair it. The old sleazebag will probably get off on it. Cool air washes over my scarred ass cheeks as Dom lifts my dress, bunching it at the waist.

"You nearly cost me five million dollars!" he bellows, ripping my cheap lace thong off my body. "I want to whip you bloody," he threatens though he's never physically beaten or lashed me. The sounds of his zipper lowering churns the acid in my stomach. I grip the seat firmly and retreat to that safe place in my head I always go to. His cruel words fade away as I zone out, and I barely feel his vile cock as it breaches my dry walls because I'm already someplace else.

Chapter Three
Fiero

"You've gone mad," Rico says, standing at my side at the curb as we watch the old Lincoln pull out onto the road. "I should have you committed. What the hell were you thinking?" Incredulity mixed with concern splays across his face.

"I have to have her," I say, shrugging because I don't know where this has come from except it's instinctual.

"She's not yours to have," he argues as we jog across the road to where my car is.

"She's all mine next weekend, and it's agreed with her husband." Slipping off my jacket and bow tie, I toss them on the back seat before climbing behind the wheel.

Rico shuts the passenger door with more force than necessary. "She doesn't agree, Fiero, and that's all that matters. It's not like you to blatantly disrespect any woman. I don't think you should start now."

"She agrees, Rico," I tell him, checking my mirrors before maneuvering out into the quieter nighttime traffic. "Her body was doing all the talking. She wants me as much as I want her."

He buckles his belt and stares at me. "She's right. You are an asshole."

"I know, but I'm still doing this."

"Why? Out of all the women you could have, why her?" He shakes his head. "I don't understand it. You have never gone after any made man's wife before. Why now?"

"I can't explain it, but she sets my blood on fire. No woman has ever impacted me the way she does. One look from her, and I want to pillage and ravish every single inch of that gorgeous body."

"Well, that's just great." He throws his head back and groans.

I chuckle. "Relax, man. You're making a big deal out of nothing. I'll bring her home next weekend and give her the weekend of her dreams. I'll fuck this all out of my system and then send her back to her pig of a husband. She'll be a fond memory I'll think of from time to time." The words feel all wrong as I say them, but I'm not delusional.

This is a one-and-done scenario.

I've never wanted more from any woman, and that's not changing now.

Rico's eyes bore into the side of my face, and I cast a quick glance at him. "If you truly believe that, then you're as clueless as you are crazy and an even bigger asshole than I thought."

I'm not surprised Bianchi is struggling to accept this. He worships the ground his wife Frankie walks on and he's one of the legit good guys. "You're overreacting. I'll give her the time of her life. Take her out to the best restaurant and maybe a show. In between, I'll worship her body, showing her more pleasure than that prick has ever given her. Any objections she has will be gone within the first hour, trust me. By the end, she'll be begging me to keep her."

He rolls his eyes. "If this is what you were like as a young man, I'm glad I wasn't your *consigliere* back then."

"I was worse. Way worse." I flash him a wicked grin. "Man, the things Massimo and I got up to." I waggle my brows. "Those were fun times."

"If you say so."

"I know you don't get it because you got hitched to Frankie when you were barely out of diapers."

"Slight exaggeration, but I don't regret my decision to marry my wife. Best thing I ever did was put a ring on her finger and knock her up." He tilts his head to the side, eyeballing me as I take the turn for the road leading to my house. "You should be finding a woman to settle down with, not chasing a woman who already belongs to another."

Irritation bats at me. "She doesn't belong to him. She loathes him, and he doesn't appreciate her."

"Yeah." A heavy sigh leaves his lips. "I picked up on that too. I'm betting theirs was an arranged marriage and she was forced into it by her parents."

"No betting or digging required. One hundred percent that's how that happened. There's no way a woman like Valentina willingly chose marriage to that dick."

"Want me to find out?"

I shake my head and look over at him while I wait for my front gates to open. "Why bother? I told you this is a one-off, and I meant it. Her marriage is none of my business."

"I still can't believe you paid that much for her."

I drive slowly along the short drive toward my two-story Spanish-style hacienda. "I'd have paid four or five times more if I had to."

It's barely a dip in the ocean of my finances. I majored in financial investment during my undergraduate studies, and I put my knowledge to good use. Massimo and I invested wisely, which is how we were able to start our own business, Rinascita, in our early twenties. It's hugely successful and it's made us very rich.

Combine that with our earnings from our *mafioso* criminal enterprises—namely our Colombian drug production facility in Cali—and we're obscenely wealthy. I have my own personal property development portfolio, and I continue to invest heavily in the stock market. It's all paid off, and I'm more than comfortable. I have more money than I know what to do with. Five million is chump change to me. I'd have paid way more for the pleasure of Valentina's company if I'd had to.

Rico's eyes almost bug out of his head as I pull my car into one of the bays in my parking garage. "You are literally insane," he says.

"It's not like I'm struggling for money, and that prick needs it." I shut off the engine. "I hope he uses some of it to buy a new car. That piece of shit looked like it was falling apart."

"How bad is his gambling debt?"

I rub the back of my neck. "It's considerable, and the cartel is apparently running out of patience."

"That could cause issues for D'Onofrio and for us in a larger context."

"I'm aware," I say before getting out. Rico joins me. We walk toward the side door that leads into the house. "I have informed the board Dom is problematic and I'm handling it." The intel on the cartel is new, but I'll update the board on that after my weekend with the stunning Valentina in case I need to use that as leverage for a little longer.

"I'm sure they weren't expecting you to bail him out and bed his wife in the bargain."

I slam to a halt and turn to face him. "No one is to know about that deal. This stays between us."

"My loyalty is with you, and I would never discuss your private business. You know that."

I do. Rico is one of the most trustworthy men I've ever

encountered. I resume walking. "Just ensuring we're on the same page."

"For the record, I want to state this is a really bad idea, and on a personal level, I completely disapprove. You are railroading that young woman, and it's not right."

"Your disapproval has been noted," I say, punching the code into the alarm keypad and stepping foot in my house.

Rico emits a deep sigh. "But it doesn't change anything."

I let a smirk run free. "You got that right. Next weekend, Valentina Ferraro is mine and I intend to make the most of my time with her."

"Show me who you have on your list," I demand of Vitto the following morning as we sit across the table from one another out on the patio area at the rear of his house. It's a glorious day, and I'm hoping to finish up here early to go for a run on South Beach, followed by a swim.

"Do we have to do this now?" Vitto rubs his temples while nursing his usual ginger hangover cure drink. "Can't it wait until Monday? I didn't crawl into bed until five." He pouts like a toddler on the verge of throwing a tantrum.

And this is why the board sent me to mentor this goon. Despite his failings, I quite like the man. He's not a bad guy, just lazy, unambitious, and out of his depth. He's had no one to show him the ropes, having been thrown in the deep end when his father died suddenly two and a half years ago, leaving his playboy heir in charge years earlier than he was expecting. He really needs to get his act together and fast. We can't have a weak link in a key territory, and Vitto knows he's on borrowed time.

"You've got to quit the partying, Vitto." I take a sip from my coffee as I study the man. "And quit with the womanizing. It's not a good look for a don, and it doesn't do anything to foster confidence with the board."

"I never wanted to be a don," he grumbles, staring out at acres of pristine manicured lawns.

"Not everyone does, but you are where you are, and there's no point bitching about it. Your men are looking to you for leadership, and you're not providing the right kind of leadership or setting the right example."

"I'm relating to them," he argues, dragging a hand through his chocolate-brown hair. "How is showing them I'm on their level a bad thing?"

Grant me fucking patience. I count to ten in my head before replying. "You're not on their level. That's the whole point. You're their boss. The most powerful man in the state of Florida, and you need to start acting like it. The Commission is not going to allow mismanagement to continue for much longer, which is why we need to do this now. You need to appoint a new *consigliere*, and you need to step up and quit all the bullshit. Russo's been dead for almost seven months, and you haven't appointed a replacement. That should have been done immediately, and while we're at it, we should consider Ferraro's replacement too."

His eyes widen. "I'm not replacing Dom. He's my right hand, and if you think things are mismanaged now, it would be ten times worse without my underboss."

Debatable. "I'm talking about succession planning. You need to be prepared for all eventualities. If Dom dropped dead tomorrow"—like if he was taken out by the cartel for unpaid gambling debts—"where would that leave you?"

"Cesco would take over. He's his heir, and he's champing at the bit for more responsibility."

My brow furrows. "How old is he?"

"Nineteen."

"He's not Valentina's son then." The words are out of my mouth before I can trap them.

"Dom's kids are from his first wife, Marguerite. She died six years ago, and he married Valentina a few months later."

I could extract intel from Vitto without much effort, but I'd rather get my information from one of his *soldati*. I'm more likely to get the full picture that way. "You can't seriously think a nineteen-year-old could be appointed as your underboss?"

He rolls his eyes. "Of course not! But Dom isn't going anywhere for years. By the time he retires, Cesco will be of age and all trained up."

I thump him on the arm. It's either that or knock him out cold. "Nothing is guaranteed, and you need other options in case anything happens sooner. After we've hired you a *consigliere*, we'll discuss other potential successors for the underboss role."

He opens his mouth, to object, no doubt, but I cut across him, confirming the end of that particular discussion. "Give me your top three names."

He reels them off, and two are on the list I have compiled. "I have Caruso and Pucci too, but DeAngelo is an unreliable drunk, and he'd make a terrible adviser."

"He works well with Dom, and he's been around the block. He's got a lot of experience."

"That is of fuck all benefit if he's too trashed to form intelligent decisions or share that experience." Taking a pen, I draw a line through his name. "He's out. I think you should consider Davide Gallo."

"No way. Absolutely no fucking way."

"What is your beef with him?"

"I don't—"

"Darling! There you are!" Diana D'Onofrio totters across the patio on high heels, sporting a tight, short bubblegum-pink dress and a head of big blonde curls that barely move as she walks. She's pretty, if you're into over-the-top surgically enhanced, high-maintenance women.

I inwardly groan, praying for an intervention. I cannot stand that vapid woman. A part of me understands fully why Vitto constantly cheats on her.

"I'm busy, honey. Was there something you needed?"

She attempts to toss her hair over her shoulders, but it refuses to budge under the mountain of hairspray clinging to her bleached-blonde strands. "I just came to say hi and goodbye." She giggles as she leans down and kisses her husband before turning her attention to me. "Hello, Fiero." She puffs out her chest before leaning down and kissing my cheek, her lips dangerously close to my mouth.

I cough as I'm enveloped in cloying perfume that almost chokes me.

"It's Don Maltese," Vitto corrects her for the umpteenth time.

"Don't be so silly." She straightens up, touching my upper arm for a few lingering beats as she stares at my mouth. She hasn't outright hit on me, but she's cutting a very fine line. If I gave her any indication I was into it, she'd be all over me like a rash. "Fiero and I are friends."

That's news to me, but she's inconsequential, and it's not worth going into battle. "It's fine, Vitto. Forget about it."

"Where are you going?" he asks.

"To brunch with the girls." She repositions her dress so her fake boobs are bulging out of the top. I turn away, repulsed by the sight. I'm a boob man through and through, but they've got to be natural. No offense to any lady with fake tits, but they don't do anything for me. I'd take a small pair of real tits over a large pair of fake ones any day.

"Did you invite Valentina?" He arches a brow.

An instant scowl appears on his wife's face, and I pay more attention. "Do I have to?"

"Be nice, Di. You know she doesn't have many friends here."

"I wonder why that is," she murmurs in a nasty tone under her breath.

"Invite her." Vitto levels his wife with a stern look. "And be nice. If you welcome her into your circle, the other wives will too."

"Why do you even care?" She folds her arms across her chest and glares at her husband.

Some silent communication passes between them I can't read. "She's my underboss's wife, and she doesn't get out much. Would it really kill you to invite her occasionally?" he says a few beats later, and I can't help thinking that's for my benefit.

"She doesn't fit in, Vitto, and the others don't like her. You don't need me to spell out why."

"That's enough, Diana," he snaps, unfurling to his full height until he's towering over his much shorter spouse. "I don't like giving you orders, but it's necessary. You will invite her, and you *will* include her." The "or else" part is left off, which is a shame as I'd love to know what he'll do to her if she doesn't play ball. And why he seems so invested in Valentina. Knots twist in my gut at the thought he might be sleeping with her. *Is this why Diana is so hostile and resistant?*

I don't know Valentina, but something tells me she would hate that Vitto is going to bat for her like this. Especially if she *is* fucking her husband's boss. I doubt she wants to spend time with Diana either. They seem like oil and water.

"Fine."

"Good girl." Vitto grabs his wife and plants a hard kiss on her lips before swatting her on the ass.

She stalks off with a face like thunder.

Vitto reclaims his seat, cocking his head and expecting me to ask. But I'm not going there with him.

"Right." I lean forward, pulling the paper toward us. "Where were we?"

Chapter Four
Valentina

S taring out the window, I block the inane chatter surrounding me wishing genies were real and I had three wishes. Though I'd only need one to free myself from this hell that is my so-called life. We've been here hours, and I swear I've lost a few brain cells listening to these women. We have nothing in common, and I know they don't want me here. They're being forced to accept my company because I'm Dom's wife.

"Oh, look," Diana says, pointing one long slim finger at the window. "There's Fiero." We all swivel to watch the glorious specimen that is Fiero Maltese as he jogs along the boardwalk in the tiniest pair of training shorts I've ever seen. Sweat glistens on his bare chest, and my previous assumption wasn't wrong.

I could easily eat my dinner off his six-pack.

Damn. There is no point denying it. He's sex on legs, and I'm so screwed next weekend.

"He's so fucking hot." Darlene's dreamy tone matches the nauseating expression on her face.

"If I got my hands on him, I'd handcuff him to my bed and ride him to death," Kim announces to a chorus of giggles.

"I want to run my fingers through that gorgeous hair and drag my nails down his back as he pumps me full of his cum," Beth adds with drool clinging to the corners of her oversized lips.

"I bet his dick is huge." Kim fans herself as Fiero moves out of our line of sight.

"I bet he more than knows what to do with it too," Vanna says before slurping the dregs of her cocktail through a straw.

I agree, which is one of the reasons I'm so screwed.

"He's finding more and more excuses to drop by our house." Diana preens like a peacock. "He's constantly eye-fucking me, and it's only a matter of time before I give in to him."

A laugh bursts from my lips before I can stop it. *Does she honestly believe any of us buy that bullshit?* Everyone at our table turns to look at me with expressions ranging from shock to disbelief to disgust. To hell with their judgment. I'm only thinking what they're all thinking, but none of them will ever have the balls to say. They suck up to Diana like she's royalty and it irritates me to no end.

"Finally have something to say, *Tina?*" Diana's cutting glare drills into me, but I'm used to fending these kinds of looks from her. She isn't subtle in her dislike of me, and the feeling is mutual.

Time to end these forced lunches once and for all. "If it was true he wanted you, you'd be throwing yourself at him the first chance you got."

"She joins her husband in one brief conversation with him, and all of a sudden, she thinks she's the expert on Don Maltese," Kim snidely remarks, swiveling in her chair so she can insult me to my face.

"She probably thinks she stands a chance," Darlene contributes, and they all laugh at my expense.

Darlene never wastes an opportunity to put me down. She

was best friends with Dom's first wife, and while I understand her loyalty, why am I being punished for Dom's actions? It's hardly my fault he claimed a new wife only three months after losing his first one.

"No one wants used goods, *Tina*." Vanna waggles her finger in my face.

"I'd be careful throwing shade, Vanna. Unless you're happy for all your dirty little secrets to come out," I retort, enjoying watching her face pale.

Yes, bitch, I know you're fucking Don D'Onofrio behind your best friend's back.

I won't divulge what I know from eavesdropping on my husband's conversation with his despicable son because causing shit for the don is not a smart move—and I owe Vitto—but Vanna doesn't know that.

"He does want me," Diana blurts, looking ready to throw down with me. "You haven't been here to watch it going down. Your obvious jealousy is pathetic."

I can't contain my laughter this time, throwing my head back and cackling because it's one of the funniest things I've heard in forever.

"Stop it!" Diana hisses, stretching across the table. "You're drawing attention."

I force myself to calm down because Dom would not be pleased if it got back to him his wife wasn't playing her part in public. Appearances matter to my husband—he doesn't get the irony—which is why he keeps racking up huge gambling debts. He's desperately trying to get enough money to buy us a new car, continue the much-needed repairs on our house, buy me nice things purely so he can show me off, and to continue to fund the weekly parties that have contributed to the rapidly declining state of the Ferraro ancestral family home.

"Why on Earth would I be jealous of you, Diana?" I fix her

with a rare genuine grin. The gloves are off now, and I'm done holding back. I'll deal with the consequences later. "Every part of you is fake from your over-sprayed dyed hair to your ridiculous hyena laugh. Your husband constantly cheats on you, and your desperate attempts to claim his attention have failed. You organize regular lunches so you're not rattling around that big house by yourself because you're lonely and you have nothing to do. Your intelligence level is right up there with a fourth grader, and you have the personality of a dead fish. You bore everyone to tears with your constant attention-seeking behavior and your uneducated contributions to conversation."

I don't mention her inability to deliver her husband an heir because I'll never use that against any woman, no matter how horrible that woman has been to me. "I'm not jealous of you, Diana," I confirm, grabbing my bag and pushing my chair back to stand. "I pity you."

Steam is practically billowing from her ears as I move to walk away.

"How dare you speak to me like that!" she shrieks, seemingly unworried about an audience anymore. "I am the don's wife, and you will show me the goddamned respect I deserve!" she screeches, thumping her fist on the table.

Planting my palms on the table, I lean forward and put my face all up in hers. "I'll show you respect when you start showing me some." I push off the table and straighten up. "I already know that day will never come, and I really couldn't care less." I place the strap of my purse over my shoulder as my gaze trails Diana and her friends. "Don't bother inviting me again. This charade ends now."

I'm silently patting myself on the back as I leave the restaurant, glad I finally put that bitch in her place. Should have done it a long time ago, but I didn't want to ruffle any feathers. It feels good to speak my mind. It's like a switch flipped last night, and

I'm remembering the girl I used to be. I haven't decided if it's a good or a bad thing yet.

"You've got to be kidding me," I mutter to myself when I reach the parking lot and discover the Lincoln is gone. Pulling out my cell, I find a text from Dom confirming he needed Bruno and to get a ride home with Diana. "Asshole," I hiss under my breath as I order an Uber from my phone.

I walk away from the restaurant, not wanting them to see me slumming it in an Uber. *Wouldn't that be the scandal of the century?* I head out onto the boardwalk, confident the driver will find me as the app tracks my location.

The boardwalk is teeming with people, the beach packed to capacity, and the sun is beating down on my shoulders as I dodge kids on scooters and stressed parents pushing strollers. I'm regretting wearing high heels to lunch, wishing I'd at least thought to pop a pair of flip-flops in my purse.

I exit the boardwalk five minutes later and flop down onto a bench on the sidewalk to wait for the car. Checking the app, I see he hasn't moved much in the time it took me to walk here. Traffic is obviously brutal. Brushing damp strands of hair off my clammy brow, I curse my stupidity in leaving it down because my head is hot and beads of sweat cling to the back of my neck. I rummage in my purse for a hair tie, wishing I'd thought to grab a bottle of water from the restaurant before I left.

My heart jumps into my throat when a car screeches to a halt at the curb. I whip my head up, narrowing my eyes at the flashy red sports car as the driver-side window lowers.

"Get in." Fiero's deep seductive voice sends shivers racing through my body.

"No." My response is automatic the instant our eyes connect and that freaky electrical charge sparks in the space between us. I'm not putting myself in close quarters with this man so he can try to take something else from me.

"Valentina." My name flows off his tongue like melting chocolate, and it's a miracle I don't melt onto the sidewalk. How he manages to also make it sound threatening is true skill.

"It's not Friday, and you can't tell me what to do."

"I'm holding up traffic," he growls as a few car horns blare. "And I'm not arguing with you in the middle of the street. Get. In. The. Car."

"Make me." I throw my middle finger up at him as I walk off, and I've shocked even myself. Dom would shit his pants if he saw me right now. Unfortunately, that only spurs me on.

A car door slams behind me, while other vehicles continue to blare their horns, and I glance over my shoulder, my pulse ratcheting into coronary-inducing territory when I see a furious Fiero coming after me. I react on instinct, ripping my heels off and running in my bare feet. I race across the pedestrian crossing, with no direction in mind, conscious of pounding footsteps behind me. My only motivation is to lose him and lose him fast.

"Stop!" Fiero roars, and I pick up my pace, ignoring the stinging pain in my right foot as I run over something sharp.

"Hold the bus!" I yell, spotting one up ahead. I push my limbs harder, holding my purse and shoes against my chest as the footsteps behind me draw closer. The doors of the Metrobus are starting to close as I reach it, but I manage to hop on in time. Fiero's angry face stares at me as the bus drives off, and I breathe a sigh of relief as I slump against the door, attempting to regulate my breathing. I'm panting. My dress is stuck to my back, and I'm sure I'm red-faced and my makeup is half melting off my face, but I don't care. I'm counting this as a win.

Inquisitive eyes watch me as I swipe my bank card to pay my fare and walk past the first few full rows, trying not to wince at the stinging pain in my foot. I claim a seat on the edge of a row beside an older woman with two grocery bags on her lap. She offers me a small smile before turning to look out the window. It's my first time on a Metrobus, and I have no clue where it's going or how I'll get home because I can't call Dom to come rescue me. He'd throw a hissy fit if he knew I was on public transport.

I cancel the Uber and slip my feet into my shoes without looking at the injury I've collected. I'll deal with that later. Picking wispy strands of hair from my brow, I smooth it behind my ears while taking deep breaths to calm my racing heart. My mouth is parched, and I would literally kill for a bottle of water right now.

Ten minutes later, just as my heart rate has returned to normal, my ears prick up at the sound of someone revving an engine outside. Trepidation drips down my spine as I look out the window, horrified when I see a flash of red speed past us. My heart is pounding again, crashing against my rib cage as an ominous sense of dread crawls over my skin.

Screams fill the air as passengers are jolted forward in their seats when the driver suddenly slams hard on the brake. I grab the back of the seat in front of me as my head whips forward and back, and my ears protest the loud screeching sound from outside as the tires spin on the overheated asphalt in the effort involved in stopping.

Everyone looks around as the bus finally stills, but I'm staring straight ahead in a bit of a horrified daze.

He is legit insane.

Fists pound on the bus doors, and butterflies swoop into my stomach.

"What the hell do you think you're doing?" the driver shouts after he opens the doors to the madman on the other side.

"You have something of mine." Fiero storms onto the bus wearing his teeny training shorts with a white sleeveless training top that clings to his broad chest and toned abs and highlights the most delicious arm porn, which is not something I should be focusing on, not after the ass just called me *his*. He is clearly delusional as well as insane. I spy several women sitting more upright in their seats and some openly drooling, and I roll my eyes, wondering if this kind of female reaction follows him everywhere. "I'll just retrieve her so you good people can be on your way," he says, flashing a blinding grin as he makes his way toward me.

"Fuck off back to New York, asshole," some brave soul calls out, and I silently high-five him and concur with his opinion.

Fiero ignores the guy with the dreadlocks, making a beeline for me. His expression is furious, and I swallow back nerves. *He wouldn't hurt me, would he?*

"Get up," he says in a lethally cool tone when he reaches me.

I don't protest even though I want to tell him to go fuck himself. I know when to pick my battles, and this isn't the place. I follow behind him quietly, ignoring the curious looks and envious stares.

"Sorry for the trouble." Fiero slaps a wad of notes into the driver's hand and his scowl instantly transforms. The driver smiles, nodding at the crazy fucker who just stopped a public bus to grab a girl who isn't even his.

My eyes are out on stalks as I stare out the front window to where Fiero's very noticeable red sports car is parked horizontally a few feet in front of the bus, blocking the entire lane and gathering massive attention.

Don Maltese is seriously crazy, and my husband made a deal to hand me over to him for a few days.

What the hell has Dom gotten me into?

Chapter Five
Fiero

I spin around when my foot hits the road, facing the bus as I grab the stubborn woman by the waist and haul her over my shoulder.

"Put me down!" she yells, wriggling and trying to get free.

"No. I don't trust you not to run off again." I slap her ass over her short blue dress before banding my arm around her upper thighs to hold her in place. Glancing down, I frown at the little trickle of blood running over the edge of her shoe.

"This is kidnapping." She beats on my back with her small fists, and delicious tremors coast over my skin from the contact. My dick stirs behind my damp shorts, and I will the beast to calm down. These shorts hide fuck all, and the place is thronged with families and innocent kids.

"Scream for help then," I suggest as I reach my car. Stunned silence greets my words just as I thought. She won't risk making a scene.

A crowd has gathered around my car, which isn't surprising. My Aston Martin Vantage is the latest model with a twin-turbo V8 engine and a custom interior including a state-of-the-art entertainment system. There aren't many of them in Miami. "Get lost." I glare at every single person as I stalk toward the passenger door with my treasure, pleased when they all scatter without delay. Carefully, I deposit Valentina in the cream-colored leather passenger seat, catching a whiff of peaches from her hair as I lean across her to grab the seat belt. I momentarily close my eyes and inhale deeply.

Yep, I've got it bad.

She swats at my hands when I pull the belt across her body. "I can do it!"

"My car. My rules. I'm buckling you in." My fingers brush against her chest as I fit the belt into place, and my cock jerks a few times in excited anticipation. I cannot wait to get her to Long Island and spend the weekend exploring every inch of her.

"Don't touch me," she snaps, narrowing her eyes and glaring at me. But her chest is heaving, her taut nipples are pressing against the front of her dress, and she's squeezing her thighs together like she's at a workout class.

Her body can't lie—she is feeling this as much as me.

"Or what?" I purr, leaning down into her face.

"Or I'll claw your eyes out."

My lips tip up at the corners. "I'd pay good money to see you try, kitten."

"You already have," she retorts, attempting to stare me down. "You'll get to witness it firsthand very soon."

"I look forward to it, honey," I truthfully reply before pressing my face into her hair and sucking in a deep breath.

A choked sound fills the car as the bus driver presses down on his horn, joining the slew of other angry drivers trapped behind him.

Oops. Better get out of here before the cops show up. It's a miracle they haven't already. Not that I'm worried. We have the cops in the palm of our hand now, thanks to my timely intervention when I first arrived in Florida.

"Did you just sniff my hair?" Her face contorts as she stares at me like I've just sprouted horns on my head.

"Yep. Get used to it, kitten. When I get you to New York, I'll be all up in your personal space." I slam her door closed and race around the hood of my car, quickly climbing behind the wheel. I waste no time revving the engine and flooring it out of there.

"I think you're determined to give me whiplash today," she murmurs as she jerks forward in her seat, restrained by the belt.

I ease up on the accelerator. "This wouldn't have happened if you'd just done what you're told and got in the car when I first pulled up." Taking my eyes off the road for a second, I stare her straight in the eyes. "Disobey me again, and you're getting spanked."

The leather squelches under her delectable ass when she turns to face me. "In case it missed your attention, you're not my husband, and you have no authority to tell me what to do." She jabs her finger in my direction as I slow down when we approach the junction. "And before you throw out you have five million reasons to do so, again, that is completely irrelevant until Friday."

"Tell me, kitten, is it me who brings your claws to the surface, or was the face you wore last night a mask to hide your true personality?"

"Don't pretend to know me, and you can quit analyzing me too. You won't figure me out because I won't let you, and I'm certainly not giving you any ammunition," she spits as the car rolls to a stop in traffic at the lights.

I take advantage of the brief driving interlude to put my face all up in hers. "I like my women feisty, so keep fighting me, honey. All it does is turn me the fuck on." Before she can second-guess my move, I grab her hand and place it over my now rock-hard crotch.

Her eyes widen, and her throat bobs in an audible swallow.

"Feel that, kitten?" I drag her hand back and forth along my hard length. "That's what your words do to me, so by all means, keep it up."

She snatches her hand back, and I let her go as the lights change and traffic starts moving.

"There is something very, very wrong with you," she whispers a few beats later, and I throw back my head and laugh.

"Don't pretend you didn't enjoy that." I cast a quick glance at her, loving having her sitting beside me. She looks so perfect at my side, like she was born to be there. Her hair is a little wild, her makeup fading, and that dress she's got on is way too old for her, but she still looks like my every wet dream come to life. I think she could rock up in a garbage bag and I'd still want her. "I bet you're imagining what my monster cock will feel like sliding between those slender thighs, pushing through those pouty lips, and driving into that pretty little puckered hole of yours." The lights change, and I drive through the junction and take a left.

Her mouth hangs open as she stares at me, and I wish I could enjoy the view, but I need to keep my eyes on the road before I wrap my pride and joy around a palm tree and never get to experience nirvana between the sheets with Valentina Ferraro.

"What's the matter, kitty cat? Got nothing to say to that?" I ask after a few silent beats.

"I'm not dignifying that with a response." She lifts her chin and levels me with a challenging look.

I'm so intrigued by this woman, especially because I can't figure her out. "You don't need to reply. Your body is doing all the talking for you."

Her eyes glisten with anger as she folds her arms across her chest and turns away from me to the window.

"Tell me about yourself," I say, deciding to try a different tactic.

"No," she replies, continuing to give me the cold shoulder.

I quietly chuckle before speaking. "Valentina Sara Ferraro née Baresi. Twenty-four years old. Eighteen when she married the recently widowed Dominic Ferraro. Parents Vincenzo and Emiliana. They clearly were fucking like bunnies to produce ten kids within thirteen years and—"

Her head whips around, her furious gaze pinning me in place. "What are you doing?"

"Telling you what I've learned."

"Just stop."

"Tell me one thing and I will." I grip the wheel tighter. "Why did Don Pagano Senior arrange a marriage contract for the daughter of a *soldato* from Detroit to an underboss from Miami?"

Her nostrils flare, and her eyes flash with blatant rage. Interesting. I glance between her and the road, willing her to reply because the current Don Pagano had no clue why his father did that when I posed the same question to him this morning.

I was up half the night researching the woman beside me, desperate to know everything about her. While it's not unheard of for older men to marry beautiful young women purely for how they'll look on their arm, I'm sensing there is more to this story, and I want to know all the details.

"Why do you want to know?" Suspicion threads through her tone.

"Call it curiosity."

"Are you like this with all the women you pay for?"

A grin eases across my mouth. "Don't play cute, kitten. You know you're the only woman I've ever paid to spend time with. First and last."

"I don't believe you."

My smile expands into a full-grown smirk as I take the corner heading toward the pharmacy. "Yeah, you do. You saw last night what women are like with me. You know I don't have to pay for female company. I just snap my fingers, and they come running."

"You are the most arrogant man I've ever met."

"It's not arrogance if it's true."

"We'll have to agree to disagree."

"I know what you're doing," I say as I near my destination. "Stop deflecting and answer the question."

She purses her lips for a second before replying. "Because he was a pervert."

It's not much of an answer but enough to churn the bile in my stomach "Elaborate," I demand as I stop at the curb in front of the pharmacy.

"No." Her eyes hold mine with confidence that belies her age, making me wonder exactly what's happened to this girl that she's so hardened already. "You have your answer."

"I'll find out," I say, killing the engine. "You might as well tell me."

"I owe you nothing. Knock yourself out, Gage."

I drum my fingers on the wheel, titling my head and arching a brow as I look at her. "Gage?"

A genuine smile lifts her lips, lighting up her entire face, and I bask in the glow emanating from her. It's like being sucker punched in the chest and the dick at the same time.

I want all her smiles.

I want to be the one to *put* all those smiles on her face.

I want to spend the rest of my life making her smile because it feels like my sole reason for existing.

Fucking hell. If Massimo were privy to my current thoughts, he'd probably keel over in shock before having a field day with them. Not that he's in any position to throw shade. Catarina has him completely pussy-whipped and proud.

"Earth to Gage."

I come to as Valentina snaps her fingers in my face.

"You zoned out, and you had this really creepy look on your face."

Awesome. I run my fingers through my hair. Maybe Rico is right, and I *am* going crazy. What the fuck is this woman doing to me? "Tell me," I growl.

She shakes her head and bites her lower lip, and I'm done. I need to get the fuck out of here before I strip her bare in the middle of the day, in full view of others, and fuck the living daylights out of her.

"I'll leave that one for you to work out."

"Stay put," I instruct as I open my door.

"Wait." She grabs my arm, and it's like a streak of lightning shooting over my skin. She yanks her hand back, and I think she might have felt that too. "Why are we here?"

"I'll leave that one for you to work out," I tease, climbing out and instantly locking the car.

I whistle under my breath as she bangs on the window, shouting obscenities I can't hear.

I don't delay in the pharmacy, grabbing the items I need and hightailing it back to my car. Valentina is slumped in the passenger seat with her arms folded across her chest and a petulant look on her face.

I chuckle to myself as I get back in.

"You're an asshole," she hisses.

"So, you've said." I hand her a bottle of water before setting mine in one of the cupholders and depositing the bag with the rest of my supplies in the small middle compartment.

"I want to go home," she says, uncapping the bottle and drinking greedily.

"I'll take you." *With a short detour first.* I start the engine and maneuver out onto the road.

Chapter Six
Valentina

"I don't live here," I state when Fiero stops in front of unfamiliar tall wooden gates.

"I know." He flashes me one of those grins he seems to reserve for charming women before pressing a button on a key fob. "I do."

My eyes pop wide in surprise. "*Are* you kidnapping me?" I was only half joking earlier.

"Would you like me to?" His face radiates mischief, but there's a hint of sincerity there too.

I narrow my eyes at him as we drive up a driveway enclosed by palm trees on both sides. "Don't ask stupid questions."

"It's not a stupid question," he says, driving around a small water feature and parking directly in front of the entrance door. This house is gorgeous. It has two stories, with archways and pillars, painted cream and a muted orange. Flowering shrubs and neat beds surround both sides of the sprawling property, confirming it's well maintained. Fiero cuts the engine and leans across the console so there are only a few inches between our faces. "Do you need rescuing, Valentina?"

I can't tell if he's playing with me or serious. "You don't strike me as the knight-in-shining-armor type."

"What do I strike you as?" He lifts a brow, humoring me.

"An arrogant asshole with a god complex who's used to getting anything his heart desires even if it means trampling over others and sacrificing human decency to get it."

Laugher rumbles from his chest, and his eyes twinkle, and fuck him for being so temptingly good-looking. It's hard to drag my eyes from him, but I do before I succumb to his questionable charm.

Warm fingers brush my chin as he turns my head so I'm facing him. "Oh, kitten. We're going to have so much fun together."

I glare at him and shove his hand away. "Stop touching me, and why am I here? You said you'd take me home, so take me home."

"No, and this is just a pitstop." Grabbing the pharmacy bag, he gets out, runs around the hood of his car, and opens the door for me. Before I can move a limb, he unbuckles my belt and scoops me up into his arms.

"Put me down!"

"No." He holds me tighter before closing the door of his expensive car with his sneakered foot. I'm forced to wrap my arms around his neck as he walks on large beige-colored paving stones toward the door. "You're injured," he adds.

"It's only a little cut, and I'm not a damsel in distress."

"I'll be the judge of that," he murmurs, opening the door. A blast of cold air hits me when we step inside, and it's a welcome cure to my overheated skin.

"Do you own this place?" I ask as he strides through a wide glass-domed entryway. Sunshine spills into the bright airy space from overhead, showcasing a myriad of marble tables with various vases adorned with colorful blooms. Underfoot, his feet squeak on beige porcelain tiles.

"Affirmative."

"You're so weird."

Cue more laughing. "I've been called many things, but weird is a new one, kitten."

"Stop calling me that!"

"No." He waggles his brows as he strides past a ginormous kitchen with white and gray gloss cabinets and expensive marble countertops. Dishes are piled high in the sink, and various items clutter the top of the island unit.

"Okay, Gage." Two can play that game.

Fiero flashes me a set of perfectly straight, perfectly white teeth, and I'm suddenly conscious of how close we are. A light dusting of freckles is scattered on the bridge of his tan nose, and a small, thin jagged scar resides on one side of his top lip. I'm all pressed up against him with my nose brushing the side of his hair. He smells like saltwater and peppermint and everything I should steer clear of. "Put me down," I command again.

"Never," he whispers, holding me tighter against him as he walks into a large living room with floor-to-ceiling windows and a black-leather L-shaped sectional positioned in front of a giant TV and entertainment center. Various items of clothing litter the floor, and the top of the coffee table is covered with half-empty takeout cartons and discarded beer bottles. Magazines are stacked in a pile to one side of the couch as Fiero gingerly sets me down, placing my legs lengthways on the soft leather.

"I should probably apologize for the mess," he says with an impish grin, looking completely unapologetic.

"You need a cleaner."

"You offering?" he asks as he carefully removes my shoes.

"Is this the part where you tell me five million dollars is not just for lying on my back and spreading my legs?"

He has the nerve to look offended. "Don't be so crass."

"You're the one who told me you'd be filling all my holes!"

"Jesus, kitten. Wash your mouth out."

"Did you or did you not say that?" I ask, pushing my body up with my hands.

"You're a lady, and ladies don't speak such vulgarities."

Oh my god. *Is he for real?* "I'll add hypocrite and archaic to the list of adjectives I use to describe you," I bark, watching as he removes supplies from the bag.

"You have a list?" He waggles his brows, and I scowl at him. "I'm flattered."

"Don't be. It's the opposite of flattering."

"I don't believe you." He dazzles me with his signature grin, and my ovaries swoon. "Hold still." Taking my injured ankle, he lifts it onto his bare thighs, and I bite back a gasp as fiery tremors shoot up my legs from the skin-to-skin contact. It's worse when he inspects my heel with gentle fingertips, and I chew on the inside of my mouth to stifle my moan. "You have a cut, but it's not deep."

"Okay." I cringe at my high-pitched tone, especially when Fiero looks up and grins. He knows how he affects me, and he's going to milk it nonstop.

I have never had such a strong physical reaction to any man ever before. Not even Damiano, and I was seriously hot for my high-school boyfriend. Pain spears me through the chest even now as I recall how that relationship was the catalyst for everything that subsequently happened to me.

"This might sting a little."

I brace myself as he cleans the wound with a sterile wipe, and it does sting, but it's nothing compared to the injuries I've sustained before. I'm quiet as I watch him pat the cut with a gauze pad and apply ointment and an adhesive bandage. His callused palms linger on my feet as his eyes trail a path along my bare legs. I swallow heavily, and the air is thick with electrifying tension. His gaze captures mine, and I forget how to breathe. He is so beautiful, and I'm captivated by his wide blue eyes and the heated intensity of his stare. My pussy pulses and clenches with raw need, and thick desire curls deep in my lower belly when his fingers begin to travel up my legs. My breath hitches, and my heart pounds. Warmth invades my flesh every place where he touches me, accompanied by sizzling tingles that crank my desire to dizzying heights.

When his fingers breach the hem of my dress, I snap out of my lust-filled daze and clamp my hand down firmly on his to stall his upward trajectory.

We stare at one another, neither of us moving, both drowning in the potent chemistry we share. My eyes plead with him to stop, and his seem to say *never*. My heart is thrashing wildly around my chest cavity, and my panties are damp with the evidence of my arousal, but this can't happen. I'm married and his deal is only temporary.

Fiero withdraws his hand and averts his eyes. "There." His voice is deeper, gruffer. "You'll live."

"Thank you," I whisper over the unexpected lump in my throat.

We stare at one another as that frisson of desire continues to charge the air around us. He opens and closes his mouth a few times before speaking. "Hang out with me for a while."

I'm surprised to see a slightly vulnerable look on his face. "I need to get home." Dom keeps me on a tight leash, and he's not going to be happy to discover I was with Fiero. It's not part of the deal. Plus, he'll be expecting his dinner on the table. His mother always had a formal dinner on Sunday evenings and it's a tradition he's forced me to continue.

"Hmm." He scrubs a hand over his prickly jawline. "Maybe I will kidnap you after all." His flirtatious grin is doing wild things to my insides, and I really need to get the hell out of here before I do something I'll regret.

"I don't recommend it. Not unless you want to earn the wrath of every made man in Miami. The men are very loyal to Dominic." I plant the seed and wait.

He tips his head to one side as he carefully puts my shoes back on. "Loyal to Dominic, not Vitto?"

"Don't put words in my mouth. Of course, the men are loyal to Vitto. He's their don."

He stares at me for a few charged beats before standing. "I'm grabbing a quick shower. Make yourself at home. There are drinks in the refrigerator if you want one." He sets my feet on the ground and gets up fast, quickly leaving the room.

I flop back down on the couch, sucking in huge lungsful of air. *What on Earth is happening?* I hate I'm attracted to the man who thinks I'm a commodity he can buy on a whim. I hate my brain is being hijacked by my body. I hate my body is in full insta-lust mode and craving a man who is old enough to be my father.

My cell vibrates in my purse, and I sit bolt upright, cursing under my breath when I take it out and see the caller. I briefly close my eyes before answering because not answering isn't an option. I still remember the punishment he delivered last night, and I'm not in the mood for a repeat tonight. "Dom," I say in my most pleasant tone as I hit the speaker button, holding the phone up in front of my face.

"Where are you?" he roars.

I'd lie if he didn't have a stupid tracker embedded in my arm. "I'm at Don Maltese's house," I say, frantically spinning plausible stories in my head.

"It's been almost two hours since lunch ended, and you were supposed to go straight home with Diana." That cunt must have ratted me out. I swear, someday, soon if I have my way, Diana D'Onofrio is getting what's coming to her.

"I left early not realizing Bruno wasn't outside. I was making my way back inside the restaurant when I tripped and hurt my foot." My words rush out as I concoct a believable story on the spot. "Don Maltese had been out running, and he happened to be going to his car at the same moment. He saw I was injured and insisted on driving me. He stopped at a pharmacy to get supplies for my foot."

"That doesn't explain what you're doing at his house!"

"He was supposed to take me home, but he drove me here. I couldn't exactly do anything, Dom. He sits on the board of The Commission, and he's one of The Five. I can't disrespect him. That's what you've always drilled into me about our world."

I hold my breath, hoping he accepts this version of the truth.

"Did he fuck you?"

"What? No!"

"You're telling me the man who paid five million to fuck you took you to his house and didn't lay a finger on you? What kind of moron do you take me for, Valentina!" I hold the phone away from my face as bile swims up my throat.

"A moron who doesn't understand the workings of a deal," Fiero says, stalking into the room with a look of thunder on his face. He's wearing ripped jean shorts and a fitted black T-shirt with black and white sneakers on his feet. Dragging a hand through his damp hair, he grabs the cell from my hand. "Do you always speak to your wife like this, Dominic, because I've got to say I'm not much liking it."

"With all due respect, my marriage is none of your business, Don Maltese. Valentina was very wild when she first arrived, and I had to teach her some manners. We have an understanding, and I reign her in when her rebellious side rears its ugly head."

Heat creeps up my neck and onto my cheeks.

"She needs a firm hand to keep her in line, and she likes it, don't you, darling? You like obeying your daddy, don't you, baby girl?"

I want the ground to open and swallow me.

"Valentina." The warning is clear in my husband's tone.

"I do, Daddy," I say, my voice breaking. "I do," I repeat in a more confident tone.

"See," Dom says. "My baby girl is naturally submissive. She just needed me to coax it from her."

Inside, I'm laughing bitterly. I don't think there's a submissive bone in my body. Dominic just trampled all over my fiery personality and forced me to play it his way. I've done what was necessary to survive, but Fiero brings out a side of me I've kept hidden, and it's one of the main reasons this deal is so dangerous for me. I might not live to see twenty-five if I can't leash my true temperament around my controlling husband.

A mix of emotions is playing out on Fiero's face, and I don't like any of them. I look down at my hands, closing my eyes and wishing for that genie again.

"My wife is needed at home," Dominic says, his voice singing with egotistical authority. "We have family dinner every Sunday at five, and Valentina needs to start cooking."

"I'll take her home now," Fiero says and then he hangs up. Silently, he passes the phone to me. "Let's go. We wouldn't want *Daddy* missing his precious dinner."

Chapter Seven
Fiero

H urt splays across her face, mixed with shame, and I instantly want to retract my words, but the damage is already done. I shouldn't have taken it out on Valentina. It's not her I'm angry with. I want to kill that fucking bastard with my bare hands. I want to smash his head into something hard and watch as his brain bleeds out of his skull.

The entire drive to the Ferraro house, I'm devising creative ways to murder that prick in my mind. The journey is fraught with tension. Valentina is sullen, quiet, embarrassed. Hiding behind her mask again, and it's making more sense now. I'm seething, my rage fueled by jealousy, which is a new emotion for me. Watching Valentina succumb to that asshole was heartbreaking. I think I'm beginning to understand her more, and though I was teasing earlier, I'm starting to realize she *does* need rescuing.

My brow puckers as we drive through rusted old iron gates that have seen better days. Things don't improve as we drive up a long driveway filled with potholes and bordered by neglected gardens. The house comes into view when I round the bend, and at first glance, it's an impressive gray-stone, two-story mansion.

The closer we get to the building, the less impressed I am. Thick ivy covers huge sections of the walls, helping to disguise the chips and fractures in the stonework. The window frames are crumbling with several cracked glass panels. Paint is peeling from the solid front door, and there is no water gracing the ornate water feature out front. I park on gravel, to one side of the door, watching as Dominic and a younger man step out of the house.

Valentina is stiff at my side, her nails digging into her thighs through her dress. My frown deepens as she unbuckles her belt with fumbling fingers. My hand lands on hers of its own volition, and her eyes snap to mine. She's so beautiful even with the hauntingly vacant look in her eyes.

I pull my hand back when her door is yanked open.

"Watch it," I bark at her husband. "This car is worth a lot of money. You break something, you pay for it."

"Funny," Dominic says, helping his wife out of my Aston Martin. "I was going to say the same to you."

Is he seriously comparing my car to his wife? What a dick. I get out, my feet crunching on the unforgiving ground as I round the car.

"This is for you." Dom thrusts a wrinkled piece of paper at me.

Fury is instantaneous as I read the messy handwritten invoice. "What is the meaning of this?" I ask in a lethally cold tone, pinning him with a sharp look.

His conceited smile irritates me to no end, as does the possessive grip he has on his wife's arm, and I'm only finding more reasons to gut this motherfucker. "Did you think my wife's time was free?"

Horror washes over Valentina's face as the realization dawns.

"We have a deal," I remind the asshole.

"That deal doesn't begin until Friday morning."

"Do you charge every man for spending time with your wife?" I'm growling as I look at the bill for over $156,000.

"There is a price, yes," he replies without hesitation, and I'm frowning again.

What the hell? Is he actually pimping Valentina out? My hand is wrapped around his throat before I've even contemplated the move. Valentina is quiet as I shove her husband up against my car, silently trying to talk myself off a ledge because as much as I want to murder the bastard I can't. There are rules. Rules my buddy has to uphold as president of The Commission.

"Let my father go," the younger man says stalking toward me. "Release him now, or I'll put a hole in your head," the little shit adds, prodding my temple with a gun.

"Cesco, no," Valentina says.

"Do you know who you're threatening, boy?" I ask, keeping my hand firmly locked around his father's neck. This must be the nineteen-year-old son Vitto mentioned. Dominic is grabbing at my wrist, but my hold is tight because he's overweight and unfit, and I could do this all day and not break a sweat.

"I know who you are, Don Maltese, and I have respect for you, but that's my father. You don't get to come to our home and strangle him and expect me to do nothing. He's my *father*. I would die to protect him." His hand doesn't falter as he stares at me with confidence and determination.

It's more than Dominic deserves, and this little shit has way bigger balls than his old man. Reluctantly, I release Ferraro, and his son lowers his weapon.

"My father means no disrespect, Don Maltese, it's just the way things are done around here."

"Well, things are going to change." I level Dominic with a warning look as I ball up his invoice and throw the paper at his face. "Wives are to be revered."

Dominic rubs at his neck, not containing his utter hatred for me, and I love it. Maybe if I give this guy enough rope, he'll hang himself. He's already in enough hot water as it is being in debt to the cartel. I think a little reminder is in order. "All it will take is one phone call to Vitto and the board, and you're done, Ferraro. Don't try this bullshit again." Bile crawls up my throat watching Valentina rush to her husband's side, snaking her arm around his back as she whispers in his ear. "You can make it up to me by inviting me to dinner," I add, deciding to stick around. I don't trust Dominic not to punish Valentina in some way, and I want to learn more about the family dynamic.

"I apologize for any disrespect, Don Maltese," Cesco says, extending his arm. "I hope we can put this behind us."

I accept the young man's hand, shaking it firmly. I understand where Vitto is coming from now, but this young pup still has a lot to learn. "A piece of advice, Cesco," I say, still pumping his hand. "Don't pull a gun on a don no matter the circumstances. Not everyone is as understanding as me. Next time, you could find yourself six feet under." I release his hand on one final warning look.

"I appreciate the advice, and it's been noted." He nods once before turning to his father. "I will see you for dinner, Father, Valentina." His words and his expression are respectful in the extreme, but his lips curve at one side, ever so slightly, as he glances at his stepmother, and I don't like the way his gaze quickly rakes over her.

I watch as he stalks off and disappears around the side of the house.

Valentina stares after him, wearing her usual mask, but I can feel her bristling under his unwanted attention.

It struck me earlier that Valentina is most likely a well of information. She's around these men a lot I'm guessing if her earlier comment about the men's loyalty being with Dominic is true. Valentina has been a silent observer for years. She's smart, and I bet she knows her fair share of secrets. I hide a smile behind a cool façade as I realize I now have a reason to explain my deal should I need to offer one.

"You're welcome to join us for dinner, Don Maltese," Dominic says, still fixing me with a hateful look.

"Thank you. I accept."

As soon as we enter the house, Valentina disappears to start cooking, and I demand a grand tour from my gnarly host. Dominic grinds his teeth and clenches his fists, but he attempts to act civil as he shows me around. I keep my distance as we walk through his home, his stale body odor tickling my nostrils and making me throw up a little in my mouth. I can't even think about him putting his hands on Valentina without retching and wanting to impale him on a spike and watch his life force slip away.

Ferraro babbles away as we walk, explaining the origins of various pieces of furniture and the myriad of old paintings and pictures tacked to the walls. He's very knowledgeable about his ancestral home and proud of it, but I sense his shame as he shows me around. And he should be ashamed he's let it get into such a state of disrepair. He can't be short of money. Florida is one of our wealthiest territories, and as Vitto's underboss, he would enjoy his fair share of the profits. This all points to a lifelong gambling addiction unless he's doing something else with his money. I vow to dig deeper. If he's hiding anything else, I'll find it.

This house dates back to the early nineteen hundreds, he tells me, but it is obvious from the wood-paneled ceilings, black-and-white-checkered floors, ornate chandeliers, worn patterned rugs, and exquisite tapestries housed in elaborate gold frames hanging on the walls.

The neglect is evident everywhere. Tiles are cracked and stained underfoot, the copious dark wood paneling, which is heavily featured on walls and ceilings, is chipped and faded and in need of obvious repair. The sweeping banisters that lead up both sides of the large lobby sway when I touch it, and the stairs creak worryingly as we ascend the steps. Scaffolding is mounted against the banisters on the other side, and the wood has been restored on the lower half. It's literally like men downed tools midway through the job.

He ran out of money to continue.

Upstairs is dark, gloomy, and humid despite the presence of air-conditioning units. None of them are operational, and I'm understanding Ferraro's body odor problem a little more clearly now. Though it's nothing regular daily showers wouldn't fix. A couple of buckets sit strategically under small holes in the roof, ready to capture rain during one of Florida's legendary summer showers. It can be stupidly hot here with humidity as thick as syrup, and the heavens will open, dumping rain on the land below for fifteen or twenty minutes, and then it clears up as quickly as it came on, and the sun resumes baking everyone.

It's nuts and has to be seen to be believed.

My concern for Valentina only ramps up the more we explore, and my anger at Jacopo Pagano for sending a young girl into this environment is mushrooming. Pity he's dead. I'd have enjoyed punishing him for forcing Valentina into this life.

"How did your first wife die?" I ask Dominic as we make our way back downstairs.

"Why do you want to know about Marguerite?" Suspicion threads through his tone.

"I'm just making conversation," I lie.

"If you must know, she had a heart attack."

That's what I've heard. "She was young for that to have happened."

"She had a heart condition since birth," he says, taking a left when we reach the lobby.

"It must have been upsetting for your children." I watch him carefully.

"They were devastated."

"I imagine accepting a stepmother so soon after their mom died was hard for them, especially one so close in age."

He slams to a halt, narrowing cold eyes on me. "I married quickly for my children. They needed a mother, and I don't like your insinuation."

"I'm not insinuating anything. Just stating the facts, or have I been misinformed?"

He resumes walking, his shoes clacking noisily off the tiled floor. "My children are my everything, Don Maltese. There isn't anything I won't do for them."

"Yet your two daughters don't live here with you."

He stops walking again, slanting me a heated glare. "Not that it's any of your business, but they live with their grandmother in Jacksonville. They were only five and three when Marguerite died, and they were too much for Valentina to manage."

So much for needing a new mother for his kids. I'm not buying the bullshit he's peddling for one second.

"Their grandmother had lost her only child and her husband within eighteen months of each other. My girls give her purpose, and she draws great comfort from raising them. It was the best solution."

"I see." I don't. How can his children be *his everything* when he gives the two youngest away? Ferraro is old school. I'm betting if they were sons they'd be living here.

"What's that?" I ask, stopping in front of a window that faces onto the rear of the property. Rows of tilled land sit behind a low wooden fence in front of a large greenhouse.

"That's Valentina's vegetable patch."

"It's very impressive." It's bigger than any vegetable patch I've ever seen, including the one at the Mazzone estate that Natalia Messina cultivated.

"She planted it when she first came here. It made her happy, so I let her get on with it."

I very much doubt that.

"Come." He lifts one shoulder. "It's time for dinner."

The dining table is already set for dinner when we enter the grand room. This room is sumptuous and relatively recently renovated by the looks of it. Thick red velvet curtains drape the windows, offering views of the other side of the rear gardens. Someone—Valentina, I guess—has been maintaining the lawn, and gardening tools and a mat lie on the grass before one of the circular flowerbeds. The old mahogany table glistens under a coat of new varnish, and there isn't a mark on it, but it's clearly a family heirloom. The highbacked seats have also been repaired and reupholstered along with most all the dark furniture in the room. Overhead, the stunning chandelier is magnificent, bathing the room in bright light. New rugs and soft furnishings finish the look. It's still very traditional even with the few more modern pieces.

I take a seat as instructed to the left of Dominic who is, of course, sitting at the top of the table. Cesco arrives then, greeting us both pleasantly as he sits beside his father on the other side. The door behind the table opens, and Valentina appears, looking stressed and hot. Her hair is in a messy bun on the top of her head, and wispy strands cling to her damp brow. Her cheeks are red, and the muscles in her arms flex as she carries a large, heavy, lidded silver container to the table. I get up to help her when it's obvious neither her husband nor stepson are going to, lifting the container and placing it on the middle of the table.

"Sit down," Dominic commands when I move to go after his wife. "You're our guest. Valentina knows what she's doing."

"That thing weighs a ton, and I'm helping her." I don't give him any option, pushing through the door into the old kitchen. The double stove is new, as are some of the pots and pans, and the chunky wooden cabinets have been repainted, but most everything looks like a throwback to the last century. Delicious aromas swirl through the air as a harassed Valentina looks over her shoulder at me.

"You shouldn't be here. He'll get angry."

"Do I look like I give a flying fuck?" I stride toward her, plucking a large lidded platter from her hands.

"You should. He'll consider it an insult."

I arch a brow and grin. "Again? Do I look like I care?"

"You must have a death wish." She lifts another smaller silver container, but it still looks heavy.

"Leave it. I'll carry them in. You get the plates."

"I'm not as weak as you seem to think I am." Pointedly ignoring me, she lifts the container and stomps off.

Stubborn woman.

"You're injured."

She scoffs, turning to face me when she reaches the door. "I have a tiny cut on my foot. I'm hardly incapacitated. I do this every week. I'm more than capable," she says, pushing through the door using her full body weight.

Dominic and his son pause mid-sentence, and I'm guessing they were discussing me. How flattering.

Valentina and I ferry silver containers back and forth until everything is laid out on the table. Valentina removes the lids, and my mouth waters at the multitude of different vegetables and meats before us. It seems like an excessive amount of food for only four people. I bite my tongue as Valentina serves slices of succulent beef and lamb onto each of our plates before taking her seat beside Cesco, across the table from me. We help ourselves to roast potatoes, creamy mashed sweet potatoes, cheesy cauliflower, broccoli with bacon and almond flakes, honeyed carrots, and plain green beans. A delicious rich gravy, which Valentina confirms she made herself, accompanies the meal.

She's a tremendous cook, and everything is delicious.

Conversation is largely focused on business as we talk in between eating. Valentina is quiet but tense. Every so often, she squirms a little in her chair, and her face turns pale. My attention narrows on her stepson. Cesco smiles affably, but I don't trust it.

"Excuse me!" Valentina hops up abruptly, her chair screeching across the floor. "I need the bathroom." She all but runs from the room. I keep my focus trained on Cesco as he laughs and jokes with his father, not trusting him for a second.

By the time Valentina returns, we've all finished eating. Dominic isn't happy she's been gone so long, but he doesn't say anything. I imagine my presence has stalled his scathing tongue.

"That was delicious, thanks, Valentina," I say.

"You're welcome." Her meek voice and timid smile aggravate me. This isn't who she is. *What the fuck is going on in this house, and what has her husband done to make her act so subservient?*

"Clear the table and fetch dessert." Dom leans back in his chair, rubbing his swollen belly as he levels his wife with a cautionary look.

Valentina gets up and begins stacking plates.

"Don't you have staff to do that?" I inquire, lifting my glass of water to my lips. Now that I think of it, I haven't seen a single employee during my grand tour of this crumbling mansion.

"They're on vacation," Dominic blurts, grabbing his wine-glass and knocking back a large mouthful of red wine.

Shock renders me speechless. He doesn't have any staff. *Is Valentina expected to manage this large dilapidated house all by herself?* Briefly, I wonder who looked after the house during the period she was in Sicily tending to her ailing grandmother.

"Let me help," I say, standing.

"That's not necessary," Dominic barks. "No made man is coming into my home and doing the cleanup. That's a woman's job, and my wife is more than capable. Sit down, Don Maltese, or you'll insult me."

I want to tell him to go fuck himself, but I have a better idea instead, and it's best Valentina is not here when I make my second proposal to her husband.

Chapter Eight
Valentina

I t's a miracle I keep it together as I clear the table especially after throwing up what little I ate in the bathroom. But I hold it together until all the dishes are removed from the dining room, and then I collapse against the kitchen counter, breathing heavily as I squeeze my eyes shut and ward off tears. My fingers find their way to my silver locket, and as I rub the cold, shiny metal, I feel my panic and fear subsiding.

He's getting braver, and it's only a matter of time before he takes what he wants. I feel dirty, and I badly need a shower. My heart is racing, and my hands are shaking as I set about getting dessert, removing the meringue, bowl of fresh chopped fruit, and whipped cream I prepared earlier from the refrigerator.

I need to run now. Screw waiting another year until I've saved enough money. I'll take what I have now and make the best of it.

After assembling the pavlova, I put it on the silver cake stand and walk toward the dining room, stopping at the door when I hear the tail end of the conversation my husband and Fiero are having. The door is only slightly ajar, but it's enough for me to hear what's being said.

"Dominic, you're not stupid, and I don't think you have a death wish. I made myself perfectly clear last night. This isn't a negotiation. I'm telling you now it's two million extra and I take Valentina with me tonight. I told you I'm needed urgently in The Big Apple, and I won't have time to return to Miami until next week. Most made men would just take her, but I'm making this gesture as a show of respect to you."

It's such bullshit. How dare they both sit there, after enjoying a meal I slaved over, and negotiate a trade like I'm cattle. They both make me sick. If it wouldn't sign my death warrant, I'd riddle both their bodies full of bullets.

"The math doesn't add up," Dominic huffs. "I told you it's seventy-eight thousand, one hundred and twenty-five per hour, based on the rate *you* set when you said five mil for sixty-four-hours. This new deal is for five days, give or take an hour. That's 9.375 mil. I'm not accepting two. It's a goddamn insult to my intelligence. I know my wife's worth. If you want to take her tonight, that's the price."

"I should just kill you," Fiero says on a growl. I don't need to see his face to know he's furious because I hear it in his tone.

Right now, I wish he *would* kill my husband. Anger is quick to resurface. It's not enough that Dom humiliated me on the phone and gave a fucking invoice to Fiero for the time we spent together today. Time Don Maltese spent taking care of me. Oh no. My husband has to go the full mile and actually work out the value of each hour Fiero spends with me, ensuring he gets every penny he believes he's owed.

This is a new low, and now Dom's got a taste of trading me for money, he's rubbing his hands gleefully at the prospect of using me to beef up his empty bank account. I know what my future looks like, and I'd rather die than let it happen. I didn't think things could get any worse, but this proves I was wrong.

I'm not staying here to become a glorified prostitute, handed over to the highest bidder.

This is my one chance to get away, and I'm not wasting it even if I won't be able to see my plan through to the very end.

"I will pretend you didn't threaten me, Don Maltese. I'd hate to have to report that to the board of The Commission."

"Be my guest, Dominic. They'll kill you themselves when they hear you're in bed with the cartel."

"I'm not in bed with the cartel!" Outrage underscores his statement. "I'm in debt to them! It's completely different."

"I doubt my colleagues would see it that way. I'm doing you a favor, Dominic. I'm giving you the means to pay some of the debt and the time to sort your shit with the cartel and walk away before it blows up in your face. Don't look a gift horse in the mouth. It's 1.5 mil and Valentina comes with me now."

"You said two!" Dom's panic roars to the surface. He is such a fool to think he can make someone like Fiero Maltese bend to his will.

"Now I'm saying 1.5. Keep arguing and it'll keep going down."

A pregnant pause ensues for a few seconds.

"Valentina! Where is our dessert?" Dom roars, and I almost drop the cake stand.

Tears prick my eyes, and I'm tempted to grab the cake knife and stick it in my husband's chest. I think Don Maltese would probably let me get away with it, but Cesco wouldn't. That man is the devil incarnate. If I kill his father now, he's in charge of me, and I'd rather suffer ten of Dom over one of his nasty offspring.

Forcing the tears to subside, I thrust out my shoulders and enter the room.

"What took you so long?" Dom shouts, taking his frustration out on me as usual.

"I had to assemble it," I say with bite, deliberately not apologizing.

"Watch your tone, baby girl, or Daddy'll have to remind you who's in charge."

"Valentina." Fiero eyeballs me with intent. "You're coming with me now. Go pack."

"Stay where you are," Dom hisses. "Nothing is agreed."

Cesco leans back in his seat with his legs kicked out in front of him, smirking at me as the two men battle for supremacy. I already know who's going to win, and I want Fiero to take me now. New York is my ticket to freedom, and I'm ready to grasp it with both hands.

With lightning speed, Fiero has a gun pressed to Dom's temple. Cesco straightens up immediately, reaching for his weapon. "Pull that out and your father's dead," Fiero coolly says, curling his finger around the trigger. Cesco stalls with his hand on his gun. "Give it to Valentina and don't try anything. I'm a trained sniper and weapons expert. I'll kill you and your father in a heartbeat if you try to pull a fast one."

My pulse is racing in my neck and blood rushes to my head, making me lightheaded.

"Don't bother." Fiero has a tight grin on his face as he cautions Dom. "I took the bullets out of your gun when we were on our tour."

I glance down to where Dom has his fingers curled around the holster strapped to his hip, getting a real thrill out of Fiero besting him and his son.

Cesco slaps his gun into my palm, eyeballing me with a silent message. If he thinks I'm siding with him and his father against Fiero Maltese, I have given him too much credit.

"Walk around the table slowly, Valentina, and hand me the gun," Fiero says, sounding and looking completely unruffled.

I obey without protest because it suits me to leave with him tonight, so I don't fight him.

"Good girl," he says, making me instantly want to withdraw my words and extract my claws.

Oh, Dom does not like that. His nostrils are flaring, and he's frothing at the mouth.

"Get your things, Valentina. We're leaving in five minutes."

I don't need to be told twice. Racing out of the room, I take the creaky stairs two at a time and barge into my bedroom, quickly grabbing the suitcase from the top of my closet. Grabbing clothes haphazardly off hangers, I stuff them into my case, adding the couple good dresses I have along with the matching shoes. Shoving some underwear in the case, I rush into the bathroom and quickly dump my toiletries into a washbag and toss it on top of the clothes.

Pressing my ear to the bedroom door, to ensure no one is coming, I move my bed to one side, lift the loose plank from the floor, and retrieve my stash of cash and the white pill bottle, hiding it in the middle of my clothing. Then I sit on the case to close it, push my bed back into position, and grab my purse. Before leaving my room, I remove my hair tie, drag a comb quickly through my messy hair and spritz some perfume. I wish I'd had time to shower and change, but Fiero seems in a hurry to get out of here, and I am too.

"I'm ready," I say in a breathless tone as I run into the dining room.

Fiero stands, emptying the bullets from Cesco's gun before handing it back to him. He speaks to my husband without looking at him, which is a huge disrespect. Inside, I'm silently cheering Fiero on. No one has ever taken my side and stood up to Dom before. Everyone sees how he treats me, and they don't interfere.

Cowards and perverts, the lot of them, with one notable exception. I still don't know why *he* helped me, but I'm grateful.

"I'll wire the extra 1.5 to you tonight, and the rest of our agreement remains intact."

Dom nods tersely, understanding there is no choice. Even if I planned to come back, I wouldn't return with the look he throws my way. It promises weeks of his unique brand of punishment, and I'm done being his toy.

"Let's go." Fiero comes up to me and takes the case from my hand.

"Wait, baby girl." Dom stands, and knots twist in my gut as he approaches me. "Daddy deserves an extra special goodbye." Yanking me forward, he bands his arms around my back and smashes his disgusting mouth to mine, forcing his tongue between my lips and almost choking me. I instantly zone out, having trained myself to do this from an early stage. Grabbing my ass, he squeezes hard as he thrusts his groin at me, and then thankfully it's over. Dom presses his mouth to my ear. "Keep your legs open and your mouth shut, Valentina. Think of your family."

"Enjoy the city, *Mom*." Cesco feigns politeness as he pulls me from his father's arms. My skin squirms like a thousand fire ants are dancing across my flesh when he presses his mouth to my cheek in a kiss. "Your cunt is mine when you come back," he whispers in my ear while keeping a fake smile plastered on his face. "Daddy can't help you this time." He kisses my other cheek before releasing me, and it's a miracle I'm still upright. Terror skips through my veins at an alarming rate.

I will throw myself in front of a train before I ever step foot in this house again. Death would be the lesser evil.

"We'll see you Sunday," Fiero says, taking my elbow and steering me out of the room. The others don't follow. When we're out of earshot, he says, "Breathe, Valentina. You look like you're going to pass out."

Taking What's Mine

I draw air deep into my lungs, feeling the stress leaving my shoulders the closer we get to the door. But it's a false sense of relief. I fully understand I'm jumping out of the frying pan and into the fire.

The pretty flight attendant greets Fiero warmly as we board his private jet that is taking us to New York. Me, less so. I don't miss the derisory way she stares at me. I know I look a mess, but it's not very polite to acknowledge that. She takes our luggage, scoffing silently as she takes in my battered, old Louis Vuitton case, disappearing to stow it somewhere.

"After we're airborne, you can take a shower and change," Fiero says, gently pushing me down into a plush gray leather seat. He buckles me in before heading into the cockpit where I hear him greeting the pilot like he's a friend. Perhaps he is. I know very little about the Maltese boss.

Fiero returns and claims the seat across from me, putting his seat belt on.

Miss Hostile materializes, eyeballing Fiero like he's her next meal. My eyes narrow of their own accord when she touches his arm and bats her eyelashes at him. "What can I get you, Fiero?"

"Just two waters for now. Thanks, Mimi."

"Everything is on the menu tonight, sir," she purrs in a contrived seductive voice, lowering her eyes to his crotch. "Nothing is off-limits."

Wow. *Could she be more blatant or more desperate?*

"In case your eyesight is failing, I have a companion, and you're being rude and presumptuous." Fiero levels her with a dark look that warns her to behave as he pointedly removes her hand from his arm. "That will be all, Mimi." He dismisses her and returns his attention to me. I don't miss the poisonous look she sends my way before she stalks off.

"Do you have a thing for young women, Don Maltese?" I ask as the door closes. "Or is it a flight attendant thing?"

His teasing grin comes out to play. "Jealous, Valentina?"

I snort out a laugh. "Hardly."

"Liar."

"Asshole."

The grin slips off his mouth as the plane begins moving. "What did Cesco do to you at the table?"

All the blood leaches from my face and I avert my eyes, staring out the window as my heart pummels my rib cage. When I'm composed enough to speak, I don't look at him when I say, "I don't know what you're talking about."

"Don't do that." He leans forward, gripping my chin firmly but gently, turning my face so I'm forced to look at him. "Neither of us are stupid."

I swallow thickly over the lump wedged in my throat. "It doesn't matter. Drop it."

"It matters to me," he says in a growly tone.

I drop my eyes to my lap.

"Valentina." He lowers his voice. "Did he touch you?"

"I don't want to talk about it," I whisper, horrified when tears well in my eyes.

He releases my face and stares at me as we taxi down the runway. "I'll kill him." He says it so calmly and casually, like how one would make small talk. "I'll kill both of them."

"That's a bit extreme," I say even though I'd have no issue if he killed them. It would sure make my life easier.

"Is it?"

Not really. Air whooshes out of my mouth, and my stomach dips as the plane takes off into the sky. "I know how to handle

Dom and his son," I quietly say. "I don't need anyone to fight battles for me."

"Don't you?" He unbuckles his belt and stands.

I stare straight into his eyes as I say, "I can fight my own battles."

"You shouldn't have to." Sadness lingers behind his words as he extends his hand. "Come on. I'll show you where the shower is."

Chapter Nine
Fiero

"Wash your mouth out with that." I hand Valentina a bottle of mouthwash when we enter the en suite bathroom from the bedroom. It's small with just a sink, compact cupboard, toilet, and a shower cubicle.

Her eyes narrow to slits, and I'm happy to see her resistance returning. It means she's being real with me, and I'll take that over the shell of a woman I witnessed back in that hellhole. "Are you going to dictate everything I do because I'll fight you every step of the way."

"Good." I press a kiss into her hair on instinct. "I look forward to it."

She eyes me circumspectly. "You mean that."

I lean against the doorway, trying not to fixate on her mouth, but it's hard. I need to taste her. It's all I've been thinking about in the twenty-four hours since I first set eyes on her. Valentina has fully hypnotized me, and I'm unnaturally consumed with her.

It's more than a little concerning.

My cell pings, and I straighten up. "I always say things I

mean." I jab my finger at the bottle of mouthwash. "Rinse the taste of that fat fuck from your mouth. It belongs to me now."

"I hate you," she hisses, spewing venom at me through her words and her expression.

"You want to hate me," I correct, "but you can't because you want me as much as I want you." I take a step back. "Freshen up, Valentina. I'll leave some clean clothes on the bed for you." Closing the bathroom door behind me, I extract my cell and answer Rico's call. I step out of the bedroom, not risking Valentina overhearing. "Bianchi."

"Are you on your way home?"

"We just left Miami. We're due to land in La Guardia just after eleven."

"And she's with you?"

"Yes." I eye Mimi warily as I retake my seat. She's hovering in the aisle, waiting to pounce. "Hold on a sec," I tell my *consigliere* as I eyeball the flight attendant. "I need privacy. Make yourself scarce, Mimi."

"Fiero, I—"

"Now," I command, not having to raise my voice for her to understand.

Hurt splays across her face before she turns around, pulling the curtain and retreating to her small space to the left of the cockpit.

I knew I shouldn't have fucked her last week. She's been flirting with me for months since she was hired to replace Jordan. Hiring a female flight attendant was a bad idea, but Jordan is sick, and he couldn't give me much notice. He recommended her from his commercial flight days, and I hired her without giving it too much thought. She has clinger written all over her, and screwing her in a moment of craziness is biting me in the ass now.

"Fiero, you there?" Rico asks, reminding me he's on the end of the line.

"I'm here."

"Problem?"

"Not for much longer." I'll have to replace her, but I'll talk to Zumo at home about it. He can break the news to her and handle the recruitment. I have no time for female histrionics. Right now, Valentina is my priority. As is ensuring her presence in my life this week is hidden from those who are better off not knowing.

Rico sighs. "You fucked Mimi, didn't you?"

"It was a moment of madness."

"You seem to be having a lot of those lately. Sure you're not going through a midlife crisis?"

"Honestly, I'm not sure of anything right now." I blow air out of my mouth as I slouch in my seat, glancing out the window at the dark night sky.

"Yet you still took Valentina."

"By agreement."

"So, Valentina is fully on board now?"

"She couldn't get out of that place quick enough."

His heavy sigh filters down the line as I cross my feet at the ankles. "This isn't good, Fiero. Massimo will flip his shit when he finds out."

"*If* he finds out."

"You two are thick as thieves. Are you really going to keep this from him?"

"It doesn't sit right with me, but I have no choice."

"How do you plan to play this?"

I rub the back of my neck. "We'll stay in Long Island."

"You told her you'd show her a good time. She's never been in the city, and you can't keep her locked up the entire time."

Watch me.

"I'll figure something out. For now, just arrange for Zumo to meet me at my house." I can't keep this from my little brother. As my underboss, he needs to be fully informed.

The instant I end the call, Mimi appears, depositing herself uninvited in my lap. She moves in for the kill, and I twist my head in time so her lips land on my cheek instead of my mouth. It takes effort to be gentle as I lift her off my lap. "Stop this."

"What's wrong?" She reaches for me as I stand, but I grab her hands, encircling her wrists and keeping her away from me. "Why are you being like this?"

"I made it perfectly clear after I fucked you it was a one and done. You said you understood."

"I can't stop thinking about you." Her eyes glisten as she lowers her gaze to my crotch. "Sex with you was out of this world. I know you felt the same things I did."

I bent her over a chair and fucked her roughly from behind. I only kissed her once, at the end, as a form of thanks. It was like every other emotionless sexual encounter I've had these past few years. It was a release, nothing more, and I haven't given her a moment's thought since.

I don't want to hurt her, but she needs to get the message. I glance over my shoulder, checking that Valentina is still in the bedroom. Turning my head to Mimi, I stare coldly at her. "It meant nothing to me. I needed to fuck, and you were there. I haven't thought of you once since it happened, and I have zero interest in a repeat. It was nothing special." I'm being kind because the sex was crap, and immediately after, I wondered why I bothered.

Hurt instantly transforms to anger. "It's because of that slut, isn't it?"

"Watch your mouth." Releasing her hands, I shove her up against the wall and grip her chin tight. "I have noticed the way you're treating my guest. Try it again, and you'll see a very different side to me, Mimi." Her lower lip wobbles as tears well in her eyes. I release her and step back, my anger fading. "I'm sorry you thought there was more to it, but I was very direct with you.

You need to forget about it and do the job I'm paying you to do. I need Valentina's case. Get it for me now."

"If you change your mind—"

"Have some self-respect, Mimi. I won't change my mind, now go." Valentina must be out of the shower by now, and she needs clean clothes.

Mimi heads away without further protest, and I breathe a sigh of relief. Sinking back into my seat, I finish my water and silently take the case when Mimi returns and hands it to me. She disappears, looking upset but behaving. Maybe I won't have to replace her after all if she can be mature about this.

My hand moves to my stomach when a sudden wave of nausea churns in my gut. My stomach cramps, and for a second, I think I might puke, but it subsides as fast as it came on. Weird.

I open Valentina's case, frowning as I search through her messy belongings trying to find something for her to wear. These clothes are mostly old and worn and all but a couple of dresses and shoes are from a chain store—cheap and of poor quality. My hatred for Dominic Ferraro elevates another notch as I finger trashy thongs, panties, and bras. A woman like Valentina deserves to have the finest silk and lace gracing her delectable body and the most stunning designer clothes to make the most of her gorgeous figure.

My frown increases when I find a large brown envelope stuffed with cash in the middle of her case. *Did he give this to her, or has she been hiding it from him?* My mind is spinning theories as I put it back and close her case after extracting a light white cotton dress and a pair of tennis shoes. I grab a white bra and panties, vowing to take her entire case and burn it all when we get to my house.

Making a note of her sizes on my phone, I ponder which twin to call and press the button for Caleb. Joshua Accardi—one of the twin dons of the Accardi *famiglia* in New York—is my partner in managing the drug supply chain for the *mafioso*, and I normally wouldn't hesitate to call him for help. But Joshua plays by the rules, and I can't involve him in this. His more reckless twin thrives on rule-breaking even if Caleb is somewhat of a changed man since he got married and knocked his new bride up. Of the two, Caleb is more likely to help without it being a crisis of conscience.

"Maltese," Caleb answers, sounding out of breath. "This better be good."

"Bad timing?"

"You could say that. What's up?"

"I need a favor, and I need this to be kept between us."

"Now I'm all kinds of intrigued. Shoot." I hear a soft female voice in the background. "Make it snappy. My wife needs me." I can guess why. In the past, Caleb would have made some crude remark, but he treats his wife like a queen, and he'd never disrespect her by saying anything vulgar. I used to joke Caleb was the son I never had because he reminded me so much of myself at his age. Seeing how love has transformed him is nothing short of miraculous. I've never wanted that for myself.

Until Valentina.

My thought shocks the shit out of me, and I force it aside, unwilling to analyze it now.

"Dude, you there?"

"Yeah. I need Rachel McConaughey's number. Can you text it to me and let her know I need a favor?"

Rachel McConaughey heads one of the top female global clothing brands, and she recently expanded her line to include shoes, bags, and lingerie. The Accardi clothing brand is one of the best-selling male brands, and the twins have the best contacts in the industry. Rachel helped Joshua out recently when he needed stuff for his wife, Gia, and she was happy to accommodate, so I'm hoping she'll be amenable to doing me a favor too. I'll make sure it's worth her while, paying handsomely for the personalized service.

Valentina deserves the best, so she's getting the best.

If I didn't have to keep her hidden, I'd take her to the store so she could pick items herself. But that's not an option. I can't parade her nonstop around the city and expect to keep it a secret.

"You got a woman we don't know about?"

"It's complicated."

Caleb chuckles. "It usually is. Okay. Consider it done, but you owe me, Maltese."

"Wouldn't expect anything less." After ending the call, I grab Valentina's clothes and head to the bedroom. My stomach is queasy again, and I hope I'm not coming down with a bug.

My breath stutters in my chest when I enter the room, discovering Valentina curled up in the bed fast asleep. Glossy ink-jet hair fans around her head on the pillow. She must have blow-dried it before climbing under the covers in her underwear. That hideous blue dress she was wearing is draped over the end of the bed, and I'm adding it to the pile for burning.

Carefully, I perch on the edge of the bed and watch her sleeping like a bona fide creeper. She looks even younger in slumber, with her fingers clutching a silver locket around her neck, and for the first time, I consider how wrong it is to crave her. She's almost twenty years younger than me, and I'm old enough to be her father. That should be enough to deter me, but it isn't. My blood is alive, singing a song that's just for her, and my fingers twitch with an insurmountable urge to touch her. In my head, a voice is urging me to claim her, and I don't think I'm strong enough to resist.

I wanted her to myself, and now I have her, I'm not holding back.

Very carefully, I reach out and finger the ends of her hair, being careful not to wake her. Air trickles out through her slightly parted pillowy lips, and I can't resist dusting my mouth lightly and quickly over her tempting one. She tastes of mint and cherries and the natural floral scent wafting from her body.

She's so perfect, and I have never craved another human as much as I crave her. If she were awake, I would eat her alive, and it would not be enough.

It'd never be enough.

I'm not sure I'll ever get my fill of this woman.

I've been deluding myself into thinking a few days would satisfy me.

Valentina stirs a little, and I hold myself still, my face hovering just above hers, raking my gaze over every beautiful part of her. Her olive skin is so perfect, unblemished and untainted, and I'm struck dumb by her beauty and the innocence that clings to her in sleep. The elegant curves of her face are begging for my touch, and it's becoming harder and harder to deny what I want and need.

Yeah, I'm definitely fooling myself if I think this is temporary.

What I'm feeling is not temporary.

It's not just lust either.

I want to smother her, cherish her, protect her, love her.

My thoughts terrify me like I've never been terrified before.

Especially because they feel *right*.

I've made up my mind. I'm not sure how I'm going to pull it off, but I'll figure out a way.

I'm not giving her back.

She's *mine*.

Consequences be damned.

Chapter Ten
Valentina

I'm warm and sated as I snuggle into my pillow, feeling more content than I have in ages. The steady thumping at my ear almost lulls me back to sleep until a fresh minty, citrusy scent mixed with spicier notes tickles my nostrils, and I suddenly jerk my eyes open.

"Shh, honey." Fiero's hold tightens where he carries me in his arms. "Go back to sleep. We're nearly there."

I shouldn't nestle closer into his chest or cling possessively to his shirt, but it's been a long time since I've felt anything close to comfort in a man's arms, and I'm too sleepy to resist. My eyelids close and I succumb to blissful darkness once again.

When I wake next, I'm in the passenger seat of a helicopter as Fiero flies us over what I assume is New York City and we're both wearing headphones.

"Oh my god," I murmur in a sleepy tone. "What's going on?"

Fiero chuckles, smiling as he glances at me. "You're safe, and we're nearly home." His voice rings clear in my ears.

"You're a pilot?" I stupidly ask.

"I am, and I'm experienced, so don't look so panicked."

"I've never been in a helicopter before," I admit, stretching my legs and frowning when I see what I'm wearing. My head whips up to his. "Who dressed me?"

"I did." Solemn eyes meet mine. "I didn't think you'd want Mimi doing that."

I instantly scowl, and his lips tip up at the corners. "Watch the sky!" I blurt, and laughter bursts from his chest.

I grab the soft, blue blanket sitting on my lap, pulling it up over my shoulders and tucking it in around me, briefly contemplating yanking it over my head to shield my embarrassment.

"I could fly this chopper in my sleep, kitten. Relax, and you have no need to be jealous. You won't see Mimi again. I'm firing her."

My eyes pop wide. "Because of me?"

"Partly." His reply is terse on purpose.

"You fucked her."

"Watch your mouth, Valentina. A lady doesn't curse."

I flip him the bird. "Who says I'm a lady?"

"I do." He glares at me. "Continue to challenge me, and I'll be making good on that spanking threat."

I bite down hard on my lip and avert my eyes, looking out the window of the helicopter to avoid looking at him.

Tense silence fills the air.

"Valentina."

I ignore him, straining forward to see the landscape below.

"Valentina." His tone is sharper and laced with frustration. "Look at me when I'm talking to you."

"Fuck. You," I reply as if on autopilot.

"I plan to. I'll fuck this rebellion from every bone in your body."

He gets his wish when I swing my hate-filled gaze on his face. "You'll have to tie me down to do it, and it still won't work."

"Is that how Dominic did it?" he asks, and all the blood leaches from my face.

Horrific memories of that first night in the Ferraro household return to haunt me. It's been years since I've let myself think of it, but the more I'm around Fiero, the more everything I've spent years blocking out is seeping through the steel walls I've erected to keep them out.

"What has happened to you in that house, Valentina?"

"I don't want to talk about him or that house." My words sound hollow to my ears. "You took me to fuck me, so just fuck me. I don't get why you have to talk to me. I don't get a say anyway."

He curses under his breath. Guess it's okay for him to curse, because he's not *a lady*. Such double standards sicken me, but it's often the way of this world even if I have heard tales of how progressive New York is.

"Let's get one thing straight," Fiero says, glaring at me again. "You are here because I want you here, and it's not just for your body. Secondly, everything we do will be consensual because I'll never force you."

"Then we won't be fucking," I retort, "because I'd rather kill myself than be your whore."

A growl spews from his lips. "I should take us down and put you over my knee right now." He glances quickly at me, and his expression has softened a little. "Don't ever refer to yourself as a whore again."

"Why not? You paid for me. I am a whore."

"You are not a whore, and I only paid for you because you are married."

"And if I wasn't?"

"I would have claimed you as mine the instant I locked eyes on you. I would have dragged you into a private room and fucked you until you saw sense and realized we were meant to be together."

His words shock the shit out of me. "You don't even know me."

"That doesn't matter. We'll discover everything about one another in time. I know what my heart wants, and in that moment—and every moment since then—my heart only wants you."

He looks as shocked as I'm feeling, but he quickly composes himself. "Unfortunately, you *are* married, and I couldn't steal you away from a made man without his permission, so I was forced to do this. But I haven't bought you, Valentina, and you are not a whore. What happens in New York will only happen if you want it. I have never forced any woman, and I won't be starting now."

I spin in my seat so I'm facing him more clearly as we dip lower in the sky. "So, if I say no, if I refuse to have sex with you, you'll just accept it after paying all that money?" I'm sure my skepticism is written all over my face.

"It's not about the money, and you won't refuse me. You want this as much as I do."

Fiero helps me out of the helicopter after we've landed on the helipad in the middle of expansive manicured lawns. A man dressed all in black with a rifle strapped across his body approaches, reaching down for our luggage. "Welcome home, boss," he says, slanting a quick, inquisitive look my way.

"It's good to be back," Fiero says. "Take those to my room," he adds, and the man nods and heads off. Without asking, Fiero scoops me up into his arms and strides across the grass toward the imposing house in the near distance.

Lights are dotted all over the property, highlighting its perfection. The house is two stories, composed of gray brick with triangular roofs of different shapes and sizes. White-framed windows are numerous and wide, facing the dock to my right. I spy a speedboat and a larger craft at Fiero's dock, and my mind starts plotting escape routes. *I've never even been on a boat, let alone driven one, but it can't be too hard, right?*

My eyes scan the area, taking everything in. The property seems very big, bordered by copious trees and dense woodland on three sides. Although I see a gray stone driveaway to the right of the house, I can't see the front entrance gates from here. I'm guessing it'd be way easier to escape on water than on land, but I'll keep my options open. As soon as Fiero leaves me alone, I'll be checking the place out thoroughly.

The garden is set across three levels, and we're on the lower one when we pass a cute stone house with an abundance of hanging baskets and colorful pots housing different flowers.

A fragrant scent tickles my nostrils, and I inhale deeply, savoring the familiar smell. Back home in Detroit, I had zero interest in flowers or gardening, but it became my salvation in Miami. A place I could escape to when I was silently screaming inside and my lungs felt like they were bursting from holding so much in. Dom begrudged the money I spent on seeds and gardening supplies until I pointed out how much money we were saving growing our own vegetables, and then he stopped bitching. Dom likes to entertain a lot, and he always ensures there is money for food and drink, but he's happy to cut corners where he could. "Who lives there?" I ask as we stride past the place.

"It's a guest cottage," Fiero says, jerking his head to the right as we pass a large pool with a small structure at the back of it. "That's the main pool and pool house. There's another pool on the first level of the house.

"I see it," I say, noticing the infinity pool up ahead. Fiero takes the first set of steps up to the next level of the garden, holding me tighter and closer to his chest. "I can walk you know."

"I like carrying you, and I know you're tired."

A yawn leaks from my mouth as if on cue, and Fiero chuckles.

"You have a nice home," I supply as we ascend the second set of steps and head toward the front door.

"Thank you. When I'm not in Miami, I live in my penthouse apartment in the city during the week and escape here on the weekend. It's my sanctuary."

I stare into his face. I'm not sure what to make of Don Maltese. He's a bit of an enigma, and not entirely what I was expecting.

Fiero finally puts me down to open the door, lacing his fingers through mine as we step inside his palatial home. He closes and locks the door behind us as I attempt to wrench my hand from his, but he keeps a firm grip of it. My face contorts into a scowl when delicious tremors shoot up and down my arm and warmth sinks into my palm from his touch. I hate how natural it feels to hold his hand and to be touched by him. I hate how every part of me comes alive when he looks at me or puts his hands on me, mostly because I don't hate it at all.

I'm confused. He confuses me, as does the potency of the chemistry between us. I don't have much to compare it with as the only man I've been with by choice was Damiano. I was crazy about him when I was seventeen, but I don't remember his touch setting me on fire like Fiero's does.

"You must be hungry," he says, leading me into a large bright kitchen with white painted cupboards and stainless-steel appliances. After lifting me onto a stool at the island unit, he heads straight to the large refrigerator and opens the door. "What would you like?" he asks, inspecting the contents of his packed fridge. "We have lasagna, chicken pasta, vegetarian curry, or lamb and vegetables."

"I'm not that hungry." My eyes drift to the large clock mounted on the wall, and I'm surprised it's not later.

"Don't lie." He dumps a few plastic containers with hand-written labels on the counter. "You barely ate any dinner."

What little I ate came back up easily after my battle with Cesco under the table, but Fiero doesn't need to know that. "I'm not eating a full dinner at midnight," I say, stifling another yawn. "I'll never sleep with a full stomach."

"I make a mean grilled cheese." He places his palms down on the counter. "Will you eat that?"

"Why do you care if I eat?" I tuck my hair behind my ears, placing a hand over my mouth as another yawn slips free.

"You're under my care, and I plan to look after you well. I'm making us a snack. If you don't like grilled cheese, I can probably scrabble something else together."

Warmth blossoms in my chest at his words. I'm still angry he bought me, but after his earlier explanation and this, it's getting harder to hold on to it. It's been a long time since anyone cared whether I was hungry, or cared period, and it's nice to know this man isn't just some savage who brought me here to spread my legs and service him without any regard for my welfare. I'm under no illusion. He's a dangerous made man, and in my experience, they're mostly selfish pricks with little respect for women. I doubt Fiero is much different. This is probably an act to butter me up, but I'll take it because I'm just that desperate for affection.

I'm walking a slippery slope, and I've got to be careful around this man. Appeasing him is the smartest option if I can pull it off. I offer him a genuine smile. "Grilled cheese is good. Thank you."

He stares at me as if in a daze for a few seconds before shaking out of it. "Coming right up."

He returns the containers to the refrigerator, before gathering the ingredients he needs to make our grilled cheese. We don't talk as he sets about making our sandwiches, putting them on the griddle, and then cutting them in half and sliding them onto plates. "What would you like to drink?" he asks, setting a plate in front of me. "I've got water, juice, coffee, and a variety of herbal teas."

"Do you have peppermint?" I ask, and he nods. "I'll have that, thanks."

I inhale the gooey, cheesy goodness as Fiero puts the kettle on, moaning as I sink my teeth into the first bite.

Fiero's shoulders stiffen as he stands with his back to me. A few beats later, he casts a glance over his shoulder. His expression is carefully controlled. "Good?"

"Very," I mumble in between bites. A satisfied smile crawls over his delectable mouth, and his entire face comes alive. He's so gorgeous I almost choke on the piece of sandwich in my mouth. He is incredibly sexy with that cheeky boyish grin, the mischievous glint in his big blue eyes, mop of white-blond hair falling over his brow, and the layer of dark stubble coating his jawline. My fingers twitch with a need to explore, and I wonder how I'll survive a week in this house with him and not succumb to his charms. I have a feeling when he fucks me I'll never be the same again, and the thought is troubling in the extreme.

I never thought I'd ever be attracted to an older man, but I barely even register that fact when I'm with him. He turns my insides to mush with one heated look, and his touch is like lightning, supercharging every inch of my body and amplifying desires that have long lain dormant.

I am so screwed.

I could fight it, refuse to let him touch me, and see if he's a man of his word, but pacifying him is a smarter move. If I keep him happy and distract him with sex, I can snoop and plot my escape. I'll try to zone out, like I always do during sex, but I have a feeling that'll be impossible with Fiero. I'm terrified with one touch I'll be putty in his hands. I'll have to find some way to detach myself from the act. To view it purely as a physical release and not read more into it. After all, he only wants me to sate his lust, and he fully plans on giving me back.

He has no idea I'm never returning to Miami.

And I can't contemplate the consequences for him if I escape while I'm under his care.

Fiero is a big boy, and he outranks Dom; he'll figure a way out.

Chapter Eleven
Fiero

"Sleep in this," I say, walking out of my closet holding a white T-shirt. I'm not letting her sleep in that tatty shit that is supposed to pass for a nightdress I found in her case. I thrust the shirt at her, and she throws it on the floor like it offends her.

"Did you go through my things?" she shouts, looking instantly panicked. Her case is open on my bed as she glares at me.

"I didn't pry," I lie. "I just opened it to grab clean clothes."

"You undressed and redressed me." She turns to me in her bare feet, crossing her arms over her chest. One hand reaches up to curl around her locket. "That is a massive violation of my privacy."

"We already discussed this, and I didn't look," I lie again.

I mean, I set out with that intention, but I couldn't help looking, and fuck me, I have never seen a woman more beautiful. It took everything in me to leave her sleeping on her back while I dressed her and not part her thighs and feast on her tempting flesh. When I take her for the first time, she'll be fully conscious and aware of everything I do to her, every pleasure I tease from her silky, smooth flesh. I want her panting and screaming and writhing underneath me. Nothing less will be acceptable.

Her eyes narrow in suspicion. "You don't really expect me to believe that, do you?"

"What's it matter? I'll be seeing everything very soon."

"I thought I had a choice?" She tightens her arms around her body and bites her lower lip.

"You do, but you'll choose me." I stalk toward her and pull her into my arms, pressing my body all up in hers. "Stop fighting this. *Us.*" I yank her firmly into my body, grinding my hips against her so she feels the semi in my pants.

"I'm tired." She attempts to wriggle out of my grasp.

"I know." I slam my lips down on hers without warning, covering her mouth in a slew of passionate kisses. I can't get enough of her. She tastes like heaven, and every nerve ending and tissue in my body is electrified with the need to take her and make her mine, but I meant what I said. I won't force her. I'm seconds from pulling back when she stops fighting me, going slack in my arms, and her lips part as I lick across the seam of her mouth. My tongue drives through her lips, tangling deliciously with hers as all the blood in my body rushes south, and I'm straining painfully against the zipper of my black cargo pants.

She's clawing at my back and pressing her tits against my chest as she meets me hungrily, kiss for kiss, tongue for tongue, whimpering and moaning into my mouth as she rubs against me.

This. This is all that matters. I could devour her whole, and it still wouldn't be enough to sate this unquenchable craving for her. My hands long to travel the length of her body and mold to her exquisite curves, but I don't have the time to devote to her now, and I refuse to rush this.

We've got the rest of forever because I meant what I promised myself earlier.

I'm not giving her back. She's *mine.* Now and forever.

I yank my lips off hers as that thought lands front and center, frying my brain and inducing rare anxiety. *Fuck. Fuck. Fuck.* I thought I had everything worked out in my life, but one look at this woman, one taste of her divine mouth, and I'm fucking undone, coming apart at the seams and questioning everything I thought I knew about myself. I drag my hands through my hair and gulp over the lump lodged in my throat. It's quite possible Rico was right, and I *have* lost my mind.

"Get some sleep," I growl, stepping away from her. "And put my shirt on." I don't wait for a response, all but running out of my bedroom, slamming the door shut behind me.

I stalk downstairs and grab a cold beer, adjusting my painful hard-on behind my pants. I'm just wondering if there's time to rub out a quick one when my *soldato* at the gate calls to tell me my brother just arrived.

Guess I have my answer. I drain the beer and toss the bottle in the trash before walking to the front door to greet my brother and underboss.

"Walk with me," I say when he approaches, and Zumo readily falls into step alongside me, heading toward the walking trail at the rear of the house. I had walking-slash-jogging trails installed a couple years after I bought this place so I could take advantage of everything the property has to offer. My men patrol the grounds twenty-four-seven, so it was practical as well as indulgent.

Sensor lights embedded in the cream-colored stone path light up the second we set foot on it.

"What's got your panties in a bunch?" Zumo eyes me with a mix of concern and amusement.

"I'm wired and horny, and I need to walk this restless energy off."

He quirks a brow. "So, call someone. Head back to the city to fuck it out of your system."

"No can do." I point back at the house. "The reason I'm all screwed up is back there in my bed."

Zumo slams to a halt, his eyes widening instantaneously. "What the fuck? You have a real woman in your bed?"

I snort out a laugh as I keep walking. "As opposed to a fake woman?"

He speeds up to catch me. "It could be a sex robot. They're very realistic now with proper pussies and assholes and—"

"Stop." A shudder works its way through me. "I should shoot you for even daring to suggest it."

"You never bring women here. That custom-fit sex room you spent a fortune on has never been used. Excuse me for being fucking shocked."

"You and me both, brother."

Zumo stops walking again, and I slow down, turning back to face him. "What's going on?" he asks.

"Rico thinks I'm having a midlife crisis." I run a hand along the back of my neck. "Maybe I am."

Zumo's features soften though amusement still glimmers in his eyes. "It's okay to change your mind, Fiero. It's okay to let a woman in. Honestly, this is a good thing. A great thing." He would say that. He's always been more into relationships than casual fucking. Bet he won't be thinking that in a minute when I spill the beans. "We were all worried you'd remain a bachelor for life."

That had been the plan, but now? Now I'm all mixed up. "You enjoy gossiping with our sisters as much as any woman. You sure you don't have a pussy?"

"The only pussy in my vicinity is the one currently warming my bed, so can we move this along? Who is this woman and why am I here?"

I give my younger brother the CliffsNotes version, watching

as his expression changes from elation to shock to fear to amusement and disbelief and a host of other emotions.

"You *are* going through a midlife crisis. Are you fucking insane? You paid over six million dollars for one week with a woman when you turn women down left and right? She must be some woman."

"She is."

"Well, damn." He surveys me more closely. "You've got feelings for her."

"All the feelings are trapped right here." I grab my junk and smirk. It's an asshole move, but I'm not exactly myself right now.

"Bullshit." Zumo steps closer. "Utter bullshit."

Air whooshes out of my mouth in a loud sigh. "I know. I'm screwed. So fucking screwed."

Sympathy splays over his face. "I hate this for you. You finally find a woman you want for more than just sex, and she's already fucking married. This won't end well, Fiero. You should put her back on a plane to Miami before you do anything. You can't fuck her. You won't want to give her back."

I'm not confirming I've already decided she's *not* going back.

"It'll just be sex. I just need to fuck this craving away and it'll be fine."

"You've pulled some stunts in your time, brother, but this might be the craziest of all."

Debatable, but my little brother isn't privy to all my escapades.

"The board will have your balls for this, Fiero. We don't treat women like this in New York. Bennett and Massimo have worked hard to introduce equality, fairness, and respect and to include women more in our world. This shits all over that notion."

"Which is why they can't know. I promised her dinner and a show, and I want to take her to some of the main sights, but the rest of the time, I'm keeping her here away from prying eyes. I need your help to keep this a secret. I need you to handle a few things for me and to cover my back when I need it."

He slaps me on the back, agreeing without hesitation like I knew he would. "You got it, brother. Whatever you need, it's yours."

When I return to the bedroom after Zumo has left, Valentina is asleep in my bed in the tatty black cotton nightdress and not my soft white shirt. That's still lying in a crumpled heap on the white carpet.

She's such a defiant little thing.

One part of me welcomes her rebellion, but the other is frustrated she'll obey that fat fuck she calls a husband and not me. *Would it have killed her to sleep in my shirt?* I want her in my clothes, and cheap cotton has no place nestled up close to such perfection.

A wicked grin trips over my lips as I strip down to my boxers and pad downstairs to the kitchen, rummaging in the drawers until I find what I need. Ana will bust my balls for messing up her organization, but I pay her to sort my shit, so she won't complain too much.

Returning to the bedroom, I set the scissors down and very carefully peel the comforter back, revealing Valentina to me. She mumbles in her sleep, and while it'd be easier to do this while she's unconscious, I'm not opposed to her waking either and fighting me. But she merely turns over onto her back and settles into the land of nod, leaving me to execute my dastardly plan in peace.

I stifle my chuckles as I carefully cut the nightdress up the front, holding it out from her body so I don't accidentally hurt her. It falls to the sides, exposing her bare body to me, and my dick instantly thickens, blood surging through my veins at the sight of such perfection. Natural tits with small rose-colored nipples salute me, and my mouth waters at the thought of tasting all that soft flesh. My eyes rake over her flat stomach and lower to her beautiful pussy, my mouth salivating at the fine strip of shaved dark hair and her toned thighs and long slender legs.

I'm painfully hard, and my cock spasms, thrusting involuntarily with the need to plunge into her wet warmth. I squeeze the head of my dick, and precum leaks from the tip. Knowing I need to deal with it this time, I snip the thin straps of her dress and cut the rest fully away before dumping the ragged threads into the black bag I also brought from the kitchen.

Valentina must be exhausted since I managed all that without her waking. I blow her a soft kiss before carefully covering her with the comforter. Then I head into the bathroom and jerk off into my hand to visions of my sleeping beauty with her mouth latched around my cock.

Returning to the bedroom, I head into the closet and tip the contents of her shabby case—bar the cash envelope, toiletries, and pill box, which I leave alone—into the bag and head outside, making a beeline for the gardener's shed.

I pull a steel drum outside and dump the bag inside. "Who's got a lighter?" I ask into the darkness, knowing one of my *soldati* will hear me.

"I've got you, boss." Dino steps forward from the trees, fighting a smirk as he scans my boxer-clad form. "Here." He slaps a cheap red plastic lighter in my palm, and I grab an item of clothing from the bag and hold it up as I set it on fire. Then I dump it into the drum and watch with smug satisfaction as every stitch of clothing Valentina came here with goes up in flames.

It feels prophetic, and I wish I had dragged her out of bed, kicking and screaming, to watch her old life start to burn.

Chapter Twelve
Valentina

S nuggling into the warmth of the bed, I inhale the fresh floral scent from the pillow as I slowly wake. Cool air kisses my cheeks as I stare in initial confusion at the large airy bedroom until it all comes back to me. Heat seeps into my skin from the large palm pressed firmly against my tummy from behind, his long fingers dangerously close to my most intimate parts that are bare like the rest of me.

What the hell? I know I went to sleep in my black nightie. That asshole must have removed it while I was unconscious. I'm usually a light sleeper, but I guess I was really out of it last night. It's been an exhausting weekend, so it's not altogether surprising. My eyes scan the floor and the room at large, but it's nowhere to be seen. The shirt he gave me to sleep in lies in the same crumpled heap where I left it, and that'll have to do. I attempt to free myself from his grip, but Fiero pulls me back flush against his body, and a strangled sound rips from my lips when his morning wood presses up against my ass.

Holy fuck. He's naked too. *Of course, he is.*

I work harder to wriggle out of his grip, but it's in vain.

"Where you going to, kitten?" he asks in a sleep-drenched tone, sliding his leg over mine as both arms band around my waist, caging me. His lips find my neck, trailing a slew of drugging kisses up and down my rapidly overheating skin.

"I need to pee," I protest, pushing at his arms to free myself.

"We need to talk about your language, kitty cat," he purrs, nestling his head into the crook of my neck.

"We need to talk about my lack of clothing," I pant, briefly closing my eyes and praying for strength I already know I don't have.

"What's there to talk about?" Moving quickly, he slides me underneath him. Heat rolls off his bare flesh as he holds himself above me, his inked arms solid as his palms sink into the mattress, and his erection pokes at my lower stomach, dangerously close to where my pussy is throbbing in instant need.

Oh god. How am I expected to resist when I can feel his hardness pressing against me?

He slowly rakes his gaze all over me. "Nope, can't see any issue." He flashes me a dazzling smile, and his eyes crease at the corners. It's like getting sucker punched in the heart and the pussy at the same time. His eyes darken with lust, and his tongue darts out, wetting his full lips. "I want you," he growls in a wickedly seductive tone. "I want to gorge myself on you until I've sampled everything on offer." He drops down on his side, pressing himself up right up against me, igniting tingles all over my body as he draws circles on my bare tummy with his warm fingers. "I want to feast on your tits," he adds, his hand coming up to cup my right breast. He tweaks the hardened peak. "Suck and bite your nipples." His eyes bore into mine as he gropes my body, sending a slew of fiery tremors cascading across my skin.

My chest heaves as I fall under his spell, watching with bated breath as his hand travels lower. A whimper flees my mouth when his fingers skim through the strip of fine hair on my pussy to rub up and down my slit. "Play with your clit," he continues, swirling his fingers around the tight bud of nerves. "Finger your cunt." He maintains eye contact as he slowly drives one finger inside me, and I'm melting into the bed. "Lick, suck, and tongue your pussy until you squirt all over my face. I'll lap it all up and drink it all down." His finger pumps slowly in and out of me, and my inner walls clench around it. "And then I'll slam inside you, pounding so fucking hard I'll hit your womb, over and over, ruining you for all other men." He withdraws his finger and smiles, arching a brow and watching the red flush stealing over my skin and my pathetic attempts to regulate my breathing.

My mouth is dry, and my ability to speak seems to have evaporated.

"Got nothing to say to that, kitten?" he asks before plunging his finger in his mouth and sucking hard, moaning and licking it clean.

Liquid lust floods my pussy, and I'm so wet I'm afraid I'm drenching the sheets. "I need the bathroom!" I blurt, sliding off the bed and scrambling to my feet, careful to keep my ass hidden.

Fiero chuckles. "Hurry, baby." A look of sheer wantonness washes over his face as his pupils dilate, and he licks his lips, his gaze roaming my body with blatant lust.

I snatch the shirt from the floor and shimmy into it.

More laughter rumbles from his chest. "Don't bother, it'll just be coming off again." He props up on one elbow, and the comforter slides down the bed, exposing him in all his masculine glory.

Fuck. Me.

Fuck my life.

My eyes pop wide as I inspect his body fully for the first time. My god, he's too beautiful to be true. Ink covers both arms, one side of his neck, and his upper chest. Every part of him is ripped, toned, and tan from his broad shoulders to his sculpted chest and abs leading to tapered hips and oh, wow. *Wow.* He's huge and pierced, and my legs almost buckle under me.

A thin layer of dark hair extends from his chest, down the center of his stomach, and lower. He's well groomed, which is a welcome change from my norm. I squeeze my thighs together as I visually feast on his long thick hard cock. It jerks under my gaze, and a bit of precum leaks from the crown where two piercings exist on either side.

I almost come on the spot. I've never been with a man who has cock piercings, and I'm salivating at the prospect of feeling it inside me.

Hell. I am truly screwed. Completely and utterly fucked already.

This man is unraveling me, and I don't know if it's a good thing.

"Like what you see, honey?" He wraps one large hand around his erection and strokes it slowly. "This is all for you."

He's going to be the death of me. With my heart racing, I rush into the bathroom with my cheeks on fire and my pussy clenching and unclenching in anticipation.

I brush my teeth, splash water on my face, and drag Fiero's comb through my hair. I'm sitting on the toilet peeing when he saunters casually into the room. "Get out!" I shriek, moving my hands to cover myself. My cheeks inflame, and I stall mid-flow, too embarrassed to pee in front of him.

"Don't be shy, kitten." He fills a toothbrush with toothpaste before looking over at me. "I want nothing between us. No clothes. No secrets. No reservations." He turns on the faucet. "You're mine, Valentina, and you don't need to be embarrassed around me."

"I don't know you."

"We're rectifying that." He shoves the toothbrush in his mouth. "Pee," he says in a garbled tone, pointing at me.

I can't hold it forever, so I look down at the floor and finish my business. I flush and wander to the second sink, avoiding his probing gaze as I wash and dry my hands. His fingers gently encircle my wrist as I move to walk off. He shakes his head, spitting out toothpaste and rinsing his mouth with water. "Stay," he commands, walking to the toilet where he proceeds to pee in front of me with a cheeky grin on his face.

He has no shame. I focus on drinking my fill of his naked body from behind. The rear view is every bit as impressive as the front. Firm, tan skin molds over broad shoulders, defined muscles on either side of his spine, a toned ass, and powerful thighs. His ass cheeks flex as he grins at me over his shoulder, and I fidget and shift on my feet when my arousal drips down my inner thighs. This shouldn't turn me on, but it does.

He scrutinizes me with laser-sharp focus while washing and drying his hands. I'm rooted to the spot, staring at him like a deer in headlights. How I ever thought I could zone this man out is beyond me. I'm completely out of my league, and this is like nothing I've experienced before. Butterflies swoop into my belly as lust coils low in my core and my heart starts running a marathon.

"You're so incredibly beautiful, Valentina," he says in a deep, dark tone laced with desire. His fingers trace lightly up my neck as he moves my hair aside. "So stunning I don't have the right words to describe it." Leaning in, he grazes his teeth slowly and seductively along the column of my neck. I arch on instinct, gripping the counter behind me so I don't fall on my jelly legs to the ground. Fiero nips and bites my earlobe, and a throaty gasp flees my lips.

In another fast move, he lifts me onto the counter and pushes my thighs apart. His lips are on mine the next second, and it quickly descends into a frenzy. His mouth is unforgiving as he drinks from me, holding my face in his warm, firm hands and tilting my head back. Heat rolls off him in waves as he stands in between my legs, pressing his hard chest against me while ravishing my mouth and obliterating every resistant bone in my body.

I couldn't stop this now if I tried.

It's as inevitable as the sun rising every morning.

The last of my rebellion flees, and I give in to him and the intense consuming need to feel his hands and his body all over me.

This is happening, and I might as well enjoy it—for the short while it will last.

Chapter Thirteen
Fiero

I can't hold back because I've lost all control. I'm high on lust, delirious with desire, and I can't stop kissing her, eating her mouth like I want to swallow her whole. Her kisses set my blood on fire, and every muscle in my body is straining with powerful need. I've never felt this way about any woman before, and my inner beast is demanding I take her and brand myself all over her gorgeous body so she knows who she belongs to. I had planned on taking this slow and gentle, easing her into giving herself to me, but I'm incapable of going slow, and it's not what she needs anyway.

Valentina wants me, but she'll talk herself out of it if I give her even the slightest opportunity for doubts to form. I need to hit her over the head with our chemistry—metaphorically speaking—and continue to demand and take until she accepts we are inevitable. I have accepted that truth, and though parts of me are still freaking out, I won't deny what's staring me in the face any longer.

I was meant for her, and she was meant for me.

That fat fuck will not stand in my way.

I want her and I'm having her. End of.

I'm guessing no one has ever properly taken care of Valentina. I'm going to show her she can hand her pleasure to me, and I'll have her soaring on a cloud of ecstasy every time I lay my hands on her.

Tearing my mouth from hers, I grab the hem of the shirt and rip it from her body, leaving both of us naked. "I want you to trust me with your pleasure." I lift her left leg and bend it at the knee before setting her foot flat on the counter. "Give control to me," I calmly request, lifting her other leg. "I won't hurt you, and I won't push you beyond what you're comfortable with. Let me do this, and I'll have you screaming my name over and over as you come again and again and again."

Vulnerability ghosts over her face, and she chews on the corner of her lip, looking down at where she's fully exposed before me. "Eyes on me, kitten," I say, purposely not lowering mine. "Give me your consent and control."

I'm expecting her to resist, but I'm pleasantly surprised when she concedes.

"Okay," she whispers, her lower lip wobbling.

Leaning in, I press a soft kiss to her lips before resting my brow on hers. "Trust me. I'm not going to hurt you. I'm going to worship you like the queen you are."

Her chest heaves, and she gulps while looking directly into my eyes. "I don't trust you with anything but this."

"That's okay." I tuck her hair behind one ear as my other hand cups her breast. "It's smart, and I'll prove myself to you in time." I take her mouth again, greedily, hungrily, driving my tongue through her lush lips as I fondle her tit and tweak and pinch her nipple. She squirms on the counter, panting into my mouth, and I'm betting she'll come in record time once I touch her.

Sinking to my knees, I stare at her cunt with my cock

weeping and begging for attention as my gaze runs over all that glistening pink flesh. I swipe my finger up and down her slit, coating my skin with more of her salty-sweet nectar. "You're dripping." I drive one finger into her pussy, tugging on my dick, with my free hand, as her wet warmth hugs my digit. Fucking hell. She won't be the only one coming in record time unless I get a grip. "So greedy," I purr, adding another finger and pumping them in faster.

She grips the edge of the counter, leaning back against the mirror.

"Watch me," I instruct, my gaze flicking between her flushed face and her slippery cunt. I add a third finger, and she emits a delicious moan as she squirms. "Don't move." I plunge my fingers in and out while squeezing my dick just under the head to slow things down. I lean in and lick at her clit in time to the pumping of my fingers. Then I pull back, chuckling when I see the startled look on her face. Pressing my face to her cunt, I inhale deeply. "Nirvana," I murmur before licking a trail up and down her slit. Then I part her folds with my thumb and forefinger, squeezing my dick again, and dive in, eating her all up. She tastes like heaven on my tongue, and I'm ruined. Completely destroyed and obsessed. I devour her, and she lets me, giving herself over to me fully as she writhes, moans, and whimpers while bucking her hips and thrusting her eager little pussy into my face.

Sitting up a little, while still on my knees, I grab the back of her thighs, spreading her wider and keeping her in place as I continue eating her out like a savage. My tongue plunders her pussy as I drive in and out of her with my sanity hanging by a thread. Lowering one hand, I squeeze my dick again, not trusting I won't come all over the floor like a horny teenager.

Taking her feet one at a time, I drape her legs over my shoulders and pull her right to the edge of the counter. My face is buried in her cunt, her juices coating my lips and my stubble, and

I'm drowning in bliss. Nothing tastes better than this. Feels better than this. Her breathing is elevated, the flush on her face grows deeper, her chest heaves, and I know she's close. Her thighs start trembling, and I growl against her succulent flesh. "Come for me, kitten. Right fucking now." Rubbing her clit with rough fingers, I pinch it hard when her inner walls start contracting around my tongue.

She screams my name as her thighs close around my face and her back arches, her gorgeous tits jiggling with the force of the orgasm cresting her body. I lap at her juices, milking every drop as my eyes remain glued to her face.

Watching her come is perfection.

I want to do it for the rest of my life.

Her awestruck gaze lights a spark under me, and I spring up, grabbing my aching cock and bringing it to her entrance. I hold it there for a second, leaning over and crushing my lips to hers, letting her taste herself on me. "Taste that?" I say when I break our lip-lock, straightening up and putting the tip of my dick into her pussy. "Tastes like mine." I slam inside her, relishing her scream as I grab her hips and hold her steady while I pound into her, over and over. The feeling of her tight walls hugging my bare cock is heaven on Earth, and I can't get enough.

"Fuck, fuck," I rasp, digging my nails into her hips as I ram into her like a crazy man. "You feel that, kitten?" I peer deep into her eyes. "You feel me owning you? You feel my cock marking you inside forever?"

"Fiero," she cries, arching her back, and I bend down, sucking her tit into my mouth. My tongue rolls around her nipple before I bite down hard on it.

Her scream was probably heard by my men outside, but they know better than to disturb me.

I continue pounding, feeling a familiar tingle at the base of my spine as I move my mouth to her other breast. I suck hard on her flesh, wanting to leave a visible mark. When I'm happy with my work, I claim her mouth again while rotating my hips and plunging deep. The sounds she's making are music to my ears, and they only crank my arousal even higher. I lift her body a little, hitting her at a deeper angle, and we groan together.

"Oh my god. I'm going to come again." Confusion wars with amazement on her face as I fuck her.

"Wait for me." I grab both tits and squeeze them hard. "I fucking love these. I'm adding a tit-fuck to my list." My balls lift and stars spark behind my eyes. Lifting her more upright, I bring our bodies in closer together. "We go together, baby. When I tell you." I slow down and look at my body moving inside hers. "Watch," I command, and she dips her chin to where we're joined. Watching my cock thrusting in and out of her almost undoes me. "My dick is covered in you," I pant as I slide out and then push back in, going deep, deep, deeper.

"Fiero." The word comes out desperate.

"Does my cock feel good in you, baby?"

She throws back her head as her hands wind around my neck. "So good. Too good."

"No such thing," I pant, driving in deeper as I pick my pace up again. "Wrap your legs around me, kitten, and hold on tight." She does as she's told, and her obedience sends warmth flooding my chest. She readily succumbed to me, and it's the best damn sex of my life. It's no wonder I'm addicted to her. "Not before me," I warn again, grabbing her waist and driving into her at full force. I fuck and fuck and fuck her. Pounding, driving, thrusting, and it's not enough. It'll never be enough. I want to drown in her and the sensations she's coaxing from my body.

Sweat drips down my spine, and little beads cling to my brow. She gyrates her hips in time with my thrusts, and that's it. I can't restrain myself any longer. I shove myself into her so deep it feels like I'm permanently embedded there. Then I move my hand in between our bodies and rub her clit in sync with the rampant slamming of my hips. My balls lift farther, my spine locks, and I shatter. "Now, Valentina!"

Like the good little kitty cat she is, she explodes all over my dick while I roar out my release, almost blacking out as I pulse and throb inside her, depositing my seed deep. She clings to me as she rides out her climax, and my hips only stop moving when I'm completely sated.

Holy hell. What the actual fuck was that?

She looks up at me with tears in her eyes, and pain splinters my heart. "Did I hurt you? Was I too rough?"

"No," she whispers, shaking her head. Tangled strands of inky hair cascade over her flushed shoulders. "You didn't hurt me. That was..."

She's as speechless as me. "Yeah, it was, baby." I sweep my fingers across her gorgeous face.

"I never knew sex could be like that."

I brush a few tears from her cheeks. "Would you believe me if I said I didn't either?"

A faint smile accompanies her soft giggle. "I actually think I would."

I press a soft kiss to her lips. "You're perfect, Valentina."

And I'm definitely never giving you back.

Chapter Fourteen
Valentina

Fiero leaves to answer a call, and I'm glad to have a few moments to myself. That was like an out-of-body experience, and I'm stunned silent. I've never orgasmed during sex, and it's no wonder people are addicted to fucking if that's how it's supposed to feel. Every part of me still tingles from his touch, and I can't help smiling as I recall the possessive way he claimed me. I usually hate when men are rough with me, but I couldn't get enough of Fiero. I wanted it harder, deeper, filthier. My body is a little stiff and sore as I climb off the counter and turn to face the mirror, barely noticing the woman staring back at me.

My fingers gently prod the growing bruise on my chest, and another smile trips across my lips. I should not be applauding that kind of barbaric display of ownership, but it's hot when Fiero does it. It's as if he wants the world to know about us and he wants to keep me. The smile slides off my mouth. I can't afford to think like that, and I shouldn't want him to keep me. I don't. I want my independence. I want freedom from this world and the men who want to cage and chain me.

"What the fuck is that?" Fiero's harsh tone drags me back into the moment, and fear is a dagger driving a stake through my heart as he pushes me down over the counter with my ass on full display.

"Fiero, don't, please."

"No." His fingers are tender as they move lightly over the scars covering both ass cheeks and the very tops of the backs of my thighs. "Did he do this to you?"

"Yes," I semi-lie. I do have them because of Dom, but it wasn't by his hand.

"You're not going back to him," he snarls, lifting me gently, his soft touch at odds with his angry words.

No, I'm not, I silently agree, but I'm not staying here either. "I have to. The deal was only until Sunday."

"I don't care. I'll find a way to make it work."

"You'll start a war."

He stares deep into my eyes. "You're worth it."

My heart soars, trying to beat a path out of my chest. The conviction in his eyes does weird things to me. I feel something shifting inside me, and in this moment, I know I could fall for him, if I let myself, but I can't. "I'm not," I whisper before I can stop myself. "I'm really not."

"Don't say that," he snaps, reeling me against his naked body. "You *are* worthy, and I'm not giving you back to that monster. I'm keeping you." His eyes flare with dark obsession. "When did this happen and why?"

I turn stiff in his arms. "I don't want to talk about it."

"Nice try. Go again." He narrows his eyes in warning.

"I've blanked it from my mind and bringing it up will only upset me."

A muscle clenches in his jaw, and he steps back, dragging his hands through his hair. "You *will* tell me, Valentina," he says, opening the shower door and reaching in to turn the water on.

"You will tell me everything, but I won't force you to tell me today." He tests the water and steps aside. "Get in."

"Ask me nicely."

"No. Get in."

"Make me."

He flashes me that signature grin, and in a split second, I'm up and over his shoulder. Fiero slaps me across the ass as he steps into the shower stall. "Remember what I said about fighting me, kitten?" My body slides slowly down his as he sets me on my feet, and his fresh erection almost pokes a hole through my stomach. He grabs his dick and tugs on it. "You turn me on with that sassy mouth." He rubs his thumb along my lower lip. "I think I'll claim that next, but first, I'm going to wash you."

He turns me around, pulling my back flush against his front as he eases us under the water. The warm water is a balm to my achy body, and I give up fighting, resting my head back on his shoulder as he washes me carefully with a soft cloth and citrusy shower gel. "Give me a list of the toiletries you like, and I'll get them for you," he says while meticulously washing up and down my arms.

Whichever is the cheapest. "I don't have a list, and I brought my own things. Or I'm happy to use yours." I shrug. I'm really not that fussy.

"I want to spoil you." He lifts one breast and then the other, washing me carefully, and my heart is pounding like crazy.

"I don't need to be spoiled," I say in a breathy tone as he swirls the cloth over my belly.

"Which is all the more reason I want to do it."

"Fiero."

"No." He spins me around, pinning me with a fierce look. Water cascades over us from above. "You're not going back to him, end of. You're staying here with me."

"This is insanity," I murmur, my eyes widening when he crouches before me and begins washing me from the feet up.

"It is, but it feels right." His eyes lock on mine as he trails the cloth up one leg. "Don't lie and say you don't feel it. It's written all over your face."

"That doesn't mean we should fucking do it," I hiss because he's confusing me and making me want things I can't ever have.

"What did I tell you about cursing?" he says, sliding the cloth up my inner thigh.

I thrust my arm out to cling to the wall when he cups my pussy with the cloth and drags it back and forth.

"You're showing your age, old man."

Fiero scowls before leaning in and softly biting my inner thigh. "Careful, kitten. I'll put you over my knee and spank it out of you." He moves on to my other thigh and down my leg.

"Please don't do that," I quietly say in a moment of vulnerability. "I don't want to be spanked or..." I trail off, squeezing my eyes shut as the sound of the leather belt meeting my sore skin reverberates in my ears.

"Look at me."

I open my eyes, and he's right in front of me. "I know they are whip marks, and I would never do that to you if you didn't want it." He cups my face in his hands as steam swirls around us. "But you might want to consider conquering that fear to control it. Creating new memories to replace the old ones." He presses a hard kiss to my lips. "Just think about it."

I chew on the inside of my mouth as he turns me around and begins shampooing my hair. After he rinses it, he adds some conditioner and moves me out of the stream of water for a couple of minutes. His fingers massage my scalp, and I lean back against him, more content than I can ever remember feeling. His fingers are magical, and I'm completely under his spell.

When I'm all done, he refuses to let me wash him, quickly

attending to his needs before pushing me down on my knees and bringing his dick to my mouth. I don't usually like giving head, but watching Fiero come undone as I hollow my cheeks and suck him deep into my mouth is a heady feeling.

Grabbing handfuls of his ass, I work his skillful cock, my head bobbing up and down his long, thick length. Fiero swivels his hips, driving through my lips in tune with my movements, and I gag when his dick hits the back of my mouth. "That's it, baby. Choke on my cock."

I almost choke on his *words*, and he chuckles before releasing a strangled groan when I cup his balls and rub one finger along his taint. His eyes flash with heat, and he pulls out abruptly and yanks me to my feet. His lips are on mine instantly, and we grab one another as we kiss like we'll never get to do it again.

Then I'm shoved against the wall, my boobs smooshed against the tiles as he kicks my legs apart and drives into me with no warning. He fucks me brutally, savagely, and I'm sure his fingers will leave bruises on my hips, but I don't care because it's everything, and I relinquish control, letting my body accept everything he's giving.

When we're close, he wraps a hand around my throat from behind and straightens me up, pulling me back against his body as his hips pivot, and he fucks into me harder and harder. "Perfect," he growls in my ear before grabbing it with his teeth. "So fucking perfect and all *mine*."

Releasing my neck, he grabs my hips with both hands and fucks me so hard my legs almost go out from under me. One hand reaches up, squeezing my boob, and then he's rubbing between my legs while ramming his dick into me, and my orgasm races over me with little warning. I scream, buck, and writhe as I succumb to the most amazing sensations zipping all over my body. Then Fiero roars, jerking his hips and cursing as he spills his seed inside me.

"Holy fuck," he rasps, pulling out and wrapping his arms around me. "I think you might fuck me to death."

"What's the matter, old man?" I ask, turning in his arms. "Can't keep up?"

"That's it," he says, turning off the water. "You're definitely going over my knee."

I scream and race out of the shower, giggling when he scoops me up from behind and wraps me in an overlarge, soft, fluffy white towel.

Fiero deposits me on the bed just as his cell pings again. Snatching it up, he frowns and scrubs the back of his neck. "I've got to take this. I'll be right back." He stalks out of the room with a towel wrapped around his slender hips and beads of water rolling down his back.

I return to the bathroom and grab a smaller towel to dry my hair. I brush my teeth again and run the comb through my damp hair, securing the towel at the front of my body as I pad to Fiero's closet to get my things.

Panic presses down on my chest when I open my case and find most of my belongings missing. I open the envelope with trembling hands, breathing a sigh of relief when I see all my cash is intact, but the feeling is fleeting. If he looked inside the pill bottle, I'll have some explaining to do, and I'm sure he's already wondering what I'm doing with a big wad of cash. Or maybe not. I can always lie and say Dom gave it to me to go shopping.

Taking my toiletries bag, I climb to my feet and look around the large closet, wondering where Fiero hung my clothes. I walk past rows of dress shirts and suits, jeans, shirts, tees, and sweaters, trackpants and hoodies, and training gear, and he has a full row of jackets and coats as well as rows of shoes and a display drawer full of ties and another one with watches and cuff links.

I'm momentarily caught off guard by the myriad of biker leathers, pants, jackets and boots, and a visual of Fiero dressed all in black on the back of a motorcycle sends a fresh wave of desire shooting through me.

Shaking myself out of those dangerous thoughts, I circle around the space, but I can't find my clothes. They're not here, and I just know that arrogant ass has done something with them. They are the only clothes I brought with me, and I need them. I don't have extra money to splurge on buying new things.

In the blink of an eye, my lust is replaced with red-hot rage, and I'm going to throttle him.

"Valentina."

Charging out to the bedroom, I slam into him, shoving him in the chest a few times. "Where the fuck are my clothes?" I yell.

He opens his mouth to chastise me, and I beat on his chest with my fists. "Don't fucking say it. I'll fucking curse if I fucking want to." The irony is I never cursed in Miami. It was a habit I grew out of as an adult, but Fiero pushes my buttons like no one else, and I'm subconsciously pushing his buttons right back. "What the hell did you do with my things?"

He walks to the bed and drops down on it. "I set fire to them." He looks almost angelic sitting on the end of the bed in his towel, like his actions are normal. A bundle of clothes rests beside him.

"What?" I splutter, planting my hands on my hips as I glare at him. "That better be a joke."

"It's not." He grins, and I lose it, screaming as I lunge at him. I jump onto his lap, slapping and punching him. He laughs as he easily gains control, grabbing my wrists and flipping me onto the bed, pinning me with his large body. "If this is your idea of foreplay, I like it." He waggles his brows, and I growl.

"I'm never having sex with you again. I hate you!"

This seems to amuse him to no end, and that only enrages me further. Angry tears prick my eyes. "Fuck you, Gage. You had no right. Those were my things." Tears spill over my eyes onto my cheeks, and his amused smile disappears.

"Valentina." He sits up and hauls me into his lap. "Kitten."

"Stop calling me that." I try to climb off him, but his strong arms hold me in place.

"I'll buy you new things." He grips my chin forcing my face to his. "Those clothes were fucking rags."

Hurt and shame take turns slapping me in the face. "Maybe to you. They were mine, and you had no right to do that. I don't want you buying me new clothes or anything." I avert my eyes while trying to wriggle out of his arms.

"I didn't do it to hurt you, baby, but no woman of mine is wearing anything less than the best."

"I'm not fucking yours," I roar, the ire stoking inside me again. "I'm not fucking anyone's." I thump at my chest, only now realizing the towel has come lose and it's pooled at my waist. "I belong to me. Only me. No one else will ever own me, and that includes you."

"Wrong, but we'll have to argue about it another time. I need to go to the office."

"Great, so you're just leaving me here naked and helpless and chained to your bed, I suppose."

His eyes twinkle mischievously. "Can't say I'd mind, but this isn't a prison, and I have some clothes for you." He releases my wrists and jerks his head at the clothes on the bed. I frown as I examine the pale pink tee and denim skirt, and bile swims up my throat.

"I'm not wearing some other woman's clothes," I snap as jealousy kicks me in the teeth. "How many women are you fucking anyway?"

"Only you."

It does little to comfort me, and jealousy and anger charge through my veins like a wrecking ball. "You fucked me without protection, you asshole!" I swat at his chest, but he grabs my wrists again.

"Stop hitting. It's not very ladylike. You're clean, and I am too, and you have an IUD, so stop making an issue out of a non-issue."

Tension instantly thickens the air. "You know this how?"

He heaves out an annoyed sigh. "I don't have the time for this petty crap." Lifting me off his lap, like I weigh nothing, he dumps me unceremoniously on the bed.

"Fiero!" I jump up as he gets off the bed, uncaring the towel falls to the floor. "How do you know that?"

"That fat fuck you call a husband told me." His biceps bulge and strain as he opens and closes his hands. "The same time he was telling me I could do whatever I wanted to you as long as I didn't mark your face." He turns around and yells before slamming his fist into the wall, putting a hole in it.

I grab the towel, holding it up to my chest as I step away from him.

His face falls as he watches me. "You're not in danger from me, Valentina. I won't hurt you." He grabs handfuls of his hair. "You've got to stop pressing my buttons."

"I thought you liked my sass."

"I like your sass in the bedroom. I'd prefer your obedience outside of it."

"You're a fucking prick, just like every other man I've ever known." I'm awash with rage, and every nerve ending in my body bristles with anger. I feel like screaming and throwing shit, and I'm barely clinging to my sanity.

He mutters something under his breath before briefly closing his eyes. When he reopens them, he seems calmer. "If it helps, no other woman has ever shared that bed with me, and the only women who have come into this house are my sisters, my house-keeper, my mother, and my best friend's wife. I've never fucked anyone without a condom before, and I wouldn't have fucked you bare if I wasn't clean. I'd never risk your health like that. Those clothes belong to my youngest sister. She won't mind you borrowing them. Now if there's nothing else, I need to get dressed."

He stomps off into his closet, leaving me hurt, pissed off, and even more confused than before.

Chapter Fifteen
Fiero

"Thanks for coming in on short notice," Massimo says from the head of the conference table where we are gathered for an emergency sitting of the board in downtown Manhattan at Commission Central HQ.

"What's going on?" Bennett Mazzone asks, clasping his hands in front of him on the table as he leans forward a little in the chair.

Ben was the first president of the reformed Commission, and he mentored Massimo for years, ensuring a smooth transition from our first president to the next. They are still close, and Massimo confides in Ben more than anyone else when it comes to serious matters. It's clear, on this occasion, that Ben is as much in the dark as the rest of us.

Originally, The Commission comprised the dons of each of the five New York *famiglie*. The current New York dons are yours truly, Massimo Greco, Bennett Mazzone, Cristian DiPietro, and Caleb and Joshua Accardi. It's a good mix of youth and experience, but we felt we'd achieve greater unity across the US if we expanded the representation. So, eighteen months ago, Dominic Mantegna from Chicago, Dario Agessi, the Philly don, Volpe from Pittsburgh and Pagano from Detroit were voted onto the board, and so far, it's verifying the decision was a smart one.

"Don Salerno received troubling information that has potentially far-reaching consequences. He's dialing in from Vegas shortly."

Ben's brow creases, and I'm guessing he's wondering why his ex-*consigliere* and close friend Alesso didn't call him directly.

"The intel just cropped up," Massimo says, knowing exactly where Ben's head is at.

The screen on the wall lights up as Alesso joins our meeting. I fiddle with my tie as I lean back in my chair and wait for things to kick off.

After initial small talk, Massimo gets straight to the heart of the matter. "Share the intel you shared with me earlier with the board, please."

Alesso nods and clears his throat. "A trusted source within my *famiglia* came to me a couple of weeks ago with information he had gleaned from one of the *soldati* who was friendly with one of the guys loyal to Cruz."

Everyone shifts uneasily in their chairs, now suspecting where this is going. My gaze instantly whips around to Massimo, and we share a look—one that worries me.

Everyone knew Cruz DiPietro was in bed with the wrong people, and he was heavily involved in a ton of shit that went down recently. We figured there was more to it, but we haven't been able to link Cruz to anything else. One of the main reasons I was sent to Florida was to discover what he'd been up to, but I have uncovered jack shit, and it's obvious now that Vitto D'Onofrio wasn't in on anything.

I wonder if we're about to find out what else Cruz was up to.

Alesso resumes speaking when he has reclaimed all our attention. He looks completely calm when he says, "Cruz was working with the cartel."

All the blood drains from my face. "Sinaloa?" I ask though I don't really need an answer.

Alesso nods.

"In what capacity?" Cristian asks. Cristian is Cruz's younger brother and the DiPietro don for New York. They weren't close, and Cristian was sickened by the things his older brother did in the run-up to his death.

Alesso's gaze flits to mine briefly. "Everyone knows the fentanyl market in Vegas is owned by the cartel. The authorities have been on their back for years, and they almost drove them out of the territory."

"Pity they didn't," Agessi says, picking a piece of lint off the sleeve of his suit jacket.

"They caused them enough issues with supply chain and distribution that the cartel had to get creative."

"That's what Cruz was really using the airplanes for?" Joshua asks, arching a brow.

A few years before his death, Cruz bought a couple airplanes he said were for personal use, but none of us ever believed that.

"Cruz wasn't bringing the drugs in from Mexico," Alesso confirms. "The cartel was bringing them in via a different route. Instead of driving them over the border directly to Vegas, they were driving to a number of small towns in Utah where they have a few warehouses. They were driving the goods to Vegas from there, but Cruz was flying some supplies from Vegas to Miami for distribution in Florida."

Fucking hell. A muscle pops in my jaw as dread pools in my gut.

"Why get involved in this?" Pagano asks, drumming his fingers on his thigh.

I kick my legs out, crossing and uncrossing my feet at my ankles as I try to figure this out in my head. We knew there was a connection between Vegas and Miami because Cruz was flying there weekly to supposedly party with Vitto. But Cruz working with the cartel puts a completely different spin on it. I sit up straighter, digging my nails into the arms of the chair as my knee bobs up and down.

"What was in it for Cruz?" Caleb props his elbows on the table.

"I'm not sure. He was getting paid handsomely for the air shipments, but we all know Cruz wasn't doing it for the money," Alesso says.

"I want to kill that motherfucker all over again." Caleb cracks his knuckles, his blue eyes darkening. To say the twins hate Cruz is an understatement, but they have good reasons.

"Still causing problems from the grave," Cristian says, shaking his head.

"Unless there's anything else, we'll let you go, Don Salerno," Massimo says. Alesso nods, his gaze drifting to Ben and Caleb briefly before he ends the video call, and the screen goes black.

Popping the top button of my shirt open, I loosen my tie before it strangles me. I clear my throat, knowing I can't keep what I know hidden any longer. All of this is obviously connected, and the board needs to know. "I discovered something recently that involves the cartel in Miami, and my guess is it ties back to Cruz."

All heads swivel in my direction, giving me their full attention.

"Dominic Ferraro has a nasty gambling addiction, and he's up to his eyeballs in debt to the cartel."

Massimo scrubs his hands down his face and shakes his head. I know this kind of crap pisses him off. We're worked so hard to legitimize our operation and to conduct ourselves in a more respectful manner, but there are still too many rotten eggs.

It's all starting to make sense in my head now even if I don't have all the answers yet. "They don't let enemies sit at their table, which means..."

"He's a friend," Caleb says.

"Or an ally," Ben says.

"Is Vitto involved?" Massimo asks.

I shake my head. "The guy is a womanizing playboy masquerading as a *mafioso*, but he's not dirty. I'd stake my life on it. He doesn't know about Ferraro's gambling problem or the cartel debt. I haven't found a shred of evidence linking D'Onofrio to the Sinaloa cartel."

"We have to assume Ferraro was working with Cruz on the ground in Miami for the cartel," Volpe says before taking a sip of his water.

"I don't like making assumptions," Massimo says. "We need concrete evidence to go after Ferraro."

"How much does he owe?" Joshua asks.

"Twelve mil is what I've heard."

"How the fuck does an underboss in one of our wealthiest territories get himself into so much debt?" Disbelief threads through Pagano's tone.

"Because he's a fucking idiot." I remove my tie and toss it down on the table.

Caleb smirks in my direction.

"Is this why you were asking me about his wife?" Pagano adds, and I want to pump him full of bullets because I asked him to keep that between us.

Massimo cocks his head to one side, staring at me.

"I'm doing my due diligence on the fucker, exploring every possible angle," I say, avoiding looking at my best friend as I deliberately omit the largest part of the truth. "His son and heir recently came to my attention, and I'm going to look into Cesco too because he's an ambitious little shit who could buy and sell his papa."

"What about the wife?" Our president drills me with a look.

"I'm still checking her out." *Literally*. I inwardly cringe.

"So why are you here?" Massimo asks, applying silent pressure because he suspects I'm hiding something.

"I have things to attend to in the city, but I'll return to Miami next week, and I'll make some calls after we're done here. Get a few guys to shadow Dominic and Cesco and see what that throws up."

"You being away for longer than usual could be a good strategy," Cristian says, frowning at the screen of his cell phone as it lights up.

"They might be keeping their noses clean while you're there," Joshua agrees. "Afraid you'll find out what they're up to. Could be why you haven't found anything in months."

"You should stay away for an extended period," Caleb says, struggling to hide his grin before he bites into an apple. "Let's give them enough rope to hang themselves," he adds over a mouthful of fruit.

Around the table, everyone nods, and I can't believe it worked out in my favor. I'm sweating bullets because I've never kept anything from Massimo before, and this isn't sitting right with me. I don't like deceiving him, but I can't tell him about Valentina. He'll be furious because it's a complete asshole move, and if it comes out, it'll weaken our rep. Especially if it turns out Dominic is betraying his *famiglia* and everything *La Cosa Nostra* stands for in the US.

"D'Onofrio needs to be replaced," Ben says, getting up to make himself a coffee. "You've given him enough time, and he hasn't stepped up to the plate."

"I don't think he wants to," I admit. "I think he's waiting for us to step in and appoint another don. His heart isn't in it."

"His father would be so disappointed in him." Volpe joins Ben at the coffee station.

"Is there anyone competent enough to replace him?" Massimo asks.

I nod. "Davide Gallo would make an excellent don though Vitto will resist his appointment. They hate one another though I haven't discovered why yet."

"When you return to Miami, get closer to Gallo." Massimo taps his pen off the arm of his chair. "Subtly sound him out."

"Will do."

"We're going to need a new underboss too," Agessi says. "And I presume there's been no *consigliere* appointment made yet either?" Dario looks over at me.

"No. Vitto's been dragging his heels for weeks."

"A fresh new leadership team will work wonders for the territory," Ben says. "Maybe this is a blessing in disguise."

"Not if Dominic has made us a target for the cartel," Cristian says, rubbing at his tired eyes. I'm guessing his son is still not sleeping well at night.

I wonder how much of Elio's issues are connected to the trauma he experienced when he was only a few months old. Elio is Cruz's son, and Cristian immediately stepped up and took responsibility for the child when he became an orphan. Cristian is one of the good guys, and he didn't hesitate to make a lot of personal sacrifices to do right by the boy. He has only gone up in my estimation in the past year.

"We need to know what the cartel is planning," Massimo says. "I don't have a good feeling about it."

"None of us do," Pagano says.

"For now," my buddy says, eyeballing me, "set up the surveillance on the Ferraros. Include the wife too." I deserve an award for not even blinking.

"Do they have trackers?" Ben asks, reclaiming his seat and

setting his coffee down on the table. Ben's Caltimore Holdings company has developed next-level technology we use to safe-guard our businesses and our men. A lot of *mafioso* in the US have tracking chips in their bodies that can pinpoint their loca-tion, and it's come in more than handy over the years. However, we don't enforce it. It's left up to local territories to decide whether they are compulsory or optional.

"No, but I'll get something put in their cars."

"Stay away for a couple of weeks, but then I want you back there," Massimo says. "We need someone trustworthy on the ground. If the cartel is involved and they're planning something, we need to find out before we're embroiled in another war."

"I'll get to the bottom of it," I promise, hoping the things I've done haven't made everything worse.

Chapter Sixteen
Valentina

I'm a prisoner. Granted, my cage is way nicer than my usual one, but I'm still trapped here, and my hope for escape is rapidly fading. I've explored every inch of Fiero's home and grounds while he's been gone today, and he has the place locked up damn tight. The dock might still be an option, but I'll have to convince Fiero to take me out on his boat so I can figure out how to navigate it. If he plans to disappear on me every day, I don't see how I can make that a reality.

Returning to the house after my exploration outside, I take a shower and make a sandwich before settling down with my phone to call my cousin and my siblings. Except I can't because my cell has no coverage and it's not letting me connect to the Wi-Fi. I'd use Fiero's office if I could get into it, but I'm guessing it's one of the two locked doors I discovered on my tour.

Frustrated and pissed off, I borrow some training clothes I find in one of the spare bedrooms—clothes I'm guessing belong to his sister—and then I take my frustration out in Fiero's home gym, pounding the treadmill like a madwoman, only stopping when sweat coats my body like a second skin.

After showering and redressing in the borrowed tee and denim skirt and my own tennis shoes, which escaped the purge, I head into the kitchen, figuring I'll bake something to keep myself occupied. It's either that or raid Fiero's wine cellar and drown my sorrows. It holds appeal. Imagining Fiero returning home to find me trashed and his wine stash missing a few expensive bottles is almost worth risking it. I'm sure he wouldn't find it very *ladylike*, and I almost do it for that reason alone. Except I need to keep my guard up, and I've already decided it's smarter to just play nice and keep him on board.

So, I'll bake, and when he returns later, I'll try to keep my anger on a leash.

His kitchen cabinets are well stocked, his refrigerator and freezer full of labeled home-cooked meals, and it's obvious he has a housekeeper. Unless his mother and sisters get his groceries and cook for him, but I doubt it. After setting the ingredients for cupcakes on the counter, I pull out drawers in search of an apron when there's a gentle knock on the door. My head whips up, and I'm instantly on guard when I find a guy dressed in black standing in the kitchen doorway. It's the same guy who greeted us when we arrived last night.

"Sorry to disturb you, miss." He glances briefly at the rings on my ring finger. "But I have some deliveries for you."

I frown. "I didn't order anything."

His lips kick up at the corners ever so slightly. "The boss ordered them for you. I'll have them brought into the living room."

"Oh. Okay." I blink several times as he walks away, wondering what's going on. *What is Fiero up to?*

Heading out into the living room, I slam to a halt when I reach the entryway, my eyes almost bugging out of my head as I watch three armed *soldati* traipse in and out of the large homey room carrying boxes with the Rachel McConaughey brand stamped all over them. Fiero said he was going to replace my clothes, but I didn't think he meant *this*. I clutch the door frame as I watch them deposit box after box on the floor over the rug centered between three cream-colored leather couches. My heart crashes against my chest cavity when two clothes rails are wheeled into the room, each holding a ton of covered items on hangers.

The man from the kitchen returns, carrying a massive bouquet of red, purple, and pink roses and a shiny gold box. "The boss wanted me to give these to you personally. He's been delayed longer than expected, but he'll be home for dinner." I stare at him in shock as I accept the flowers and the gold box in a bit of a daze.

"Um, thanks," I murmur quietly.

He stares at me for a few seconds, looking like he wants to say something, but he just smiles and nods, and then they all walk off leaving me surrounded with the physical evidence of Fiero's insanity.

I'm still in a daze as I bury my nose in the roses, inhaling deeply and sucking the heady scent into my lungs. On wobbly legs, I head toward the couch, maneuvering around boxes to flop onto the soft leather. Keeping the roses tucked into my chest, I examine the gold box. White Plains, handmade confectionary and chocolates is printed on the front, and the address is a Connecticut one.

Opening the box, I find the most perfectly crafted chocolates. Two layers with a mix of dark, milk, and white chocolates. Bringing the box to my nose, I sniff them, and a laugh bursts from my throat at the thought of any of Fiero's *soldati* watching me right now. I'm acting like a crazy person or a woman who has never received flowers or chocolates from a man before. I glance quickly over my shoulder, but I'm alone thankfully.

Plucking a dark chocolate from the box, I pop it in my mouth, and my taste buds explode with bitter chocolate and vibrant peach flavors before I bite down on a nut. It's like heaven on my tongue, and I squeeze my eyelids shut, savoring each flavor as it melts in my mouth. I slowly open my eyes after I swallow, fighting a sudden bout of tears. A lump clogs my throat. This must be what it feels like to be spoiled and cherished.

This means so much to me, which is pretty pathetic.

It's sad that one of the nicest things anyone has ever done for me comes from a man who bought me.

I hug the flowers tight, fighting potent emotion. Fiero didn't have to do this. He didn't have to do any of this. I'd have opened my body to him without gifts, but *this*...all of this shows he cares, at least on some minor level, and I don't really know what to make of it.

I walk to the kitchen with the flowers and find a large glass vase in one of the cabinets. I take my time arranging the flowers until they look pretty. I can't keep the goofy grin off my face as I carry the vase back to the living room where I place it on the coffee table. I take a picture with my cell; I'm not even angry I can't send it to Nina because Fiero has somehow disabled my phone.

"I definitely need wine for this," I mumble to myself as I survey the mountain of boxes in the room which is starting to look like a massive project. Returning to the kitchen to grab some scissors, I pour myself a large glass of wine from the bottle of chilled white wine I find in the refrigerator, and then I head back to tackle the rest of my gifts.

I sit on the floor and drag the first box toward me with excitement bubbling in my chest.

I don't know how long I've been unpacking, but I've managed to drink half the bottle of wine while I uncovered everything Fiero bought me. It's so much. Too much, and I'm feeling overwhelmed. There are cosmetics, toiletries, a wild variety of shoes, sneakers, bags, lingerie, sleepwear, loungewear, and so many clothes I don't know how I'll ever wear them all. He thought of everything. I have shirts, blouses, skirts, pants, jeans, sweaters, cami tops and matching short sets, bikinis and swimsuits, and a mix of light summer dresses, casual maxi dresses, and exquisite formal dresses that have me drooling and panting.

It's all expensive, made from the finest materials, sourced from the best brands, and everything is the correct size meaning he must have checked that before he burned my stuff. He's thoughtful in a way I didn't expect.

I can't even guess how much money he spent. I don't want to. I'll probably just induce a panic attack. All I know is no one has ever done anything this nice for me before. It's the opposite of what I'm used to, and I don't know how to process everything I'm feeling.

It feels like I'm in a movie and the director is going to call cut at any second because this is a fantasy. This isn't real. I'll have this for one week, and then it'll all be gone. It's the worst form of cruelty. To dangle all this before me and then have it ripped right out from under me. I know Fiero did this out of the goodness of his heart, and it's so sweet and thoughtful, but it's everything I'd ever dared to dream of, and the thought of having it so fleetingly guts me.

The house. The man. The romantic gestures. Fiero spoiling me. It's all perfect.

But this isn't my reality, and it never will be.

Sobs burst straight from my soul as I fall apart on Fiero's living room floor, crying over everything that's been denied to me all because I chose to date the wrong man in high school. If I'd never met Damiano, I'd still be in Detroit, living a far simpler life, but at least it'd be my own.

I give in to years of pent-up grief and cry my heart out.

That's how the older woman finds me, sobbing and hiccupping with tearstained cheeks, sitting in a pile of expensive things in a borrowed shirt and skirt.

"Oh dear." She sets a grocery bag and her purse down on the couch and rushes toward me. "Whatever's the matter, *tesoro?*" She kneels beside me and instantly wraps me in her arms.

She's a stranger, but the delicate scent of her perfume mixed with the tender warmth of her hug reminds me of my *nonna* in Sicily, and I cry harder, clinging to her, too comforted to be embarrassed.

She peers at me with concerned blue eyes. "Are you hurt, Valentina?"

"No." I sniffle and shake my head, attempting to get a grip. *What must she think of me?* I gesture around me. "It's too much. It's overwhelming."

"Ah." Her lined face softens as she smooths a hand up and down my back. "My Fiero is a good and generous man. He looks after those he cares about."

Her Fiero? Oh fuck, this must be his mother. I hastily swipe at the dampness on my cheeks. "I'm so sorry, Mrs. Maltese. I swear I'm not usually such a basket case."

Her smile is affectionate as she takes my hands and squeezes. "I'm not Fiero's mama. I'm Ana, *tesoro*, Fiero's housekeeper, though I've looked after him so long I consider him my son."

"Oh, well it's nice to meet you, and I'm sorry you found me like this." I emit a brittle laugh. "I was just having a moment."

"What the hell is going on, and who the hell is she?"

At the harsh tone, I swing my gaze to the woman standing in the doorway, carrying a briefcase, with a small purse over one shoulder, staring at me with narrowed eyes. The red skirt suit she's wearing is expensive, clinging to her slim figure, highlighting her ample chest, the subtle curving of her hips, and her long shapely legs. A string of pearls rests around her neck, matching the bracelet on her right wrist. Her dark hair is pulled into an elegant chignon, highlighting her exquisite heart-shaped face. Wide gray-blue eyes stare at me with unconcealed suspicion. She's absolutely stunning, and she radiates confidence as she walks across the room with her shoulders held back and her head held high.

Ana stiffens slightly, sliding her arm around my shoulders in a protective gesture. "Sofia. Fiero didn't mention you were dropping by."

"I don't need an appointment to see my own brother, Ana," she scoffs, not even looking at the woman, keeping her venomous eyes locked on mine.

I'm guessing Fiero has more than one sister because there's no way the clothes I'm wearing belong to this woman.

"Who are you?" she snaps, looming over me. "And why are you wearing Tullia's clothes?"

I get to my feet because I won't be looked down on by anyone. Especially not this haughty bitch who thinks she's better than me. I help Ana up before eyeballing Fiero's sister in warning. My instinct is to release my claws and snark back at her, but she's Fiero's family, and I don't think he'd like it. Best not to make an enemy if I can help it. "I'm Valentina, and Fiero gave them to me. He said she wouldn't mind if I borrowed them."

"Who. Are. You?" she repeats, enunciating her words while running her gaze over my tearstained face.

"I'm Fiero's...guest." I figure he wouldn't like me divulging the details of our deal to his bitchy sister, and I'm not giving her ammunition to feel justified in looking down on me.

"Are you always this obtuse?"

"I'm *not* stupid, which is why I'm not telling you anything else. You want to know who I am? Ask your brother."

"Fiero wouldn't appreciate your tone with his *signora*," Ana says, shocking me. I wonder exactly what Fiero has told her about me.

"She's not his *signora*," Sofia scoffs again. "She's someone's wife!" Her eyes latch on to my rings.

"Maybe I'm *his* wife," I retort without thinking it through.

Her lips pull up in amusement. "Not a chance in hell. My brother is an eternal bachelor. He'll never marry." She squares right up to me, and I brace myself for whatever is coming because I know it won't be pretty.

"I know who you are. *What* you are. Tell me?" She tilts her head to one side. "How long did you wait before spreading your legs for my brother?"

"Sofia!" Ana gasps. "You cannot say such things."

She ignores Fiero's housekeeper, boring holes in my skull with her poisonous eyes.

I keep a neutral expression on my face as I glare at her, making it obvious I'm not answering.

A bitter laugh leaves her glossy lips as she looks all around. "You must really have done a number on my brother because he doesn't usually bring his whores home or give them anything more than his cock." She jabs her finger in my face. "You're nothing but gold-digging trash and—"

"Want to say that to my face, sis?" Fiero barks, storming into the room with a thunderous look on his face.

Chapter Seventeen
Fiero

I stuff my clenched hands into my pants pockets before I strangle my sister with my bare hands. "Apologize to Valentina right now," I say, my gaze dancing between Sofia and Valentina. My kitten's cheeks are damp, her skin blotchy and my heart sinks. She's been crying, and she looks on the verge of tears again. Hurt is written all over her face, and I will tear strips off my sister for this because her hideous words have put this look on her face.

"Now, Sofia," I say through gritted teeth as I watch my oldest sister getting ready to dig her heels in. God help whatever man ends up with my fiery sister because they'll certainly have their hands full with Sofia.

"I'll apologize when you explain what's going on, *if* it's warranted."

Spoken like a true attorney. "Don't push me, Sof." I caution her with my eyes. "Apologize or leave my house, and I'll revoke your guest pass permanently."

My men at the gate have a short list of preapproved visitors. No one else gets through my gates without explicit permission. I value my privacy, and I don't mess around with security. The *mafioso* have plenty of enemies, and every member of the board is high on their target lists. I never give them any opportunity to come after me, which is why my property is as fortified as Fort Knox.

Sofia's eyes widen in surprise. She can tell I'm serious.

I whisper in her ear. "She's important to me. Fix whatever mess you just created."

She stares at me like I'm a stranger for a few beats before she turns to Valentina. "It seems I have misread the situation. I apologize for the assumptions I made and any hurt I caused. I am fiercely protective of my brother."

Valentina's entire demeanor changes, and her shoulders relax. "I respect that, and I appreciate the apology. No hard feelings."

"I'm just going to make a start on dinner," Ana says, tugging on my arm and pulling me down closer. "Give her a hug, she needs it," she whispers.

I know she's not talking about my ball-busting sister, so I walk over to Valentina and reel her into my arms. I tip my head down and drag my gaze over her stunning face. "You were crying. Are you all right?"

A blush steals over her cheeks. "I'm fine." Her soft tone winds around my heart, tugging and squeezing. "I got overwhelmed," she blurts, raking her gaze over the clothes and other stuff I had delivered. "I can't believe you did all this. It's so sweet and generous, but it's too much, Fiero. I don't need all these clothes."

I kiss the tip of her nose. "You needed things, and I enjoyed spoiling you."

She swallows heavily, looking conflicted for a moment before her features soften. "Thank you. It's very thoughtful. No one has ever done anything like this for me before." Her expression turns sheepish. "No man has ever bought me flowers or chocolates or anything." Her voice cracks, and a fresh delicate flush creeps onto her cheeks. "It means a lot to me."

The way she's looking at me will be forever cemented in my mind, and I want to put that expression on her face every day for the rest of my life. "You're welcome." My heart beats to a new rhythm as I slowly lean down and kiss her, pouring everything I'm feeling into every sweep of my lips. This kiss is unlike any I've ever experienced. It's full of emotion and joy and purity and warmth, and I hold her closer, never wanting to be away from her.

"Ahem." My sister coughs, ruining the moment, and I break our kiss, glancing at Sofia with transparent annoyance. "I didn't drop by for the hell of it. I need a favor. Can we talk in your office?"

Valentina slips out of my arms, and I instantly feel cold. "Talk to your sister," she says. "I'll be busy moving all this stuff."

Hauling her back into my body, I press a quick, hard kiss to her lips. "Leave the heavier stuff for me."

She rolls her eyes. "I'm not an invalid, Fiero. I'm perfectly capable of carrying all this myself."

Out of the corner of my eye, I spy Sofia's lips twitching.

I swat Valentina on the ass. "What did I say about sass?" She pouts, and I laugh. "Move stuff around in my closet to make room for your new things. I don't care how you clear out the space."

She opens her mouth to object, no doubt to tell me that doesn't make sense as she's leaving on Sunday, but I don't want to hear that bullshit, so I clamp her lips shut with my fingers. "Nope. Remember what I said this morning?" Her brow furrows, and I've clearly still got work to do to convince her I'm genuine. "No arguing."

She expels air from her mouth before she says, "Okay."

"Good girl." I kiss her lips again. "That wasn't so hard, now was it, kitten?"

She glares at me, and I'm chuckling as we leave her in the living room. Sofia's high heels click off the dark hardwood floors as we walk side by side down the corridor toward my office. She doesn't say anything, just looks over at me a few times wearing an inquisitive face. I know Sofia is reserving it for when we're in private.

I unlock my office door and usher her inside, locking it after me.

"What's going on, Ro?"

I walk to the far right of the long, wide room, scanning the multitude of screens that project the feeds from the cameras mounted all over my property. The only places I don't have cameras are the bathrooms and guest bedrooms.

"It's better you don't know," I advise as I check the screens quickly. Satisfied all is in order and the property is secure, I turn around and walk to the other side of the room and sit down behind my desk. My sister takes the vacant chair across from me, depositing her briefcase and purse on the ground.

"I'm involved now, so you might as well tell me."

"You're not involved." Removing my jacket, I hang it on the back of my chair. "You didn't see her. She doesn't exist."

Sofia sits up straight, pinning me with a shrewd look. My sister is gorgeous, elegant, and smart, and she has her fair share of admirers, but she's focused on her legal career, and getting involved in the family business is not her cup of tea. Nor is marrying and settling down. In that regard, we've always been alike, so I know she's puzzled and trying to figure it out.

"I have never known you to bring a woman here or to shower her with gifts. I've never seen you act like you just did with *anyone*. You're in love with her," she proclaims, watching me like a hawk to see how I'll react.

Sof is like a dog with a bone when she gets her teeth into anything. She's not going to let this drop, so I might as well give her something. "I think I might be." It's the first time I've even admitted it to myself.

Shock is splayed across Sofia's face, and when she opens her mouth, nothing comes out.

I chuckle as I lean back in my chair, crossing my feet at the ankles. "Don't tell me I've rendered the notorious Sofia Maltese speechless. I'll need to note this moment for posterity."

"I *am* shocked, Fiero. All I have heard from you, over and over, for years, is that you're not interested in settling down or getting married. I can count on one hand the girlfriends you've had over the years. You don't do this. You fuck them and walk away without a backward glance."

I wince a little. She's not wrong, but it all seems so frivolous and callous now.

"What makes Valentina so special?"

"Everything, Sof. Everything about her calls to me on every level. I just want to be with her, protect her, love her, adore her."

"I'm sorry I misjudged her. I was taken aback, and my first thought was she was manipulating you somehow."

I snort. "I'd like to see any woman try." Though, to be fair, Valentina will probably have me wrapped around her finger in no time. I remember how quickly Massimo became pussy-whipped.

"She's young."

I arch a brow as I stare at her. "That's a bit rich coming from you." Sofia never dates guys her own age; they're always older.

She smirks. "FYI, my current fling is a good bit *younger* than me."

Now it's my turn to look surprised. "Are you sick or some-thing?" She flips me the bird, and laughter rumbles from my chest. "And I thought you were a lady."

She flips me off again, and I roll my eyes. "I wasn't criticizing your choice, Ro, merely stating a fact."

"She's twenty-four." I wet my lips. "Do you think that's too young for me?"

"You know what I think. Age doesn't matter. It's all to do with the person. With the connection you feel. Whether there's a spark in the bedroom. If they make you laugh. Make you happy. Those are the things that matter."

"She makes me feel things I've never felt before. When I'm away from her, I can't stop thinking about her, and when I'm with her, I can't stop touching her," I blurt, instantly feeling like a pussy. I'm close to both my sisters, but Sof and I don't do this. We discuss business and family. I'm more likely to have an emotional conversation with my younger sister Tullia. She wears her heart on her sleeve and regularly comes to me for advice.

Sofia's face lights up in a way I rarely see. "That's good, right?"

"I think so." I scrub my hands down my face. "It's making me crazy and more than a little irrational at times."

"It's definitely love then." My sister is grinning, but it quickly fades. "Who is she married to?"

"A prick who doesn't deserve her." I dig my nails into my thighs. Any time I think of that bastard Ferraro, I instantly turn feral. I've been considering options—ways to extract Valentina from her marriage and fast—all day. I could offer to pay him to divorce her, but Valentina would hate that, and it wouldn't be the best start to our new life together. She's already pissed at the deals I made, and I don't think offering another one is the right course of action.

Plus, if he's up to no good with the cartel, I can't hand him a large chunk of money to aid his goal.

Which really only leaves one option. Personally, I think it's a two-birds-one-stone scenario, but the board might not see it like that. On this occasion, I'm thinking it'll be easier to ask for forgiveness than permission.

Sofia's mouth hangs open. "Please tell me you didn't kidnap her from another made man?"

"I didn't. He knows she's with me. We have his permission."

Her nose scrunches in disgust. "I don't have words." She'd have a few choice words for me if she knew I signed a contract and paid 6.5 mil for that permission. "What husband would do that? Is he gay or in love with his mistress?" she asks.

"Possibly," I lie. "Anyway, enough about me and Valentina, what favor do you need this time?"

Removing a folder from her briefcase, she slides it across the table to me. "This guy has cropped up in a case I'm working on. I had my usual PI dig around, but he didn't find anything. I'm not buying it. This guy has shady written all over him. Can you take a look?"

I often help my sister out on the downlow. Though my undergraduate degree is in business, specializing in financial investment, I attended courses online in my thirties to add an IT post-grad to my list of accomplishments. I had to step up when Massimo became president because he no longer had the time to manage that part of our business. "I'm busy this week, but I'll ask Allante to cover it."

Allante is a PI friend of ours, and we've worked with him for years. Massimo and I own a stake in his burgeoning business, and he's as trustworthy as they come. If I'm not available, and it's not something we want to do formally through Ben's IT services, we pass the work to Allante.

I stand, wanting to go to Valentina. I've missed her today. "When do you need the intel by?"

"End of the week if possible." She gets up. "The case goes to trial soon, and I'm trying to wrap up the loose ends."

"It was good to see you," I say, bundling my sister into a hug.

"Good to see you too." She holds me tight. "We must arrange a night out with our siblings. It's been too long."

"It has. I'll ask Zumo to arrange something in the next few weeks."

She grabs her things and walks to the door.

"Sof," I call after her. She stalls with her finger on the lock. "Don't tell anyone about Valentina. Especially not Tullia." I don't like hiding it from my little sister, but she'll be too excited to keep it a secret. I'll tell her when it's safe to do so.

"That's a given."

"Just for now until I sort things."

"Be careful, Ro." She flips back the lock as she drills a look at me. "Don't do anything reckless. You've worked too hard to jeopardize everything now."

"I'll try." I won't lie to my sister's face.

No, you'll just do that to your best friend.

"I'm happy for you, and I hope it all works out."

"Me too," I say, rubbing at the tightness spreading across my chest long after my sister has exited the room.

Chapter Eighteen
Valentina

I'm almost finished putting everything away in Fiero's closet when he arrives, sliding up behind me and wrapping his arms around my waist. My pulse races when he nuzzles his face in my neck and audibly inhales, drinking me in. "I missed you today. Sorry I was gone so long."

"I'm mad at you," I say, reminded of earlier. "Why does my cell not work, and why can't I connect to your Wi-Fi?"

He spins me around in his arms and tips my head up. "We need to keep your presence here a secret. I can't have you talking to anyone and telling them about the deal."

"I already told you I wouldn't tell anyone." I shove at his chest, needing space. When I'm all wrapped up in him like this, I can't think straight. He bamboozles me with his explosive touch, panty-melting kisses, and gorgeous face. "In case it's escaped your notice, I'm not exactly happy you *bought* me. It's not something I'll be publicizing."

He squeezes my ass, banding his arms tighter around me. "And I told you I only did that so I could take you with me. I would never have *bought* you if you were a single woman."

"No, you'd just have kidnapped me instead," I snap.

"Maybe."

I stare at him in horror, and he laughs, the sound doing funny things to my insides.

"I'd have tried to charm you, and if that didn't work, I'd most likely have kidnapped you," he admits, and at least he's honest.

"You'd keep me prisoner, just like you are now."

He scowls. "You're not a prisoner, kitten. You're free to come and go as you please."

"Right." I cock my head to one side. "So, I can leave tomorrow when you're gone all day and go sightseeing?"

"Well, no." He steps back, clawing a hand through his hair, sending strands of messy blond hair tumbling across his brow. "You have the run of the house and grounds, but you can't leave my property."

I huff out a dry laugh. "Like I said, prisoner." I poke at my chest and storm out of the closet.

"Valentina." He reaches out, grabbing me from behind, and then I'm up and over his shoulder. He swats my ass. "It's for your protection. I know it's frustrating, but it won't be forever. I just want to keep you safe."

"Put me down, asshole." I pound my fists on his back. "You just want to keep me locked up here!"

Fiero throws me down on the bed and crawls over me, stretching my arms above my head and gripping my wrists. His body pins me to the mattress, and his dick hardens against me almost instantaneously. "Fuck, you turn me on so much," he says, burying his face in the crook of my neck while gyrating his hips against me.

"Stop distracting me with sex," I rasp, trying to stop my eyes from rolling back in my head as he plants a slew of feather-soft kisses up and down my neck.

"It seems to be the only time you're reasonable and will listen to me."

"Reasonable!" I shriek, digging my nails into his back through his white dress shirt. "You're the most unreasonable man I've ever met!"

"Doubtful," he murmurs, dragging my shirt down a little with his teeth. "Fuck," he says, staring down at my chest. "I love seeing my mark on your skin. It's hot."

"You have issues."

"Bite me."

"Okay." Flashing him a maniacal grin, I stretch up and sink my teeth in his neck, biting hard.

He grunts and groans on top of me as I pierce his skin and draw a little blood. His erection is straining against his zipper and digging into my crotch, dampening my panties and causing an instant ache to form in my groin.

"You little vixen," he says when I pull my mouth free. His lips crush mine as he rotates his hips, pushing his hard-on into my pussy through our clothes.

All logical thought escapes my mind, and I'm reduced to a mass of quivering cells. We attack one another with our lips and our hands until we're both naked and his fingers are pushing inside me.

"Such a good girl. Always so wet for me." His voice drips sex, and my cunt hugs his fingers tightly as he thrusts them roughly in and out of me. "Need you now, baby. Over you go."

I'm flipped onto my stomach with my head in the pillow and my ass in the air. Fiero swipes my slit with his tongue, and a strangled moan leaves me. He is so fucking good at that. Without warning, he slams his cock inside me, and I scream.

"Shush, quiet, kitten. We don't want Ana to think I'm murdering you and come rushing into the room."

"Oh god," I whimper as he pounds into me with savage force.

"You undo me, kitten. I won't ever get enough." He grips my hips as he ruts into me over and over and I'm quickly climbing that high. Covering me with his body, he grabs my face to the side and kisses me passionately before dropping a line of hot kisses along my spine. He rubs my clit with two fingers, and my inner walls suck him in. "Are you close, baby?"

"Yes," I pant, rocking back against him as he plunders my pussy.

He lifts my ass a little higher, hitting a different spot inside me, and I lose the ability to speak, to think, to hear. Blood rushes through my body, pooling in my core, and I'm moaning and crying and pleading as he rubs my clit faster and harder and fucks me deeper, deeper, deeper. The instant his slick finger breaches my ass, I detonate, my body shattering under the intensity of the most blissful orgasm.

Fiero roars his release, continuing to pump into me. As I feel his hot seed lodge deep inside me, a loud sob rips from my mouth unbidden, along with a silent wish that I didn't have an IUD and he just impregnated me.

I'm shocked by my thoughts and barely aware he's pulled out and is now cradling me in his arms as tears pump out of my eyes and down my face.

What is this man doing to me? I feel like I'm losing my sanity again, and I can't go back to that place.

"What's wrong?"

I clutch at his sweat-slickened skin, hating feeling so vulnerable and helpless. I shake my head, forcing myself to calm down.

"Valentina, please." His voice is deliberately soft, coaxing me with his dulcet tone and his comforting touch running up and down my back. "Don't shut me out. Tell me what's troubling you?" His fingers grip my chin, forcing my gaze to his. "Did I do this? Did I hurt you?"

"No. Sex with you is incredible, but it's making me too emotional."

"I'm feeling the same things."

His adoring gaze melts me, and in this moment, I never want to let him go. Snuggling into his body, I feel safe and secure and... loved. His fingers brush my hair back off my face.

"Tell me what you're thinking?"

"I want a baby," I blurt, instantly horrified it just spewed from my mouth.

Shell-shocked eyes latch on to mine.

"Oh god. I'm sorry." I bury my face in his neck. "I shouldn't have said that."

"If it's what you were thinking, I'm glad you said it." He runs his hand along my hair, and it's amazingly soothing. "Don't be afraid to speak your truths to me, kitten. I want to know everything about you."

"I..." I lift my head and peer deep into his eyes. "When I felt your sperm inside me, I wished I didn't have an IUD and you'd just knocked me up. How's that for crazy?"

The most gorgeous smile appears on his face. "Glad it's not just me." He dots kisses all over my face. "Why don't you have any babies, kitten?"

My heart falters, and pain spears me all over.

Cupping my face, he stares at me with concerned eyes. "Tell me."

I wish I could tell him the whole sordid story, but I won't be able to get out of bed for days if I tell him everything. "I hate my husband, but I'd have let him knock me up if it meant I could have babies to love." I stare off into space, turning numb as I confess this truth.

Fiero strokes my face, my back, my arms, and my hair, patiently waiting for me to speak.

I tip my face up to his. "Dom insisted on birth control. We

were only married a few weeks when he told me he didn't want any more children. He has his heir." My lip curls, and I'm aware I'm probably saying too much, but I don't think there's much harm in telling Fiero this.

"He said he was over raising kids. Cesco was thirteen when I moved in, and he'd just initiated. He was largely independent. The girls were younger and needed more care and attention. They were confused and hurting and missing their mama. I tried to be there for them, but I wasn't who they wanted. Dom would shout at them and tell them they were too soft when they cried for Marguerite. Then one day, their grandmother showed up and took them away, and I never saw them again. That was five years ago."

"He made out you didn't want them or couldn't cope, but I knew it was a lie."

"They are sweet girls, and I already loved them. They were the reason I got up out of bed each morning. If it hadn't been for them, I think I would've thrown myself off the roof of the house that first year."

"Will you tell me?" Sincerity bleeds from his eyes, and I want to confide in him.

"It's not a pleasant story."

"I already know that."

I nod just as Ana hollers that dinner is ready.

"Rain check." Fiero lifts me off his lap and onto the bed. "Stay put." He dashes into the bathroom, returning a few seconds later with a warm cloth he uses to clean between my legs. Then he pats me dry with a small hand towel before planting a tender kiss on my lips. "Wear a pretty dress. We'll eat outside."

We head into the closet together, and I remove a white silk and lace bra and panties set from the drawer. It's pretty and the material feels so soft to the touch. I've never had any lingerie that wasn't basic or cheap, so this is a major thrill. Fiero's eyes are out on stalks as he watches me put them on.

"Fuck." He adjusts himself in his boxers as his heated gaze rakes over me. "I need you again. If it wasn't rude to let Ana's dinner go cold, I'd push you up against the wall and impale you on my cock." He prowls toward me, and I'm rooted to the spot, incapable of moving. "You're so sexy." He kisses me ravenously as his hands mold to my curves, and if he doesn't stop, I'll have to change underwear already.

He pulls back, rubbing at his face. "Damn, I'm insatiable for you." I flush all over, and a full smile spreads over his mouth. "You look good enough to eat, baby, but you've got to cover up before I pin you to my bed and never let you out of the room."

Doesn't sound too bad to me.

I blow him a flirty kiss as I pluck a pretty pink summer dress off a hanger and slide it over my head. The straps are wide enough to cover my bra straps, and it has a fitted top that only shows a hint of cleavage before it falls gently to my knees. It's soft to the touch, feminine, and pretty, and I feel like a million dollars in it. After slipping my feet into a pair of nude wedges, I spritz some of my new, expensive perfume, dabbing it at my wrists and both sides of my neck.

Fiero hasn't taken his eyes off me, and he's still standing in his boxers, sporting a massive bulge, when I turn to face him. The goofiest smile slides over my lips. "I thought we didn't want to waste dinner?"

"You're so beautiful, kitten. You steal all the air from my lungs."

Warmth mushrooms in my chest, and I'm practically floating on a cloud as I traipse into the bathroom to fix my hair and apply a little makeup. Butterflies turn loops in my stomach, and this heady rush is entirely new. I suspect I know what it means, and it's dangerous in the extreme, but right now, I don't care. Fiero Maltese is slowly bringing me back to life, and there isn't a single bone in my body that regrets it.

Chapter Nineteen
Fiero

I can't stop looking at her. It's like an addiction. Everything she does seduces me, ensnares me, mesmerizes me. A girlish giggle filters into the nighttime air as she smiles at me. Her gorgeous face is flushed with color, her eyes bright and alive, her smile warm and genuine. It's a far cry from earlier. "Stop staring at me and eat!" She jabs her fork in my direction. "This salmon is so good, and you're letting it go cold."

"It seems I'm only hungry for one thing." Snatching her free hand, I bring it to my mouth.

"You need to eat, old man. How else will you have the stamina for me?" she teases, and I lightly graze my teeth across her knuckles.

"Brave, kitten. Very brave." I'm beginning to think she's sassing me on purpose so I'll fuck her. She seems equally as obsessed with me, at least in the moments where she's not lost in her head and fighting whatever demons plague her. Valentina is keeping a lot of secrets. That much I know for sure now.

"I'll make you a deal."

Her glare is instant, and I burst out laughing. I sling my arm around her shoulders and press a kiss to her delicate cheek. "Come on, baby, you know it's our thing now."

"It better not be."

"I'll eat if you tell me how you came to marry Dom."

She pushes her half-eaten plate away. "Way to ruin my appetite."

I scowl. I'm not the only one who needs to eat. With the things I have planned for her, she'll need every ounce of energy. "Let's finish dinner, and we can talk after."

Her chest heaves up and down. I lean in and kiss her. "Eat, baby. You need to eat too."

We eat in companionable silence after that, and the salmon, baby potatoes, and green vegetable medley Ana prepared is delicious.

"It's so peaceful here," Valentina says, finishing before me. Her gaze roams beyond the patio to the gardens below and the dock below that. "The only sounds are the birds chirping in the trees and the gentle roll of the water. I've always lived in cities or places with lots of noise. This is idyllic."

"I'm glad you like it. I feel the same way, and I come out here as often as I can. I don't like the bustle of the city. This place soothes my soul."

"How long have you lived here?"

"Almost seventeen years. I bought it shortly after Massimo and I moved back to the US."

She lifts her wineglass as her brows climb to her hairline. "You lived overseas?"

I swallow the last bite of food and dab my mouth with my napkin before turning to give her my full attention. Perhaps if I open up to her, she'll open up to me. "Let's move to the couch, and I'll tell you all about it." I pull back her chair and help her to her feet, grabbing the wine cooler and my own wineglass. We settle in one of the soft outdoor couches to the left of my patio. I top off our wineglasses and put the bottle back in the cooler on the table.

"Your house is stunning," she says as I pull her closer and slide my free arm around her shoulders.

"I've spent a lot of time adding to it and redecorating over the years. The outdoor spaces are some of my favorite things about the property." As I lean back, with the woman who has captured my heart snuggled into my side, drinking the delicious crisp sauvignon blanc and surveying the gorgeous grounds of my home and the stunning view before us, my heart fills with pride and happiness.

Life really doesn't get much better than this.

"You bring peace to my soul, Valentina," I say, looking down at her. "I can't remember when I ever felt this contented."

"Same," she shyly agrees.

"You belong here. With me."

Silence greets me, and I don't like it. My words don't appear to be getting through to her at all.

"Tell me where you lived before here," she says in a blatant redirection, but I'll allow it.

"Massimo and I left home at eighteen to go to college overseas. I got a business degree, and Massimo got an IT degree. We invested wisely and heavily during our college years, amassing a considerable amount of money. After we graduated, we started our own business, which we have grown very successfully."

"What exactly do you do?" she asks in between sipping her wine.

"Initially we imported Italian goods into the US, like olive oil, cheese, pasta, herbs. Today our business is focused on real estate, property development, and drug production, shipping, and distribution for the *mafioso* in the US." This shouldn't be news to her. Every *famiglia* across the US is supplied by us from our production plant in Cali, Mexico.

"No wonder you can afford all of this."

"I have more money than I know what to do with," I admit.

"That must be nice."

"It's nice to not have to worry about it. To be able to take care of my family and know they'll always be provided for. But I lead a busy, stressful life, and juggling all my different responsibilities is challenging."

"Is that why you never married?"

I take a healthy mouthful of wine, crossing one leg over my knee. I curl my arm tighter around her, peering into her piercing green eyes. "It's not the main reason."

"What is?" Her fingers curl on my chest. "You're a real catch, Don Maltese, and all the women love you."

Do you?

"I'm not interested in them."

She playfully swats at my chest. "Stop deflecting. You know you could have any woman. I'm betting you've been with your fair share." She quirks a brow in silent question.

"I'm nearly forty-four, Valentina, and I haven't been a saint, but these past few years, I haven't been with many women." I brush my thumb across her lip, wanting to plant a couple of seeds now. "I use a sex club in the city if I want to fuck, but I haven't been there for months."

Her cheeks pink, and it's adorable. "A sex club. Hmm."

"Does that disgust you?"

The stain on her cheeks darkens. "No."

"Then why the look?"

"No reason." She looks down at her lap, and I'm not having that.

"Valentina," I growl. "Stop fucking lying. Tell me what you're thinking."

Her nostrils flare as her gaze meets mine. "Right now, I'm

thinking you need to lose that tone with me, Fiero, and your double standards piss me the hell off."

I know what she's doing, and this time, I'm not going to let her, so I count to ten in my head to calm down. "Sorry, kitten." I nip at her ear. "I just need you to be honest with me. You can deny it all you like, but we're at the start of something special here, and I want no secrets between us."

"I can't possibly satisfy you, sexually, if you're used to frequenting sex clubs," she blurts. "I'm not into voyeurism, public sex, or kinky sex, and I—"

I kiss her lips to shut her up, continuing to kiss her until I feel her melting in my arms and her panic subsiding. Then I pull back, taking our near empty glasses and setting them down on the table. I haul her into my lap and snake my arms around her.

"First, you are perfectly capable of satisfying me sexually even if we spend the rest of our lives having vanilla sex. Sex has never been intimate for me, Valentina. It's pleasure for pleasure's sake alone. With you, sex is emotional and transcendental in a way I've never experienced." I press my lips softly, fleetingly to hers. "You did that, so trust me when I say you are more than enough for me."

"You say all the right things." She nestles her head on my chest.

"It's no lie. I'm telling the truth." I boop her nose, and she glares at me, swatting my hand away. I chuckle, staring at her peering up at me with stars in my eyes. I truly am losing it, and Massimo is going to have a field day with this whenever I'm able to tell him about her. "Secondly, unless you've tried it, you don't know if you have any particular kinks."

Her cheeks pale, and her voice trembles when she says, "Or it's forced, and you know it's definitely not one."

"What happened wasn't consensual, was it?" I'd already reached that conclusion by her reaction and the fact whoever whipped her was either inexperienced or did it on purpose to leave those scars.

She nods.

"Then my point stands. I will never force you to do anything, but if you're willing to play with me, we can explore different things in a safe, controlled manner in private. I won't ever take you to a club, and I won't ever share you. I see the way your body responds to me, kitten, and I think you're kinkier than you know. You just need time to experiment, but if you don't want to, or you do and you don't like it, then I'm perfectly fine with vanilla sex for the rest of my life."

I truly hope no camera has captured that statement because the people who know me would lose their shit if they heard what just came out of my mouth. But I meant it. I wouldn't agree to that with anyone but her.

I want a future with Valentina.

A life I never imagined for myself is now painting itself in front of my eyes, and I want it all. My kitten as my wife. Her belly swollen with my babies. Our house filled with children and tons of laughter.

"You can't be real," she says with tears in her eyes. "This is just a dream, and I'm going to wake one morning and be back in hell."

"No, baby." I run my hand up and down her arm. "You're not going back there. I know you don't believe me, but you'll see."

"How, Fiero? How is it possible?"

I kiss the tip of her nose. "That's for me to figure out. You don't need to worry about it."

"What are you going to do?" she whispers.

"It's better you don't know." I've worked out what I have to do but not the how yet—though I have a few ideas.

"I don't want you to get hurt."

"No one is hurting me." I thread my fingers through her long, wavy, black hair. "When I was overseas, I spent time with a training facility in Nepal. I'm an experienced sharpshooter, proficient with knives and guns and combat. I train regularly and keep myself fit. I take security precautions, and if anyone threatens me, I have the IT skills to ruin them before they come for me. No one has ever gotten near me, and that's not changing anytime soon. Dominic is the one who should fear me. It's not the other way around."

"You need to watch out for Cesco. He's the dangerous one."

"In what way?"

She sits up straighter, resting her hands on my shoulders. "He's power hungry and smart in a way his father isn't. Cesco plays the game way better than Dom. Dom lets his emotions rule him too often, but Cesco is an emotionless bastard, so he doesn't have to worry about that. I think he's a psychopath and he wants complete control. When he succeeds Dom as underboss, I fully expect him to target Vitto. He'll either kill him or marry any daughter of his to get his hands on Miami."

"He's said this to you?"

"No, but I'm a decent judge of character, and I hear things. I observe a lot."

I had suspected as much. I think Valentina may be the key to all this. I want to ask her about the cartel and if she knows the extent of Dom's involvement, but I need to know something else first. "Has Cesco hurt you? Touched you?"

She shakes her head. "It's not like that."

"Then what's it like? What was going on at dinner last night?"

She sighs heavily, reaching for her wineglass as she slides off my lap. Her troubled eyes pin mine in place. "I'll need more wine if we're going there."

Chapter Twenty
Valentina

Fiero pours the dregs of the wine into my glass before heading into the kitchen to grab a fresh bottle. It gives me time to sort through my thoughts and decide how much I can tell him. My gut is telling me I can trust him. That I should tell him everything and he'll protect my family, but I just can't do it. I've known this man a few days, and it's not long enough to prove this is all true.

Fiero is an older, experienced made man and one of the most powerful, most dangerous men in our world. This could be an elaborate ruse to get me to confess everything I know so they can take Dom down. He could discard me when he gets what he wants, and I'll be the one left paying the price.

No, I can't tell him everything.

There is too much at stake, and I just can't risk it.

I'll stick to my personal story as that's the safest, and I'll play dumb if he asks me about anything *mafioso* related. That is the best way to protect myself and my family.

After he returns, he pours more wine into both our glasses before reclaiming his seat. I snuggle up against him because I love being close to him and distracting him with intimacy and sex is the best tool in my arsenal.

"I'm ready whenever you are," he says, curling his arm protectively around me again.

"Cesco first hit on me when he was fourteen. I was nineteen, and Dom was away on a business trip. He wasn't forceful, and he backed off when I told him it was inappropriate, but I knew it wouldn't stop there." I gulp back a large mouthful of wine.

"I told Dom when he returned, and he hit the roof. He beat Cesco black and blue and warned him not to touch me again." I bark out a laugh. "My husband is such a hypocrite. It's okay for other men to touch me when it suits him to play that card, but his son is not allowed go there because it's disrespectful to his father."

Tension instantly bleeds into the air, and I stare off into space as I wait for him to ask it.

"He lets other men touch you?" he chokes out.

Looking toward the boats bobbing at the dock, I slowly nod.

"Valentina." His touch is feather soft as he directs my face to his. "I need you to look at me, honey."

"It's hard to speak about this, Fiero. The only person who knows anything is my cousin Nina. Are you sure you want to hear this? You might not feel the same way about me again."

"There is nothing you could tell me that would change the way I feel about you." He hugs me tight to his chest and his warmth seeps into my body, heating my suddenly icy bones. "Don't be afraid, and don't be ashamed," he adds, tilting my face up to his. "Whatever happened is not on you. I already know you've done what you had to do to survive. There is no shame at all in that."

Pressure sits on my chest, and tears prick the backs of my eyes, but I refuse to let them fall. I've done enough crying in front of this man, and it's embarrassing. After this past year, I thought I had shed every single tear I had to give, but it seems I was wrong.

"Dom has a gambling problem, as you know. He was already broke by the time I arrived, and things haven't ever been better. You saw the state of the house, the car, the clothes I was wearing. Any time he gets money, he gambles believing he'll double or triple it, but he always fucking loses. It's an endless vicious circle."

"I'll let that slipup pass this time." Fiero cautions me with his eyes, and I can't help smirking. "Miami is one of our wealthiest territories. Dom gets his fair share of the profits, so what the hell is he doing with it?"

"He blows most of it on parties. It's his way of keeping the *capos* and *soldati* loyal to him. Everyone knows to show up on Fridays at our place—the men, Dom's friends, contacts, and people he's trying to network with. Dom provides the drink, drugs, and the hookers. All bought on his dime." Hatred toward my husband rages inside me. I worry my lower lip between my teeth and work up the courage to say this next bit. "They play cards, big money stakes, and if my husband loses and he doesn't have the cash to pay up, he offers me instead."

The wineglass slips out of Fiero's hand, dropping to the stone patio floor and smashing upon impact. "It's okay," Fiero says into empty space. "We're okay." He stands, carrying me in his arms, and walks us over to the other couch. His entire body is rigid with tension, his jaw taut, eyes flaring with dark anger, his mouth pulled into a grim line. He puts me down and sits beside me, resting his elbows on his knees and cradling his head in his hands. Tension simmers in the air, and pain pulverizes my heart.

"Told you you'd feel differently," I whisper before knocking back my wine.

"No, baby." Fiero's tortured eyes land on mine as he moves in closer to me. He leans in and kisses me. "That's not it. I'm furious with Dom and with myself." His Adam's apple bobs in his throat. "No wonder you hate me. I'm no better than him or any of those men."

"You're not like them," I rush to reassure him. "I won't lie and say I'm not disgusted you propositioned my husband and effectively bought me, but you're not fucking me in lieu of a cash debt; you're doing it because you want me, and you've already treated me better in two days than my husband has treated me in six years."

"That doesn't make it right!" he yells, hopping up and pacing the ground. "Fucking hell." He rubs his hands continuously over his face and through his hair. Then he rushes to my side, kneeling in front of me. "I'm so sorry, Valentina. I would have found another way if I'd known."

"It's okay," I say, and I mean it. I'm not happy about the deal, but his motives were driven by need for me, and maybe it's wrong, maybe I'm too messed up to see it clearly, but no one has ever fought for me or wanted me this much to go to such lengths. Only Fiero.

"It's not okay, honey." He sits down beside me again. "It's very far from okay. I've made mistakes with you, but I'll make it up to you. I'll treat you like a queen, give you everything your heart desires and more. I'll worship the ground you walk on and never make you feel like this again. I swear." Bringing my hand to his lips, he dusts kisses all over my skin, sending a rake of fiery tremors shooting up my arm.

"You're speaking like we're forever when we both know we're not."

"Quit deluding yourself. We *are* forever, and we both know it."

"All I know is you're crazy."

"Guilty as charged, but so are you, baby. Deny it all you

want, but we both know the truth. Now quit deflecting and tell me the rest. I want a list of names by morning."

"What?" I splutter.

"I want to know who these men were."

"Why?"

"So I can fucking annihilate them for daring to touch what is mine."

I think there's a compliment mixed in with that misogynistic crap, but again, I'm clearly a nutjob because I love he wants to get violent to seek revenge for me. Not that I can let him. "I'm not giving you names. I can't in most cases because I blocked them all out. It's the only way I could hold on to my sanity. They fucked my body, but I never let them get into my head."

"What about Vitto?" A muscle clenches in his jaw. "Has he touched you?"

I shake my head. "No. Vitto is always kind to me. He wouldn't do that."

Disbelief is etched all over Fiero's face.

"I'm sure you're aware Vitto is not loyal to his wife, but he doesn't force women, and he's not into it if it's not completely consensual. Besides, Dom would never offer me to him. It's a matter of pride. I've heard him bragging how his wife is sexier and more desired than the don's wife."

Fiero's face scrunches in disgust. He heaves out a heavy sigh, scrubbing a hand along his prickly jawline. "How many?"

"Don't ask me to tell you that."

"I'm so sorry, Valentina." He lifts me carefully into his lap, hugging me close. "You should never have had to endure that. That's not how things are supposed to be done now. The Commission has made their stance very clear. Wives are to be cherished and adored and respected. Dominic is going to regret every single thing he's subjected you to."

"I hope so." My voice is timid, my body exhausted. I'm feeling drained, and I haven't even explained half of it.

"The scars," he says.

"Yes," I whisper, praying he lets it go.

"Just don't mark her face." He briefly closes his eyes. "That motherfucker is going down, and you'll give me the name of the sadistic prick who whipped you."

His face flashes before my eyes, and a shudder seizes hold of my body. As long as I live, I'll never forget that evil bastard. Outwardly, he was handsome and dashing, but inside, he was ugly as sin.

"He's already dead."

Fiero grips my face and peers deep into my eyes. "Is that the truth?"

I stare right back at him. "Yes."

His tongue darts out, wetting his full lips, lips that have already given me so much pleasure. I rest my head on his shoulder and huddle closer to his chest.

"What did Cesco do yesterday?" he asks after a few silent beats.

I swallow back bile. "He forced my thighs open under the table and touched me. I jumped up before he reached my panties."

"I'm adding him to my kill list," Fiero calmly replies.

I lift my head and examine his face. He truly means that. "I wouldn't lose a second's sleep if any of those men died."

"Good."

"But you can't take both Dom and Cesco out. I don't want you risking everything you've achieved for me."

He presses his lips to my brow. "I'll handle Dom first and then deal with Cesco when the timing is right, but that little shit doesn't get to live."

I should probably be appalled, but all I feel is relief. I want them to die, and if Fiero makes it a gruesome death, even better. I convey that with my eyes before covering my mouth to stifle a yawn.

"I know you're tired, and this is hard to share. Thank you for telling me." He kisses my brow. "I just need to know one final thing, and then the subject is closed."

"Shoot."

"How did you end up in an arranged marriage to him? How did he even know of you?"

"My high-school boyfriend's dad decided he wanted me for himself, and after manipulating the situation and making my boyfriend believe I'd cheated on him, his son publicly broke up with me and kissed my best friend in front of me at a party. His dad offered to drive me home, and I accepted because I was distraught and had no other ride. He tried to force himself on me while driving me home, but I fought him off."

Fiero's eyes blaze with anger, and if the bastard wasn't already dead, I'm guessing he'd be adding him to his kill list. "I heard he was a sick pervert who preyed on young girls."

My eyes narrow to slits. "You know who it is?"

"Vitto told me Jacopo Pagano was the one who negotiated the contract. It doesn't take much to connect the dots. Pagano's son is on the board of The Commission, and he's never had anything good to say about his deceased father." Fiero sits up straighter and alarm is etched all over his face. "Fuck." His expression turns pained. "Was Louis your high-school boyfriend?"

"How can you be an IT expert if you're that bad at math?" I tease.

Fiero's shoulders instantly relax. "Thank fuck. I'd hate to have to kill another board member. That one might be difficult to pull off without getting caught."

"Louis wasn't around when I was going out with Damiano. He'd left home a few years before, was already married with kids.

I never even met him. Damiano was an oops baby, born to Mrs. Pagano when she was forty-six and her youngest child at that point was fifteen."

"And Damiano believed whatever bullshit his father fed him?"

"Yep." I tuck my hair behind my ears. "He hero-worshipped his father. Don't know why. He was a blatant creep. I didn't know he was behind the lies until he fessed up in the car. I said I was going to tell Damiano, and he said, 'Be my guest, he'll never believe you over me.' He was evil to his core. I celebrated the day he died." My fingers dig into my thighs, and rage is a snarling beast in my veins like always when I think of that monster.

"How bad was it?"

"Bad enough considering I was pretty innocent back then." I'd given Damiano my virginity, and we'd slept together a few times, but I wasn't experienced or mature in the ways of our world back then, and what his father tried to do terrified me. "He groped my breasts through my shirt, pushed my skirt up, and was clawing at my panties when I hit him over the head with his son's basketball trophy. He was out cold, and at first, I panicked that I'd killed him. I didn't know what to do, so I just ran off and raced home. I didn't tell a single person what happened, and he mustn't have either because no one came knocking on our door."

"He timed his revenge instead," Fiero says in a clipped tone.

"Yes." Bile claws up my throat. "My father didn't tell me he was approached about a marriage contract because he knew I wouldn't want to leave home to marry a man who was the same age as him. For ages, I believed it was my own fault for not telling my daddy what Damiano's father tried to do. That if he'd known he wouldn't have agreed." Tightness spreads across my chest. "But I was lying to myself. My father would still have agreed. He's only a *soldato*, and you don't refuse your don."

"It's not your fault." Fiero forces my gaze to his. "Please tell me you know that now."

"I do." I hear how feeble my protest is. It's hard to have much self-respect when you've suffered the things I have. "Ironically, it was Damiano who introduced me to Dominic at a fundraiser at a hotel in Detroit. I was so giddy that night. I was wearing one of my mama's dresses, and I'd splurged on new shoes. Daddy had paid for me to get my hair and makeup done. I remember feeling pretty and important as Damiano paraded me around the ballroom, introducing me to some of the most powerful men in the US." I shake my head, disgusted at my naivety. "I was so stupid. A little girl completely out of her league in a brutal world she didn't understand. Dom told me later he saw me that night and knew he had to have me. His wife died six months later, and he was immediately on the phone with his old buddy Jacopo."

"What lucky timing for Dominic," Fiero deadpans, and I answer the unspoken question.

"Dom killed his first wife. He staged it to look like suicide, but he gave her the pills and the alcohol and told her if she didn't do it he'd put a bullet in her skull."

"He told you this?" Fiero rubs warmth into my chilly arms.

I bob my head. "Promised I'd suffer the same fate if I didn't please him and obey his every command."

"He told me she had a heart attack."

"That's the lie he tells outsiders to hide *the shame*. Within our circles, the story is she killed herself, and most probably believe it because by all accounts he treated her even worse than me."

"He's a piece of shit, and his time is running out."

"If you're asking for my permission, you have it."

"I know, kitten." He presses his lips to mine in a soft kiss. "What about Jacopo?"

"He escorted me from Detroit to Miami for my wedding. My

family couldn't afford to come, so they put me into the hands of one monster to be given into the hands of another. I shook the entire time on the plane. I was terrified. I knew he had something awful planned for me. Jacopo was watching me like a hawk, and I expected him to pounce but he waited until we got to Dom's house. I was a complete basket case by then, shaking and trembling with fear." Tears well in my eyes as I think back to the night before my wedding.

"You don't have to tell me. It's okay." Fiero hugs me close, dotting kisses into my hair and whispering soothing words.

When I have relaxed a little, I rest my cheek on his chest and tell him the rest. "Dom took me to his room and stripped me naked in front of Jacopo, and then he held me down while his buddy violated me. The entire time, Jacopo taunted me with how Damiano was now dating my best friend and planning to marry her because she wasn't a cheating slut like me. After, Jacopo returned the favor for Dom, and they kept going in rounds for hours." My tears are all gone when I lift my head and fix emotionless eyes on my Gage. "He broke me that night and every night since. Now there is nothing left of that naïve, innocent eighteen-year-old girl who stepped foot on the plane that night."

Chapter Twenty-One
Fiero

I carry Valentina to bed, helping her into a red silk nightie and cradling her in my arms all night as she sleeps fitfully. I barely sleep, only grabbing a few minutes here and there. I'm too tortured with images of everything she's been through to switch off my brain. Jacopo Pagano is lucky he's already dead because he'd be on top of my kill list along with Dominic Ferraro.

I'm fully at peace with the decision I've reached. Even if it comes back to bite me on the ass, that's okay. Dominic Ferraro is living his last week on this Earth. He just doesn't know it.

Looking down at the woman sleeping in my arms, I make a silent vow to ensure no one ever hurts her again. No man will ever touch her but me. If anyone looks at her with even a hint of lustful intent, I'll scoop their eyeballs from their sockets and make them choke on them. I hold her closer, dusting some kisses in her hair, careful not to hug her too tight so I don't wake her. It's still early, and she needs to sleep.

Reluctantly, I peel myself away from her and tiptoe into my closet, grabbing a pair of training shorts. Taking one last glance at my sleeping beauty, I head to my office and begin to set things in motion.

I call my assistant first, promising her a bonus when she protests being woken at five thirty a.m. After ensuring she's got everything set up for tonight, I tell her to reschedule my day. I'm not leaving my kitten alone. Not after last night. She's bound to be all up in her feelings, and I want to be here to support her as she processes everything. Questioning her about Dom's activities will have to wait for now.

Then I place a call to my guys in Miami asking if anything interesting has cropped up. They began shadowing Dom and Cesco yesterday. They don't have anything yet but promise to update me the second there is something to report. Next, I call Rico and ask him to handle a few things. He asks about Valentina, and I tell him she's fine, but I don't say any more. If Rico doesn't know, he can't be implicated.

Lastly, I send a message to Natalia Messina to make an appointment for her to come out to the house on Friday. Nat is Caleb and Joshua's mom, and she's a doctor at the private hospital we own in the city. Her husband, Leo, is Ben's under-boss. Nat provides private medical care to our small inner circle, and she's the only one I'd trust with my kitten.

Finally, I summon Zumo and Caleb to my house, telling Zumo to pick up his best friend and explain everything to Caleb on the way. My brother is fully up to speed, and our meeting will be quicker if all parties are on the same page.

They arrive shortly after six thirty, and after checking to make sure my kitten is still asleep, I usher them into my office and close the door.

"I presume you know everything and you're okay with it if you're here." I eyeball Caleb, trusting I was right to bring him into this.

"You know me. I'm always down to kill a few motherfuckers." He flashes me a wicked grin and cracks his knuckles.

"You're a husband now with a baby on the way." Caleb's wife Elisa is due to give birth in August, six days after Joshua's wife Gia is due to give birth to their baby. "It's okay if this is too much to ask. I understand." I know Caleb can be trusted to keep it a secret even if he doesn't participate.

"I'm all in, Fiero."

"As I am, brother."

I nod my gratitude toward Zumo before swinging my gaze back to Accardi. "What we're doing is unsanctioned. This could jeopardize our standing or even our positions on the board."

Caleb props his butt on the edge of my desk, flicking strands of dirty-blond hair out of his eyes. "The guy is corrupt to his core, and he's in bed with the cartel. We'll torture him for intel, and you'll find the evidence retrospectively. Then we'll go to the board and explain it, and they'll let us get away with it." His voice resonates with cool confidence.

"Are you very sure, Caleb?"

"Dude, seriously." Caleb clamps his hand down on my bare shoulder. "All in means *all in*." His expression sobers. "I talked to Lili on the way. Don't worry I didn't give her any names or specifics, but I gave her enough info to explain the kind of man Ferraro is, and do you know what she said?" His eyes twinkle with pride and delight, like always when he talks about his wife, his Lili.

I roll my eyes. "Always so dramatic."

"Hah! I think you're giving me a run for my money these days."

Can't really argue that. "Go on."

The laughter fades again. "She said to riddle him with bullets and make sure he was properly dead."

"What have you done to that sweet girl?" I tease. Stories of

Caleb and Elisa fucking in the blood of our enemies is legendary in our community. Not sure it's something her father, Don Salerno, relished discovering that day when he burst into the dungeon to rescue her.

"My love is still the sweetest, kindest, most adorable woman I know, but she doesn't tolerate cruelty and abuse. She cried when I told her the things your girl has had to endure."

My girl.

Warmth spreads across my chest, and my lips tip up.

"Holy fuck." Caleb chuckles, nudging my shoulder. "I seriously never thought I'd see the day you fell, but you've fallen hard, my friend."

"I have."

Zumo grins wide. "Told both of you it would happen, and you never believed me."

"Says the guy who moves from one longtime girlfriend to another without ever getting hitched. What's up with that, buddy?" Caleb waggles his brows.

"I'm still searching for *the one* and enjoying myself on the journey."

"I'm happy for you, man." Caleb squeezes my shoulder. "I used to idolize you when we were younger because you got all the pussy and you never got attached. It's only in the last few years I realized how lonely you must be because I became you, and it wasn't all it was cracked up to be."

"I didn't have much chance to consider it, because I was distracted with work, but you're right. Valentina coming into my life has shown me how empty my existence has been."

"Not anymore."

"Are you two pussies done with your bleeding hearts?" Zumo asks, his tone laced with amusement. "I have a meeting with the *capos* this morning, so let's move this along."

We talk through the pros and cons of the plan I've come up with, tweaking it until we're satisfied.

"We should probably run this by Rico." Zumo leans back in his seat. "In case we've missed anything."

"I'd rather not involve him." If this goes haywire, I don't want to take him down with me.

"I agree. The plan is solid." Caleb stands and stretches his back.

"Fiero?" A gentle rap on the door accompanies her sultry voice.

Caleb and Zumo share a grin and some silent communication, and before I can stop him, Accardi is striding across the room and opening the door.

Valentina jumps back, slapping a hand to her chest as she stares wide-eyed and open-mouthed at Caleb. "You startled me." A blush steals over her cheeks as she looks sheepishly at me. "I'm sorry. I didn't realize you had visitors."

"Where's your robe?" I work hard not to shout, but she's standing in my hallway in front of my brother and Caleb in the red nightie. It's revealing as fuck, molding to her tits, curving around her hips, and hitting her mid-thigh. She's flashing far too much skin, and her nipples are trying to poke holes through the silk. Her hair is tussled from sleep, and with that delicate flush on her flawless skin, she looks sexy as fuck, and it should be for my eyes only!

"Cover your eyes," I bark, glaring at Caleb and Zumo.

Her eyes widen to saucers as Zumo arches a brow and Caleb lets his grin run free.

"Valentina, I assume," he says, completely ignoring me as he extends his hand toward her. "It's so lovely to meet the woman who has brought this guy to his knees." He jabs his thumb in my direction as I frantically search my office. My breath is oozing out in heavy spurts, and my heart is racing. "I can totally see why," the fucker says, taking her hand and lifting it to his mouth.

"Put your lips anywhere on her body, and I'll have to shoot you, Accardi," I snap. "Let her go." My hands clench into balls as a tsunami of emotions rushes through my veins.

Caleb ignores me, *again*, brushing his lips across her knuckles.

Zumo is watching me with a mix of amusement and concern as I lose it while Caleb is grinning and milking this for all it's worth. Poor Valentina just looks confused.

Spotting my jacket where I left it yesterday, I snatch it from the back of my chair and rush across the room. Barreling past a laughing Caleb, I dig my elbow firmly into his ribs on purpose. He stumbles back, grunting.

Yeah, buddy, not laughing now, huh?

"What the hell were you thinking?" I ask my kitten, covering her in the jacket. It falls to her knees, and I button it in the front, but it still shows far too much of her cleavage.

"I didn't know they were here, and you're overreacting."

I push her behind me so they can't see.

"Fiero. You're acting crazy. They were only looking at my face."

"Don't care."

"Man, I'm so glad you called me. I wouldn't have missed this for the world." Caleb cracks up laughing.

"Fiero. You're smothering the woman. For fuck's sake, we weren't looking at her like that. Give us some credit." Zumo shakes his head, looking at me like he might be considering committing me. "Introduce me."

"Fiero. I'm all covered up, look." Valentina tugs at my arm, and I reluctantly release her, spinning around to inspect her before I'll even consider stepping aside. She's wearing a soft smile, clutching the sides of the jacket together so it completely covers her torso. My eyes skim down her bare legs. "Fiero." Her tone is more forthright, her smile a little harder. "I know you're protective, but you can't wrap me in cotton wool or hide me from the world. Are you going to stop me wearing minidresses or bikinis?"

"Of course not." Her smile expands. "As long as we're not going out and we don't have company."

The smile fades, and she squeezes her eyes shut momentarily. "You're being unreasonable, but we'll discuss this later. Introduce me to your friends." She holds out her free hand. "Please."

I kiss her lips quick before grasping her hand and turning us around.

My brother smiles at her with affection. "I'm Zumo. This nutjob's brother. It's nice to meet you, Valentina. I'd shake your hand, but..."

"You value breathing," she replies, her lips twitching. "I see the resemblance now."

"Please," I scoff. "I'm way hotter."

"Think you mean way *older*." My brother leans against the doorway, smirking.

Ignoring him, I turn to Caleb. "And this is..."

"Don Caleb Accardi," she says in a breathy tone. "I probably shouldn't admit this in front of the caveman, but when I was growing up, my friends and I had mad crushes on you and your twin. Those campaigns you modeled for were—"

"Kitten, no one wants to hear this," I growl, covering her mouth so she can't spew more of that bullshit. I briefly consider getting the gun from the drawer in my desk and shooting Caleb in his overly smug face.

"I do." Caleb flashes me a wide grin.

"Same," my traitorous brother announces.

"Thought you were leaving," I snap.

"This is the best day ever." Caleb rubs his middle finger up the bridge of his nose because he's just that childish.

Not that I'm one to speak, at the moment.

I know I'm acting insane, but I can't help it. Jealousy stabs holes in my heart, and I'm not used to these emotions. I'm not fully equipped to handle it. And it's more than that. I don't want anyone looking at her with anything less than the respect she deserves. Valentina has had enough men objectify and abuse her, and it's not happening on my watch. But I'm being a tad unreasonable because I know my brother and Caleb would never treat her like that.

"Thanks for that, kitten. I'll tell my twin you were asking for him," Caleb says, and Zumo pulls him back as I lunge at him.

"Get control of yourself." Zumo slams his hand into my chest to hold me back. "You'll scare her away if you're not careful." He shakes his head. "I've never seen you like this. It's a little disturbing."

"It's okay, Gage." Valentina pushes me back, peering up at me with doe eyes. "Just take a deep breath."

Her big green eyes trap mine in place, and I suck in lungsful of air, calming down when I pull her against my chest, hugging her tight.

Caleb and Zumo are smiling.

I shrug. "She makes me crazy."

"Happens to the best of us," Caleb says.

"We'll see you Thursday," Zumo adds, and I nod before they walk off.

"Well, that was an unusually troubling-slash-entertaining way to start my day," Valentina jokes, tipping her head up.

"Sorry." I run my hands up and down her arms. "I don't seem to be able to help myself when it comes to you." I push my hands into her hair. "How are you feeling?"

"I'm okay. I hate talking about that night, but it was kind of therapeutic in a way."

I kiss her brow before scrutinizing her face. "I've rearranged my day so I can be here with you."

Her eyes light up. "You have?"

"Yep." I grab her ass over my jacket. "I'm going to make you breakfast, and then I'm taking you out on my boat. Later, we're going into the city for dinner and a show."

She emits the most gleeful squeal, and her entire face is glowing.

I am so in love with this woman, and I hope everything goes according to plan because I don't know how I could continue to live without her if it doesn't.

Chapter Twenty-Two
Valentina

I trace my finger back and forth along the indent on my ring finger, wondering if I'm tempting fate removing my rings this early. But I don't want to go out with Fiero tonight wearing them, and I've already decided I'm not going back to that pig, so there's no reason to wear them any longer. When the timing is right, I'll mail them to Dominic's daughters. The engagement ring is a family heirloom, and it belongs to the Ferraros.

Exiting the bedroom, I head down to the kitchen.

"Perfect timing," Fiero says when I step onto the tiled floor. "It's just ready. I set the table outside." He glances over his shoulder from his position at the stove, and his blue eyes instantly darken with heat. "Fuck, you look beautiful."

My cheeks warm as I drop my beach bag on a stool. "Thanks." I'm wearing a light white and blue summer dress with cap sleeves and a cutout triangle on the back. My feet are encased in flat bejeweled silver sandals, and I tied my hair up into a ponytail.

"Did you pack swimwear?" he asks, dividing his attention between me and the skillet.

"I'm wearing a bikini."

"Show me," he growls, abandoning the stove to turn fully around.

I'm contemplating lifting my skirt to flash him my bikini bottoms when he shakes his head and adds, "Don't."

I arch a brow.

"If you show me, I'll have to fuck you, and we won't be leaving the house today." He points toward the sliding doors. "Go before I pounce on you."

I'm giggling and smiling as I walk past him, squealing when he smacks my ass and growls under his breath.

I tip my face up to the sky as I make my way toward the table on the patio. It's a gorgeous day and there's barely a cloud in the sky. It's warm but a lot cooler than I'm used to. I make a note to grab a cardigan before we leave in case I'm cold on the boat.

My heart starts doing cartwheels when I reach the table to find a large bouquet of lilies waiting for me. Lifting the arrangement to my nose, I inhale deeply, absorbing the sweet floral scent with a hint of spice and citrus. My fingers are trembling as I open the card, reading the messy scrawl.

You make me so happy, kitten.
Always yours, Fiero.

I place my hand over my chest, where my heart is thumping wildly, and I'm smiling through blurry eyes. This feels like a fairy tale and I never want it to end.

"Okay?" the man himself says, setting a tray down on the table.

"Yes." Putting the bouquet down, I fling my arms around him and hug him tight. "You make me happy too," I whisper, almost afraid to verbalize it in case I jinx myself. "Thank you."

His strong arms wind around my back, and he holds me close. "You're welcome." His fingers lace through my hair, and he tilts my head back before kissing me tenderly. His eyes radiate with so much emotion when he breaks our kiss and just stares at me. "I want you by my side forever, Valentina." He cups my cheeks. "I mean every word I say to you. You're mine, and I'm yours, and I'm letting nothing stand in our way."

"I want to believe it, but nothing good ever lasts long in my life, and I'm afraid to trust this."

"I get it, but I promise I'm going nowhere, and I'm a man of my word." He kisses me again before breaking our embrace. "Breakfast is getting cold. Eat."

I place the bouquet in one of the empty chairs and sit down to eat the breakfast Fiero prepared. A plate of bacon, eggs, toast, tomato, and mushroom has never looked more appetizing. He's made mimosas, and there's coffee too.

"This looks delicious. Thank you." I could really get used to this.

You're not hanging around, a little voice whispers in my ear.

"It's not much. My cooking repertoire is limited, and I'm nowhere near as skilled as you in the kitchen."

"I come from a large family, and I'm the eldest girl. I learned to cook from a young age, and I regularly helped Mom with dinner," I say before cutting a piece of bacon and popping it into my mouth.

"Are you close with your family?" he asks, spearing a mushroom.

"I'm close with my sisters. I call them all the time to check in. My brothers are harder to connect with now they're teenagers and initiated. They're rarely around when I call, and when I manage to talk to them, I get one-word answers."

"Sounds like typical teenage boys."

"Yeah." I scoop up a forkful of the creamy eggs.

He lifts a brow. "And your parents?"

I swallow the food in my mouth before replying. "Growing up, I was close to both parents. I was dad's first *principessa*. Mom used to confide in me and rely on me a lot as more and more babies kept arriving. I looked up to her until they handed me over to Dom, and I just can't forgive them for it."

"That's understandable but sad. When did you last see them?"

"I haven't seen my parents or my siblings since I was eighteen."

A muscle pops in his jaw as he sets his silverware down. "Are you saying Dominic never arranged for them to visit or you to visit them?"

I nod as I sip my mimosa. It's delicious, and I barely resist the urge to knock it back in one go. "My family doesn't have the money to fly everyone to Miami, and Dominic is stingy with any money he has. Besides, I didn't want any of my siblings around the scene in the house." A shudder works its way through me. "I didn't want any monster taking a shine to one of my sisters. I'd never forgive myself if they ended up in the same situation as me."

"Yet he gave you money before coming here." Fiero drinks from his coffee cup as he stares me straight in the eye.

I could lie, but given everything I've said about my husband, it wouldn't be believable, and I can tell Fiero is suspicious. "He didn't. That's mine. I've been stashing it for years. I wanted to be prepared so when an opportunity arose to escape I could take it. I didn't leave it in case anyone went snooping in my room."

He nods, and from his expression, I can tell he's pleased I was honest. "You don't share a room with him?"

"No, thank fuck."

"Language," Fiero snaps, and I roll my eyes. "Why?"

"Why'd you think? He likes to entertain hookers, and a wife just gets in the way. He tried to involve me at the start, but I fought him. Wouldn't touch those women or let them touch me. Eventually he gave up and put me in my own bedroom. It's probably the only win in my entire marriage, but it was an important one."

"I'm setting my plan in motion tomorrow, and I expect Dom to show up here on Thursday where we'll be waiting for him." I'm not sure what he sees on my face, but it's enough to have him take my hand and squeeze it. "He won't see you. You'll be safe in my panic room. You won't see or hear a thing. I promise."

"I'm nervous. What if something goes wrong?"

It's not just my welfare at stake if this goes belly up. I don't care he's going to die. It's something I've thought about a lot, and my conscience is clear. Dom is a monster, and he deserves it. I'm not overly worried he's left any plans should he die early, because my husband is not an organized man, but the threat is real all the same, and there's a small part of me that's worried he might have set something in motion. And Cesco is a wildcard. I don't know how much he knows and whether he might intervene and do something or say something. I'm hoping he'll be too busy trying to persuade Vitto to appoint him underboss in his father's stead to focus on me.

I won't survive if anyone gets hurt because of me. It's why I can't fully relax, and I won't until Fiero has dealt with both of them.

"I've known men like Dominic my whole life. I grew up with a prick like him, and I know how he'll react. If I'm wrong and he doesn't take the bait, I'll find another way of handling him."

"Your father was like him?"

Fiero removes his hand and lifts his mimosa to his lips, draining it. "They share some traits."

"I'm sensing your childhood wasn't a happy one," I say, picking up my fork and resuming eating.

"It wasn't unhappy per se, but my father and I never saw eye to eye. I was a bit rebellious as a teenager, and while I enjoyed being *mafioso*, I didn't always obey the rules. That pissed him off, so I kept rebelling to annoy him." He looks out toward the water. "It backfired in a major way when he replaced me as his heir with my brother Armani." His Adam's apple bobs in his throat, and his fingers grip his chair tightly.

"I can't believe he did that. It's so disrespectful to you."

His jaw is tense when he turns to look at me. "It was, but truth be told, Armani was a better candidate. He was steady in a way I wasn't back then. More mature than me too, and he was a good son. He followed orders without much argument. It was always obvious my father preferred him to me."

"Is that why you went overseas to college?"

His head bobs. "Massimo's father was an asshole too, and we both wanted to put distance between us and our fathers."

"But you're the don now."

Pain bleeds from his eyes and his pores, and his hurt is palpable.

"You don't have to talk about it," I rush to reassure him.

He moves his chair back and reaches out, grabbing me by the hips and lifting me onto his lap. His arms instantly band around me. "I don't want secrets between us." His lips meet mine in a brief, sensual kiss before he rests his brow against mine. His chest heaves, and his pain is palpable. "Armani died in the warehouse bombing years ago," he admits in a strangled tone.

Everyone in *La Cosa Nostra* knows about that bombing. It

wiped out so many dons and heirs from across the states, and it was a very tumultuous time in our history.

"I'm so sorry, Fiero."

"It should have been me."

My brow crinkles. "It's not your fault he was appointed as heir instead of you, and I'm sure it wasn't your fault he was there that day. If anyone is to blame, it's your father or the prick who set the bomb."

"He was my younger brother, and it was my job to protect him." He thumps a closed hand over his chest. "I shouldn't have acted like such a fucktard as a teen. I should have toed the line. Then Armani wouldn't have been the heir, and he wouldn't have lost his life."

"Fiero." My hands clasp his face. "He could have lost his life at any time. It's the risk every made man takes in our world. If it'd been you, we wouldn't be here now. You wouldn't be rescuing me from my nightmare, and I wouldn't be feeling alive for the first time in years. All those people you employ in your business wouldn't have jobs, and The Commission would be sorely missing your skills and experience. What happened to Armani is tragic, but it's not your fault, and please don't wish it had been you. I'm sure everyone who loves you says the same thing. It's not your responsibility to bear."

"I don't think the guilt will ever leave me," he quietly says.

"Is this why you never married?" I examine his tortured face. "You think you don't deserve to be happy because your brother died?"

He gulps audibly and shrugs his shoulders.

I hold his face firmly, peering deep into his eyes. "You deserve to be happy, Fiero. I didn't know your brother, but I doubt he'd want you to deny yourself happiness. From what you've told me about him, he'd want you to live *for him*, to embrace everything life has to offer because it can end in the blink of an eye and it's too short to deny yourself anything."

"You're so smart. So good. Kind and compassionate. So perfect." He slams his lips to mine in a searing-hot kiss I feel all the way to my toes. We're both panting when we break apart. His gaze snares mine with intensity and determination. "God, I fucking love you," he says, shocking both of us. "I really fucking love you."

A pregnant pause ensues as we stare at one another. I wonder if my face is reflecting the same host of emotions his face is. A radiant smile trips over his mouth, expanding as he holds me closer and tighter.

"I know we barely know one another, but it's what I feel in my heart, and it doesn't feel wrong to say it." His lips brush against mine. "I don't expect you to say it back. Not yet." He places his palm over my heart. "You've been hurt, and you don't trust easily for good reason. I know it'll take time, and I'm okay with that. Just open your heart and give in to the possibility. That's all I ask. Don't shut me out or discount what we share because I know you feel this thing between us too."

"I do, but it's overwhelming and intense, and I'm feeling so many things. For years, I was numb, emotionally closed off, because it was the only way I could survive. You've torn down my walls, Fiero, and everything I've kept trapped is breaking free. It's a lot to handle, and I need to process it in my own time and my own way."

He dots kisses all over my face. "Like I said, I'm going nowhere, and after Thursday, we'll have all the time in the world."

Chapter Twenty-Three
Fiero

"**Y**es, right there, baby," I pant, gripping her hips tighter and grinding up inside her. Her tits bounce all over the place as she rides me slowly and enthusiastically. Valentina pivots her hips as she slams down harder, and I'm seeing stars. I already took her twice earlier on the boat, and I'm still insatiable. I'd literally spend twenty-four-seven buried balls-deep inside her if I could.

I sit up and scoot back to the headrest with her still on my cock. Then I lift my knees, nestling them against her ass and her back to hold her upright as I thrust up inside her, hitting her deeper at this angle.

"Yes, Gage. That feels so fucking good."

Gage. I've definitely got a bone to pick with her over that. I googled it, discovering he was the older man who propositioned Woody Harrelson's character in *Indecent Proposal*. His ending will not be mine, and she's going to lose the name or end up over my knee.

"Watch your mouth, kitten," I rasp, exploring her body with my hands as we fuck. "And quit calling me that old man name."

"If the shoe fits," she rasps, smiling before she groans loudly when my cock surges forward as I push in deep.

The moans coming out of her mouth as I sweep my palms across her flat stomach and up along her rib cage almost have me coming on the spot. A line of sweat rolls down my back, and my heart is working overtime, but it's the best workout, and I'm down for changing my daily routine.

She shivers when my palms land on her tits, grinding down on me when I play with her nipples, tweaking and pulling them between my thumbs and forefingers. Shoving my face in her chest, I pound up inside her as I kiss and suck her breasts, grazing my teeth along her nipples and lightly tugging. Her pussy clenches around me hard, and I have to stop thrusting for a few seconds to slow this down.

When I'm back in control, I suck on the hickey on her chest, ensuring my mark doesn't fade.

"Fiero," she says in a breathy tone that sends shivers coasting all over my body. "I'm close."

"Not without me, baby." Circling my arms around her back, I reach up and wrap my hand around her hair, tipping her head back and exposing her neck to me. I lavish kisses all over the elegant column of her neck before releasing her hair so I can kiss her plump lips. Kissing has never been something I've indulged in much, but I'm fucking addicted to kissing Valentina. I could do it for hours, and it still wouldn't be enough.

Her inner walls grip my dick, and I know she's almost there. Breaking our kiss, I stare into her eyes as I thrust up. "I'm taking over." Grabbing her hips, I slam her up and down on my cock in sync with my thrusts. "Eyes on me, honey." Our gazes lock, and I'm mesmerized by the look in her eyes as I fuck up into her over and over. Nothing feels as good as her bare cunt gripping my dick as I pump in and out. "Ready, kitten?"

"Yes. God, yes," she moans, still keeping eye contact.

"Good girl." I rub her clit with two fingers, moving them fast when I feel my balls lock up and a familiar tingle at the base of my spine. "I love you." I press down on her bundle of nerves, and when her thighs start to tremble and her body shakes, I pinch her clit hard as I simultaneously drive up inside her deep and explode.

Valentina screams, falling apart on my dick as I empty inside her. Our sweat-slickened skin is stuck to one another, and my heart is racing in my chest, the same way the vein in her neck is pulsing and throbbing.

"I think you fucked me into a coma." She drops her head to my shoulder and drapes her arms around me.

"You wouldn't be talking if you were in a coma, kitten." I rest my chin on her head and hold her close against me.

"A semi-coma then," she murmurs in a sleepy tone.

"Not sure such a thing exists."

"Oh, shut up. You fucked me good."

"I know I did, baby." I hug her closer. "The day I stop fucking you good is the day I die."

"So sleepy." Her warm breath kisses the side of my neck, and my deflating dick jerks a little. "No, no, no. No more."

A chuckle teases my lips. "Have a nap. There's a little time before we have to leave."

"Mmkay."

Reluctantly, I lift her off me and lie her down on top of the bed. She's out for the count the second her head hits the pillow. Grabbing a wet cloth and a hand towel from the bathroom, I clean her up before tucking her under the covers. She looks so gorgeous, all sexed up and messy, and I can't resist snapping a pic on my phone.

After grabbing a quick shower and pulling on a pair of shorts, I head into my office to attend to a few things, keeping an eye on the time. I have a text from one of my men in Miami, so he's my first call.

"Boss, I've got something," he supplies the second he picks up.

"I'm listening." Leaning back in my chair, I give him my full attention.

"I followed Cesco Ferraro late last night to a warehouse twenty miles outside of Miami. I couldn't get any closer without being spotted, but he met someone there. They pulled up in a blacked-out SUV and drove straight into the building, so I couldn't see who it was, but I got a pic of the plates."

"Send it to me along with the coordinates of the warehouse, and I'll do some digging."

"Okay. I assume you want me to keep tailing him."

"Absolutely. Just ensure you're not made."

"Will do, boss."

I hang up and wait for the information to come through as I log into my system. He got a clear shot of the plates, and I quickly hack into the police database using the alias I set up a couple years ago for this very reason. I type the registration into the field and press enter, unsurprised when the search comes back empty. Fake plates. It's not unexpected. I log into another system and upload the picture of the vehicle and the plates and set it to run. It'll take a few hours for it to search street and road cams, but hopefully by the time we return from our night out, I'll have something.

I check in with Zumo, Rico, my assistant, and the office manager at Rinascita before a quick call with Joshua Accardi to go over a few things, and then I make my way back to the bedroom to wake my sleeping beauty.

Valentina hasn't budged in the bed, and she looks so cute snuggled into the pillow with her hands under her face.

"Kitten." I lean down and kiss her soft cheek. "Time to wake, baby." She doesn't stir, not even when I kiss her lips and lightly shake her shoulders. A wicked grin slips over my mouth as I peel back the covers and stare hungrily at her naked body.

She is truly stunning.

Like a piece of expensive art you're itching to touch but afraid you might damage.

I trail a line of kisses from her neck, across her collarbone, and down to her tits. I suck one nipple into my mouth, and she moans, flipping onto her back and mumbling in her sleep. My grin is full force as I move lower, kissing down along her stomach until I meet the promised land.

The second I lick a path along her pussy, her eyes pop open, and her legs automatically part for me.

"Such a good girl," I murmur, driving one finger inside her. "Always so fucking wet for your man."

"Fiero." Her voice is drenched with desire, and I wish I had time to fuck her again, but the schedule is too tight. Just as I think it, my cell pings with a notification from the gate that the hairdresser and makeup artist have arrived.

"You awake now, baby," I ask, adding another digit to her cunt.

"Fuck me," she rasps, arching her hips. "Fuck me now."

"No can do, love." I pump my fingers in faster. "But I can ease this ache."

She pouts and grumbles when I remove my fingers, and I chuckle as warmth blooms in my chest. Peeling the covers fully back, I lie down on my stomach between her legs. "Pull your knees to your chest and hold them there," I command, beyond pleased when she readily obeys. I stare at her pussy and her ass, licking my lips in anticipation. All that pink glistening flesh is mine and mine alone. No man will ever see this or touch this ever again. No one but me.

Mine. Mine. Mine.

"Prepare to have your world rocked, kitten," I say before diving in.

I feast on her pussy with my lips, my fingers, and my tongue, dry humping the bed as I eat her out. She's writhing and whimpering and shoving her pussy in my face, and it only cranks my arousal to dizzying heights. My hips are grinding into the mattress, and I'm hard as steel. Her walls tighten around my tongue just before she shatters, and I add a finger into her wet heat as I suck hard on her clit.

Valentina screams out my name, over and over, and the possessive beast inside me fucking loves it. I'm leaking precum and close to finishing just from devouring her, which never happens. Keeping my tongue on her cunt, lapping up her salty-sweet juices, I slowly push the tip of my finger into her tight hole, feeling her constrict around me as I gently probe the inner edge of her ass. She screams louder, her hips bucking up, and my finger slips in a little more.

Fuck. She's so fucking tight. Gradually, she comes down from her orgasmic high, and her body settles back down on the bed. I keep my finger in her ass, softly driving it in and out a centimeter or two.

"Fiero," she pants, looking down at me through a tangle of messy hair. "Is your finger in my ass?"

"It is, my love." I push it in a little more, and she gasps. "I want to take you here."

She squirms a little, and her face scrunches up. "I don't really like anal."

"Because it hasn't been done right." I press a kiss to her quivering pussy as my cell pings again, no doubt alerting me to the visitors at my front door. Sighing, I withdraw my finger and crawl up the bed, kneeling over her. "You still trust me with your pleasure, right?"

She nods, her eyes fixated on my dick as I start stroking myself over her chest.

"Then trust me when I say you will love it, and once we go there, you'll be begging me for more."

"Arguable," she whispers before her tongue peeks out, wetting her lower lip. Her eyes are out on stalks watching me jerk off over her.

"I'll prove it," I pant, pumping myself harder in my hand. "Fuck." I throw my head back as my balls tighten and my body prepares for release. "Close your eyes, kitten." I don't want any stray cum landing in her eye and causing an irritation. "Lie still, baby." Stars burst behind my retinas as my dick strains, my balls lift, and tingles shoot up and down my spine. I spurt ropes of cum all over her tits as my cell pings with an incoming call. "Fucking hell, kitten." I collapse on the bed beside her, propping up on one elbow to admire the view. "You can open your eyes now."

She surveys the mess I made on her chest with amused curiosity before swiping a finger through the sticky semen and sucking it into her mouth.

"Fuck. Me."

"Gladly," she says, smirking. "But someone spoiled my fun."

"What happened to *no more*?"

"I had a nap. Now I'm all energized and raring to go."

"Now she tells me," I deadpan, rubbing my cum all over her chest until it's coating her breasts in a glistening layer. "Go shower, babe. The hair and makeup people are below, and I left a dress, shoes, and lingerie in the closet for you."

"Hair and makeup?"

"Up, Valentina." I climb over her and haul her to her feet. "We're already running late, and we don't want to miss the start of the show."

Chapter Twenty-Four
Valentina

Standing before the full-length mirror, I don't recognize myself. My hair and makeup are on point, the black and gold dress is to die for, and it hugs my body as if it was custom made for me. It's retro nineteen-twenties style hitting me mid-thigh. The gold diamante clips holding back the soft waves in my hair compliments the outfit perfectly. The sky-scraper heels make my legs seem longer and I won't have to stretch to look up at Fiero so much tonight.

I feel like a million dollars, and I'm as excited as a kid on Christmas morning.

"Holy fuck." Fiero's eyes are dripping with admiration as he steps into the room. "I'm not sure I can let you out looking like that." His gaze slowly trails up my legs, heating my skin all over.

"Compromise, remember?" I remind him of the conversation we had on the boat this afternoon.

"If any man dares ogle you, I can't be held responsible for my actions," he warns, reeling me into his arms.

"You promised you'd be more reasonable." I place my hands on his chest, over his dress jacket. He's wearing a black suit with a black shirt, open at the collar. The jacket has a small green border around the edges and the cuffs. "You look hot."

"You're beautiful. Most stunning woman I've ever seen."

My heart melts. "Thank you for going to all this trouble. You're spoiling me."

"You're worth it." He lifts my hand and kisses my knuckles. "Our car is waiting, but I have one thing to do first." His eyes glint mischievously. "Bend over the bed, kitten, and pull your dress up."

"Why?" My gaze narrows in suspicion as I step back from him.

"It's for your pleasure. Just trust me like a good girl and get into position."

Hoping I won't come to regret this, I do as I'm told. Cool air kisses my ass cheeks as Fiero drags my black silk panties down to my ankles.

Pushing my legs apart, he chastises me when I look back over my shoulder. "Face forward and hold still. Don't move." Butterflies swoop into my chest as adrenaline courses through my veins in anticipation.

I can't help flinching when something cold is drizzled in between my ass cheeks.

"Don't move," he repeats, parting my cheeks with one hand.

A blush steals over my face at how exposed and vulnerable I am right now, but I trust him with this. I barely resist the urge to squirm when he rubs his finger up and down my crack, smoothing the lube all over me. "Breathe deeply, baby, in and out, nice and slow, relax those muscles for me."

He breathes with me, and I concentrate on each inhalation and exhalation as he slowly inserts the tip of his pinky into my ass and warms up my hole. "That's it, kitten, just keep breathing and remain calm."

His finger slides in deeper, and I feel myself contracting and relaxing. "Slow breaths, baby, in and out, just like that." He pushes through the next ridge of muscle until his finger is fully inside. "That feel okay, honey?"

"Yes."

He moves his slick finger in and out a few times before adding another digit and then another, stretching me before he fully withdraws. "Keep breathing and stay relaxed," he adds as I feel something larger breach my hole. "This will feel more intrusive at first but relax your muscles. That's it, kitten," he says in a provocative, dark, and sultry tone while pressing the object in farther.

My heart is beating like crazy, and my pussy is clenching and unclenching as he pushes it fully into my ass.

"Good girl." He kisses my pussy lips, and I almost face-plant the bed. Then he wipes my cheeks with a tissue, pulls my silk panties back up my legs, and helps me to my feet before fixing my dress into place. "That feel okay?"

"It's a little weird. Is it a plug?"

He nods. "It's for beginners, so it should feel okay. Just give your body a little time to adjust to the sensation."

I bite on the inside of my mouth. "You want me to wear this tonight, all night? Are you going to fuck my ass later?"

"Yes, and not tonight." He kisses the end of my nose. "We're warming up to that." He brushes a quick kiss to my glossed lips. "Grab your purse. We're leaving now." He walks into the bathroom, and I hear the tap running a few seconds later.

I almost take a tumble in my heels when we step outside to discover a shiny black limousine is waiting. "I thought we were keeping a low profile?"

"It's not unusual to see limousines pulling up on Broadway,

and I'm willing to risk it because I want tonight to be special." He pulls me in close as the driver gets out to open the back door. "It's our first date. I want it to be memorable. Something amazing we can tell our kids and grandkids about."

Thank God he's holding me as he escorts me to the car because I'm sure I'd face-plant the ground for real this time.

"You want kids?" I ask when we're settled side by side in the back with the privacy screen up.

"I want them with you," he confirms, opening a bottle of Cristal champagne and pouring it into two flutes.

I'm rendered speechless as I accept a glass of bubbly.

"To us. To making memories." He clinks his glass against mine, and I take a large mouthful to avoid responding.

I'm so confused. Today, I got him to show me how to navigate the boat, and he even let me pilot it for a while. *I have a way to escape now, so why doesn't that make me happy? Why am I considering staying? Am I that easily bought?* I strongly believe that Fiero is not doing this for any reason other than to make me happy. I no longer believe there's an ulterior motive. He's a good man, but he's also quite demanding, and though it feels like I've known him forever, I haven't. I don't really know him. *What if I give him a chance and stay after he kills my husband and it doesn't work out? Will he let me go or trap me here? I might only have this one chance to escape, and how can I even be considering not taking it?*

"I'm coming on too strong," he says, lightly touching my chin. "I'm scaring you."

"A little," I admit.

He releases a frustrated sigh. "Why do I feel like I'm being tested and if I don't pass you'll disappear like mist when the sun rises?"

"It's not a test, Fiero. All this talk of forever and babies and being yours is freaking me out a little."

"I just want everything with you. Is that so bad?"

"No." I caress his smooth face. He shaved for me. "But this is all happening superfast, and you've got to give me time."

"I'll try."

I roll my eyes and take another sip of champagne.

"What? I can't help it. I've waited my entire life for you, Valentina. I don't feel like waiting any longer."

"You're very romantic for a playboy."

"Reformed playboy. I haven't been that man for years."

"You continue to surprise me," I truthfully admit, accepting a top off as we enter the outskirts of the city. "Thank you for doing all of this. It's extremely thoughtful."

"Nothing is too much trouble for my kitten." He leans in and kisses me before pulling back and staring at me strangely.

"What?"

"I don't want to ruin tonight by introducing any topics that will upset you, but I need to ask one thing."

I instantly sit up straighter, my gut informing me I won't like this. "Ask me." My tone is harsher than I intend, and I shift on the seat, feeling the plug moving inside me.

"We need to have a talk tomorrow about Dominic and things you might know."

My mouth turns dry as I nod. "Okay."

"Cesco went to a warehouse last night about twenty miles from Miami. He met with someone we couldn't identify. Do you know anything about a warehouse and who it might be?"

I shake my head. "I'm not privy to those kinds of conversations. I don't know about any warehouse," I say, forcing a smile and knocking back more champagne. I try not to fidget under his examining stare, and I will the heat creeping up my neck to fuck off.

"Okay. Have a think about anything you might know that

could help. Even the smallest detail that might seem irrelevant could help."

"I will," I promise, already searching my mind for things I can say and moving the stuff I can't say into a different mental folder. I glance out the window, biting my lip as the Cristal sloshes uncomfortably in my stomach.

"Hey." He threads his fingers through mine. "I don't want to put a dampener on our night." He slides his arm around me and kisses my temple. "Forget I said anything."

―――

"That was amazing. Wow. The acting, singing, and dancing was superb, and the staging and lighting was incredible and all the costumes." I glance down at my dress before throwing my arms around Fiero. "You chose this for tonight, didn't you?"

"I asked Rachel if she had anything that might vibe with *Moulin Rouge* and she sent me that."

It's on the tip of my tongue to say I love him because he blows me away with his thoughtfulness, and what I'm feeling right now can only be love. But I hold back, that cautionary part of myself urging me to rein it in.

"Thank you, Fiero. Thank you so much." I press kisses all over his face, uncaring I'm leaving glossy lip marks on his skin. "I have never enjoyed anything as much."

"We'll go weekly," he says, clasping my hand and leading me out of the private box. "We'll hit up every new Broadway show as it opens."

He's only giving me more reasons to stay. *How will I leave him when he's my Prince Charming come to life?* A wave of pain crashes over my chest, pricking my heart. "That would be amazing."

He looks at me a little funny.

"I need to use the bathroom before we leave."

"No problem." He holds me close as we join the crowds and make our way downstairs to the lobby. I'm conscious of the fullness in my back passage with every step. "Keep your eyes on your own date," he snaps a few beats later, and my head whips around to the couple beside us on the steps.

The man is similar in age to Fiero, I'm guessing, and the woman looks to be in her early thirties maybe. They're wearing matching wedding bands, so they're clearly married. Her mouth turns down as she quickly glances at me, pain skittering in her eyes before she trains her gaze on the carpeted floor.

"Look at my woman again, and it'll be the last thing you do," Fiero threatens in a menacing tone.

A muscle clenches in the man's jaw before the tension fades, and he makes a slow, deliberate perusal of my body.

Is he crazy or stupid?

All the fine hairs lift on the back of my neck, and bile churns in my gut. It's the very definition of undressing someone with your eyes, and it sickens me because once again some pervert is salivating over me, and I know Fiero is going to do something reckless.

He doesn't let me down.

Moving around me, he presses a gun discreetly into the man's side. "You have a death wish, asshole?" he snarls, glowering at the man who's not looking so cocky anymore. The woman still has her eyes on her feet, so she has no clue what's going on. Thankfully, there is no one behind us, the crowd in front of us instead.

"I told you not to look at her, and you have the nerve to eye fuck her in front of my face?"

A subtle click rings out, and I react on instinct, placing my hand tentatively on his back. "Don't shoot him," I quietly say. "He's not worth the trouble."

At my words, the woman's head jerks up, her eyes wide in

shock. The crowd below has moved to the next level, and we're all alone up here now. I have no idea if they have cameras.

"I'm sorry," the man splutters, looking like he might shit his pants.

"Apologize to her," Fiero snaps, jerking his head at me. "But don't look at her while you do it."

Oh my god. He's ridiculous.

"I'm sorry. It was an asshole move. Please forgive me," he says, looking at Fiero.

"Now apologize to your wife for disrespecting her."

The man frowns.

"You can look at her when you say it," Fiero adds.

"I'm sorry, Sarah." He barely looks at his wife, and it's less sincere than the apology I received. What a dick.

"Until the next time," she mutters.

"If he doesn't treat you right, you should leave him," I say, standing alongside Fiero. I don't know her circumstances. Perhaps she's trapped like me, but I feel the need to say it anyway.

"Wallet," Fiero demands, eyeballing the guy.

"What?"

"I don't need your money. I want your license."

"Why?"

"Just do it, Alistair," his wife encourages.

Reluctantly, he hands it over. On Fiero's instructions, I remove the man's license and take a pic with Fiero's cell phone. Fiero slaps the wallet back into his hand with a warning look. "Say anything about this, and I'll come for you. Next time, I won't be so charitable."

"We'll tell no one."

Fiero hands a business card to the woman. "That's my number. If you ever need help, call me." Fiero swings his gaze on the man. "That invitation isn't extended to you."

He purses his lips, glowering at Fiero, which is more than a little stupid.

"Get out of my sight, you pathetic sack of shit." Fiero uses his jacket to conceal his gun as he slips it back into the holster at his hip. "Before I change my mind and shoot you."

The man doesn't need to be told twice, taking his wife's elbow and leading her down the steps.

"Was all that really necessary?" I ask.

"Yes." Fiero takes my hand, and we descend the steps together. "No man is ever objectifying you again."

"As much as I love your determination, it's not cool to pull a gun on a man in such a public space."

Fiero pushes me up against the wall. "Aw, kitten, are you worried about me?"

I swat his chest and glare at him. "Don't patronize me! You're not above the law."

"Don't worry, baby." He ignores my attempts to wriggle away from him, tucking me firmly under his arm. "We have the police commissioner on speed dial, and half the cops in the city are on our payroll. We keep our noses clean, but on the rare occasions we run into trouble, they tidy it up."

"The guy was a dick. You'd do better just ignoring him," I say as we step into the half-empty lobby.

"Not my style, kitten," Fiero says, crowding me against the wall again. His palms rest on either side of my head while he cages me in with his body. "Kiss me," he demands the same time an unfamiliar male says, "Fiero? What are you doing here?"

Chapter Twenty-Five
Fiero

Fuck. I push off the wall and thread my fingers through Valentina's, scrambling to come up with a plausible explanation, but there's no point. Massimo will see through any lies in an instant. I didn't want him to know partly because it could jeopardize his position on The Commission, but it's too late now. He's already an accomplice even if I give him no details.

Valentina's eyes are wide, and fear is written all over her face the second she sets eyes on my best friend. Of course, she can tell who he is. Everyone within *La Cosa Nostra* knows what The Commission president looks like. Catarina is by Massimo's side, raking a politely inquisitive gaze over my date.

I squeeze my kitten's hand and pull her in flush to my side. "I could ask you the same thing," I say, smirking at my buddy. "Didn't think this was your scene either."

"I've wanted to see *Moulin Rouge* for years on Broadway," Cat replies, sending a warm, assuring smile in Valentina's direction. "I snapped up tickets the instant I heard it was returning for a limited run."

"Introduce us," Massimo says, scrutinizing my face as if a load of zits has just popped up all over my skin.

I'm tempted to use a fake name, but I won't do that to my kitten. "This is Valentina."

Massimo's pleasant façade doesn't falter for a second, but I know him inside and out, same way he knows me, and he knows the name isn't a coincidence. He knows who she is.

"These are my good friends, Massimo and his wife, Catarina."

"My friends call me Cat." Cat thrusts out her hand, shaking Valentina's. "It's lovely to meet you."

"Likewise." Valentina has composed herself, and her tone is confident, her expression cautious but friendly.

"Nice to meet you." Massimo leans in, pressing a kiss to her cheek, and a growl tumbles from my lips unbidden.

Massimo quirks a brow while Cat is full-on beaming now. I stare at my buddy for a few beats before turning to Valentina. "Go to the bathroom, kitten. I'll be right here when you come back."

"Okay." She grips the strap of her purse, moving to walk off, but I reel her back, clasping her face and kissing her deeply.

"Now you can go." I tap her ass, fighting a smirk as her eyes narrow ever so slightly at me.

We watch her walk toward the bathroom in silence, and tension is thick in the air. As soon as she's out of sight, Massimo rounds on me.

"What the hell is going on, Fiero?" He drags a hand through his hair. "Have you lost your goddamned mind?"

"It's possible."

"What don't I know?" Cat's confused gaze bounces between me and her husband.

"That's Valentina Ferraro," Massimo says. "She's married to

the Miami underboss who's up to his fucking neck in secrets and debt to the cartel."

Shock splays across her face. "She's married, Fiero? What are you thinking?"

"I love her." I just put it straight out there. I'm not going to bullshit them or insult their intelligence by using the excuse I took her to drill her for intel on her husband as it's disrespectful to all parties and Massimo will never believe it now anyway.

Massimo almost keels over in shock. "What?"

"I. Love. Her." I fold my arms over my chest and sharpen my gaze on him. "Didn't think it would ever happen for me, but she stole my heart the second I saw her."

"How long has this been going on?" my buddy asks, shoving his hands into the pockets of his dress pants.

"Not long, only a few days, and Dominic knows."

"Okay, now I'm seriously intrigued." Cat runs her hand up and down her husband's arm in a soothing gesture.

"No hitting," I preface before I give them a summary of what's gone down.

Cat punches me in the gut the second I've finished explaining. "What is wrong with you?" She looks completely horrified. "You have railroaded that poor woman! How could you do something like that?" She shakes her head, and I'm not gonna lie, but the look of disgust on her face makes me feel ashamed. "I feel like I don't know you at all, Fiero. You've always been so respectful towards women but this, this, sickens me."

"I know it was an asshole move, but that was before. It's different now, and everything that has happened between us is consensual. You do know me, Cat. You know I'd never force myself on any woman, no matter how I feel."

"What kind of husband agrees to something like this?" she snaps as Massimo pulls her into his arms, offering comfort.

"You know what kind, *mia amore*." Massimo smooths a hand

down her long, wavy dark-blonde hair. "I'm pissed too, but we know Fiero. We know he's been treating her like a queen, and there's more to it than meets the eye."

"I have and there is." I glance over at the bathroom.

"She's been in there a while. Can you check she's okay?" I ask Cat. "Talk to her a bit. And then join us for dinner so we can explain it more fully."

"We'll do that," Massimo says. "Cassio and Armis are at the house, they'll watch the younger ones."

Cat kisses Massimo, shooting me some serious stink eye before she stalks off toward the bathroom.

"I want to say I'm happy for you, but she's married, and this situation is as complicated as it gets."

"You think I don't know that? It's why I didn't want to say anything. You need to stay out of this."

"I can't now." He stands beside me. "How does this end, Ro?"

"Me and her together forever in a house full of kids."

He rocks back on his heels as his brows climb to his hairline. "I'm so completely blindsided."

"Me too. This has come out of nowhere, but it feels so fucking right." I level him with a direct look. "She's not going back to him."

"You'll start a goddamned war." His jaw pulls taut before he cleaves a heavy sigh. "Whatever you're planning, stop. We'll figure this out. Find a diplomatic way to make this work."

I bark out a bitter laugh. "Diplomacy doesn't work with that abusive asshole."

"How bad is it?"

"Not as bad as what Cat endured but bad enough, which is why I'm not putting her back on a plane."

He scrubs his hands down his face. "You sure know how to pick your moments, dude. This is the last thing I need on top of everything else right now."

I'm sensing he's not talking about business. "What's going on?"

"Something's up with Cassio, and he won't talk to me or Cat. I'm trying to play it cool, but he's openly hostile, and every time he snaps at Cat, I can't hold back. He can treat me like crap if he likes, but he's not treating his mother like that."

Before we can discuss it any further, the ladies return, and we walk toward the entrance doors together. Cat stops a couple feet away from the door to message her kids with an update while Massimo calls his driver to follow our limo to the steakhouse.

"They can't know my plans for Dominic," I whisper in Valentina's ear while we loiter in the lobby as we wait for my friends.

"I'm not stupid, Gage. I know who Massimo is, and I've heard all the stories about Catarina Greco."

"What did she ask you?" I inquire, opening my cell and retrieving the number for the restaurant.

"She just wanted to know if I was safe and being looked after and if things were consensual. I told her they were and that I don't want to return to Miami and the nightmare I was living."

I slide my arm around her shoulders. "I didn't want Massimo to know because it compromises him. The only way I can protect him now is by keeping him out of my plans even if he suspects what I'm going to do."

"Will he stop you?"

I shake my head. "He'll trust me to cover my tracks, and he'll bust my balls after the fact, but he won't tell me not to do it. Not with the things you've had to endure. If we weren't dealing with the cartel issue, he'd haul Dominic to New York and force him to file for divorce because of the things he's done and the shame he's brought to the organization."

"But we can't risk that now because we don't know what he's

planning with the cartel," Massimo says, catching the tail end of our conversation. "Unless you can shed light on anything?"

"I don't know much, but what I know, I already promised to tell Fiero tomorrow."

Massimo drills her with a look I know well, and I shove her behind me, snarling at my best friend. "Quit that shit. This is the only night I can take Valentina out, and I promised her one night where we wouldn't discuss this. I've got it handled, and you need to step away and let me deal with it."

"It's your mess. You *should* be the one to handle it." Cat pops her cell in her purse. "I mean no disrespect to you," she adds, facing Valentina.

"Let's call a spade a spade." Valentina loops her arm through mine. "It *is* a mess."

"Glad we all agree on something," Massimo says in a grumpy tone.

"Let's talk in the car. It's too open here."

When we step outside, the *soldati* working our protective details tonight fall into line around us, only pulling back when we're all securely seated in the limo. They'll shadow us to the restaurant in their vehicles.

Massimo pours champagne for the girls while I place a call to the restaurant advising them to upgrade our table to a larger one. When I end the call, he hands me a cold beer.

"I'd like to say something," Valentina says, lifting her head and staring at my friends. "And then I'd really like it if we didn't talk about my husband for the rest of the night. It'll only put me in a bad mood, and Fiero has gone to so much trouble to make this night special for me." Her smile is genuine as she turns to me and kisses me softly and sweetly. We break apart, staring at one another as our potent chemistry surrounds us in an electrifying bubble that feels safe but is only illusionary. She squeezes my hand before refocusing on my friends.

Cat is grinning, all previous ire forgotten, though I'm sure she'll have more choice words for me another time. Massimo is deep in thought, hiding his emotions behind a well-practiced mask.

"I'm not going back to Miami." Her voice projects confidently. "I left Miami with the sole purpose of never returning." She casts a quick glance at me. "I've been saving money for years and plotting escape. This was the perfect opportunity to get away from him."

"I suspected as much," I admit.

"I know you did." She turns on her side, sucking in a soft gasp as the plug moves in her ass, I'm guessing. "I, ah." She's flustered now, losing her train of thought. I circle my arms around her, anticipation building as I think of what's to come. I didn't do anything in the theater, wanting her to get used to the foreign object in her ass before I up the ante.

"Relax, kitten," I murmur before dropping a kiss to her temple.

"And now?" Massimo asks.

"Now?" She eyeballs my friend head-on. "Now I have a reason to stay right here."

"You haven't known one another long." Massimo watches her closely as he sips from his beer, effortlessly slipping from president mode into best-friend mode.

Cat whacks her husband on the arm. "If you know, you know."

"Says the woman who ran off on me for five years and then spent months resisting when we reconnected." My buddy shoots a knowing look at his wife.

"I had my reasons."

"You did, *mia regina*."

Valentina smiles. "It's been fast, but it's like we've known each other way longer, and it feels right in a way nothing has before."

I press a lingering kiss to her temple as love swirls through my veins.

"You're soulmates," Cat says.

Massimo snorts, and I glare at my buddy.

"I like that." I lean forward and kiss Cat on the cheek. "I like it a lot."

Cat speaks directly to Valentina. "You've been living a nightmare with that monster, so it's only right you now get to experience the dream with your Prince Charming."

Massimo snorts again, and his wife thumps him hard in the arm this time.

Valentina clears her throat. "I hope this isn't inappropriate, but I've seen the picture. I know what you did to your abusive first husband, and I want you to know you've always been my hero. At times when it felt like I couldn't go on, I thought about you, and what you did spurred me on. It gave me hope there was a way out. That I could free myself and put it behind me, just like you did."

Cat grasps my kitten's hands. "We're going to be the best of friends, Valentina, and if I can do anything to help, you only need to ask."

Chapter Twenty-Six
Valentina

We have only just taken our seats at the table when it happens the first time. The plug in my butt *vibrates*, and I quickly slap a hand over my mouth to trap my shocked gasp. My eyes dart to Fiero's. He's sitting beside me on one side of the large circular leather booth perched against the window, offering magnificent views of Central Park, while his friends sit across from us.

"Are you okay?" Cat asks, her brow puckering in concern.

"Fine." I wave her concern away. "I just felt a little nauseous there for a second." It's only a little white lie, but I still hate telling it.

"I felt a little ill on the plane from Miami," Fiero says, snaking his arm around the back of the booth behind me as he scoots in closer. "Hope we're not coming down with something."

Guilt slams into me, but I keep a pleasant smile plastered on my face.

Cat pours some water from the jug into a glass and hands it to me. "Our daughter Bella is sick with a terrible bug right now. I hope you haven't caught the same thing."

The plug vibrates again, and I jump in my seat, starting to sweat a little. My pussy and my ass are clenching, and lust coils low in my belly. "Me too," I say, hoping they don't hear the tiny wobble in my voice.

Fiero presses his mouth to my ear before opening his palm, showcasing the small black remote he is holding. "Relax those beautiful muscles, kitten, and sit back and enjoy."

Enjoy? While we're in public? Is he insane? "Not here," I whisper.

"I'm in control of your pleasure, remember?"

I am going to kill him. He can't do this the first time I'm meeting his friends! *How does he expect me to sit here and not squirm or moan?*

"No outward movements," he purrs in my ear, as if he just read my mind. "I know you're good at pretending, kitten, so keep that skilled mask on your face, and don't give the game away." He nips at my earlobe. "It's half the fun."

"Should we leave?" Massimo asks with a glint in his eye.

"Absolutely not." Fiero shakes his head. "We'll try to behave, but it's hard. I can't keep my hands off her."

"I know things are complex," Cat says, "but I'm sure you'll work it out. You look amazing together, and it's so good to see you this happy, Fiero. It's all I've ever wanted for you."

Fiero pins her with a dark look. "I think Cat is remembering the few times she forced me into blind dates," he says. "Every single date was an unmitigated disaster, and she finally got the message and stopped trying to play matchmaker. I know your heart was in the right place, Cat, but none of them worked because none of them were Valentina." He looks adoringly at me, and I almost melt into the leather underneath me. "I know now I was always waiting for her."

"How far the mighty have fallen," Massimo quips, waggling his brows.

"Stop it." His wife nudges him in the ribs. "That was so romantic." She looks me straight in the eye. "I always knew Fiero had this side hidden deep inside him. It just took the right woman to bring it out."

"It's not like you can throw shade, buddy," Fiero says, pressing the button.

It takes enormous effort not to flinch, move, or show anything on my face, but I work hard to conceal what's going on under the table because making a good first impression on Fiero's best friends is important to me.

The waiter arrives, and we place our food order. Meanwhile, Fiero is pressing that button like he's got trigger finger, and things are getting interesting down below.

The sommelier arrives with our wine, and we're quiet as he pours the expensive French white wine into our glasses. Apparently, he's matching wines with our food, and we'll sample a different variety with each course. It'll be a miracle if I can walk straight when we leave here. Or walk at all if Fiero keeps up these vibrations.

We're chatting casually as we drink, and I'm enjoying their company enormously even if I'm sweating under my dress and clenching my thighs together as heat builds in my panties. I gulp back a large mouthful of wine when Fiero's hand lands on the inside of one knee and begins inching up under my dress. He's talking business with Massimo, looking cool as a cucumber, while I'm trying hard to concentrate as Catarina tells me all about her four kids. "I'd love to see some pictures," I say, squeezing my thighs together and trapping Fiero's hand when he reaches the apex of my legs.

"I've got tons on my phone," she says, rummaging in her purse while Fiero easily forces my thighs apart, and his fingers find their way to my panties.

I knock back more wine as he rubs me over the silk while

stimulating the plug in my ass, and I'm starting to panic I'll come and make a scene. "Relax," he whispers while kissing my temple. "Stop fighting and trust me."

Letting my legs loosen, I discreetly widen my thighs, and he immediately takes advantage, slipping two fingers under the silk and pushing them inside me. I take another large mouthful of wine, and it's taking enormous self-control not to react to the things he's doing to my body.

"Take it easy," he says. "Drink more water."

If he wasn't fingering me under the table, I'd tell him to take a hike, but I don't think I can speak in an even tone, so I just agree.

Cat leans across the table to show me her phone, and I sit forward, admiring her kids with smiles and nods as she flits through pictures with a swipe of her finger. Meanwhile, Fiero is casually chatting with his friend as if he doesn't have his fingers inside me and he isn't pressing the plug remote every few seconds.

My composure is slipping, and it's showing.

"Are you sure you're feeling okay?" she asks. "You're sweating."

I take the escape. "I do feel a little hot. I'll just go splash some water on my face."

Fiero is forced to drop his hand and let me out of the booth. I feel his eyes glued to my hastily retreating form as I make my way across the large, busy restaurant toward the corridor that leads to the bathrooms.

I'm breathing heavily, my pussy and ass squeezing and contracting because the remote control is still working even with distance between us. There is no bathroom, per se, just a row of single-occupancy gender-neutral toilets with their own doors. Finding an unoccupied one, I throw myself inside, but before I can shut the door, I'm being pushed back inside by a six-foot-four caveman. Fiero's nostrils are flaring, his pupils dilated, and the bulge in his pants is growing in front of my eyes.

"Naughty kitty," he says, locking the door behind him and gripping my hips. "Did I say you could leave?"

"You can't be serious! I was close to coming!"

"I should make you wait until we get home," he says, tearing my panties down my legs and over my shoes. "But I'm too fucking horny." He sniffs my panties before shoving them in his pocket.

My jaw slackens. "What are you doing?"

He smirks. "Smelling what's mine." He hoists my dress up to my waist. "Fucking what's mine." His hand lands hard on my butt, and I shiver all over as the movement of the plug sends tremors of desire ricocheting everywhere. "This will be hard and fast, baby. Bend over and stick your ass in the air." He presses the remote, and the vibrations penetrate deep.

Fucking hell. I'm panting and sweating and so aroused it feels like I'll come without touch. I should not agree. This is a Michelin-starred restaurant, not to mention we've just abandoned his friends at the table. But I'm too worked up, and I *need* to come.

"Now, kitten." He slaps me again, and I cry out, my legs turning to jelly with the intensity rocking through my core.

I bend over and hike my ass up, spreading my legs and gripping the counter. His hand wraps around my mouth the same time he slams into me without warning. "Breathe through your nose for me, baby." My scream is muffled against his palm, and all I can do is hold on for dear life as he fucks me roughly from behind.

I'm already saturated, and every nerve ending is on fire, so when he twists the plug in my ass, I shatter immediately into a thousand sparks as the singular most intense climax of my life powers through me. His free arm slides around my waist, and he's the only reason I'm still standing. I can't feel my legs, and I'm exhausted, as if I just ran a marathon.

"Fuck, kitten, I can feel the aftershocks. Keep squeezing me. That's it," he rasps, pounding into me harder and faster. "Hug my dick, baby. Strangle my cock." His hands land on my hips, and I'm seeing stars as he rams into me like a crazy man. He throws his head back and clamps his lips shut as he falls over the ledge, filling me full of his cum in the bathroom of one of the most salubrious restaurants in The Big Apple.

He cleans me up using tissues and helps me back into my panties while I wash my hands and try to fix my makeup and tame my hair. Standing behind me, he cups my boobs through my dress. "You look gorgeous, but there's nothing you can do to wipe that freshly fucked look off your face."

I turn around and punch him. "You're evil."

Laugher rumbles from his chest. "There are plenty of reasons to reach that assertion, but that right there is not one of them, baby."

"I don't know what I'm going to do with you," I say as he washes and dries his hands.

"I can think of plenty of things," he says, flipping the lock and taking my hand as we exit the room.

To my utter humiliation, there is now a line for the bathrooms and I'm sure my blush is noticeably evident even through my makeup.

"I'm going to kill you," I hiss as we walk past several curious faces. I pick up a few amused smirks from the men and envious glares from the women. I'm close to snarling at an older woman who is blatantly eye fucking Fiero even though he's holding hands with me.

"Are your claws going to come out, kitty cat?" he whispers in my ear.

"Unlike some people," I say, giving him the evil eye as we head back out into the restaurant, "I know how to restrain myself." I lower my voice as we walk toward our table. "But under different circumstances, in a different place, I'd have knocked her the fuck out for daring to stare at you like that."

"For God's sake, Valentina. Watch your mouth!"

"I'll make you a deal," I say, slowing down before we get back to our table. "I'll watch my language if you agree to give me that remote."

"You strike a hard bargain, but deal." He slips the remote into my purse. "I want that back when we get home," he adds, snatching a quick feel of my ass.

Our appetizers are on the table when we reclaim our seats, and I'm grateful I ordered a salad because Fiero's crab cakes look cold. Massimo and Cat are already finished with theirs, and they're looking expectantly at us.

"Sorry about that," I say, sure my cheeks are flaming.

Fiero chuckles and I glare at him. *And you know what?* His friends need to know he's the rude one, not me. I'm going to own this because I've done nothing wrong. The heat on my face subsides as I lift my chin and let my gaze dance between husband and wife. "You can blame Fiero. He's been playing with me under the table the entire time, and he followed me to the bathroom to fuck me."

"Language, kitten." Fiero tugs on a piece of my hair. Pride mixes with amusement on his face, and he doesn't give a shit I just divulged that to his friends.

"I was wondering if that's what was going on," Cat says.

"It's really rude and not the impression I wanted to make."

"There's no judgment here," Cat quickly asserts.

Fiero snorts out a laugh. "It'd be quite hypocritical if there was."

I have no clue what they are referencing.

"Did you ever hear the story of how we met?" Massimo asks.

I shake my head as I tuck into my salad. Although we had a large lunch on the boat, it was hours ago, and I'm ravenous now.

"Massi loves an opportunity to tell this story." Cat grabs her wineglass, fighting a smile.

"Cat propositioned me in an airport lounge, and we fucked in the disabled bathroom while the man she told me was her husband kept guard outside."

"Get out!" My admiration for Cat has only gone up.

Fiero is wolfing down his crab cakes like he's competing for the *Guinness Book of World Records*, listening avidly.

"You propositioned *me!*" Her tone is laced with indignation.

Massimo boops her on the nose. "I think your memory is a little rusty."

"You're insane. You spent an hour eating me with your eyes, and I might have moved things along but only because my flight had just been called."

"Tomayto, tomahto." Massimo shrugs, grinning at his wife.

Cat rolls her eyes before a calculating, mischievous look washes over her face. She leans toward Fiero. "Did Massi ever tell you about the dream I had about Vikings?"

"Shut your mouth, woman." Massimo's hand slides instantly across his wife's mouth.

"You been keeping secrets from me, brother?" Fiero asks, finishing his appetizer and dabbing the corner of his mouth with a napkin.

"You really want to go there?"

Fiero pulls me in close to his side, wrapping his strong arms around me. "Nah, we're good."

"Thought as much."

The rest of dinner passes uneventfully, and all too soon it's time to leave. I've really enjoyed tonight, and I really like Fiero's best friends.

Cat envelops me in a warm hug as we stand on the curb by our cars. "Let's do lunch when everything settles down. In the meantime, call me anytime if you need anything."

"I'd like that, and I will."

We switch phones and add our numbers.

"If you're bored this week at the house, watch *The Last Kingdom*." A dreamy expression materializes on her face. "You can thank me later."

Chapter Twenty-Seven
Fiero

I'm late waking the next morning, which is unusual because I'm an early riser. The bed is cold beside me, and when I emerge in the kitchen a few minutes later, I find out why. "What's all this?" I gesture toward the multitude of baked goods resting on plates, mesh trays, and cake stands along my counter.

"I wanted to thank you for all you've done for me, so I've made you breakfast and baked a bunch of stuff. Hope you have a sweet tooth."

"I do." I wrap my arms around her, dipping down to lick a blob of white icing off her cheek. "You didn't need to do this, but thanks."

"Go sit and I'll bring it out."

I hug her closer. "I didn't like waking up without you by my side, but seeing you wearing my shirt at my stove, making use of my kitchen, makes me happier than you know."

"I don't want to step on Ana's toes, but I'd really like to cook dinner for us at night. I've got nothing else to do while you're working and busy with the other stuff."

"I'll talk to Ana. She'll be fine. I'm sure she'd enjoy the extra time to relax." I kiss her lips. "I've got a few things to do after breakfast, but we're going out this afternoon."

"We are?" Her face glows, and I'm addicted to how she looks right now. Her hair in a messy bun on top of her head. Streaks of flour smeared across her brow and more icing sprinkles dotted around her face. My black shirt swamps her, but she looks ridiculously sexy. She has tons of clothes now, but she chose to wear my shirt from last night, and it does funny things to my insides. The apron tied to her front is spattered with the remnants of all the things she was baking. Her long legs are bare, encased in a pair of simple white flip-flops, and I just want to eat her all up.

She's delicious. Precious. *Mine.*

"I love you." It comes so naturally to say it.

Her features soften. "I know you do." She cups my face. "You're so hot and sexy. I could stare at your handsome face all day long."

"You do wonders for my ego, kitten."

"Bullshit." She wriggles out of my embrace. "Your ego is more than healthy. You don't need me showering you with compliments."

I laugh, feeling lighter than I have in ages. "True, but I like hearing them from you."

"Where are we going this afternoon?"

"Out on my bike to the city. I'm going to show you some of the sights." Massimo knows, and while he won't tell anyone, he was the main person I was terrified to bump into it. Now it's happened, I figure we can risk another day in the city. I want to show Valentina around, and it has to be today because I'll be tied up the rest of the week.

After a yummy breakfast of chocolate chip pancakes with strawberries and the most delicious lemon vanilla muffins, we have a quick fuck in the shower and get dressed before parting for a few hours.

Taking What's Mine

I set my plan in motion, placing a call to Dominic Ferraro to tell him I'm not giving his wife back and he can sing for the rest of the money. I tell him to expect to be served divorce papers in due course. My men in Miami are aware to shadow his every movement and report to me. I'm relying on his hotheadedness to take the bait and come to me. I make a few other calls and attend to some urgent things before rejoining Valentina downstairs.

The kitchen and outdoors area are clean and empty, with no sight of my kitten. I go searching, eventually finding her in the cinema room. Her attention is riveted to some Viking show on the big screen, and she barely acknowledges my arrival.

"I'd like to have that talk before we leave," I say, pausing the show and claiming the seat beside her.

"Okay." She pulls her knees to her chest, her bare feet resting on the large leather seat highlighting her pretty pink toenails. "But I don't really have much to say."

"Anything could help."

"You asked me before where Dom's money went, and I told you he spent it on parties and hookers, etcetera, but he also pays the *soldati* under the table."

"What do you mean?"

"He gives them a second wage that he pays from his own share of the profits. He's been doing it for the past couple years."

"Why?" I have my theories, but I'd like to hear what she has to say.

"My guess is he's buying their loyalty because he plans to take Vitto's place one day."

"He's a fool if he believes that'll work. That's not how we operate anymore."

"Dom is old school, and he's not always smart. He has it in him to be calculating, but like I said, he lets his emotions rule him too often."

"Anything else?"

"Not that I can think of," she says, her gaze unflinching.

"What about the warehouse?" I'm hoping she knows something other than what I've found out so far. The warehouse is owned by a Spanish company I suspect is a front. It'll take time to trace the real owner, but I am all over it. We sent a drone in, but the windows are fully blacked out, and we couldn't see inside. All entry points are padlocked, and there's a full security system with keypads on each door. We could break in, but then they'll know we're onto them. It's better to sit and watch in the hopes of catching them in the act.

My online search showed the car cropping up in a few places before it disappeared without a trace. I'm guessing they're switching out fake plates on a regular basis, and as it's a popular SUV and there are no distinguishing stickers or identifiers on the vehicle, there is no chance of finding it again unless it reappears at the warehouse.

"I told you I don't know of any warehouse."

She's putting up a good front, but her little eye twitch gives her away. She knows something and she won't tell me. *Why? Is she still planning to leave? Is Dom threatening her to force her silence? I know she wants him dead so why isn't she fully cooperating? What is holding her back?*

I was hoping to have something concrete to come at Dominic with. It'll be easier to crack him if he knows I already know what he's been up to. But it's looking like we're going to have to go at him empty-handed and hope our interrogation and torture techniques do the job.

I haul her into my lap. "You can tell me anything, kitten. You don't have to be afraid. Nobody is hurting you or your family."

She frowns. "My family? What about them?"

"Don't get mad, but I spoke with your father earlier."

She stiffens in my arms and attempts to pull free, but I clamp my arms around her, keeping her where she is.

"I didn't give him anything. I told him I would explain it when I could, but you were under my protection and by extension his family was too. He accepted it at face value, and he's agreed to keep this confidential. A team of twenty men should be landing in Detroit shortly. They will keep your family safe. Nina too, I promise."

"Why? I don't understand."

"You're precious to me, and I know how much you care about your siblings and your cousin. I wanted to give you peace of mind in case Dominic is using them to threaten you. Is he?"

She shakes her head, and I know it's a lie. I work hard to temper my frustration. "You don't have to be scared, Valentina." I caress her face. "Whatever it is, I can protect you. Dominic doesn't have half the resources or the smarts I have. I can easily outwit him, but I can't do it blind."

"There isn't anything else to tell. But thank you for taking care of my family. It definitely gives me peace of mind."

She's not going to give in now, so I drop it for the moment. Let her think it through and hopefully whatever she is hiding she'll feel comfortable telling me soon.

"I know your relationship is fractured with your parents, but your dad was really upset and worried about you. I didn't give him details, only to say your marriage wasn't a good one and I'd removed you from a bad situation. I warned him not to call Dominic. I told him we were handling it and it needed to be kept on the down-low."

"He was only saying that because it was you. My dad hero-worships those in leadership. He's probably building a shrine to you as we speak."

Her words are tinged with bitterness, but there's a lot of pain too. I won't ever push her to reconcile if she doesn't want to, but her father was genuinely upset, and he didn't come across as an uncaring man. If he was a prick like mine, I'd understand it, but I think he thought he was doing right by his eldest daughter, that she had the prospect of a better life with a wealthy underboss than marrying a *soldato* and leading a simpler life. I suspect Dom has been keeping her from her parents on purpose, but I could be wrong.

"He cried on the phone, honey." I brush hair out of her eyes. "It didn't appear to be an act."

She worries her lip between her teeth as her face contorts painfully before smoothing out. "I really don't want to talk about him, Fiero. It hurts me too much, and what's done is done and can't be unchanged."

"I didn't bring it up to upset you."

"I know you didn't." She turns into me, resting her head on my shoulder. "Can we go now? I want to climb to the top of the Statue of Liberty."

"There are one hundred sixty-two stairs to get to the top. Sure you're up for it?" I joke, wanting to defuse the tense situation.

"I'm more than up to the challenge. It's why I'm wearing sneakers," she says pointing to the new pink sneakers resting on the floor at her feet.

"Okay." I stand with her in my arms, carefully setting her down. "I just want to ask one final thing and no more talk of the fat fuck for the rest of the day. How many men will he take with him for protection?"

"You mean coming here?"

I nod as I place her in the seat and crouch in front of her to put her sneakers on.

Her brow furrows as she thinks about it. "He has little regard for the *soldati* despite how he acts with them. He won't lose any sleep over his men, so I guess he'll bring at least eight, maybe ten."

I had a similar figure in my head. "We'll be prepared." I hold out my hand. "Come on, we've got a busy day ahead of us."

Chapter Twenty-Eight
Fiero

I 'm lost in thought as I check my weapons in my office while waiting for Zumo and Caleb to arrive. Dominic's plane is due to land at La Guardia shortly, and he'll be here within a couple of hours.

Yesterday was one of the best days of my life. Valentina loved my Harley, and I'm picturing regular bike rides, hikes, and picnics in our future. I'll probably invest in another motorcycle. One that caters specifically for passengers because most of the bikes in my garage were chosen for speed, not comfort for passengers. Apart from my sisters, I've never taken any woman out on one of my bikes. Feeling Valentina pressed all up against me from behind, her slim arms locked around my waist, and hearing her whoops and hollers had blissful contentment seeping bone-deep.

Seeing the awe in her eyes on Staten Island and the childlike exuberance on her face as we stood at the top of Lady Liberty and admired the spectacular view is something I'll never forget. I took her to the Top of the Rock too, and we looked down on Central Park from up high. A quick trip to St. Patrick's Cathedral rounded off our sightseeing, but there is still so much to show her.

When everything has settled down, I'm vowing to take her everywhere. I loved introducing her to The Big Apple, and I can't wait to show her all the other magical sights of my city. We stopped at a local Italian restaurant on our way back to Long Island, sharing antipasto and the most delicious meat cannoli, before heading home where I spent the rest of the night buried deep inside the woman I love.

It's easy to get jaded with this life. To forget the simple pleasures. Having Valentina in my life reminds me to appreciate and enjoy the minor things I tend to take for granted.

"Any news?" Valentina asks, materializing in the door of my office. Her eyes skim over the rifles, equipment, and boxes of bullets strewn across the table.

"He'll be landing shortly," I say, glancing briefly at my Rolex.

She nibbles on her lips and wrings her hands together.

"Come here." I open my arms, and she runs across the room in her bare feet, flinging herself into my arms. "It's okay, honey." I hold her close, running my hands up and down her back while dusting kisses into her hair.

"I'm scared. What if something goes wrong?"

She looks up at me with big doe eyes, and I just want to wrap her in cotton wool and keep her away from a world that's only ever hurt her. A streak of flour crosses one cheek, and I love how comfortable she's getting in my home. *Our* home. She's been baking all morning while I was busy working.

"It won't, but if it does, we'll regroup and figure a new way out."

She bites on the corner of her mouth.

"Your family is safe," I reassure her. "They're all at your parents' house under armed guard, and that's how it'll remain until any and all threats are dealt with."

"It's not them I'm worried about."

236

"Who else?" I tip her chin up, watching a war rage behind her eyes.

"Dom's *soldati*. They are innocent, and the thought of them dying so I can be free doesn't sit right with me. Many of them have young families."

I smile at her. "We're not going to harm his *soldati*. Contrary to what you might believe, I don't like shooting innocent men either." It's debatable how innocent they are. At least some of them must know something about the cartel or the warehouse, so keeping them alive is more advantageous than killing them anyway. "Caleb and I are trained snipers. They won't be killed or even harmed. I promise."

She frowns, opening her mouth to ask for more details, but I shake my head. "It's better you don't know."

She rubs at her chest, and I lean down and kiss her, taking my time leisurely brushing my lips against hers until I feel her relaxing.

"Is this a bad time?" Accardi says, and I hear the amusement in Caleb's tone before I see it on his face when I break our lip-lock and look up. He's leaning against the doorjamb, my brother just behind him.

"The plane landed early," Zumo says as both men enter the room. "We need to get into position now. They'll be here in an hour."

Valentina stiffens against me, and I massage the knots in her shoulders.

"Hey, kitten." Caleb ambles toward Valentina. "You look super cute today."

She does. She's only wearing yoga pants and a slouchy off-the-shoulder tee with her hair up in a messy bun and no makeup, but she's adorable.

And *mine*.

"Fuck off, Accardi," I snap. "Don't think I won't shoot you. I can take those motherfuckers down myself if I have to."

"Don't wind him up today." Zumo whacks Caleb on the arm before snatching my love out of my arms and hugging her.

"That goes for you too!" I bark at my brother.

"Jesus, Ro. Take a goddamned chill pill. I'm only giving the girl a hug." He releases her immediately upon spotting the aggression on my face.

"You've got it bad, man." Caleb chuckles.

"So, quit riling me up, and keep your fucking hands off her," I say through gritted teeth.

"You still holding on to your sanity living here?" Caleb asks Valentina, smirking.

"Just about," she jokes, leaning back to touch my face. "I'm still training him, but I quite like his possessiveness."

Zumo groans. "Don't feed the beast."

"Too late for that." I flash him a smug grin while wrapping my arms around my kitten and hugging her tight.

"Is that flour on your face, kitten?" Caleb asks, and a snarl rips from my chest.

"Call her that, again. I dare you." I drill him with a pointed look.

"Caleb." Zumo warns his friend and Caleb holds up his hands in surrender.

"I'll stop. I like my head attached to my body. You're just too easy to fuck with these days and I have to get my kicks someplace."

I shove my middle finger up at him.

"Don't leave without finding me," Valentina says, her gaze flipping between Caleb and Zumo. "I've been stress-baking all morning, and I have a box of cupcakes and other stuff for both of you. My way of saying thanks for helping Fiero with this."

I've never seen grown men turn into puppy dogs so fast. They're only short of drooling and whimpering at her feet.

"Elisa will love you forever," Caleb says. "She's been craving sweet things all during her pregnancy. I'll love you forever too 'cause she's gonna be all over me like a rash when I show up with home-baked goods."

"Jesus Christ." Letting Valentina go, I scrub my hands down my face. "Go set up before I shoot you to shut you up. I'll escort Valentina to the panic room and follow you up to the roof."

"See you later, cutie pie." It's an improvement on kitten, but only just. Caleb waggles his brows and exits the room, grabbing his bag from the hallway before disappearing.

"Don't worry about Fiero." Zumo squeezes her shoulder because he's seriously got a death wish. "Nothing will happen to him or us. Our plan is solid."

"Be safe," she tells him before he leaves to convene with my *soldati* in front of the house to give them their orders.

I hold Valentina's hand as we make our way to the basement where I had a specialized panic room built years ago. Tension bleeds into the air as I unlock it and let her inside. Ana restocked the cabinets and refrigerator in the small kitchenette, and there's a ton of food, snacks, and drinks.

"This is fully bulletproof, fireproof, and soundproof. The walls are built around reinforced steel," I explain as I pull her into the homey space. "This is the main living space." I gesture around the carpeted room with an L-shaped velvet sectional, large wall-mounted TV, and a few end tables with lamps. A bunch of fresh flowers sits on top of the display unit against one wall. "You have access to the same streaming options as upstairs, so you can continue watching that Viking show." I'll need to have words with Catarina because my kitten is quickly becoming as obsessed as Massimo's wife. At least, it might help to distract her today.

"There's a small kitchen and eating area through there." I point to my left. "A bedroom and bathroom in there." I point to the right. "And that door at the back of the living room leads to the tech center."

"Tech center?"

"You can access the cameras all over my property from that room. There's also a phone and laptop in case you need access, and the panic button on the wall links directly to the local cop station. The code to open the door is on the wall." I pull her into my arms. "I don't advise you to go in there. Don't look. Stay here and fantasize about the hot Viking, but you better be imagining him as me."

A giggle meanders through the air. "Always, babe."

My heart melts at the endearment. "I've got to go, kitten." I claim her lips in a hard kiss. "Try not to worry. I promise I'll be fine, and if anything goes wrong, no one will get to you in here. We should have Dominic and his men under our control in minutes. When the first phase is done, I'll send Zumo to apprise you, but don't leave here until I come and get you. The people I trust know the code to the door. If someone is asking you to open up, they're not to be trusted."

"Okay. Please be careful." She winds her arms around me, pressing her face to my chest and hugging me tight. "I feel sick imagining something happening to you."

"I can relate." I hug her tight before releasing her. "I'll see you soon, my love. Relax and take it easy." It pains me to leave her, but getting distracted worrying about her isn't smart because that's how mistakes are made. She's safe here, and I can concentrate on ending the prick who has made her life a living hell.

"You have some nerve showing up at my place, Dominic," I say into the phone, sticking to the script. So far, it's playing out how we want. Dominic is at the front gate in a black van with an unknown number of men. My *soldati* knew to call me when he arrived. "How'd you even find it?" The answer is obvious, but I let him believe he's the big man. I want him to think he's caught me unaware so it'll be too late when he realizes he's walked into a trap.

"My wife has a tracker."

"She told me she didn't have one," I lie.

"You're the fool who believed her." His smarmy tone rubs me the wrong way, but he won't be the one laughing soon.

"I'm not giving her back."

"We had a deal, and this wasn't part of it. You can't just take my wife. At least not without negotiating a fee."

I fucking knew it. Caleb's eyes flare darkly from his position beside me on the roof. He's been listening to everything. "You have some nerve, Ferraro. I should tell my men to shoot you."

"You can try, but I didn't come alone, and I doubt you'd appreciate a shootout in front of the neighbors and the street cams."

"Fine." I heave out an annoyed sigh on purpose. "Put me back onto Daniel."

"Let them through," I tell my *soldato* and hang up.

"He's a fucking prick. You sure we can't riddle him with bullets right now?" Caleb seethes.

"Trust me," I say, getting into position behind my mounted rifle. "I'd love nothing more, but we need him alive to get the answers we need. We'll get creative torturing him. Make him suffer before he dies a slow and painful death. That fat fuck doesn't deserve a quick death."

Caleb moves into position a few feet away from me, lining his eye up to the scope the same time I do. Zumo and the bulk of my men are hiding in the trees near the front door of my house while the rest of my *soldati* guard the gate and the perimeter in case Dominic has grown a strategic brain overnight and has covered all bases. I doubt it, but it pays to be on the safe side. It's why I called in extra reinforcements this morning. Men I can trust to keep this confidential until I'm ready to approach the board.

I train my gun on the van as it rounds the bend in my driveway, knowing Caleb is doing the same. The vehicle rolls slowly up to my house before stopping a few feet from the front door. Dominic and his men are cautious as they climb out on both sides of the van, and we don't waste a moment. Zumo and Dino shoot out the tires on the van the same moment I take aim at Valentina's prick of a husband.

Dominic goes down screaming the instant I shoot his kneecaps out. His men look all around, unsure where the bullets originated from, shooting haphazardly in all directions. Dominic is roaring at them in between screams of pain. The instant a gun appears in his hand, I shoot it from him, taking half of one hand with it.

Oops. My bad.

He's howling now and clutching the bloody stump to his chest. If my guess is correct, Valentina is watching this on the screen in the panic room, and I hope she's enjoying the show. Dominic should be ashamed to call himself a made man. He's a pathetic piece of shit who deserves everything coming to him.

"Now," I tell Caleb, and we open fire. He aims left of the van while I aim right. It's ridiculous how quickly we shoot the weapons from their hands. A few of Dominic's men produce backups, but we shoot them from their fingers before they can use them to target my crew. Zumo and his team swoop in, surrounding and outnumbering the ten men as they tackle them to the ground, inject them with the sleeping aid, and cuff them.

Zumo's team carries them to the van while two of my men

search Dominic for other weapons before hovering over him with their guns pointed at his head.

A low buzzing sound pricks my ears, and my head tips back as I look up. Caleb spots the drone the same time I do, instantly shooting it out of the sky. We watch as it hits the ground and auto-detonates. We peer over the ledge of the roof, watching as any and all evidence goes up in flames. "Fuck." Accardi drags a hand through his hair. "Will you be able to get any intel from it?"

"Can't do anything with charred remains."

"He must have brought it with him," Caleb surmises.

"I don't think it's his style. Dominic is old school, but we'll ask him."

"If he's important to the cartel, it could be theirs?"

"It's possible," I agree, packing up my stuff. "Let's worry about it later. We have more pressing concerns right now."

By the time we make it downstairs and outside, the van has left to take the unconscious men to the safe house, the drone remnants have been boxed up and stored in the shed for me to examine later, and Dominic is waiting in the underground dungeon built under my guesthouse.

"That went smoothly," Zumo says when we reach him.

"Except for the drone," Caleb says.

"It's a complication, but we didn't kill anyone. I'm not overly worried. How's our guest?"

"Furious and bleeding from his wounds. We stripped him and tied him to the chair. He's already pissed himself."

"Good. Check on Valentina. Let her know it went well and we're interrogating Dominic. Tell her it could take a while, but I'll come to her as soon as I can. I want her to stay there until Dominic has been fully dealt with. We'll keep the extra men here for a couple days. I want eyes and ears on every part of my property in case he had contingencies."

"You got it, boss."

"Call Ziti in Miami," I add. "See if he's got eyes on Cesco. I'm wondering if he's behind the drone."

"I'm on it," Zumo says before taking off.

"He's a natural underboss." Caleb smiles proudly at his friend.

"He's taken to it like a duck to water," I agree as we make our way toward the guesthouse. "He'll make a good successor when my time comes to retire."

"Look at you, old man. Talking retirement now."

I flat-out punch him in the face. "Less of the old man."

He chuckles, dabbing at the blood trickling from his nose. "I forgot you're only as old as the woman you're feeling."

"I can still shoot you," I growl.

"Is that any way to repay me for going out on a limb for you?"

We walk down the steps. "You know I'm grateful, and I owe you, but that doesn't give you a free pass to flirt with what's mine."

"It's all good fun, dude." He wraps his arm around my neck. "Lighten up. There's no need to be so serious. You know I'm only messing."

"I can't help it where my kitten is concerned," I admit as we enter the guesthouse and head toward the door leading to the basement. It's usually padlocked and secured to keep it away from prying eyes. "I'm aware I'm irrationally obsessive, but I'm not apologizing. She's mine, and everyone needs to know it. I see red when any man even enters her airspace." I yank the door open.

"You're so fucked, man." Caleb laughs as we walk down the stairs.

"Tell me something I don't know."

I shake hands with the three *soldati* waiting downstairs outside the solid steel door that leads to my dungeon and torture chamber. "Any trouble?" I ask.

"No, boss. We're watching the camera, and he was shouting and roaring expletives at first. Then he started crying." Disgust laces through his tone, and I get it. Dominic is a disgrace. An abomination. I really don't see how The Commission could be too upset with Caleb and me once we tell them.

"He brings shame to *La Cosa Nostra*, which is why he's being dealt with," I say. My men aren't privy to many of the facts, but when the truth comes out about Dominic Ferraro, they'll be glad they were involved today.

Caleb and I enter the room together, sealing the door behind us.

"You won't get away with this," Dominic hisses, glaring at me. Blood drips from the stump where his right hand should be and trickles from the bullet holes in his knees.

"You forget who you're speaking to," Caleb replies, pulling two chairs over in front of the naked, bleeding man.

His flaccid little dick flops between fleshy thighs, almost concealed by the overhang of his sizeable belly. He's disgusting, and the thought of him going anywhere near Valentina makes my blood boil. I consciously force those thoughts from my mind before I kill him with my bare hands.

"Did you really think I wouldn't tell The Commission about your involvement with the cartel and the abuse you've subjected your young wife to?"

"We had a deal," he huffs out, coughing and gasping for air.

"I don't make deals with traitors." My assessing gaze rakes over him, noting the blue tinge to his lips and his sweaty skin. "But you're alive because we don't kill men without a trial," I lie. "Fess up and The Commission will hand down a lighter sentence." Another lie. This prick isn't leaving here alive today.

"I already told you," he splutters. "It's why I need the money to pay the cartel and get them off my back."

"What's in the warehouse in Miramar?" I push, growing

alarmed as his chest heaves up and down and he appears to be struggling to breathe.

"What?" Panic glides across his face, and strangled sounds emerge from his mouth as sweat rolls down his nose and his limbs appear to tighten. His wide eyes latch on to mine, and more gargled sounds leak through his lips before he projectile vomits all over the ground.

"What the fuck is happening?" Caleb hops up and jumps back the same time I do.

"I don't fucking know."

We can't do anything but watch as Dominic's breathing gets shallower and shallower and his skin turns a darker shade of blue. Fuck. This isn't looking good. "Should we intervene?" I ponder out loud. "We need answers."

"If you're volunteering to do mouth-to-mouth, go for it, but I'm out." Caleb crosses his arms over his chest.

Dominic's body is jerking and stiffening, and his strangled breaths are fading.

Yeah, my mouth isn't going anywhere near that fat fuck. "Screw it. He can die. We'll find our answers another way."

"This is very inconvenient, Ferraro." Caleb leans over Dominic as he continues struggling for air. "You just had to be difficult, didn't you, asshole?" He kicks him between the legs. "If you're going to die, just do it."

In that moment, Dominic Ferraro draws his last breath. His wide bloodshot eyes are frozen in place. His limbs are stationary. His heart no longer beats.

"Well, that was anticlimactic," Caleb drawls, pressing his fingers to Dominic's neck. "No pulse."

"It's obvious he's dead, Accardi." I grab fistfuls of my hair as I kick Ferraro in the stomach, and the chair falls backward, landing with a thwack on the hard concrete floor. "Fuck."

"What the hell just happened?" Caleb frowns as he stares

down at the dead man. "Those injuries should not have killed him."

"Heart attack if I had to guess." He didn't lead a healthy lifestyle, and it's not completely unusual for a man in his fifties to die from a coronary.

"What now?" Caleb purses his lips.

"We can't go to the board when we've got jack shit, but we can't leave the fat fuck here either. His son will get suspicious if he doesn't return home, and I don't want Vitto asking questions either." My brain churns as I try to spin this in a way that'll buy me time to get the evidence I need to go to Massimo.

"Why not dump him back on his doorstep with no explanation. Let everyone draw their own conclusions?"

"They'll think it was the cartel."

"Exactly."

"We don't need a war with the cartel in Florida, Caleb. That's the last thing we want to set in motion."

Caleb shrugs. He's always so bloodthirsty. I thought it might have changed now he's a family man, but it appears not.

I sit back down and think. Caleb watches me without interrupting, typing messages on his phone while he waits for me to figure a way out of this mess.

I tap out a message to Zumo, asking if he's still around to come meet us.

He shows up ten minutes later, his eyes almost bugging out of his head when he sees Ferraro.

"What the fuck happened?"

"We didn't even get to interrogate him before he had a fucking coronary and died," Caleb says, kicking Dominic's stiff body.

"Well shit."

"Yeah." I stand. "I think I have a plan that might work."

"We're listening," my brother says.

"We do what Caleb suggested. Dump his body on his front door and let everyone conclude it was the cartel. When the board calls a meeting, I'll lay out a plan for neutralizing the situation. I'll warn Vitto not to retaliate until we've gleaned evidence. I'll tell him about Ferraro's involvement with the cartel and how he was buying his men's loyalty. It'll force him to keep the *soldati* and Cesco in line. He'll obey because he knows how bad this looks for him.

"We'll send more men to join our crew on the ground in Miami to keep watch over everything until I return. I'll set up a meeting with the cartel, pay them what they're owed plus interest, and smooth things over while feeling them out. I'll say we don't want a war and find out if they're agreeable to a deal that would suit both parties. In the meantime, I'll work to dig up all the dirt there is to be found on Dominic, and when everything is settled, I'll tell the board the full truth."

Both men have been listening carefully. "It's not a bad plan," Caleb says. "The board won't take any permanent sanctions against us, but this will damage your reputation with the others, Fiero."

"It'll damage yours too," Zumo says.

"I don't give a fuck." Caleb thrusts his hands into his pockets. "I have zero desire to be the future president. I'll leave that to my twin, but you do." He jabs his finger in my direction. "This will harm your chances. Massimo's term ends in four years, and I know the plan is for you to take over."

"How'd you know that?" Massimo and I have never disclosed the plans we made in our twenties to anyone except Catarina.

"It's the obvious next move," Caleb says proving he's more than just a pretty face. "The only dons capable of stepping up at the next election are you and Agessi. Maybe Mantegna. Volpe is too old. Pagano has medical issues. Ben's already been there, and the rest of us are still too young. If we do this, I don't see how it won't impact the vote. This will discredit you in some of their eyes."

"As it should," I truthfully admit. "I'm aware what this means, and honestly, being president is bottom of my list of priorities right now. If this ruins my chances, so be it." I shrug. "I've seen what a burden it is. The responsibility is considerable, and it's taken a toll on Massimo. I'm not sure I want it anymore. I've got Valentina now, and we have plans. I don't want to be an absent husband or father. Maybe this is a blessing in disguise."

They both stare at me like I've just sprouted wings, and I get it. I laugh. "I know. Fuck me." I rub the back of my neck. "Everything is changing."

"I'm happy for you, brother, and Mom will be over the moon if you give her a grandchild." Zumo pulls me into a hug, and we slap one another on the back.

"Okay, are we in agreement?" Caleb asks, and we nod.

"I still think you should talk to Rico," Zumo says. "He's completely objective, and he might think of loopholes we haven't."

"I don't want to risk damaging his reputation too. Besides, he's on vacation in France with Frankie. I'm not disturbing him with this shit." My *consigliere* is going to be very angry with me when all this comes out. Though I have kept him out of this to protect him, he won't see it like that.

"You should go home," I tell Caleb. "Your wife needs you."

Zumo nods. "Fiero and I can take it from here."

"I'll be needing that cake box." Caleb waggles his brows.

"Come on." I lift one shoulder. "Let's get Valentina."

Chapter Twenty-Nine
Valentina

"You're all good," Natalia Messina says, gently pressing down on the small gauze at the back of my neck covering my new tracker. Fiero told me earlier in the week he'd arranged for Caleb and Joshua's mom to come to the house today to remove the old tracker from my arm and install a different one in my neck. It's a new prototype and only a select few *mafioso* have them. It's not common knowledge, and news of the new chips hasn't reached Florida yet, so if Cesco, or any of Dom's men, are trying to track me, they won't be able to, but Fiero can if there's a need.

It gives me an extra layer of protection, and I'm grateful. I spoke to a few of my sisters this morning and my cousin Nina, needing to hear their voices even though Fiero has told me they're safe. He reactivated my phone and hooked me up to the Wi-Fi, and it's a measure of trust I'm grateful for.

My hair falls down my back, covering my neck. "Thank you. Are you in a hurry to leave, or would you like to stay for some cake and iced tea?"

"I have a little bit of time. I'd love that."

Natalia goes outside to the table to make a call while I fix a tray with cupcakes and small slices of key lime pie and meringue with strawberries and peaches and fresh cream. Lastly, I add the jug of iced tea I made earlier and two glasses and carry it outside, arriving just as Natalia ends her call.

"Oh my. This looks delicious."

I set it down. "Thanks. Fiero has been working a lot these past couple days, and I've been bored, so I baked." I shrug.

"Oh, I heard all about it last night on the phone," she says, helping herself to a cupcake. I pour iced tea into two glasses. "My daughter-in-law Elisa told me you sent some cakes home with Caleb. She was raving about how yummy they were."

"I'm glad she liked them." I hand her a glass and claim the seat beside her. "Fiero told me your twin sons are expecting with their wives. Are these your first grandchildren?"

"Yes. I'm so excited."

"You look way too young to be a grandmother." She's stunning with thick dark hair, curves forever, and flawless olive skin. She reminds me of Sofia Vergara.

"You're too kind, but trust me, I'm old enough. My youngest two are ten and eleven now, and I miss having babies around. There's just something about their soft skin and that delightful baby smell I'm addicted to. I always say they're easier when they're babies."

"Yeah, babies are adorable." The words sound devoid of emotion to my own ears.

She arches a brow in silent question as she bites into her cupcake.

"I'm the eldest of ten in my family. I raised my younger siblings with my mom. They were like my babies."

"Well, hopefully someday, you'll have babies of your own too."

Pain cuts a line across my chest, but I disguise it behind a practiced mask before sinking my teeth into the key lime pie. It tastes like sawdust in my mouth.

Concern splays across her face as she watches me. "I gave Fiero my word that my visit here would be confidential, and I will not breathe a word to anyone. He didn't give me any details, but am I to assume you and he are together?"

"Yes, but it's new and more than a little complicated."

"Relationships usually are." She pats my hand and smiles. Glancing at the large colorful bouquet in the glass vase on the table, she asks, "Are these from him?"

I bob my head. "Every morning, a new bouquet arrives. If he keeps this up, I'll be able to open my own florist shop."

"How romantic."

A genuine smile trips over my lips. "It is. He's blowing me away with so many thoughtful gestures. He even paid someone to drive his chocolate delivery from White Plains in Connecticut to here. He said their chocolate is your favorite and Joshua put him in touch with the owner."

"I'm addicted to their chocolate though my hips don't thank me for it." She laughs lightly. "Fiero is a wonderful man. I'm delighted he's met someone. Someone he clearly cares about."

"He's been amazing, if a little overbearing at times."

"I'm well acquainted with the type. My brother, my husband, my sons, my friends' husbands, they're all the same. I think it's in their DNA, and who doesn't want to be loved and protected like that?"

"I'm definitely not unhappy. Fiero got me out of a bad situation, and being treated like this is new for me. I'm still processing it all and how fast it's happened."

"I'm sorry to hear that but glad you have him and happy you are away from that situation. If I can do anything to help, I'm only a phone call away."

"There is one thing," I say over a smile. "Catarina told me when I met you I was to ask for your apple cake and apple cannelloni recipes, so could I have them?"

Taking What's Mine

After a run and a swim, I take a shower and settle on the couch on the patio with a romance book I found in the guest room. Fiero still isn't home, and he said he'd be late, so I haven't bothered cooking dinner yet. I already made the coleslaw and caprese salad and prepped the chicken breasts and sauce for the parmigiana. So, all I have to do is cook it and make the garlic bread. I asked Fiero to tell me when he's thirty minutes away so I can start cooking.

I'm engrossed in the book when my cell pings. All the blood drains from my face when I read the text from Cesco.

> Don't think this frees you. What was his is now mine. I'll be seeing you soon, Mom.

Nausea swims up my throat, and I race into the house barely making it to the downstairs bathroom in time. I'm shaking all over as I expel the contents of my stomach. Cesco can't force me to marry him, but he's always wanted me, and I don't think he's going to back down.

"What's wrong?" Fiero asks the instant he walks into the kitchen and sees my pale face.

I quietly hand him my phone with the screen opened to the text message while I plate our chicken. Everything else is laid out on the table inside. It's a little breezy tonight, and it felt too chilly on the patio to eat outside.

"He's not touching you." He tosses my phone down and hauls me into his arms. "Don't worry about that little shit. I'll handle him." He kisses me, temporarily washing away my fear. "Okay?" he asks, tucking a piece of hair behind my ear.

I nod even though it's not really okay. I forced Fiero to tell me everything last night. Dominic being dead is a huge relief, but it didn't go according to plan, and that's my fault. Guilt is all-consuming on several levels. "Did you arrange it?"

He sighs, holding me closer. "It's done. The body was dumped early this morning, and the news is out. I've just been hauled over the coals at an emergency meeting of the board."

"Did they buy it?"

"Yes. All but Massimo because he knows about you and he knows I'm behind this."

"Did you tell him?"

He shakes his head. "I didn't say anything, and he didn't ask, and that's the way it'll stay for now." He kisses the tip of my nose. "He's furious with me, and I don't blame him. I put him in this position."

"That's not good. I never wanted to cause trouble between you and your best friend."

"Don't worry about it. It'll blow over eventually."

"What if it doesn't?"

He shrugs, looking unruffled. "Then I'll deal with whatever cards I'm dealt. As long as I have you, I don't care."

"You can't mean that!" I shuck out of his hold to turn off the oven. "He's your oldest, closest friend."

"Nothing will change that, but if it's a choice between you or him, I'll always choose you."

My jaw drops to the floor. "Fiero, you've known me less than a week."

"It's a week tomorrow, and time doesn't matter. Neither does age. All that matters is how you make me feel and this indisputable sense of rightness I feel when I'm with you. It's like Cat said. We're soulmates."

"It doesn't make sense. You can't pick me over Massimo."

"Kitten." He reels me back into his arms. "It doesn't have to make sense if it's right. I know you're used to people not picking you, but that's not who I am. You're the most important person in my life, end of. I will always pick you. And don't feel too bad because Massimo would choose Cat over me any day, and I wouldn't want it any other way. It's how it should be."

"You're crazy," I say, stretching up on tiptoe to kiss him. "But I like your brand of crazy."

"Good, because you're stuck with me now." He takes the plates while I grab the bottle of sparkling water from the fridge and follow him to the table.

"Fuck, this looks delicious." He looks at me with so much love in his eyes that I melt.

"I like cooking for you." I hated cooking for Dom because he demanded it and he was ungrateful, rarely complimenting or thanking me. Fiero is the opposite, and he has taken such good care of me. This is the least I can do to show my appreciation. Plus, I'll die of boredom without something to occupy my time.

"You're one in a million, kitten. I'm so lucky to have found you."

"You're very romantic, Don Maltese," I say, heaping salad onto my plate. "It's most unexpected but appreciated."

"You bring out this side of me," he says, helping himself to garlic bread, salad, and coleslaw. "You make me a better man. I don't care if I've only known you a week. I will love you forever, Valentina."

Tears prick my eyes, but they're happy ones. There is no point deluding myself any longer. I'm not leaving this man. I'm staying right here where I belong. I love him too, crazy as it sounds. He makes me incredibly happy, and even if it doesn't last, I know he'll always take care of me because he *is* a good man. Besides, staying here is way safer than fleeing on my own. Dom's threat seems to have died with him, but until I know for sure, I've still got to keep my guard up. Fiero will protect me, protect my family, and it's still needed because Cesco is smart in a way Dom wasn't, and he won't give up easily.

"I've upset you." He sets his silverware down.

"No, babe. These are happy tears. I'm the lucky one, Fiero. I didn't believe my life could turn completely upside down in a week but it has. All because of you."

Fiero is at work all day Saturday, and I'm bored out of my mind. I haven't been answering my siblings' calls because there is so much I can't tell them yet and I don't want to lie. Avoidance is the best strategy for now. Clearly, they have heard the news about Dom and most likely want to know if I'm coming home now. I also ignored Vitto's call for similar reasons, but I can't be disrespectful to the Florida don either. I'll talk to Fiero about it when he's home.

My fingers curl around my locket as I lie on the couch outside reading. I must have dozed off because when I wake the sun is hanging low in the sky and Fiero is sitting in a chair watching me. He's wearing a suit with the tie missing and the top two buttons on his blue dress shirt open.

"What time is it?" I ask in a sleepy voice.

"A little after eight," he says.

I bolt upright. "Shit. I didn't make anything for dinner."

"I've got it covered," he says, moving over beside me. He pulls me into his arms, and I instantly melt. It's amazing how incredible I feel when he holds me. How protected and cherished he makes me feel. "Now I can breathe," he murmurs, closing his eyes and resting his chin on my head. I love that we both feel the same and it's on more of a level footing.

We sit like that for a few minutes in silence, and it's blissful.

Fiero glances at the time on his watch and stands, taking me with him. "Come." He holds my hand the entire journey to his bedroom and into the bathroom. I gasp at the scene awaiting me. The tub by the window is full, red rose petals resting prettily on top of the water. Notes of jasmine and vanilla tickle my nostrils from the countless scented candles covering the window.

"What's all this?" I ask, looking up at him.

"Do I need a reason to spoil you?"

"You spoil me every day," I say, not protesting when he pulls my shirt over my head and discards it on the floor. My shorts are next, swiftly followed by my panties and bra until I'm standing before him completely bare. His eyes glimmer with heat, and my core pulses with need.

A wry chuckle escapes his lips. "Is my kitten wet for me?" Leaning in, he grazes his teeth along the column of my neck.

"Always, Fiero."

He slides one finger inside me slowly, and I grip his arm. My pout is instant when he removes it, bringing it to his mouth and sucking deep. My chest heaves up and down as need floods every nook and cranny of my body.

"You're perfect." He kisses my lips briefly. "Hold that thought for later," he adds, offering me his hand and helping me into the bath. I moan as the warm scented water eases my muscles when I lie back. "Here." He hands me a glass of champagne.

"Aren't you joining me?"

"Tempting as it is, I have a few things to set up." He kneels at the edge of the tub and leans in to kiss me passionately. "Take your time and then dress in a pretty dress. Wear your hair down. Then go to the patio and wait there."

"This is all very mysterious."

He caresses my face. "All will be revealed soon." He kisses me again, and he seems nervous when he pulls back.

"What's wrong?" I cup one cheek.

"Nothing, honey. You're so beautiful, and I'm so very much in love with you," he says, nestling into my touch.

This would be a good time to tell him I love him too, but the words get stuck in my mouth. "I know" pops out instead, the lamest of lamest responses.

"Don't be late," he whispers before leaving me to contemplate what he's got planned now.

Chapter Thirty
Fiero

I'm sweating buckets in my gray suit as I wait in the rear garden of the guesthouse for Dino to escort Valentina here. I chose this setting as it's the most private on the grounds. This area is bordered by pretty flowering shrubs and trees, yet we still have a view of the dock. String lights crisscrossing through the trees illuminate the space, along with the multitude of lit candles dotted all over the stone ground. Red roses wind around the base of the golden candelabra sitting on the dressed table. Inside, the chef and waiter I hired for tonight are hiding in the laundry room under strict instructions not to come out until I get them.

If anyone knew I was doing this, they'd have me committed. But it feels right, and I'm going with my instinct. I don't care what anyone else will think when they find out. They don't matter. All that matters is us, and I hope Valentina agrees.

She steps out of the house and onto the patio looking like a goddess in a gorgeous pink strapless chiffon dress that drapes to her ankles. A large fake flower rests to the left of her waist, and there's a high split up one side of the dress, revealing one long toned, tan leg. My cock immediately springs to life, like always when she's near. Strappy silver slingbacks adorn her feet, and she's wearing her usual locket and a bunch of thin silver bracelets on one wrist and the new Rolex I bought her on the other. Diamante earrings glisten in her ears, and her hair is hanging in soft waves down her back. She's not wearing much makeup, but she doesn't need it. She's magnificent. Definitely a sight to behold.

"You look stunning," I say, walking to where she has stopped. Her gaze darts around the space, her eyes growing wide.

"What is all this?"

"Dinner." Taking her hand, I lift it to my lips.

She visibly shudders when my mouth brushes her skin, and I love how responsive she is to every touch from me.

"This is spectacular, and the view is to die for."

"I agree," I say, eyeballing her so the message is clear.

Two pink dots stain her cheeks, and I'm partial to that color on her.

"I love you." I slowly pull her into my body.

Her eyes glisten with emotion as her hands land on my shoulders. "I love you too," she whispers, and I almost lose the ability to breathe.

"You mean it?"

"Yes." The biggest smile materializes on her gorgeous face. "It's crazy insanity but no less true."

I crash my lips to hers, dipping her back a little as I kiss her deeply. We're both panting when we come up for air.

"You've just made me the happiest man alive," I say even though I haven't even proposed yet and there's still a strong chance she'll say no.

But this has got to increase the odds, right?

I help her into her chair and pour her a glass of champagne before heading inside to tell the chef and waiter we're good to begin.

We enjoy a sumptuous dinner of lobster ravioli to start, then the most delicious filet steak with accompaniments, and a rich chocolate mousse for dessert. Conversation is flowing naturally, and we're trading stories of our childhoods and steering clear of awkward topics. She manages to adequately distract me, and waylay my nerves, until I let the waiter and chef go and the moment is upon me.

It's now or never. No turning back.

The box in my pocket feels like a lead weight as I return from the bathroom having splashed water on my face and washed my clammy hands. My heart is skipping around my rib cage like an out-of-control racecar, and my collar feels tight around my neck. Most days, I hate wearing suits, but tonight is an important night, and it demanded I be as impeccably dressed as she is.

She turns slightly in her chair when I step outside, smiling expansively as she holds her flute, looking happy and relaxed, and I want to freeze-frame the way she looks tonight for eternity.

Taking her glass, I set it aside before dropping to one knee. She emits a shocked gasp when I take her hand, pull the box from my pocket, and clear my throat. "Valentina. We haven't known one another long, but I've waited what feels like an eternity to find you. I know what I'm feeling is the real deal, and I don't want to waste another day living my life without you by my side. I love you. I will love you every day for the rest of my life. I will make you happy and give you the family you've always dreamed of."

Tears stream down her face, but I can't work out how she's feeling because her face is displaying so many differing emotions. I forge on anyway. "Be my wife." I pop open the lid, revealing the three-carat princess-cut diamond ring I purchased yesterday from Harry Winston's. "Will you marry me?"

Her lower lip wobbles as she stares at me, and the longer she says nothing, the more agitated I become. "Say something," I plead.

"This is too much," she whispers, yanking her hand away and hopping up, running off before I can stop her.

I'm rooted to the spot, my heart pulverized in my chest, as pain slays me on the inside. Acting on autopilot, I clear the table, leaving the dishes piled in the sink. I switch off the lights outside and lock up the guest house before making my way back into the house. The lights are off downstairs, so I remove my shoes and head up to our bedroom. Valentina is in bed, but she's not sleeping. She's staring numbly at the wall, looking so young and lost it breaks my heart all over again.

"Can I get you anything?" I ask, cringing at how hoarse I sound.

She shakes her head, not looking at me, and I walk into the bathroom, undressing and taking a cold shower. Resting my head on the tile, I berate myself for my stupidity. *What was I thinking proposing to her so soon?* It's only been a week, and her husband just died. He was an abusive prick she was forced into marrying. It's a lot. She's still processing everything that's happened in a short period of time, and I knew she was already overloaded.

It was selfish to propose tonight, but I want her. I want her to be my wife. I want to protect her and love her in a way she's never known. *Why wait when I already know she's my future?* She's worried about Cesco coming to claim her, and her marrying me is added protection. Not that it's the reason I proposed. It didn't even cross my mind. I asked her because I love her and she's the only woman who will ever be my wife. If she says no, then that's it. I won't ever marry. I'll continue alone.

I turn off the shower when my frozen limbs start trembling,

dry myself in the bathroom, and pad naked into the bedroom. Her eyes are closed now, but she's not asleep. After heading into the closet, I pull on a pair of clean boxers and make my way to the bed. Awkward tension filters into the air as I slide under the covers. She tenses. *Goddamn it, Fiero. What have you done?* Needing to make this right, I scoot over and pull her into my arms, her back pressed to my chest. "I'm sorry, honey. I didn't mean to upset you."

"I know," she whispers, reaching out to switch off the bedside lamp, plunging us into darkness.

"I just love you so much."

"I know that too. Just let me sleep on it."

Fickle hope mushrooms in my chest. "So, it's not a no?"

"Fiero, don't push it."

"Okay." I hold her closer, nuzzling into her neck, grateful she doesn't push me away and that she's considering my proposal.

I stay up for hours, holding her as she sleeps fitfully in my arms. Eventually, I drift off, and when I wake, she's sitting cross-legged in the bed staring at me.

"I want to make a deal," she says, and I'm wide-awake now. I sit up, dropping my head back against the headrest.

"I thought you didn't like deals."

"I normally don't, but this situation calls for it. Do you want to hear this or not?"

"I'm listening, baby."

"This is a lot, Fiero."

I nod.

"And it's insanely, ridiculously crazy."

I nod again because she's speaking the truth.

"All I've wanted since the second I was forced to marry Dom is my independence. My freedom. I told you I was planning my escape, but I didn't tell you I was actively making that happen this past year. If you're serious about marrying me, you at least deserve this truth."

My brows knit together as I study her pretty face. "Go on."

"I was poisoning Dom and Cesco."

"Say what?"

"It was arsenic. You can administer it in small doses in food and drink, and it's undetected. Over time, it would have killed them. It may still kill Cesco, but he's younger and fitter than his father. I suspect that's why Dom had a heart attack on Thursday. The stress and trauma must have brought it on, but he was predisposed to it because of the arsenic."

"Kitten." I lift her into my lap. "This only adds to my reasons to want to marry you."

She barks out a laugh. "You're not worried I might poison you?"

I shake my head. "I won't ever give you a reason to."

"I was planning to escape. To use your boat to run away."

"I know that too, baby." I thread my fingers in her hair. "You made it pretty obvious with all the questions you were asking."

"I didn't have much time to plan. I thought I only had a week to run away."

"No doubt you'd have been smoother if you'd have had more time," I agree to appease her.

She narrows her eyes. "I can't decide if you're patronizing me or not."

"I mean it. You're resourceful and smart." I chuckle. "Arsenic is a classic. Real old-school. The heart attack would have seemed natural."

"I poisoned you," she says, and my brows climb to my hairline. "I couldn't separate out the food that Sunday at dinner."

"That's why you didn't eat much."

She nods. "And I threw up what little I ate, but you didn't know. I'm so sorry. You should probably get checked out. But don't go to Natalia. She likes me. I'd really like to keep it that way."

A laugh bursts from my chest. "I'll get checked out, but I doubt it's done much harm if it was only trace amounts. At least I know now why I was feeling sick."

"You should hate me.

"Impossible." I tweak her nose. "We need to get you checked out too." My laugher dies. Even if she was hardly eating any of the poisoned food and puked it back up, she might still have ingested more than she realizes. I hope it hasn't caused her any lasting damage.

"I thought you'd be mad."

"I'm not exactly thrilled you poisoned me, kitten, but I get it."

"I didn't feel overly guilty at the time because you were acting like an ass, but I've felt guilty a lot since."

"You're forgiven. Is this what was holding you back last night?" Excitement is trickling through my veins.

"In part." She worries her lip between her teeth.

"Don't do that." I pull it out gently. "You'll hurt herself. Just tell me the rest."

"I'm struggling to reconcile my wants and needs." She twists on my lap, settling over my morning wood with her thighs straddling me. "I want my independence, but I'll lose it again if I marry you."

"No, you won't. You can have all the independence you want. Marriage shouldn't be a cage. We can love one another while giving one another space. I know, I know, I'm a jealous, possessive beast at times, but it doesn't mean you'll be trapped. I want you to be your own person in our relationship, Valentina. I won't curtail your movements unless there's a security risk. I'll encourage your passions and ambitions and welcome any friendships you make. I don't want you to feel like a prisoner. I want this to feel like home. We can fly Nina and your siblings in, and you can go visit them." I hold her face and stare her straight in the eye so she understands I'm serious.

"You're not just saying this so I'll marry you?"

"Absolutely not. I want you to be happy, and I know how important your independence is to you. I would never take that away. However, there are some caveats."

She narrows her eyes.

"Just listen. I was already planning to talk to you about this. Now Dom is gone, you can go out in the city if you like as long as you use my driver and take two of my *soldati* with you for protection. I'll assign my two best men to you full-time so you can get to know them, and it'll feel less awkward. After a while, you won't even remember they're there. I want to be transparent. If you marry me, you will *always* need protection. I'm one of the most powerful men in *La Cosa Nostra*, and I'm a target. Like all the wives, you would have a protective detail, and on occasion, if it's warranted, you might have to stay housebound if there's a threat, but other than that, you are free to come and go as you please."

"I like the idea of a protective detail. I know you don't believe Cesco is a threat, but you shouldn't underestimate him. He'll be plotting something for sure."

"I've spoken to Vitto, and he's watching Cesco carefully. He hasn't left Miami." If Cesco was behind the drone, he wasn't personally flying it.

"Is that why he called me on Friday?"

I squeeze her ass as she rocks gently back and forth on my hard dick. "Vitto called you?"

She nods. "I didn't pick up. Wasn't sure what I could or couldn't say."

"I don't know why he called you. There's no need unless he wanted to offer condolences."

"I doubt it. He knew how Dom treated me."

"And he did nothing." Anger swells in my chest.

"It doesn't matter now, and he hasn't called back."

"So, what's this deal then?"

"I've been thinking all night about your proposal and my future. First, I thought it's way too soon and I can't say yes to someone I've just met. Then, I worried about losing the independence I've just regained. What people think is another consideration. It was all jumbled in my head until I realized I was overthinking it. For the first time, I have a choice. This is my decision." She thumps a hand over her chest. "And that's the very definition of freedom and independence. Who cares what anyone thinks? I'm following my heart and trusting it won't lead me astray. My heart is saying yes, telling me I belong with you and you'll make me very happy, but I can't walk into this marriage blind like I did the last one."

"You need a safety net."

Her head bobs. "I need to know if it doesn't work out I'm not trapped. I need that for my sanity, Fiero."

"That makes sense. What are you proposing?"

Steely determination is etched all over her face. "If I say yes, if I marry you, you agree to a contract that allows me to divorce you in one year if it's not working out. You'll let me go and give me five million dollars so I can get settled someplace else."

I understand why she's asking for this. This is a way to gain back her freedom if she's made a mistake. I have no issue agreeing to it because it won't ever happen. We were made for one another, and we're going to be happy. I'll die on that hill. "Make it fifty million," I say, lifting her off me and scrambling across the bed.

"What?"

"I agree but the settlement is fifty million." I hop off the bed. "If we don't work out, I want you to be comfortable for the rest of your life, baby," I say before racing into the bathroom. Yanking my pants off the floor, I drive my hand into the pocket and extract the box before rushing back into the bedroom.

"You only get crazier, but I agree."

"Great." I jump onto the bed, and she bounces all over the place. "I'll have my sister draw up the paperwork." Forcing myself to calm down, I take her hand in mine, aware I'm grinning like an idiot and completely uncaring. This is the happiest day of my life. "Now, let's do this again."

Chapter Thirty-One
Valentina

"Congratulations!" Tullia squeals, almost bowling me over as she throws herself at me in the corridor of the Manhattan City Clerk's Office—also known as Manhattan City Hall—after we exit the room where I just got married for the second time. It's only been two weeks since Dom died, but the death certificate has been issued, and Fiero knew a judge who pulled some strings to make this happen fast. "I'm so happy to have another sister. Welcome to the family, Valentina."

"Thank you for the warm welcome." I hug her back, smiling over her shoulder at Sofia and Zumo who are standing beside Fiero. I only met Tullia a few minutes before the civil ceremony got underway, and I instantly loved her. She's the opposite of her ice-queen sister. While Sofia has been pleasant and outwardly friendly since our first disastrous encounter, and she drew up the deal paperwork efficiently, ensuring everything was signed before today, I can't forget how we met. Hopefully, in time, we can both put it behind us and grow close. I won't be holding my breath though.

"Hands off my bride." Fiero nudges his youngest sister out of the way so he can pull me into his arms.

"My heart is bursting for you, Ro. This is the best day ever." Tullia beams at her eldest brother. "I can't wait until we can tell everyone."

"You can't breathe a word, Lia," Fiero warns her for the umpteenth time. "It's dangerous for me and Valentina if this news gets out before we're ready to reveal it." He shoots me an apologetic look, and I stretch up and kiss him. I know he feels bad we've had to do this in secret, without telling my family, and that he can't give me a big wedding, but I don't mind.

I love him.

I really, really love him.

The last couple of weeks have firmly cemented that.

And today is for us.

When this mess is sorted in Florida, we'll get to tell everyone, and then we can set a date for the big wedding we're planning. Fiero wants to marry in St. Patrick's Cathedral and then hire this specific wedding venue in Long Island for the reception. It's been fun these past couple of weeks discussing it and jotting down ideas. He's even found a wedding planner he wants to hire to help me with the planning.

"And you can't tell Mom and Dad," Zumo reminds her, dragging me back into the conversation.

We needed witnesses today, and it was only natural for Fiero to ask his siblings. I asked him if he wanted to invite his mother, but he was resolute he didn't. It seems his relationship with his mother isn't much better than the one he has with his father. He resents her for always having her husband's back and not standing up for him and her other kids enough.

Neither of us are on good terms with our parents. We're quite a pair.

I feel bad for Fiero that he couldn't ask Massimo and Catarina, but he's trying to protect Massimo by keeping him out of this while he works to fix everything in Miami. He's returning on Tuesday to meet with the cartel, and I'm worried sick.

"I understand, and I already gave Fiero my word. I won't say anything to the rents." Tullia's smile turns a little pouty. "I hate you all don't trust me. I'm not a little kid anymore. I can be trusted with confidential stuff."

"It's not about trust, squirt." Fiero tucks Tullia under his other arm. "I do trust you."

"You're too excitable," Sofia interjects.

Tullia glares at her older sister.

Sofia's features soften. "It's a good trait. It's a big part of who you are, and you should never change."

"But?" Tullia folds her arms.

"You get excited sometimes and blurt things out. We know you don't mean to, but this time, you've got to be extremely careful. Fiero didn't want to leave you out today. He is trusting you to keep this completely secret for now. Don't let him down."

"I don't need a lecture from you," she scoffs at Sofia.

"Okay, that's enough." Zumo steps in, shooting a warning glare between his sisters. "This is a happy day. We're celebrating, and that's the end of the bickering. Lia knows what's at stake, Sof. She won't betray the secret."

Zumo pulls her into a headlock, and I grin as I watch them. "This reminds me of growing up," I say to Fiero, beaming as I snuggle into his side. "I was always pulling my siblings apart. We're a hotheaded bunch."

"I'd never have realized," Fiero drawls, his lips twitching.

I pinch his delectable butt. "Sarcasm is beneath you."

"If you say so, Mrs. Maltese." He hauls me around to his front, pressing me flush against him, with his arms low on my back. "I love saying that."

My arms wrap around his neck. "I love hearing it." My smile is so wide it threatens to split my face in two.

"Happy?" he asks.

"Exceptionally so."

Our heads move in tandem, and our mouths meet in the most heavenly kiss. Contentment seeps deep into my bones, and my soul rejoices as I kiss my man, pouring every bit of love in my heart into every sweep of my lips. I never thought I could be this happy with any man, but I love that Fiero is proving me wrong.

The flash of a camera drags us back to reality. Reluctantly, we break our kiss but not our embrace. I cling to my husband as he clings to me, happier than I ever remember being.

"I'm framing that one," Tullia says, peering into the screen of her Nikon. She's a budding photographer, apparently, and she insisted on taking the photos today. We were more than happy to agree. "Let's get some more pics at the mural and the wedding garden across the street." City Hall has a large mural of the city in the building, and it's customary for couples to get photos taken with it as a backdrop and in front of the bronze doors at the rear of the building.

We spend a half hour taking photos in both locations before moving to this posh French restaurant housed in an atrium with a stunning arched stained-glass roof. Potted flowering shrubs are dotted around the large space adding to the delicious smells wafting in the air.

We dine on the most sumptuous oysters before sharing chateaubriand and finishing with soft and creamy crème brûlée and mini praline madeleines. The bubbly is flowing, and conversation is lively though I'm sensing some tension between the sisters. Tullia is a little prickly with Sofia while Sofia seems to be treading on eggshells around her. Tullia is also knocking back the champagne despite Zumo quietly warning her to take it easy.

I don't know if Fiero has noticed. He's only got eyes for me, and right now, he's too busy groping me under the table.

"Regretting not shoving a plug in my ass?" I purr into his ear as he fumbles with the satin layers of my gown.

"Nope." He nibbles on my earlobe. "I've got plans for you tonight that will have you soaked and struggling to walk tomorrow."

Shivers cascade over my skin. "Tell me."

He gives up on my dress, clasping my face in his hands. "It's a surprise." He kisses me tenderly. "You are the most stunning bride, and I am the luckiest man to call you my wife."

A smile runs free across my face as he looks me up and down, and there's no disguising the love, lust, and admiration in his eyes. For a fierce made man, Fiero is one hell of a romantic, constantly showering me with attention and professing his love through words and gestures.

His eyes rake over me like a sensual caress, and lust coils low in my belly as he drinks me in like it's the first time he's seeing me. My dress isn't a full formal wedding gown. I'll save that for the cathedral. This is one I picked up from Rachel McConaughey. It was a sample from the store, but she personally oversaw the alterations ensuring it was ready for me in time.

It's got a mesh lace layer over the fitted satin corset top, and the satin skirt is asymmetrical, showing my legs from the knee down at the front while the back almost reaches my ankles. The same hair and makeup people looked after me earlier, and my hair is done with a multitude of little diamante ornaments threaded throughout it. The front part is held back by a braided band, ensuring no stray strands stick to my face. My gorgeous gold high-heeled sandals are a wedding gift from Rachel, and I couldn't thank her enough for all she's done for me. It's nice to know one of the most celebrated designers of our time is also one of the sweetest women. And don't get me started on her gorgeous Irish accent. I could listen to her talking all day long.

"Earth to Mrs. Maltese." Fiero eyes me with humor as my fingers curl around thin air at my neck. I'm not wearing my locket as it clashed with the top of the dress, but it's instinctive for me to touch it, and I didn't realize I was reaching for something that isn't there.

I circle my arms around his neck, and the stunning diamond bracelet on my wrist sparkles and glimmers. It matches the drop earrings I'm wearing and the gorgeous necklace that was also a part of Fiero's wedding gift to me. It's currently residing in the safe in his office. "I'm the lucky one. You're so hot, so smart, so thoughtful, so sexy. I won the lottery the day I met you." He looks incredible today in a blue suit with a crisp white shirt. I told him to forgo a tie because he hates wearing one, so his shirt is unbuttoned at the top offering a glimpse of toned, tan skin and the ink creeping over one side of his chest.

"Is that him?" Tullia snarls in an ugly tone that doesn't seem like her, instantly claiming our attention.

Sofia looks up from her cell phone. "Don't, Lia. This isn't the time or place."

"You did it on purpose!" Tullia says in a raised voice. Her lower lip is wobbling, and tears fill her eyes as she stands, pointing at her older sister. "You knew how I felt about him, and you deliberately went after him because you can't let me have anything."

Sofia slips her phone into her purse. "That's not how it happened, and we shouldn't be discussing this here."

Fiero is frowning, his concerned gaze centered on his little sister.

"This is Ro's day. We can talk about this tomorrow," Sofia says.

Tullia hiccups over a sob, and my heart breaks for the obvious pain she's in. "You don't even care about him. He's just someone to fuck in between court sessions." She throws her napkin down. "I hate you and I'll never forgive you for this." She glances at us briefly. "I'm sorry for ruining dinner," she sobs before running off.

Sofia jumps up and dashes after her. Fiero removes his hands from my waist, moving to get up.

"Don't." Zumo shakes his head. "I'll go and sort this. Stay with your wife." He rushes off in the direction his sisters went.

"You're his *wife*?"

My head jerks up at the familiar voice, but it's been a long time since I've heard it. "Damiano?" I look at my ex in shock, instantly noting the uniform. "You work here?"

Fiero stiffens, wrapping his arm around my shoulders and pulling me in tight. He doesn't disguise his glower as he stares at the younger man.

"Yeah. I just came on shift."

Damiano has put on weight, and the muscles he worked so hard for senior year are clearly long gone. His hair is much longer than in high school too. It curls around his ears, unkempt and in dire need of a brush.

"I didn't realize you were living in New York."

"It, ah, was a recent development." He scratches the back of his head, and I notice he's not wearing his wedding ring. His gaze roams over me from head to toe. "You look beautiful."

"Fuck off," Fiero says in a lethally calm tone, eyeballing my ex. "You had your chance with Valentina, and you blew it. She's my wife, and I don't like the way you're looking at her. If we were anywhere else, I'd blow your fucking head off."

"I mean no disrespect." He holds up his palms. "I just saw Val here, and I couldn't believe it."

"On your way," Fiero says in a clipped tone.

"I didn't know," he blurts, fixing his brown eyes on me. I used to think his eyes were stunning, like melted chocolate, but they're just a boring muddy brown. Looking at him now, I wonder what I ever saw in him. "Louis told me recently what really happened at the party that night. I'm so sorry, Val. I broke down when he told me what was done to you. I'm all choked up my father hurt you like that. I'm so fucking sorry."

Fiero growls and his body is vibrating with anger. I land a hand on his thigh and squeeze, cautioning him to back down. I've waited a long time to say this to Damiano, and I don't see why I should waste the opportunity. "You didn't even give me a chance to explain," I say, holding my head up high as I address my ex. "You believed it without question, and then you kissed Florentina in front of me. It wasn't enough I'd lost my boyfriend. You had to take my best friend from me too."

"I was a fool. I worshipped a monster who stole the best thing to ever happen to me."

"I'm sure your wife would love to hear that," I say. "Where is the backstabbing bitch anyway?" I'd like to know so I can avoid her. I have nothing nice to say to the girl who was my best friend from fourth grade.

"Living in England with her new Russian oligarch husband." Bitterness laces through his tone. "She forced me to steal from my brother so I could give her the life she wanted. When Louis found out, he took everything and kicked me out of the state. I came here six months ago with nothing."

Fiero laughs, and it's a cruel taunting sound. "She ruined your life and then found a better option when you couldn't fund her extravagant lifestyle anymore."

Damiano's hands clench into fists at his side. "She played me, but I guess it's my own fault."

"You got that right," Fiero drawls. "If it's any consolation, I bet she's miserable with that old prick she married, and she'll be traded in soon for a younger model. If you ask me, sounds like she did you a favor."

"She aborted my baby before she ran off!" he hisses. "Excuse me if I don't agree."

"Watch your fucking mouth, boy." Fiero drills him with a dark look. "Unless you want to be looking over your shoulder for the rest of your life."

"She's a touchy subject," he sheepishly says, immediately backing down.

I snort out a laugh.

Unbelievable.

"If I could go back and do it all differently, I would," he says, looking at me.

"Well, I wouldn't. You were never good enough for me, and no one compares to Fiero." I palm my husband's cheek. "Every other man pales into insignificance." I look into Fiero's eyes, and I'm instantly mesmerized. "Goodbye, Damiano," I say, not looking at him as I lean in and kiss my husband.

Fiero hauls me into his lap, uncaring we're in public, kissing me passionately because he needs to stamp his mark all over me, and I'm A-okay with that. When we finally break apart, panting and wearing matching lust-filled eyes, my ex is gone, Zumo has taken care of the check, and the tables surrounding us are clapping and cheering.

Fiero's grin is smug in the extreme as he sets me on my feet and clasps my hand. "Let's go home, my love. I have plans for you."

Chapter Thirty-Two
Fiero

"Tell me what you're thinking?" I ask, standing back and inspecting my wife as her wide eyes scan the four corners of my sex room.

I mapped out every square inch and was very specific with the interior designer I hired to create this private space. Walls covered with red and black Gothic-style wallpaper meet black-stained hardwood floors. Soft, plush red-and-gold rugs cover parts of the floor in and around the various pieces of equipment. A built-in shelving unit houses toys, lube, condoms, towels, and various other supplies. The large bed at the back of the room is dressed in expensive black silk sheets and an abundance of soft pillows and silky red, black and gold cushions. Mirrored panels over the bed should add an extra dimension to our fun. Lighting is low, sending a sultry red glow all over the space.

"I was curious what was behind the locked door, but I never imagined any of this." Her fingers sweep over the smooth edge of the St. Andrew's Cross with intrigue written all over her face.

"I probably should have shown you before we got married," I say, coming up behind her, "but I wanted it to be a surprise." I tip her chin up and angle her head so she's looking back at me. "I want to play with you, kitten."

She gulps nervously, but she can't disguise the excitement in her eyes. "Okay."

"Good girl." I wrap my arm around her waist and graze my teeth up and down her neck. "Let's take a shower first." Grabbing her hand, I lead her into the large bathroom and turn her to face the mirror over the sinks. I leave her there for a second while I choose the music, pressing the button on the wall-mounted pad when I've made my selection. Soft, sensual music filters into the background, which I hope will help to relax her. "Don't be nervous," I say as I slowly lower the zipper on her dress, feeling her trembling against my fingers. "I will take good care of you, and if you want to stop, I will."

"I trust you." She looks at me through the mirror as I push the dress off her shoulders, and it glides down her body like liquid silk.

I bend down and lift it, hanging it on a hanger at the back of the door. "You're like a sexy angel in that lingerie," I admit, staring at the generous swell of her tits in her white lace teddy. It winds elegantly along the dip in her waist and over the curve of her hips. Her legs look super long in her high heels, and I'm already painfully hard just looking at her. Her taut nipples are poking through the thin material, and my mouth is watering in anticipation. "Makes me want to dirty you all up." I spear her with a dark look full of promise. "Take it off, baby. I want to see all of you."

She maintains eye contact as she slowly peels it off her body, kicking it away. Her stance is regal as she stands before me completely bared. I've spent weeks exploring every inch of her beautiful body, but she still steals my breath every time I look at her. "You're stunning, Mrs. Maltese."

"Thank you," she whispers in a breathy voice that sends shivers racing all over my expectant flesh.

Crouching before her, I remove her shoes and set her on her feet. She watches as I undress, her tongue darting out to lick her lips while she presses her thighs together. "Horny, baby?" I purr, pressing her back against the glass shower door. My dick jerks against her stomach, and she emits a delightful whimper that almost has me blowing my load. "Shall I check?" Her legs part automatically to let my hand through. I push one finger inside her, and I'm instantly coated in the evidence of her arousal. "Drenched." I kiss her lips once and pull back. "You're such a good girl, kitten. Always hungry for my cock." Taking her hand, I wrap it around my erection, using her hand to stroke me slowly. I kiss her again before moving aside to turn the shower on.

After testing the water, I pull her in, taking my time washing every gorgeous inch of her.

"Hands on the wall and ass out," I instruct, keeping her under the cascade of water as she obeys. It never fails to ignite my blood when she does what's she told. "Part your cheeks and hold them for me." She obliges without hesitation, and I carefully wash her crack and the edge of her puckered hole before planting a kiss right there. She shivers, and I silently fist pump the air.

I quickly wash myself, and then we get out. After wrapping her in a towel, I dry every inch of her tempting body, blow-dry her hair, and secure it in a messy bun on top of her head. Then I lie her on the bed and rub scented oil all over her body until she's fully relaxed and smiling. "How are you feeling?" I ask.

"Wonderful." She peers at me with a dreamy expression on her face.

I sit on the edge of the bed and cup her tits. "I want you to know you're the first woman to be in this room, apart from the woman I hired to outfit this space."

"I was going to ask, but then I decided I didn't want to know. This pleases me."

I lean down and kiss her. "I was saving it for you." I caress her body, loving how sensitive she is to my touch. "There are a few rules for when we play in here. We'll use a traffic light system. If you are happy to continue, you say green when I ask. If you're unsure or you want me to take it slower, say yellow. If I'm doing something you don't like or you're in pain and it's not the pleasurable kind, you say red."

"I understand."

"Good girl." I press my mouth to her stomach and nuzzle my face against her warm soft skin. "I know spanking is off-limits, for now, and I'm not going to push you too far tonight. We'll go through a list tomorrow, and we can determine if there's anything else you don't want to try. For now, I'm going to tie you up, blindfold you, and fuck your ass on the bench. Any objections?"

She audibly gulps, shaking her head.

"Words, kitten. Use your words."

"No objections."

I eyeball her, inwardly smirking as she frowns. "Sir," I say. "No objections, sir."

"You can't be serious." Disbelief is etched on her face, and it lingers in her tone.

"Deadly."

We face off for a few beats until she slowly nods. My smile is instantaneous. For a girl who thought she didn't have a submissive bone in her body, she is a natural with me in the bedroom.

She squirms a little as my fingers dance over her hip and lower. "Color."

"Green." There's a slight pause. "Sir."

"That's my good girl." Helping her off the bed, I walk her over to the spanking bench and sit her up on the cushiony black padded surface. After removing what I need from the supplies unit, I switch the music to something a little more provocative and walk back to the woman who owns my heart. "Ready, baby?"

"Yes, sir."

"You please me, Mrs. Maltese," I mumble against her lips.

"I aim to please you, sir." She bats her eyelashes, pleased with herself, and I may have created a bit of a diva.

"I'm glad to hear it," I say, showing her the black silk eye mask before I put it on. "Feel okay?"

"Yes." Her breathing has accelerated, and a light flush crawls over her chest. I move her around and lie her down flat on her back, positioning her legs draping over the end of the bench. Then I stretch her arms over her head and cuff them before attaching the cuffs to the hook on the wall behind. "These are velvet-lined cuffs. They won't cut your skin if you move while I'm fucking you."

"Okay."

I pinch her nipple.

"Okay, sir."

Spreading her thighs wide, I lean down and stare at all that glorious, glistening pink flesh.

Mine, mine, mine.

A deep sense of satisfaction glides through my veins, and my cock leaks precum. I'm so turned on, but I need to take my time to get her ready. I've been training her for weeks, using the plug and playing with her hole during sex each day. She is ready for my cock, but I want her soaked and fully relaxed.

Standing, I lean over her and stroke her all over, paying extra special attention to her tits, because I'm fucking obsessed with them, sucking, licking, and pinching the hard peaks. Valentina moans, and the sound is the best aphrodisiac. I hold the tip of my dick several times to resist shooting my load all over her supple body.

Positioning myself between her legs, I stare at her beautiful cunt. Her juices are dripping from her folds, coating the insides of her thighs, and her glistening skin is the most perfect sight. "Color," I ask as I slide two fingers into her heat.

"Green," she pants, squirming on the bench.

"Hold still, baby." I add another digit and roughly pump my fingers in and out of her, reveling in the slick sounds her body makes as I plunge deeper and thrust harder. My lips suction over her clit, and I pull deep, inhaling her addictive scent. Valentina cries out, and I rip my fingers away, not wanting her to come yet. I push her knees back to her chest. "Keep your knees there," I say, drizzling lube all over her exposed crack. I rub it around her hole before pushing the tip of one finger inside. "Relax, just how we've done it before."

Her obedience is immediate and sublime. I toy with her ass for a few minutes, pushing my finger all the way in before I add another, checking in with her to ensure she's comfortable. Using three fingers, I stretch her for my girth, massaging her inner walls, and when I'm satisfied she's ready, I pull them out and bury my tongue in her hole, licking her rim and pushing my tongue a little inside.

The moans coming from Valentina are exquisite, and I'm done holding back.

"Color," I demand in a strangled tone as I pump my dick in my hand.

"Green, sir," she pants. "I'm so turned on, Fiero. Oh god."

"Breathe in and out, kitten, nice and slow, and relax your muscles," I say as I bring my cock to her entrance. "That's it." I push in a little. "Listen to the music." I bury two fingers in her cunt as I push farther into her ass. "Feel everything I'm doing to you. Just focus on the pleasure and empty your mind of everything else." I move my thumb up to rub her clit while I stroke her cunt and drive slowly into her tight hole.

I'm in heaven, and it'll be a miracle if I last long. Her warm tight walls are strangling my cock in a vise grip, and it's like nothing I've ever experienced.

Unfurling her knees from her chest, I drape her legs over my shoulders one at a time, repositioning myself in a way that should be comfortable for her. Her hips tip up a fraction, and I pull her ass down a little more on the bench, the movement driving me in deeper. She gasps. "Does that feel okay?

"I'm good. Sir."

I thrust in inch by inch, watching her face and her body for any signs of discomfort as I fill her up.

"Color, Mrs. Maltese," I say when I'm buried to the hilt in her ass, holding myself still as I check she's comfortable before moving. My cock is throbbing, aching, desperate to move, but I need to know she's okay before I start fucking her.

"Green, sir. Totally green." Her face is flushed, her chest heaving, and her legs are trembling a little, but I see no discomfort. She's fully ready.

"That's my good girl." Heady warmth surges in my body as I begin to move, pulling out slowly and pushing back in again. I play with her clit and her pussy as I pick up my pace until I'm fucking her hard, my body slamming in and out of hers as she cries and whimpers and pleads underneath me. Her pussy is dripping, the tight bundle of nerves at the apex of her thighs swollen and begging for release. I continue pounding into her, and I'm cresting the best high. Nothing has ever felt this good.

A familiar tingle at the base of my spine tells me I'm close, and I couldn't hold back any longer if I tried. "Together, baby," I pant, ramming in and out of her as I add another finger to the two in her cunt and fuck her with my fingers.

She's wailing and screaming my name as I shout my release the same time I pinch her clit, and she falls headfirst into her own climax. We push and move against one another as we ride wave after wave of orgasmic bliss, and my fingers are covered in her essence. I thrust my fingers in my mouth, groaning as her salty-sweet taste explodes on my tongue.

When we're both sated, I pull out slowly, holding her legs up by the backs of her thighs, admiring the way my cum leaks out of her ass and onto the edge of the bench. Gently, I set her legs back down and come around to her head, kissing her lips as I remove the blindfold. "How do you feel?"

"Thoroughly fucking fucked," she croaks.

"Language, Mrs. Maltese." My words are soft, matching the smile I give her. "You did real good, baby. I love you." I plant my lips against hers, kissing her tenderly. "Stay there," I command after I've released her hands. "Don't move."

I head into the bathroom to clean up, and then I wet a warm cloth and come back to clean her up. When I lift her into my arms, her head falls to my shoulder. "Do you want to sleep or play some more?"

She lifts her head, staring into my eyes. "Is that a trick question?"

I bark out a laugh. "I need to hear the words, kitten."

"I can sleep when I'm dead. I want to play, husband. What's next?"

Chapter Thirty-Three
Valentina

"Did you ever find out from Zumo what beef is between your sisters?" I ask Fiero as he drives us to Connecticut on Sunday for the baby shower. I'm nervous, and conversation will distract me.

"They wouldn't say. All we know is it's something to do with a guy."

"Maybe you should talk to them."

"No way. I'm steering well clear of boy drama. They're adults. They can sort it out themselves."

I'm fascinated watching the muscles flex and roll in Fiero's arms as he drives. He's got some serious arm porn going on, and I'm here for it. Thinking of porn has me thinking about the last couple of days and the many different ways Fiero introduced me to his sex room. I didn't think I had a kinky bone in my body, but I'm enjoying being proved wrong. My husband has mad skills in the bedroom, and I'm reaping the rewards. I stretch in my seat, and my limbs ache deliciously.

"What are you thinking about?" Fiero glances at me before he takes the next left.

"How lucky I am to have a husband who is a beast in the bedroom."

"Fuck."

"What?"

Fiero takes my hand and plants it on his crotch. "That's what. I seem to be in a constant state of arousal around you, and I can't exactly show up at a freaking baby shower with a noticeable erection, so please keep the topics non-sex-related."

"I love you so much," I say because it's the totality of what's in my heart.

His smile is full of affection as he casts another glance my way. "Love you too, kitten." He takes my hand and kisses the tips of my fingers. "I can't ever remember being this happy."

"Same." He drives one-handed, keeping his fingers laced in mine.

"Who will be here today?" I ask, nibbling on my lip.

"Pretty much everyone. Elisa's parents and younger siblings have flown in from Vegas, Gia's family will be here, along with all the other New York dons, their wives and kids."

I want to ask about *him*, but I can't single him out without raising suspicion. "What about Louis Pagano?" I inquire instead.

Fiero squeezes my hand. "He won't be here. Joshua and Caleb aren't overly close with Pagano, Volpe, or Agessi though they did invite Dominic Mantegna from The Outfit. I'm not sure if he'll be here though."

"Okay." I rub my vacant ring finger. "I know why we have to keep our marriage a secret, but I hate not being able to shout about it from the rooftops today. Especially surrounded by so many happy couples and families."

"It won't be too much longer." He takes a sharp right that brings us into Glencoe town center. "If my meeting with the cartel goes to plan on Tuesday, I should be able to wrap this up fast. A few of Ferraro's men are singing like canaries, but most don't know the specifics. I'm still piecing the last few elements together, but it shouldn't be too long before I have enough evidence of Dominic's betrayal to go to the board."

"Great." My words sound hollow to my own ears. I chew on the inside of my mouth as my skin crawls. I'm hoping Fiero gets his evidence without anything linking to me because I don't want to tell him. I know it's not wise to start a marriage with such a big secret, but I can't tell him. It could be the very thing that tips him over the edge and makes him realize how unworthy I am.

Guilt threatens to drown me, and I stare out the window at the gorgeous town as we drive toward the property the Accardi twins purchased shortly before their double wedding to build new homes for their growing families.

"We're here," Fiero announces, slowing to a stop in front of tall, thick solid wooden gates. All around the vast property are imposing high gray stone walls with a row of barbed wire running around the top. Various cameras are visible from the road, spaced at regular intervals all around the wall, as far as my eyes can see. Two men stand outside the gates, and the one with the clipboard approaches. Fiero lowers his window to talk to the man. He ticks our names off his checklist before asking Fiero to press his thumbprint into a digital scanner. When all is good, the gates open, allowing us entry.

Fiero whistles under his breath as we drive along a winding driveway, past empty field after empty field, with no house in sight. "This place is something else."

"They clearly take security very seriously."

"We all have to." Fiero clasps my hand in his, looking over at me. "Are you okay? Is something troubling you?"

"I'm just nervous. It's a lot of people to meet."

"I won't leave your side."

"Don't be ridiculous. You can't stay glued to my side, and I'm not that needy. I'll be okay. I'm well used to situations like this."

"These are my people, and they're good people. They'll welcome you warmly, and you've already met some of them. Zumo and my sisters will be here, and you know Natalia and Caleb, Massimo and Cat, and Rico will be here with his family too."

"Why do they think I'm here?"

"I've told them Cesco was a threat to you, so I moved you to my house as a protective measure. Excepting the people I mentioned, most don't know we're together."

I bark out a laugh, staring at him incredulously. "And you think you can stick to my side like glue and someone won't notice the way we look at one another?"

"I don't give a shit if anyone figures it out. It's all going to come out soon anyway."

I turn around in my seat, the leather squelching with the movement, as Fiero draws up to another set of wooden gates. Like out front, there is another gray stone wall ringing the inner circle of the property with more barbed wire and cameras on top. The twins are not messing around. I wait until Fiero has pressed his thumb to the keypad and the gates have opened to let us through before I reply. "You need to give a shit. I won't have anything happening to you. Not after you've gone to all this trouble to be careful. We need to stay away from one another, as much as possible, so we don't set tongues wagging."

"No can do, my love. I can't share the same air and not be close to you."

"We'll just stay for a couple of hours, mingle and chat, and then leave. You can manage two hours."

"I don't think I can." He pouts as he drives through the gates. Two imposing properties loom in the near distance, one on either side of the road. The styles of both houses are different, confirming the couples built homes suited to their own needs and tastes.

"You're ridiculous, but I adore you."

My husband grins at me like a loon as we drive past a large playground still under construction. My siblings would have loved a playground like that in our backyard growing up.

"Not as much as I adore you. You're my everything, kitten. My entire world starts and ends with you."

I stretch over the console and kiss his cheek. "I feel the same."

Fiero parks the car alongside a row of other expensive cars in a specified outdoor parking lot, extending to the left and right, in between the driveway a few feet from both houses. He gets out and opens my door, helping me outside before grabbing our gifts from the trunk of his Aston Martin. Thankfully, Elisa and Gia had an online gift list, and Fiero purchased their gifts, ensuring they were delivered gift-wrapped. Neither couple did a gender reveal, which I personally love.

"Let's go," Fiero says, holding both gift bags in one hand and taking my hand with the other.

I instantly wrench my hand back. "We can't."

He snatches my hand again. "The fuck we can't. I can hold your hand as a friend, kitten."

"You can't call me that either."

"I should have used a driver," he mumbles. "I'll need a beer or ten to survive today."

I can't help giggling because he's so dramatic and over the top at times.

A wide gray stone path leads from each parking lot to the relevant house, bordered by an abundance of shrubs, leading to a circular paved area with a water feature in the middle. On either side of the path are colorful flowered manicured lawns behind little stone walls.

The house on the right is a stunning, large, contemporary ranch-style bungalow. It's mostly finished though there is scaffolding on one side of the building. It's magnificent with various peaked roofs, large gray-framed windows, and several black wrought-iron balconies that extend off the bedrooms, I'm guessing.

The house on the left is a modern warehouse style with two stories built in different aspects. Industrial-type pillars prop the property up, painted a pristine white. The roofs are flat, and there is a ton of glass everywhere. Even the large upper-level balcony is made of glass. It's no less stunning than its neighbor though both are very different houses. I also spy scaffolding around the corner of this house too, confirming neither is fully finished yet but obviously habitable. I'm guessing both couples wanted to be moved in before their babies arrive.

Fiero steers me to a gray path that intersects both houses, walking in the direction of the noise. Childish shrieks and giggles mix with the rumbling of adult conversation and laughter. Contemporary music plays in the background, barely audible over the noise of such a large crowd. I grip Fiero's hand tighter, grateful for his comforting warmth. I'm not usually nervous at parties, but these are his friends, and I want them to like me.

"Wow," I whisper when we reach the large combined garden at the rear where the baby shower is being hosted. People congregate on the expansive gray marble patio, standing and talking with drinks in hand or sitting on one of the copious comfy couches or at the outdoor dining tables. Two large bounce houses are nestled on the new lawn. A rectangular marquee on one side shows a catering team busy at work. Long tables are stretched from one side of the marquee to the other with various plates of food being arranged. To one side of the marquee is an ice-cream stand and to the other a candy station. Kids and adults alike are lined up in front of both areas.

Waiters move among guests, offering canapes and flutes of champagne or beers. In the center of the patio area is a large circular wicker couch with a matching coffee table. Copious balloons line the back of the couch, swaying softly in the light breeze. The two couples are there, laughing and chatting with a few friends. A table on the left holds an enormous array of wrapped gifts, and on the other side of the couch is a small table with a cupcake stand. Warmth mushrooms in my chest when I realize they are the cupcakes I baked for today.

"Your friends know how to throw a baby shower," I murmur.

"That they do." Fiero looks equally impressed.

"There you are." Massimo and Cat materialize in front of us. Cat pulls me into a hug before her husband does the same while she greets Fiero.

Massimo glances at our linked fingers. "I thought you were here as friends," he murmurs in a quiet tone.

I eyeball my husband in a silent "see." As much as I hate to pull my hand from his, I do. I won't have Fiero jeopardizing himself, Caleb, or Massimo when we've come this far.

"Go greet the Accardis," Cat suggests. "And then I'll take Valentina with me. I'll introduce you to the other women," she says, smiling.

"Sounds like a plan."

Chapter Thirty-Four
Valentina

F iero grumbles as we walk side by side, without touching, toward the center couch, and I fight to contain a smile. I love that my husband gets grouchy because he can't hold my hand. He's a big ole softy underneath that hard lethal exterior, and I'm so happy I listened to my heart and married him. I haven't regretted it for a second.

I move a little closer, hooking my pinky around his for a brief moment. "We'll make up for it later. You can put your hands all over me all night," I promise.

"Not helping," he growls. "What did I say in the car?"

"You're acting like a big grump. It's only a couple of hours. Lighten up."

"It'll feel like eternity," he mumbles.

Soooo dramatic. I giggle and my heart is fit to burst with how much I love this man.

"Maltese." Caleb hops up as the men and women they were talking to head toward the candy station. Don Accardi walks toward us. "Good of you to come." He slaps Fiero on the back, noting his grumpy form and grinning wider.

"Hi, Valentina. Nice to see you again."

"What happened to cutie pie?" Fiero arches a brow, and I shoot daggers at him.

The two gorgeous heavily pregnant women sitting on the couch look over with curious expressions on their face.

"I'm on my best behavior," Caleb says, winking at me. "But you know I love a challenge." Sliding his arm around my waist, he pulls me away from Fiero and over to the two mothers-to-be. Pain tries to strangle my heart as I peruse their swollen bellies when they both stand to greet me, but I shove it away.

"Lili, this is Valentina. She's staying with Fiero right now."

Elisa beams at me. "You're the baker," she says. "Thank you so much for the goodies you gave Caleb for me. They were the best thing I've ever put in my mouth."

"Don't lie, baby." Caleb bundles his wife in his arms. "Second best," he fake whispers in her ear.

Elisa giggles while Joshua rolls his eyes.

Caleb's twin rises to his feet, and though he's not quite as tall as Fiero or his brother, he still towers over me in my flat sandals. "It's nice to meet you, Valentina."

He shakes my hand, and I can't stop the blush that heats my cheeks. Each twin is drop-dead gorgeous but seeing them together is something else entirely. I'm obsessed with my husband, but I'd have to be dead not to react to the Accardi dons when confronted by so much magnetic masculinity. "Likewise," I croak, cringing a little when Fiero yanks my hand out of Joshua's.

Caleb cracks up laughing as Fiero glowers at me, and I glower right back. He can't pull his usual possessive maneuvers here today. He'll give the game away in no time if he doesn't cut it out.

We stare at one another, conducting a silent conversation, neither of us backing down.

A throat clearing finally breaks our stare off. "Thanks for

sending over all these cupcakes for today," Gia says, shooting me a knowing smile. "It was a really sweet, thoughtful gesture."

My god, what must she think of me staring at her husband like I've never seen a hot made man before? I've seen their wedding photos, they were splashed all over *The New York Times,* and while the pictures are incredible, they don't do her beauty justice. Same for Elisa. Both women are completely stunning, glowing, and radiating happiness.

"You're welcome. I wanted to contribute to today, and I've been going out of my mind with boredom stuck at Fiero's house."

"I'll say," Gia adds as Fiero bids her hello.

"You both are glowing," he says, handing the gifts to Joshua before kissing Elisa on the cheek. "Pregnancy obviously suits you."

"We're lucky it's been smooth sailing for both of us," Gia says.

"And doing this with my best friend has been amazing," Elisa adds.

"That would make it extra special," I agree.

"Shoo." Gia waves her hands in Joshua's face when he returns after depositing our gifts on the table. "We want to talk to Valentina, and this is strictly a ladies-only convo." It's comical watching a heavily pregnant woman with her hands on her hips, glaring at all the men until they walk away.

Catarina comes up behind me, smiling. "I got you a drink," she says, handing me a glass of champagne.

"Thanks." I barely resist the urge to knock it back as I watch Gia and Elisa get settled on the couch.

"Come join us." Elisa pats the seat beside her, and I sit down while Cat takes the seat beside Gia.

Gia leans across Elisa, her eyes glimmering brightly. "Spill the tea, girl. What's going on with you and Fiero?"

I'm inwardly cringing again. I hate lying to these women, but it's a necessity. "We're just friends. He helped me out of a bad situation, and he's protecting me until things have settled down in Miami."

Elisa places her hand on mine, her earnest eyes shining with unshed tears. "Caleb told me a little. I'm so sorry you had to endure that, but I'm glad you are safe now. You should speak to my mom. She had a similar experience, and she might be able to help. She's around somewhere."

"I'm sorry for your pain too," Gia adds, "but you can't throw me off the scent. If I wasn't already pregnant, I would be after the intensity of that stare down. Girl, I know chemistry when I see it, and you two are on fire!"

Cat smiles sympathetically at me.

"I'd have to be blind not to be attracted to him." It's pathetic, but it's all I've got.

"He's superhot for an older dude," Elisa whispers, looking around to ensure her husband isn't around, I'm guessing. "Don't tell Caleb I said that. He's got a wicked jealous streak."

Cat breaks out laughing. "They all do. Even after all the years we've been together, Massimo still goes crazy if he thinks any other man is looking at me."

"I love it when Joshua goes all crazy jealous possessive," Gia admits. "It really turns me on."

"Oh god, don't talk about sex." Elisa visibly presses her legs together. "I thought at this stage the insane sex hormones were supposed to be dormant, but I'm still jumping Caleb every chance I get." She runs her hands over her neat baby bump. "Not literally, obvs. I can't even tie the laces on my sneakers anymore."

"That's called being hot for your new husband, Elisa," Cat says, standing and smiling. "Embrace it and have all the sex now because it'll become challenging finding time with a newborn." She tilts her head to the side. "I'm going to borrow Valentina. I want to introduce her around, and I see the other Maltese siblings have just arrived." I glance behind her, spotting Zumo, Tullia, and Sofia making their way over here. Fiero has already warned his family to keep quiet today.

I kiss and hug Fiero's brother and sisters, chatting for a few minutes before leaving them with the ladies of the moment. Cat leads me across the garden toward a table, tucked into a corner, where a few women are seated. I surreptitiously look around, pressing a hand over the tightness in my chest, relaxing when I don't spot *him*. Maybe he isn't coming after all.

My eyes meet Fiero's, and his gaze holds a question. I force a smile on my face and subtly shake my head, silently conveying I don't need rescuing. He's talking with Rico who lifts a hand and waves at me. I return the gesture, smiling at the older man. He's a nice guy, but I haven't had much opportunity to get to know him because Fiero is also keeping him in the dark to protect him.

I feel Fiero's heated gaze following me as he walks toward his siblings, and I head in the opposite direction.

"Thanks for that," I say to Catarina. "I hate lying, and I didn't know what to say."

"I knew Gia would sniff you out. She has sharp instincts."

I don't mention that Caleb has told Elisa and Elisa most likely already told her best friend because Cat doesn't know about Caleb's involvement.

God, this is a mess. Knots twist in my gut. I hate lying to everyone. Especially when they are all so nice.

Natalia rises from her seat to greet me, pulling me into a hug. "It's so good to see you again, Valentina. Thanks for coming."

"I'm delighted to have been invited," I say, smiling at the three other women.

"I'm Sierra," the gorgeous blonde says, offering me her hand. "I'm married to Ben."

"Nice to meet you."

"This is my sister Serena. She's married to Alesso. He's the new Vegas Don." Sierra smiles at the beautiful woman beside her, and though Serena's hair is dark with reddish tints, she strongly resembles her younger sister.

"Pleasure," I say, shaking Serena's hand.

"I'm Frankie. Gia's mom," the woman sitting on the other side of Natalia says. "You're very welcome, Valentina, and thank you for the cupcakes." Her eyes lower to a plate of cakes on the table. "You're giving Natalia a run for her money in the baking stakes."

"I tried your apple cake recipe," I tell Natalia as I claim the empty seat beside Serena. Cat sits on the other side of me, waving a waiter over. "It was a bit soggy in the middle, so I clearly did something wrong."

"You might have used too much baking powder or possibly opened the stove door before it was ready. Come over to my house sometime, and we can make it together."

"I'd like that." I really like Natalia. In some ways, she reminds me of my mom. For the first time in a long time, a pang of longing attacks me. I used to have a great relationship with my mom until everything turned to shit. I miss having her in my life.

The waiter arrives, handing us all a flute, and I dismiss my thoughts.

"A toast," Natalia says, and we all raise our glasses. "To Joshua and Gia, Caleb and Elisa, and their babies. Wishing them good health and good fortune and every happiness for the future."

We all clink to that. The liquid is refreshing gliding down my throat, and I settle back in my chair, trying to relax.

"So, Valentina. Tell us what it's like living with the eternal bachelor," Frankie says, her eyes twinkling mischievously. "Is it true he has a sex room in his house?"

I almost choke on my champagne.

Cat rubs my back, fighting a laugh.

"I'm guessing that's a yes." Sierra grins.

"Stop teasing her," Natalia chastises her sister-in-law and her best friend.

"You've met my husband," Frankie says. "Rico is Fiero's *consigliere*, but he tells me next to nothing about him. He's fiercely loyal, but he did let something slip one time, and I've been trying to get confirmation. Have you seen it? What's it like?"

"Hell. I need more champagne for this conversation," I joke.

Laughter filters around the table.

"More importantly"—Sierra lowers her voice conspiratorially, leaning into the table—"has he taken you in there for playtime?"

"Sierra!" Serena elbows her sister. "That's private."

"They're just friends." Cat squeezes my hand under the table.

"Puh-lease," Frankie scoffs. "You know Fiero as well as I do, Cat, and you know damn well there's no way he'd ever be able to resist her." Her warm smile is reassuring, but it does nothing to settle my frayed nerves. "You're stunning, Valentina. I bet Fiero is walking around with a constant hard-on having you living in his house."

"Want to take a walk with me?" Serena asks as I gulp down the remains of my second glass of champagne. I really should eat something.

"I'd love that." I grasp the lifeline she's extending.

"I'll take you on a tour of Elisa and Caleb's new house. They won't mind."

I half expect Cat to come with us, but she just subtly nods as I leave the table with Serena Salerno.

We duck around the cloth-covered steel fencing hiding both houses from the area where the party is taking place. "They sealed this off as construction is still ongoing in the gardens and on parts of both houses," Serena explains as we enter the rear of Caleb and Elisa's magnificent bungalow. The pool has been built, but only half the walls have been tiled, and the area around it is muddy and undeveloped.

We chat casually as Serena shows me around the house, and she has a way of really making people feel at ease. Maybe it's her soft, soothing voice or her calm, unruffled manner, but she's very easy to talk to.

After we've inspected every furnished room, she leads me back to the large, homey kitchen, grabbing a bottle of wine and two glasses before we move out to the only paved area of the garden and sit on a bench. I hold out the glasses while she pours before setting the wine bottle down on the floor.

"I wanted to talk to you privately, but this isn't an ambush, I swear," she adds, seeing the instant wariness on my face. "My first husband was an abusive monster who mistreated me for years. He died a violent death, like your husband, and I'll never forget the relief I felt knowing he was gone and couldn't hurt me or my kids anymore."

"He hurt your children?" Horror instantly washes over my face.

"He was never physically abusive with Elisa or Romeo. The damage was more psychological. Romeo was young enough not to remember most of it, but Elisa remembers. She saw more than any young girl should." She stares off into space. "Thankfully, she's strong, like you." She pats my hand. "And she's in a great place now. Happy with the man she's loved since she was a little girl. I don't have to worry about her anymore."

"They make a lovely couple." I take a sip of my wine.

"Caleb treats her like a queen, and he's a good man. Like my Alesso." Her entire face lights up. "I just wanted to say two things. I don't know if anything is going on with Fiero, and I don't need to know. It's none of my business." She grasps my hand. "I just wanted you to know you're totally safe with him. He's a good man, and there is nobody better to protect you."

"I know." A genuine smile ghosts over my lips. "I have never been treated better or felt more safe."

"That's good." She takes a drink of her wine, and so do I, and we don't talk for a few minutes, both of us contemplative, but the silence isn't awkward. After a few minutes, she clears her throat. "I was in a very bad way after my husband died. Broken. Lost. Struggling to cope and be there for my children." Her eyes drill into mine. "I don't know your specific circumstances. All Sierra said was your husband was a monster and you've endured horrific things. Most all of us have, unfortunately, suffered at the hands of various made men."

"I hope in time everyone will abide by The Commission's new policies and rulings so it becomes a thing of the past."

"A lot of good has been done, but there will always be a few bad eggs. The older generation is old-school, and a lot of them are resistant of the new ways, but they are dying out, and the younger generation is more progressive and respectful."

"True." I knock back more wine.

"Alesso saved me in so many ways. After Alfonso, I had all but given up on life, and I definitely never expected love. I was so broken and thought there was no way I could ever be happy with *any* man, but I was glad to be proven wrong." She squeezes my hand. "I strongly encourage you to go to therapy, Valentina. It helped me a lot, and I hope you meet someone as wonderful as Alesso and that your second marriage is as happy as mine."

Tears glisten in my eyes.

"I thought it might give you hope to know my story. To know this isn't the end. It's a new beginning, and I encourage you to grasp it with both hands because you deserve to be happy."

Chapter Thirty-Five
Valentina

When we return to the table, all the food has been served and Fiero is sitting in my seat at the women's table being put through his paces. "You were gone a long time. Are you okay?" he asks, reaching out to grab me onto his lap.

I fix him with a pointed look, and he scowls, sighing as he climbs off the chair to let me sit down. "I'm fine. Serena gave me a tour of Caleb and Elisa's house. It's fabulous."

"I got you some food." He moves a heaped plate in front of me. Picking up a fork, he places it in my hand. "Eat before you have any more champagne."

I barely resist the urge to tell him to fuck off. I count to ten in my head and plaster a sickly-sweet smile on my face. "Thanks for the food. Now run along. This is strictly a female zone, and you don't have the right body parts."

The ladies chuckle while Fiero looks like he wants to put me over his knee and spank the shit out of me.

"You'll pay for that later," he growls in my ear before stomping off.

"Yeah." Frankie grins wide. "You've definitely been enjoying the perks of his sex room."

"What's a sex room?" a young girl with dark-blonde hair and vibrant green eyes asks. I hadn't spotted her around the table when we returned. She's a teenager, but it's hard to pin an age on her because all the young girls look so much older these days.

"Jesus, Frankie. Can you watch what you say around impressionable ears, please?" Sierra glares at the woman across the table.

"Shit, sorry. I forgot Raven had joined us."

"We'll talk about this later, honey." Sierra brushes her daughter's bangs out of her eyes just as they light up at something over her mother's shoulder.

"Marco's here!" she screeches. "Bye!" She's up and off, running on long legs toward a tall teenager with sandy-brown hair.

"Someone, help me," Sierra laments, face-planting on the table.

Serena rubs her sister's back. "Trust me, I get it."

Sierra lifts her head, watching with troubled eyes as her daughter sidles up to the newcomer, beaming up at him like he put the stars in the sky. It's so stinking cute. "At least there was a decent age gap between Caleb and Elisa, and you knew nothing would happen when she was a young teen." Sierra rubs her temples. "There is only two years between Raven and Marco, and she is bossy and determined in a way Elisa wasn't."

"Wonder where she gets that from," Nat muses, her lips twitching as she pops a piece of chicken in her mouth.

"Your brother!" Sierra stabs her finger in Natalia's direction.

"Oh, I don't know about that." Serena smiles. "You were quite the bossy brat when you were her age, and I remember you crushing on someone older too and being quite determined."

"You don't have to worry about Marco, Sierra," Frankie says, looking over her shoulder at the two teenagers. "My youngest is way too shy and far too much into his video games to have any real interest in girls."

"He likes Raven though," Nat says, also watching the teenagers. "I've seen how they are with one another, and let's not forget raging teenage hormones. I would keep an eye on it."

"At least she's young and innocent." Frankie plucks a wedge from her plate and dunks it in chili sauce. "I still have nightmares about Sorella and Antonio. No mother should have to see that." A visible shudder washes over her.

I'm curious but not enough to pry into private matters.

Nat's daughter pulls her away to tend to someone with a grazed knee, and I pick at the food on my plate while we talk about everything and anything.

This is all so normal, and it's nice. These women are super nice, instantly welcoming me and including me in the conversation. Serena went out of her way to offer me some guidance and comfort, and I've never even met her. Catarina has been looking out for me all afternoon like a protective big sister. I've never had this before, and now I'm imagining regular phone calls, cozy lunches, and boozy girls' nights out, and warmth floods my chest.

"Look who I found," Nat says, reappearing at the table holding a dark-haired little boy in her arms. He can't be any more than two, if that. A chorus of oohs and aahs ring out as everyone gazes adoringly at the little guy. He's a cutie, for sure, chomping on a teething ring and staring shyly at all of us. Two bright red spots darken his cheeks, and I feel for him. It's hard watching them teething and not being able to do much to ease their pain. I've seen my youngest siblings go through this phase.

As if he felt me watching him, he looks up, and the instant I see his eyes, I know who he is. My heart beats wildly against my chest wall, blood rushes to my head, and alarm bells ring in my ears. I grip the side of my chair as he stares at me, awash with inner pain and struggling to hold myself together.

"This is Elio." Nat kisses the side of his head. "He's Cristian's son."

"The poor baby has been through so much," Cat says discreetly in my ear. "He lost both parents before he was one, but he's lucky Cristian is his father now and not his bio dad."

"Bio dad?" I ask in a bit of a haze, not sure why I'm seeking confirmation when I already know.

Cat leans right into my ear. "Cruz DiPietro was the previous Vegas don who died last year. He was Cristian's older brother. Cristian stepped up to adopt Elio when he was orphaned, but the child is way better off with his uncle. Cristian is one of the good guys; whereas, his older brother was a monster."

I know. I lower my head, staring at my lap.

"Massimo and Fiero loathed Cruz," she continues explaining. "They were friends for years until he betrayed Massimo during senior year of high school. I have never seen them hate anyone as much as that man, but it was justified. The things he did warranted it."

My stomach pitches, the champagne sloshing uncomfortably in my gut.

"Hello, we haven't met," a man with a deep masculine voice says, and I hear the similarity in his accent.

Wiping my clammy palms along the side of my dress, I try to fight the mounting panic attack. It's a miracle I can force my head to lift, but I do. I zone out on autopilot, retreating to that place in my head I thought was lost to me. My mask comes down, and I shove my anxiety aside to handle later. A fake smile shrouds my face. "Hi. I'm Valentina."

Out of the corner of my eye, I see Catarina looking at me with a frown.

"I'm Cristian DiPietro. Good to meet you." He extends his arm over the table, smiling at me, and all I can think is *he looks so much like him.* He's possibly a little taller and slightly less broad in the shoulders, but his piercing green eyes are almost identical as is the shade of his hair though he wears it differently. My hand is shaking as I place it in his. His large warm palm overwhelms mine, and I lose the tentative hold on my emotions the same time I lower my shields.

Cristian's face is gone, replaced with his brother's, and I'm shaking all over. Sweat beads on my brow and rolls down my spine. The surroundings are gone, faded away like they don't exist. There is only *him*, leering down at me, removing his belt, and cracking it in his hand.

My stomach twists, and I'm stumbling away blindly, off to the side, tripping over something, and falling to my knees. I throw up into a shrub. All I hear is the ringing in my ears. All I feel is the pounding in my head and the pain in my heart. My lungs seize, and I'm struggling to breathe, gasping and sobbing as an ice-cold chill tiptoes all over my body.

"I've got her," someone says, the words barely audible to my ears. Sounds of a baby crying are muted. "What the fuck did you do?" someone with an angry voice asks.

I blink as my surroundings slowly come back into focus.

"Cristian didn't do anything, Fiero," Sierra says.

"She's gone into shock, Fiero," Cat whispers. "I'm worried about her. You should take her away from prying eyes. I'll ask Nat to follow you so she can check her out."

I'm jostled against a warm chest as we move. Fiero's scent wraps around me like a blanket, and I bury my head in his shirt, clinging to the remaining threads of my sanity. Talking has ceased around us, and I just know everyone is looking at how pathetic I am.

The tears come unbidden. Silent and plentiful, soaking Fiero's shirt before we've even gotten to the car. I'm shaking, trembling, terrified, and broken all over again.

Fiero places me in the passenger seat of his car with my legs out the side, my feet resting on the gray stone of the parking lot. He hands me a bottle of water. "Use that to rinse out your mouth."

I swish water around my mouth and spit it on the ground, repeating it a few times until the gross taste is subdued. "Chew this." He hands me a piece of gum as he crouches in front of me.

I take it and chew it robotically, staring at him with tears rolling down my face.

"What's wrong, kitten?" He takes my hands, rubbing some warmth into my chilly skin. "What happened back there?"

I can't speak. I'm drained, and I don't have the energy to form words.

"It's okay." He kisses my brow. "I'll take you home."

Natalia arrives then with her medical bag, conducting a few quick checks and talking to me in a soft voice. I don't know what she asks or if I even respond. I hear her talking to Fiero in a hushed voice while I stare numbly at my folded hands in my lap, trying to ignore the pain eviscerating me on the inside.

Nat kisses my head and offers words of assurance before she leaves.

Fiero hugs me before settling me properly in the car, securing my seat belt, and placing a blanket over my legs. I pull it up, tucking it around me as he climbs behind the wheel and starts the car.

I pretend to sleep as he drives us back to Long Island, and it's late when we arrive.

Fiero carries me from the car, gently strips me, and showers me before drying my hair, brushing my teeth, and forcing me onto the toilet. Then he dresses me in a silk nightie and tucks me under the covers. "I'm losing my mind here, Valentina," he softly says, sitting on the edge of the bed. "Do I need to call a doctor?"

I shake my head. "No," I whisper, curling into a ball. "No doctor."

"Then tell me. What is going on?"

"I'll tell you tomorrow," I lie. "Just let me sleep."

He holds my face in his hands, stabbing me with a worried look. "I love you. Nothing you could tell me would ever change my mind. You know that, right?"

I nod without conscious thought.

A frustrated sigh cleaves from his chest. "Get some sleep." He kisses my lips. "I'll be up shortly."

"Fiero," I call after him. "I love you too."

It isn't too long before he's climbing into bed and spooning me from behind. He doesn't fall sleep for ages, and I suspect he knows I'm not asleep either, but eventually, his breathing slows down and his arms loosen around me. Silent tears pour down my face as I carefully extract myself from the bed without waking him.

Pain settles on my chest like a dead weight as I get dressed in yoga pants, a long-sleeved top, my sneakers, and a black jacket. Snatching a duffel bag from the closet, I throw my purse, cash, and some clothes inside.

I don't want to leave Fiero, but I can't tell him this. I hoped this secret would remain buried, but I ruined everything today. Cat's words have been on a loop in my brain since earlier. Fiero thinks there is nothing I can say that'll make him change his mind about me, *us*, but he's wrong. This will do it, and I'd rather run away than watch as that realization smashes my heart into smithereens. I don't know where I'll go, but I'll figure that out once I get away from here.

Fiero deserves better than me, and I'm doing him a favor leaving now. Hopefully, he'll see that in time.

"I'm so sorry," I whisper as I stand at the edge of the bed, taking one last look at the man who has quickly become my everything. "I love you." I blow him a kiss and creep out of the room before I break down.

Padlocking my emotions as best I can, I sneak out of the house and dart into the woods, staying close to the trees and trying to stay hidden. I don't know how many men Fiero has keeping watch at night, but I'm hoping I'll have enough time to get away before they can rouse their boss.

Racing out of the trees, closest to the dock, I push my legs as fast as they will go, running across the grass and onto the wooden walkway. Panels creak underneath my pounding feet, and adrenaline courses through my veins as I sprint toward the two crafts moored at the end. Loosening the rope from the cleat on the bigger vessel, I toss it onto the deck before jumping on board, dropping my bag, and moving to the helm.

My fingers are trembling as I punch the code into the touchpad on the console, panicking when nothing happens. Fiero explained there is no key with this model, only a code, but it's not fucking working, and I'm close to hyperventilating. None of Fiero's men has approached me, which can only mean one thing.

"Come on," I snap, punching the code over and over, crying out of sheer frustration when the boat doesn't start.

My breath hitches when the boat sways as something heavy lands on board. All the fine hairs lift on the back of my neck, and I know he's here. Leaning over the console, I give into the pain and release a flurry of tears. I can't even do this right. Wracking sobs burst from the very depths of my soul as I realize the inevitable.

Fiero says nothing at first as he straightens me up and pulls me into his arms. His large palm rubs up and down my back as I sob and hiccup and fall apart again. "I changed the code," he calmly explains, continuing to soothe me with his touch. "After our excursion because I suspected you might run, but I thought we were beyond that now." Pain flares in his eyes as he tips my head up. "I hoped you wouldn't run from me now, but you scared me earlier. I woke when some instinct forced my eyes to open.

When I found you gone, I just knew, and then Dino called me." His thumbs brush the tears from under my eyes. "You're *my wife*, Valentina. If you hurt, I hurt."

"I'm sorry." My voice is scratchy, my throat raw from too much crying. "You're going to wish I wasn't."

He shakes his head, peering deep into my eyes. "Never."

"You don't know. You can't say that." More sobs burst from my chest. "It hurts, Fiero." I clutch my sore chest. "It hurts, and I don't want you to know this pain."

"I'm already in pain, my love. Seeing you like this is killing me." He kisses me softly. "Running away is not the answer." He hugs me close. "We're a team, kitten. We don't run from our problems. We tackle them head-on."

"I'm scared to tell you this."

"I'm scared to hear it, but you need to tell me because imagining what it might be is probably worse." He eases back, taking my hand and squeezing it. "Nothing you say will take me from you. *Nothing*, Valentina. I am going nowhere." He thumps his free hand over his chest. "You own me, body, heart, and soul. I couldn't live without you now even if I tried." His eyes glimmer with unshed tears. "You're my person, and it's going to be okay. Whatever it is, we'll handle it together. You won't lose me. I promise." His eyes radiate with resolve and blatant honesty, and something settles inside me. "I already know this is about Cruz, and I have theories, but I'd rather hear the truth from you."

Chapter Thirty-Six
Fiero

My wife is shaking and shivering all over as I carry her back to the house, wearing only sweats and sneakers. I went into full panic mode when I woke to an empty bed, but I knew she couldn't have gotten far.

Knots twist in my gut at the thought of what she has to tell me. I'm not going to like it. My calls with Cristian and Cat confirmed my suspicions, but they are as in the dark as me. Seeing Cristian triggered Valentina, and that isn't anything good.

There was talk of Cruz traveling regularly to Miami because of a woman, but I didn't pay much heed to it at the time. None of us did because it was his usual MO. Which is why I never considered that woman could be Valentina, but it's looking like it probably was. Although Cruz was married, he had women stashed everywhere. He was a serial cheater. Apparently, his wife was aware, and it's not like she was faithful either.

The thought of that bastard Cruz putting his hands anywhere near Valentina sends me into a murderous rage. But it's nothing on the dark anger coursing through my veins at the thought of him hurting my kitten. It's almost more than I can bear. But this isn't about me. I need to bury my feelings and put my needs aside to be here for Valentina.

What I feel doesn't matter. She's the one who went through it, and it's my job as her husband to understand, support, and help her overcome this.

Dino opens the front door for me, looking at Valentina with concerned eyes. I nod my thanks as I step into our house, and he pulls the door shut behind us.

I walk into the living room and set my kitten down on the couch, removing her jacket and sneakers and covering her in a blanket before propping her up with a bunch of cushions. "Don't move. I'll be back."

I snag a clean top from the basket in the laundry room, slipping it over my head as I make us some hot chocolate. If she hadn't drank so much earlier, I'd make her a hot whiskey for the shock, but I'm not sure her system could handle it.

Valentina is sitting up, with her back against the arm of the couch, wrapped under the blanket, looking pale and tired when I return. "Drink this." I hand her a mug of hot chocolatey goodness. "And tell me in your own time. There is no rush." I sit at the other end of the couch, kicking off my sneakers and lifting my bare feet to the leather. I want to pull her into my lap and hold her while she unburdens herself, but I'm sensing she needs a little space, and I don't want to crowd her.

She sips her drink in silence for a few minutes before repositioning the cushions around her as she sits cross-legged. "This is good, thank you."

I squeeze her knee over the blanket as I drink my drink, trying to brace myself for this.

"I love you," she whispers with fresh tears in her eyes. "I love you so much, and I'm so sorry."

"I know, baby, and it's okay."

"I just didn't know how I could tell you. I've wanted to, but

I'm so scared you'll look at me differently. It seemed less painful to live without you than to be rejected and pushed away."

I open my mouth to protest, but she shakes her head.

"I know you aren't going to do that. I believe you, but it's hard not to feel unworthy of you, Fiero. You deserve someone better than this broken shell of a woman." She points at herself with a look of disgust that kills me.

I finish my drink and reach for her, lifting her onto my lap. Screw it. I need to have her close. Her hands grip the mug as she finishes her drink. "I love you to the ends of the Earth, Valentina. The things done to you do not diminish your worth, and you're one of the strongest people I know. You're a survivor, baby, and while it might take time to fully heal the broken parts, you are not a shell." I caress her soft skin, tucking her hair behind her ears. "You have been through a lot, and everything has changed very quickly. Anyone would struggle to cope, but you've been amazing." I press a kiss to her temple. "You're my hero, kitten, and I'm here for you now. Whatever you need to heal is yours, and I'll be with you every step of the way."

"I'm so glad we found each other," she says, setting her empty mug down. She wraps her arms around me in a tight hug. I inhale her scent and absorb the feel of her in my arms, and I know we're going to be okay.

She eases back, remaining in my lap as she wipes her tears away. Her stare is glazed, her voice lacking her usual seductive warmth when she begins talking. "I first met Cruz at a party at our house when he arrived as a guest of Vitto's. I saw him watching me. I knew he wanted me, like I knew he was more powerful than Dom, which meant at some point he'd have me. He came every week after that, and it was always the same. Intense scrutiny. Dark eyes that undressed me without shame."

I swallow back bile, holding her closer.

"The night Dom lost a card game to him, I was calm. I

knew what was coming, and I stupidly thought it would be okay." Anger dances in her gaze. She doesn't look at me as she says, "I'm embarrassed to admit this, but you need to hear it all."

I run my hand up and down her arm and kiss her cheek.

"He was good-looking. Way hotter and younger than most of the creeps Dom traded me to, and I thought at least this might not be so bad. I might enjoy it. He looks like the kind of man that might make me come."

I'm dying inside listening to this, but I hide the emotions, continuing to rub her arm and coax her to continue.

A harsh laugh rumbles from her chest. "It's true what they say. Beware of the wolf in sheep's clothing. He was worse than everyone who had come before," she whispers, digging her nails into her thighs through her yoga pants.

I gently unfurl one hand and rub her fingers.

"I don't want to go into detail. He was rough. A savage who gave zero consideration for me or my needs. He tore my clothes from my body and brutalized me all night. My tears only spurred him on. My screams made him harder."

I want to resurrect that motherfucker and torture the fuck out of him before killing him slowly, only to immediately resuscitate him so I can do it all over again.

"He whipped me with his belt that night. Lashing my back until I passed out from the pain."

I stuff my fist into my mouth, breathing heavily as I struggle to hold on to my composure.

"Dom went crazy because he had visibly marked me. Cruz smoothed it over and made a deal whereby he could have me to himself every week and he was allowed to whip my ass." She stares at me with a scarily emotionless face. "He wanted to leave marks. He preened over my scars. I loathed him with the intensity of a thousand stars."

Holding her face, I press my lips to her brow, hoping she can't feel how I'm trembling with violent rage.

"I wanted to poison him, but I was terrified of the repercussions. He wasn't like Dom or Cesco. He was much sharper and scarier. If I'd tried poisoning him gradually, he might have figured it out, and that could have tipped Dom off too. I thought of dumping a ton of arsenic in his drink and running off, but I knew they'd find me and kill me for murdering a don. So, I just had to put up with it. Until one week, he didn't show up, and that turned into two, then three."

"When he went into hiding after the debacle in New Jersey," I surmise. We knew he hadn't shown his face in Miami during that period because we had sent men to scout the territory.

Her chest heaves, and pain rips across her face.

Fuck, there's more.

"Let it out, baby." I trace my hand up and down her spine. "Let it all out."

Tears spill from her eyes as she looks at me. Her lower lip wobbles. "I discovered I was pregnant a month later."

All the blood drains from my face. "I thought Dom had you on birth control."

"I was on the pill then. The IUD only came after," she whispers. "Every other man, including my husband, used condoms. But not Cruz."

Horror whips through me like a hurricane, devastating everything in its past. My hand has stalled on her back, and I'm fighting a losing battle to remain calm.

"He switched out my pills," she whispers, averting her eyes and staring off into space. "Cruz knocked me up on purpose, just like he boasted about knocking up all those other women."

Come again? "What?"

"I knew there was a woman in New York who'd just given him an heir. He chose her for her *good stock*." A look of disgust washes over her face. "But he had backups. A lot of them. In a lot of places. He used to joke he was going to knock a thousand women up and infiltrate *La Cosa Nostra* with his bloodline."

That sounds exactly like something his arrogant ass would do. Fucking hell. This could be a potential nightmare in the future, and I can only imagine what Cristian is going to say when he hears this. "How many are there?"

"I don't know. I'm not sure he did either though I'm convinced he pulled the same stunt on other unsuspecting women."

"How did he think Dom would permit this?" It's one thing to pimp your wife out to clear your debts or for favors but letting another made man impregnate your wife is shameful. I don't think Dominic would have approved or let it go.

"I think he was planning on killing Dom and taking me for himself, but that's just a guess."

"What happened to the baby?"

Tears fill her eyes again. "Dom was going to force me into an abortion, but I couldn't let him do that. The baby was innocent."

She hacks up a sob, and I pull her against my chest, dotting kisses into her hair. I don't say anything because I have no words. This is worse than the worst thing I could have created in my mind, and I'm pretty creative.

"I went to Vitto. Told him it was Cruz's baby and he had planned it. Told him I feared what Cruz would do to all of us if he discovered I was pregnant and we'd aborted his baby. Vitto intervened. Made Dom agree to send me to my *nonna* in Sicily to give birth in secret and then the baby would be adopted. I was overseas when news of Cruz's death became common knowledge. I knew Dom would try and force me into an abortion then, so I called Vitto, and he made sure Dom stuck to the agreement."

"Where's your baby now, Valentina?"

Silent tears stream down her face. "I don't know. They let me hold him for ten minutes, and then he was stolen from my arms. I screamed at them to bring him back. I had taken one look at him and fell instantly in love."

She stares at me, looking utterly heartbroken. "He was beautiful even if he looked like his father. In that moment, I didn't care how he was conceived or who he resembled. My heart was full of love for my child. He was *mine*, and Cruz wasn't around any longer to make a claim for him. I wanted to keep him, but they said it was too late. The paperwork was done."

She breaks down again, sobbing into my shirt. "I'm so sorry, kitten. So, so sorry."

When her tears dry, she sits more upright, swiping at her eyes and sniffling. "*Nonna* collected me from the hospital, but I didn't want to leave. I was convinced my son was still there somewhere, and I was racing around, searching wards and rooms. They had to sedate me to get me into the car. I was in agony, drowning in pain, screaming and crying for my baby. It felt like someone had reached a hand into my chest and ripped my heart from my body. The pain was unbearable.

"The grief didn't go away in the following days. It only got worse. I made constant calls to Vitto, begging him to get my baby back. When my calls became crazier and more aggressive and it was clear I was losing my sanity, Vitto spoke to Dom, and after I swallowed a load of pills in an attempt to end it all, he sent me to a psychiatric hospital. I was there for a few months before they sent me back to Miami.

"Vitto told me then he'd tried to reverse the decision, but the baby was already in the system, and he had no contacts and no sway in Italy. His hands were tied. I appreciated that he tried. Especially knowing Dom would be furious if he knew."

Sounds like Vitto's guilty conscience forced him to try, but it doesn't excuse him for tolerating the way his underboss treated his wife. It wouldn't have taken much for Vitto to force Dominic to stop trading his wife to the highest bidder, but he chose to say nothing. I have lost all respect for the man and won't lose any sleep knowing he's about to be stripped of his title, power, and responsibility. He deserves it for being so fucking weak.

She slumps against me, her head on my shoulder. "Now you know. Do you hate me? Are you leaving me?"

How on Earth can she think that? It must be the trauma speaking. "Of course not, kitten." I dust kisses all over her face, wanting to bundle her up and keep her away from a world that has hurt her over and over again. She's barely clinging to me now, exhaustion seeping from every pore. It's the middle of the night. She had a traumatic shock earlier, and now she's just relived one of the most difficult periods of her life. It's no surprise she's drained physically and mentally. "What Cruz did to you, what they all did to you, is disgusting, Valentina, but how could you think I would hate you? It wasn't your fault. You are not to blame."

"But you hated him, and I had his baby."

I hide my wince in time, but it grates inside me. "He forced himself on you repeatedly and manipulated your pregnancy. It's not like you fell in love with him and willingly let him knock you up. All this does is make me hate him more and love you harder."

"People will look at me differently when they know."

"They won't, and we don't have to tell anyone if you want to keep it a secret." We have to tell Cristian and Massimo, but I'll broach that subject another time. "Can I ask you something?"

She nods, looking up at me, seeming so young in the face of all this trauma. "Does Elio look like your son? Is that what triggered you today, or was it because Cristian resembles Cruz?"

"It was Elio at first. I don't know if my son would look like him now except they both have the same dark hair. My Leandro had blue eyes when he was born, but I suspect they're green now. It was the stark resemblance to Cruz when Elio looked at me that triggered me. Then Cristian showed up, looking too much like his older brother, and when he clasped my hand and smiled, I got lost in my head, and it was as if Cruz had come back from the dead. I zoned out after that."

"Cristian is nothing like Cruz, and he despised his brother." This will devastate him all over again.

"I'm so tired," she says, yawning. "But I need to tell you more."

"It can wait, baby." Her eyelids are drooping as I lift her up. "You can tell me the rest in the morning."

Valentina passes out in my arms on the stairs, and she doesn't budge as I strip her down to her underwear and slide her under the covers. Grabbing a bottle of bourbon from downstairs, I settle in a chair by the window in my bedroom, facing it toward the bed, as I work through everything my wife just told me.

My emotions are raw. My pain is visceral. But none of it is directed at the goddess sleeping in our bed. Valentina is so strong. Not yet twenty-five and she has already experienced far too much pain and grief and suffering. How she is even able to get up each day is impressive.

No more, I vow, as I climb into bed just as the sun is setting. She will know no more suffering or pain. I'll do everything necessary to ensure she only knows happiness and peace from this point on.

I'm woken by my phone the next morning, and I quickly silence it, slowly removing my arms from around my wife. She's still in a deep sleep, and I want it to stay that way. I slip into the closet, not overly surprised to see it's after eleven, and accept the call from Dino. "What's up?"

"Boss, Don Mazzone is at the gate asking to be let in. He says it's urgent."

"Let him through." I pull on a pair of shorts, slip my feet into slides, and head downstairs to greet Ben.

I watch my fellow don and Commission colleague climb out of the back of a black Lexus, dressed in a suit and wearing a grim expression. I'm instantly on high alert.

"This isn't a social visit," he confirms as he walks up to me. "Massimo has convened an emergency sitting of the board, and I've been asked to escort you."

"What's this about?"

"I'm not at liberty to divulge that until we get to HQ."

I didn't have any missed calls from Massimo. If he couldn't warn me, then the shit has hit the fan. "You know about Ferraro."

Ben nods tersely but doesn't say anything.

"Come on, Bennett. We've known each other a long time. I know I've fucked up, but surely, you can give me something?"

He leans against the wall and sighs, his professional façade cracking. "Caleb's in the hot seat too, and he doesn't need this with a baby on the way. I wish you had come to me. I understand why you left Massimo out, but I could have advised you to take a better path."

"He was hurting what's mine, Ben. He was always going to die by my hand. You can't tell me you wouldn't have done the same if it was Sierra."

"No, you're right." His blue eyes drill into mine. "I can't."

"How bad is it?"

"Cesco Ferraro emailed us drone footage, and it's pretty damning. He's demanding the board take action against you and Caleb for breaking protocol and murder."

That little shit was behind the drone after all. He must have sent one of the *soldati* to shadow Dom and his men because he was in Miami at the time it went down. It shows cunning that might impress me if he wasn't trying to steal my reason for living. "He wants Valentina."

Ben rubs the back of his neck. "He's put in a request to marry her. Vitto has endorsed it."

That double-crossing snake. Guess he's appeased his guilty conscience after all. A smirk rolls over my lips. "Can't marry someone if they're already married." I flash him my wedding band.

"You've got balls, Maltese. I hope they're big enough to get you out of this mess." He rakes his gaze over me. "Get dressed. We need to leave."

I turn around, stalling in the doorway when he calls my name. I arch a brow as I look over my shoulder.

"Congratulations on your marriage. Never thought I'd see the day."

"You and me both, buddy." I run upstairs, debating whether to wake Valentina, but I decide against it. She needs her sleep, and she'll only freak out. So, I pen her a note instead explaining Cesco has fingered me for Dominic's murder and I'll likely be tied up with the board all day. I advise her not to worry, that I'll get myself out of this mess.

Then I walk downstairs and join Ben in his car, settling in for the journey to Manhattan.

Chapter Thirty-Seven
Valentina

I almost have another meltdown when I wake and read Fiero's note. I should have told my husband everything last night so he has the information he needs to extricate himself from this mess with the board. But I conked out before telling him the rest.

I race into my closet with my cell in my hand watching as the call connects.

"I'm guessing you've heard the news," Catarina says when she picks up.

I set the phone down on top of a shelf and remove a bra and underwear set from my lingerie drawer. "Yes. Why has Massimo let this happen? He could at least have warned Fiero." I'm a little pissed at Fiero's best friend.

"He wanted to, but he didn't get an opportunity. The intel was sent to Volpe, not Massimo, and Volpe showed up at Massimo's office, demanding he handle this immediately and that he didn't tip off his buddy. Massimo couldn't compromise himself. He knows Fiero wouldn't want that. It's why he hasn't been confiding in us, right?"

"Yes," I say, shimmying into a white, pink, and purple knee-length dress. "He knew there was a chance this could blow up before he had fixed things, and he didn't want Massimo involved. He worried it would reflect badly on him as our president and threaten his position if he was implicated at all."

"From the little I know, this isn't looking good for Fiero and Caleb."

I slip my feet into my tennis shoes, bending to tie the laces. "It's why I need to speak with Massimo. I have intel on what Dom was doing with the—"

"Don't say another word. Not over the phone," she cautions.

"Okay. Just send me The Commission's address, and I'll go speak to Massimo."

"You won't get anywhere near him, Valentina. Security is tight, and unless you're on the visitor list, you're not getting past the front desk."

"Send me his number then. I'll try calling him."

"He won't pick up. These meetings can take hours."

Panic is waiting in the wings as I wrack my brain trying to think of another option. "Fiero doesn't know everything. I should have told him, but Dom had threatened me, and later, I was trying to protect a secret about me, and it's all connected. Fiero is in this mess because of me. Please help me to help him, Cat."

"You don't need to ask. If you tell me what you know, I'll go to HQ and update Massimo. I'm at our place in the city, and it's not too far away from Commission Central. I can't go to you because Armis is home sick. He caught that bug Bella had a couple weeks ago. I can't leave him alone until the housekeeper arrives this afternoon. Could you come here?"

"Sure." I'm already running down the stairs. "Fiero has appointed me a driver and two *soldati* for protection. I'll be there as quick as I can."

"Come in," Cat says, swiftly opening her door after I rap on it. "You made good time."

"I told the driver to put the pedal to the metal. They know I'm doing something to help their boss, so they were all invested in getting me here in record time."

"I called my housekeeper, and she'll be here shortly."

"How is Armis?" I ask as she leads me through the wide hallway into an open-plan kitchen-cum–dining room–cum–sitting room. It's tastefully decorated in shades of white, gray, and cool blue with exquisite furniture and fittings and the most spectacular view over Central Park.

"His fever has come down, thankfully. Nat was here this morning, and she's given him medication. He's currently sleeping."

"I'm sorry to ask this of you when you have a sick child."

"Don't be ridiculous." She gestures for me to take a seat at the table. "Fiero is family. I want to help." She moves toward the kitchen. "Coffee?"

"Please."

"How are you feeling after yesterday? I was worried about you."

"I'm okay. A little embarrassed I broke down in front of everyone like that. Especially when it was my first time meeting most people."

"Everyone was just concerned for you. There is no need to be embarrassed."

"That's what Fiero said. We talked everything through last night." I scrub my hands down my face. "After I tried to run away like a coward too afraid to tell my husband the truth."

Cat walks over carrying a tray with two mugs of coffee, a small jug filled with milk, and a bowl of sugar cubes. The plate of pastries looks delicious, and I wish I could eat, because my tummy is hollow, but I have no appetite. My stomach is twisted into knots, and I'd probably throw up if I tried to force something down. I'll stick to coffee.

I sip my coffee as I tell Cat everything I told Fiero last night. She doesn't interrupt, only reaching out to hold my hand as I purge it all. "That's as much as Fiero knows. I wanted to tell him the rest, but I passed out before I could."

"I'm not surprised. You had a very traumatic day. I know how draining it is to share your experiences. I'm so sorry that happened to you." Tears prick her eyes. "This isn't the time, but I'll share my story some time. There are a lot of similarities."

"I'm sorry to hear that." I've heard a few rumors about the things done to her as a teenager and later when she was married to Don Conti, but I've no idea if they're all true or embellished.

"Therapy helped me a lot. If you want my therapist's number, text me for it."

"I'll probably take you up on that." Serena mentioned therapy yesterday too, and I think it might help me. I don't want to be a prisoner to my past. I want to build a future with Fiero, and I can't do that if I'm a broken mess held hostage by the things done to me.

"Tell me what I need to know." Catarina holds my hand, offering silent comfort.

"I should have told Fiero this weeks ago, but like I said on the phone, Dom had threatened me before I came here. He told me to keep my mouth shut or he'd harm my family. That was code for he'd find my baby and kill him."

"I'm glad that bastard is dead," she seethes.

"I haven't lost a wink of sleep over it. The world is a better place without him in it."

"One less monster is always a good thing," she agrees.

"After Dom's death, I wasn't sure if Cesco knew about Leandro or if Dom had made provisions to harm my son in the event of his untimely death. It's still a concern, but I should have confided in Fiero. I didn't because I was terrified he'd leave me if he knew about Cruz and the baby. It's all interconnected, and I couldn't mention certain things without it becoming obvious, so I kept my mouth shut. I was selfish because I didn't want Fiero to know. I didn't want him to push me away."

"Babe, that man couldn't even handle a couple of hours of separation yesterday. He'd never survive without you, and none of it is your fault. You are completely blameless."

"I know that now, but in my messed-up head, it was a real threat."

"It's not easy to see things logically if you're stressed or under severe trauma. It's understandable, and Fiero will forgive you."

"He asked me if I knew about the warehouse, and I lied. I have eavesdropped on Dom's conversations for years. My daddy always said knowledge is power, so I absorbed every bit of information I could get my hands on." I drink a large gulp of coffee before I get down to the nitty-gritty

"Cruz showed up in Miami wanting an introduction to the cartel. He cozied up to Vitto first until he realized Vitto had no in and he was of no use to him. Dom had just lost big to one of the cartel leaders in a card game. Fuentes had orchestrated the loss because he wanted Dom under this thumb."

"I can guess why."

"They want to take over the territory fully. I'm guessing Dom's reputation preceded him, and that was their way in. Cruz happened to show up at the opportune time."

"Of course, he did." Her eyes narrow. "He had a knack for that."

"Cruz, as you know, had plans to take over as president of The Commission and rule *La Cosa Nostra* in the US. He needed allies, and he wanted some outside *la famiglia* because he feared his Italian American partners in crime might turn on him."

"You found all this out by eavesdropping?"

I shake my head. "Cruz loved the sound of his own voice, and he talked incessantly while he was assaulting me. I was able to piece it all together from what I'd overhead and the things he told me."

"That sounds like him," she scoffs. "Go on."

"So, Cruz made a deal with Dom. He'd pay off his debt to the cartel if he made an introduction. Dom set it up, and Cruz made a deal with Fuentes whereby he'd fly their supplies in from Vegas. They paid him well for the trips, but the major part of the deal was they would assist Cruz when the time came to stage his coup and take the presidency. In return, he offered them Florida and agreed they could take over supplying *La Cosa Nostra* in the US."

"I'm not buying that." Cat gets up, taking our empty mugs over to the coffee pot in the kitchen. "Cruz wasn't stupid. He wouldn't give them that much control."

"Of course not. I suspect the cartel knew that too, but it served them to enter into an alliance. I'm sure they were plotting to take him out just like he was plotting to take them out after they'd helped him take the crown."

"Where does Dominic factor in all of this?" she asks, refilling our mugs.

"Cruz needed help on the ground, and he knew Vitto wouldn't get his hands dirty."

"But Dominic would." She hands me a fresh mug of coffee along with a bottle of water.

"Thanks, and yes, he would, and he did." I pause to uncap my water and quench my thirst. "Dom transported the supplies from the plane to the warehouses, and yes, there is more than one. I'll write out the names and coordinates for you to give to Massimo before I go. Dom was the go-between for Cruz with the cartel during the week when he was in Vegas. Cruz promised Dom Florida. He told him he could kill Vitto and install himself as don. Dom was thrilled and readily handed me over as part of the deal when Cruz demanded I be reserved for him exclusively at the weekly parties. Dom had no idea Cruz had promised Fuentes the territory. I was going to tell him. I knew he'd put a stop to Cruz coming to the house except then Cruz told me he was planning to kill Dom, Cesco, and Vitto and he'd be installing a man of his choosing to the state, like he planned to do with all states. I wasn't sure if he was playing me to keep my silence or maybe to test my loyalty to him, but either way, I chose not to tell Dom what I knew. I wanted him dead even if a part of me feared Cruz would try to keep me for himself."

"He planned to install my sister as his queen, parading Bettina's stolen baby as her own." Pain mixes with disgust on Cat's face.

I'm not sure if I should say this, but I've learned my lesson about keeping secrets. "That wasn't his plan," I quietly say.

Her eyes swing to mine. "Tell me."

"He needed Anais to execute his plan, but as soon as the presidency was in the bag, he was going to kill her and take a more suitable wife."

Her face pales.

From the things he said about his younger wife, it seemed they had a codependent, toxic relationship. "Cruz was aware of how she was perceived by others, and he said she would only drag him down."

"I always knew that was a possibility with him, but to hear he intended to go through with it." She shakes her head, averting her eyes.

"I'm sorry."

"Don't be. You have nothing to be sorry for." She tips her head to the side. "Was he planning to take you for his wife?"

"I doubt it. I'm from a lower-ranking family, and he didn't know he'd succeeded in knocking me up. He once mentioned he had his eye on a don's sister, but he never mentioned names."

"Fuck." Cat rubs between her brows. "I bet it was Tullia. He'd do it to fuck with Fiero. He had a strong rivalry with Massimo and Fiero. Caleb too, but his little sister is way too young."

"If it was Tullia, I'm doubly glad he's dead. She's so sweet, and he would have ruined her."

"I suggest you don't mention that part to Fiero. No sense in upsetting him now over something that won't ever happen."

"You're probably right." Though I'll most likely tell him. I don't want to keep any secrets from my husband. I feel so incredibly guilty I didn't tell him all this and resolve the situation weeks ago. It was so selfish and stupid, but my fear was real, and I wasn't thinking clearly. What Fiero thinks of me matters, and I thought he wouldn't see me as mother material given the circumstances. That he wouldn't want to touch me after he knew Cruz had. I should have given him more credit because that's not who Fiero is. He'd walk over hot coals and take a bullet for me. I see that now. I'm determined not to make the same mistakes again, so from now on, I'm telling my husband everything.

"What happened after Cruz disappeared?"

"Dom was forced into helping the cartel drive supplies from Vegas to Miami now they'd lost the airline route. At this point, he was massively in debt to them again, but they said he didn't have to worry about paying them back as long as he continued helping them. It's why they kept letting him join poker nights. It served them to have him further and further in debt to them."

"He was a disgrace to made men everywhere," she hisses, perking her head up when the doorbell chimes. "That'll be Lola. Let me let her in."

I finish my coffee and check my phone for updates while Catarina lets her housekeeper in, but there's nothing.

"There's one thing I don't understand," Cat says, dropping back into the chair beside me a few minutes later. "The Commission had spies in Miami. Several men were sent there to look out for Cruz and to find out what he'd really been doing in Miami. They were watching all the key players, and they infiltrated the *soldati* rank so they could ask around, but they got nothing. How was Dom doing this and not being detected?"

"Because The Commission was only focused on key players and the *soldati* were not involved. Dom kept them out of it, but no one was watching high-school seniors." It doesn't take her long to work it out.

"He was using Cesco?"

I nod. "It was Cesco's idea. He recruited a few buddies at school, and they did it all. Ferried messages back and forth and met the delivery drivers on the border and drove the vans from there to the warehouses. No one was watching them, and they did it all in plain sight."

"I hate to give either of those pricks any credit, but that was fucking genius."

"Yep." I gulp down some water. "Dom was finally wising up. After Cruz's death, Fuentes told him of the deal Cruz made and said he'd offer the same deal to Dom. He said once everything was in place they'd write his debt off. He could be don, but it would be a don of nothing if the cartel was running the drug trade in the state. Dom had no choice but to agree. He owed them a fortune, and he knew they'd just put a bullet in his head if he didn't comply. So, he was playing a long game, continuing to move drugs for the cartel using Cesco's buddies—who are not *mafioso*, by the way. They belong to a motorcycle gang—but he was planning something. I don't know the details because I was out of the country for months and I wasn't privy to what he was scheming. Just that he was planning to double-cross the cartel in some way. Fuentes is way smarter than Dom, and it was only a matter of time before they killed him except Fiero got there first."

"He killed him for you."

I nod tersely. "This is all my fault. Fiero has compromised himself for me, and I need to make this right. This will be enough to exonerate him and Caleb, right? Dom was dirty through and through, and he betrayed *omerta* and our cause. Surely the board won't hold his death against them when they know this?"

She stands. "I can't imagine they'll face serious sanctions. However, they still did this behind the board's back, and that is the issue. Not the morality behind killing a man who betrayed *La Cosa Nostra*." She pulls me into a hug. "Thank you for trusting me with everything, and I promise I'll do my best to help Fiero." She releases me. "For what it's worth, even if Fiero had known this, he still would have killed Dominic himself. He still would have faced sanction for not bringing it to the board."

"I should have told him about the seriousness of the threat the cartel poses. It's unforgivable."

Her smile is soft. "They already know, sweetie. They're making plans to replace the leadership and tackle the cartel. Knowing all the intricacies would have given them an edge, but not knowing didn't make that much of a difference, so stop beating yourself up." She touches my cheek. "I know it probably feels like you're ancient because you have lived through so much in your twenty-four years. I felt the same in my twenties. But you're still young, and you have coped incredibly well with everything thrown at you. Don't criticize yourself for trying to protect *you* and protect your *son*. It's not selfish to shield yourself when no one else was doing it."

"Thank you for listening, for understanding, for helping."

"You're my family now, Valentina. We protect our family."

I nod, choking on the messy ball of emotion in my throat. "I'll write down the details of those warehouses if you have a pen and paper."

She leaves for a few minutes, returning with a notepad and pen. "I'll just check on Armis and let Lola know I'm leaving."

When she returns, she's wearing a fitted red jacket over her black dress, concealing the holster at her waist. I hand her the folded piece of paper, and she slips it in her purse. "Let's go. I'll walk you to your car."

Cat raps on the passenger window of my SUV after kissing me on the cheek and watching me climb into the back.

"Donna Greco. Nice to see you." Dino's tone is respectful and bordering on awe.

"You too, Dino. I'm glad Fiero assigned you to protect Valentina. Take her straight home and watch out for tails." She looks back at me. "I don't trust that Valentina's stepson won't try to pull something. He has set all this in motion, and it makes me nervous."

"We'll be extra vigilant, I promise."

"I'll text you when I'm home safely," I say.

"Take care, and I'll call you with an update soon," she says before walking off.

The driver joins the traffic as I settle in the seat beside Orlo, my second bodyguard, keeping my eyes glued to the driver's side mirror, watching the cars behind us, but I don't see anyone following us.

We're only ten minutes from the house, and I'm just starting to relax when a loud noise erupts outside the car and we're suddenly spinning.

"Someone shot out the tires," Dino roars from the front. "Get down," he shouts as a vehicle slams into the side of our SUV, jolting us all forward. Orlo throws himself over me, covering me with his body. My fingers clasp the locket around my neck as I shake and shiver all over. We're slammed from the other side, sandwiched between two vehicles, and my skull rattles as the car violently vibrates before stalling.

Glass shatters in the front, accompanied by two muted pops, and I scream. My door is yanked open with force, and I scream again when someone fires two bullets into Orlo's back. He slumps to the floor, and I'm on my own now. Adrenaline kicks in, and I thrash around as I'm lifted out of the car.

"Hello, *Mommy*." Cesco shoves his face all up in mine as I'm restrained by strong arms from behind. "It's time to come home."

The last thing I see is the butt of a gun moving toward my temple, and then I black out.

Chapter Thirty-Eight
Valentina

When I wake, I have a thumping headache, a crick in my neck, and my arms ache like a bitch.

"She's awake," a man with an unfamiliar voice says, sending terror shooting through me.

Turning my head, I stare into the eyes of a man I know only from seeing him at parties at the house. He's one of Cesco's friends. A gang member. His thigh presses against mine as he grins, leering down the front of my dress. My hands are tied behind my back, and my arms throb, especially where a rudimentary bandage is wrapped around my upper left arm. Lines of dried blood are caked to my skin from where they must have opened my scar to check for the tracker.

Glancing down, I'm relieved to see my locket cradled against my collarbone, and it offers a small measure of comfort as does the tracker in the nape of my neck. Cesco doesn't know about the new trackers, so he wouldn't even know to check.

The van jolts as it pulls over to the side of the road. I slide down the bench before the dickhead sitting beside me stretches his arm out, pulling me back into his side. Two other men sit on his other side, peering forward and staring at me with naked desire.

These are Cesco's friends from his high-school days. Members of a motorcycle gang. Interesting he has them helping, not any of Miami's *soldati*. Says a lot about where their loyalties lie.

The side door opens, and Cesco climbs inside. He slides the door shut and loudly taps the black aluminum panel before sitting on the bench on my other side. "Finally." The van drives back out onto the road as Cesco grips my chin, forcing my face to his. "I was getting worried I'd hit you too hard. Pity you missed the flight. The jet my friend Pablo Fuentes loaned me was the height of luxury."

Of course, he's colluding with the cartel. He hasn't learned a thing from watching his father's mistakes.

He toys with the right strap on my dress. "You would have enjoyed it."

The strap falls down my arm, and panic infiltrates my veins. Nerves fire at me from all angles, but I stamp them down inside, wrangling my panic into a ball and shoving it behind a mental wall. A familiar mask blankets my features as I transform into self-protective mode. It's as natural as breathing after six years even if Fiero has broken through my walls so effectively. Coping mechanisms aren't that easily unraveled.

I can't see anything from the back of the van, but Cesco's words confirm I'm back in Miami. I try not to freak out because Fiero will come for me soon. Cat will notify Massimo when I fail to check in with her. Or one of the men in the car if any of them survived.

"I had plans to test out his king bed, but I'm not into fucking comatose females." Leaning across me, Cesco flips the left strap of my dress, grinning at me with heat flaring in his eyes. "But you're conscious now."

I stare numbly at him, unwilling to play this game.

"Tossing you around like a ragdoll got me all worked up though." He rubs the bulge behind his black sweatpants. "I've waited years for a taste, and I'm done waiting." Holding my chin firmly in one hand, he slams his disgusting mouth down on mine.

I zone out, going to that safe space in my mind that will protect me, not protesting or whimpering when his disgusting tongue pries my lips apart and he shoves it into my mouth. He grunts as he fumbles with the hem of my dress, pushing it up to my waist and tugging my panties aside. I'm as dry as the Sahara when he drives two fingers inside me. It hurts, but I barely feel the pain.

"Spread her thighs," a man with a gruff voice says. "We want to see."

Without breaking his kiss, Cesco forces my thighs to widen before ripping my lace panties away. Cool air wafts over my exposed flesh as my underwear falls apart at my feet.

"Damn. That's a pretty pussy," a different man adds.

"Show us her tits," the third man says. "I've always wanted to know if they're real or fake."

"They're real," Cesco pants, tearing his lips from mine. "Dad didn't want her looking like that fake imitation Diana."

"Fake or not, I enjoyed coming all over them," the first guy says to a chorus of laughter.

All three are crouched on the floor in front of us, ensuring they have a front-row seat. Bile churns in my gut as I continue to keep my emotions on lockdown.

Cesco tugs my dress down, revealing my lace bra.

"Damn," one of the guys says. "Totally real."

Cesco cuts my bra at the front, and it falls to both sides, baring my breasts.

Pain threatens to overwhelm me, but I fight to regain control as they all grope me, tweaking and tugging on my nipples. A stab of pain shoots through my chest when Cesco lowers his mouth to one nipple and bites on it. His fingers continue to pump in and out of me as they all toy with me.

With my dress around my waist, Cesco lowers me to the dirty van floor on my knees. A stained navy blanket is all that protects me from the hard floor as he shoves down his pants and boxers, presses my face into the scratchy blanket, spreads my thighs, and thrusts inside me from behind, groaning loudly.

I block it out as he violates me with his friends watching and shouting encouragement. His gross hands roam my upper body, fondling my breasts and pinching my nipples. Mercifully, it doesn't last long. He grunts as he spills inside me, and I'm grateful I didn't give in to Fiero's recent request to remove my IUD. I'll need to get tested when I'm back home because he could be carrying any number of diseases. He was always dragging different women into his bed.

"What are you doing?" he snaps, dragging me out of that safe space in my head. He flips me over onto my back, and the position is awkward with my tied hands pressing into my lower back. Cesco tucks his vile cock away, pulling up his boxers and sweats before standing, bending over so his head doesn't hit the roof.

"Going next," the guy with the cropped dark hair says, holding his erect cock in his hand as he stares hungrily at me.

I'm splayed on the floor with my breasts hanging out and my pussy on display, and it's humiliating. I've known these boys since they were thirteen. I'm sore and my nipples are hurting too. But I can't focus on that or what happened because I'll fall apart before I exact my revenge. All this has done is make me more determined. I know Fiero is coming for me, but vengeance is *mine*. I channel all my emotion into making a plan, and it distracts me from the trauma I know is waiting on the sidelines to choke me.

I hate being at their feet and so vulnerable. I can't do

anything about my top, but I close my legs, and my dress lowers a little with the movement, covering the top half of my vagina. His semen drips down the inside of my thighs, coating me in a sticky layer I itch to wash off.

"I didn't say you could have a turn." Cesco glares at him. "She's mine. You can look and grope her a bit, but you're not fucking her. Her cunt is for my cock only."

"You let us fuck that Diana bitch," the guy with the dreadlocks says.

"She was a skanky whore."

"Dude, your stepmom spread her legs for multiple guys when your dad told her to."

Cesco punches him in the face. "Shut the fuck up. She didn't have a choice, and in the future, she'll only be doing that if I'm getting well paid."

"So, how much to fuck her cunt and her ass?" the guy with messy dirty-blond hair asks.

"More than you can afford," Cesco snaps, grabbing me by my sore arm and pulling me to my feet.

I cry out as pain rips through my arm.

"Quit crying like a baby." He shoves me down on the bench, and the motion fully covers my lower parts.

"At least let me jerk off on her tits," the first guy says, pumping his dick in his hand.

"Shut the fuck up," Cesco hisses.

"We helped you kidnap her," the guy with the dreads says. "It's the least you owe us."

"You have more money than you know what to do with, thanks to me." Cesco glares at his friends. "When I end the cartel and take control of Florida, you'll be the sole supplier of drugs in the state. You'll be stinking rich, and you can buy a hundred hookers if you like."

He's legit insane if he thinks he can take on the biggest

Mexican cartel and win. Whatever deal he's made after his father's death is playing into the cartel's hands, not his. I thought Cesco was smarter than his father, but it's looking like I was wrong.

"But I'm horny, man. Come on, be fair."

"We're here," the driver says, breaking up the argument.

The guys are grumbling when they climb out, and I won't feel any remorse when I end them. Cesco grips my arm, digging his nails into my skin, as he drags me back into a house I thought I'd seen the last of.

It's dusky outside meaning it's close to eight, and I lost a good few hours to unconsciousness. It was probably a blessing in disguise.

Cesco makes a beeline for the kitchen, like I hoped he would. The guy works out a lot, and he eats like a horse. I know he loves my cooking, and I'm banking on his predictability.

This is almost too easy.

"Who else is here?" I ask.

Cesco throws me in the direction of the stove. "Just us," he confirms. "Sorry to ruin your little plan. There are none of dad's men here to run to. You're stuck with us." He stalks toward me, cupping my pussy through my dress.

I feign fright because I know he'll love it. Inside, I'm encouraging him to keep going because it's playing into my plan.

"You're mine now, *Mommy*." He bites down hard on my lip, drawing blood. His tongue darts out, licking it before he kisses me hard and thankfully fast. "We're hungry. Make dinner." He cuts the rope binding my wrists, freeing my hands.

"Fuck you," I snarl, needing to make this seem genuine. "Make your own dinner, asshole."

My head whips sideways as he slaps me hard. Then he punches me in the stomach, and I fall to the tile floor, managing to cushion my head with my hands before I make contact. Pain slams into my side, and my vision is momentarily blurry.

Cesco hauls me to my feet, snarling in my face. "Disobey me again, and I'll let them take turns fucking you."

"Please disobey, *Mommy*," the guy with dreadlocks says, much to the amusement of the other two pricks. They are passing around beers and grinning as if I'm the entertainment.

"I'll make dinner." I force my voice to sound timid and weak and let my shoulders slump forward.

"Make it quick. I'm starving." Cesco roughly grips my chin. "And don't try to escape. I have an alarm on all the windows and doors and new cameras outside. You won't get far." He drags me from the kitchen into the dining room. "Here's an added incentive to behave," he says, almost shoving me into the wide pool of blood coating the dining room floor.

Goose bumps sprout on my arms as I survey the mutilated bodies of Vitto and Diana D'Onofrio piled in a lump in the middle of the floor. Vitto's wide eyes stare at the ceiling, his fingers still pressed against the grizzly cut in his neck.

Diana's naked body is gruesome. I hated her, but I wouldn't wish this on anyone. Her throat was also slit, but not until after they defiled her, I'm guessing. Her knees are pushed into her chest, exposing her intimate areas. Bile crawls up my throat at the dried semen clinging to her folds and her puckered hole, and the caked cum coating her breasts. Her mouth is open, forming an O-shape, and I almost throw up at the thought someone was fucking her throat the same time they slit it.

"You're all monsters," I whisper, incapable of hiding my horror.

"Step out of line, and that'll be your fate. Behave and I'll give you the kind of lifestyle my father failed to provide." Cesco brushes his fingers across my face. "I don't just want to fuck you. You're going to be my wife." He kisses me again, and it's softer than before. "I love you, and I know you love me too. Maltese did me a favor. Saved me having to kill the old man myself."

I should shut my mouth. I know that, but I can't help the words that leak out. "You're too late. I've already remarried. Don Maltese is my husband, and he's going to tear you into pieces when he comes for me."

Cesco goes deathly still, and I mentally slap myself upside the head.

Stupid, Valentina.

Even if it's almost worth it to see the looks on all their faces.

For the first time, the three men aren't laughing. Their expressions range from horror to disbelief to fear.

"I didn't sign up for this," the guy with the cropped hair says, clearly starting to panic.

"He'll kill us all," Dreads says, pacing the floor.

"She's lying." Cesco stares at my bare ring finger. I hadn't worn my rings to the baby shower, and I rushed out of the house this morning without putting them on. "Trying to freak us out on purpose." He digs his nails into my arm. "Nice try, *Mommy*, but it won't work. Even if it's true, I'll see that prick on the cameras if he dares show up here, and I'll blow his fucking brains out. Fuentes has his own plans for Maltese tomorrow, but I'll placate him if he's pissed I took his kill from him."

Panic pokes at my mental walls, but I don't give in. Now, more than ever, I need to get out of here so I can warn Fiero.

"Aw, look. She's going to cry." Cesco pinches my nipple through my dress. "How could you fall for the guy who treated you like a whore? You're such a dumb bitch at times." He twists my nipple, and tears leak down my face. "I'll enjoy fucking every memory of him out of your mind." Turning me around, he slaps my ass and shoves me toward the kitchen. "Make dinner and make it good, or my belt is coming off."

Their laughter trails me into the kitchen, and I want to

scream from the rooftops. But I concentrate on my plan, humming to myself as I calmly remove ingredients for spaghetti Bolognese from the pantry and the refrigerator.

I could make this dish in my sleep, and I've got added incentive to be quick now, so I assemble the different components in record time, and it's not too long before it's all ready. I set a small portion in a bowl to one side for me before implementing the final stage of my plan.

The door from the kitchen to the dining room isn't fully closed, so I look carefully over my shoulder before I empty the arsenic powder from my locket into the meat bubbling in the stove. I'm not sure if it's enough to poison all of them. They are young, fit, and muscular, and it might require more to take them down. It should work on Cesco as I've been gradually poisoning him for over a year, but there was a break during the time I was in Sicily, so I'm not sure if it's like starting from scratch.

Better to be safe than sorry. Quietly and carefully, I extract the fake box of garlic powder from the cupboard and dump my entire arsenic stock into the mixture, stirring it around to ensure it's disguised. After putting large helpings into four separate pasta bowls, I grate tons of parmesan on top. It should completely disguise any powder that might not have been fully absorbed.

I work hard to quell my nerves as I carry the bowls into the room and set them on the table before returning to grab silverware. They are drinking beer and playing cards at one end of the table, but they move up and take their seats, wasting no time tucking in.

"You'll sit beside me." Cesco pats the space where he used to sit beside his father at the head of the table.

I glare at him as I sit down, and he laughs as he twirls pasta around his fork using his spoon. I wipe my clammy hands down the front of my apron as I return to the kitchen to fetch my dinner.

I return to my seat and begin eating, forcing food down my throat as I grow increasingly concerned when nothing happens. Sweat coats the back of my neck as they all finish eating, patting their bellies and eyeing me like I'm dessert. "I'll clean up." My voice wobbles, and they laugh.

"Such a good wifey." Cesco slides his hand between my thighs when I stand. "You deserve a reward for preparing such a delicious meal. How does a gangbang sound?"

His friends pound the table with their fists, whistling and howling and acting like the animals they are.

"Clean up and get dessert, and then we can party." Cesco drives two fingers inside me, smirking as the stacked plates in my arms shake. He makes a meal of removing his fingers and sucking them into his mouth. He's only sucking his own arousal because I'm dry as a bone.

I finally escape to the kitchen, contemplating stabbing them with the cake knife when a loud crash emanates from the dining room. Strangled shouts accompany subsequent crashing noises, and I creep toward the door, eyeing the scene through the gap. Relief pours through me as I watch all four men stumble to the floor, clutching their chests and gasping for air.

Finally.

Leave no room for error, a cold voice whispers in my ear, and I grab the cake knife and race into the dining room.

Cesco is first. He's on the floor beside his overturned chair, still conscious and aware as I loom over him wearing a smirk. "You always underestimated me. I was poisoning you and Dom. You were always destined to die by my hand, but this way is a lot more fun." I wave the knife in his face as he splutters and chokes, struggling to breathe.

His panicked eyes are bloodshot, set within a face that is slowly turning blue, as I slash the knife across his throat. It glides through his flesh more easily than I expected. Arterial blood sprays across my dress, but it's the least of my worries. Cesco emits a last few garbled sounds, and then it's lights out. I kick him between the legs. "Sayonara, asshole. Join your father in hell."

I don't spare him another thought, quickly attending to the other three and watching with sick satisfaction as their blood joins the large pool of blood already on the floor.

I don't bother wiping my fingerprints or taking the knife with me as I flee the room. Fiero will send in a cleanup crew to take care of everything.

I can't believe I just did that. I'm in a bit of a dazed state but cognizant enough to know what I need to do now.

My heart is careening around my chest as I take the creaky stairs two at a time. I search Cesco's and Dom's bedrooms in the hope of finding an old cell phone, but there's nothing. None of the landlines in the house have service anymore, and the guys' cells are all password protected, so I have no way of making a call. At least I find a gun, bullets, and enough spare cash for a taxi, which will work. Loading the bullets into the gun, I stuff it in the pocket of the hoodie I grab from my bedroom and hightail it down the stairs.

I exit the house through the rear doors because I don't know where the van driver went. He could still be out front. Nightfall has descended, and I stick to the shadows as I slowly and carefully round the side of the house. I breathe a sigh of relief when the driveway is devoid of the van, confirming I'm alone. Passing the battered old Lincoln, I wonder if I should go back and try to locate the keys, but I can't make myself reenter that house of horrors, so I take off running down the bumpy driveway and out through the gates.

I keep running, my limbs surging forward, powered by the urgency to get as far away from here as possible. No taxis appear because, of course, it would be too much to hope one would show up when I need it. So, I keep running, heading toward the nearest town. I just need to get to the twenty-four-seven convenience store to buy a phone, and I can call Fiero to come get me.

A black SUV, approaching on the other side of the road, drives across the center of the road, screeching to a halt in front of me. Panic is instantaneous as my mind immediately thinks of the cartel. Whipping the gun out, I hold it in front of me and point it at the man climbing out of the passenger seat.

"Valentina. It's okay. Fiero sent me."

Yeah, right. "Who are you?" He looks vaguely familiar, but he's not someone I know.

"I'm Davide Gallo. The board is planning to appoint me as don after they have spoken to Vitto. Your husband was the one who nominated me for the role."

That has me pausing. Our marriage isn't common knowledge, and apart from Fiero, me, and Cat, only the board knows. This seems to be legit, but I don't lower my weapon.

"Vitto is dead. Diana too."

Gallo's eyes widen.

"Cesco did it."

"Where is he, and do you need medical attention?" he asks, his eyes dipping to the blood coating my dress.

"Dead along with his friends." I jerk my head back in the direction of the house. "And this isn't my blood."

"Mrs. Maltese." A second man gets out the back of the car, holding out his phone. "I have your husband on the line. He's in the air. He wants to talk to you."

"Slide it to me," I demand, training my weapon between both men.

He nods, coming closer, keeping his eye on me as he slides the phone across the asphalt toward me.

"Raise your hands where I can see them. Both of you." I keep my gun pointed at them as I bend to get the phone. "Keep them there."

The men lift their arms without question.

I straighten up, pressing the speaker button. "Fiero?"

"Kitten, are you okay? Are you safe?" Terror underscores his words, and I've never heard him sound so scared. "Are you hurt?"

"I'm okay. I'm safe."

"Thank fuck," he blurts. The relief in his voice is transparent. "I love you, honey. I'm so sorry I didn't protect you."

"It's not your fault, Fiero, and I love you too." I wish he was here because I need his strong arms around me. The adrenaline sustaining me is fading along with my fighting spirit. My arms are shaking and my legs feel like Jello. "Are these men to be trusted?"

"Yes, baby. I vouch for them. I'm sorry it's taken me so long to get to you. We were in the meeting, and we didn't find out until Dino regained consciousness and called me."

"He's okay?" I lower my weapon and let it fall to the ground. I nod at the men, and they drop their arms to their sides.

"The driver is dead. They shot him in the head, but Orlo and Dino were hit in the back and torso, and they were wearing bulletproof vests. They sustained injuries, but they're not serious. Where is Cesco?"

"Dead. I killed him. I killed all of them."

Shocked silence greets my statement.

"How?" Fiero stutters.

"I poisoned them and slit their throats to be sure they didn't survive."

The two men stare at me in shock.

"That's my girl." Pride laces through Fiero's tone. "Remember what I asked you that first day?" he adds.

"If I needed rescuing?" I surmise.

"Yeah. I was wrong. You didn't need me to rescue you because you rescued yourself."

"I still need you, baby. I need you so much. When will you be here?"

"My plane lands in an hour. Davide will take you to the airfield, and we can go straight home after refueling unless you want to spend the night there?"

"I want to go home. I never want to see that fucking house again."

"Language, kitten. I can still put you over my knee. You deserve to be spanked for concealing that intel from me and for leaving the house without my knowledge."

"You're on speaker."

"I don't fucking care."

I roll my eyes, and the two men standing before me exchange a smile. Gallo approaches, retrieving my gun and carefully placing his hand on my lower back. "I've got her, Don Maltese. I'll bring her to you safely."

"Don't touch me," I say, pushing out of his reach. "My husband doesn't like anyone touching me but him."

"Damn straight. Gallo," he roars, "I'll riddle you with bullets if you lay one finger on her. I don't care if you're a don now. I've already gone to war over this woman once, and I won't hesitate to do it again."

"Understood, Don Maltese." He smiles at me as we walk toward the SUV. "She's definitely a woman worth going to war over."

Epilogue One
Fiero – Six Months Later

"I'm glad it all worked out for you, Fiero," Rico says, clapping me on the back as we watch our women laughing and dancing on the dance floor.

Dinner and speeches ended an hour ago, and now we're into the partying part of the celebrations. Our formal wedding day was everything I was hoping it would be and more, and from the wide smile my wife has been sporting all day, I know she feels the same.

"I'm glad the board saw reason and didn't punish you or Caleb too severely," Rico adds.

We got off lightly with fines, a one-month suspension, and a rap on the knuckles. Undoubtedly, it has damaged both our reputations, but neither of us care.

"It's wonderful to see you so happy, and Valentina has really blossomed. Love suits you both."

My lips kick up at the corners as I eyeball him. "A wise man once said he never regretted putting a ring on his wife's finger, and I couldn't agree more." My wife looks like royalty in her princess-style wedding dress, the skirt swishing around her stunning body as she laughs and twirls with her friends.

All the wives and my sisters gathered around Valentina in the aftermath of that last day in Miami, offering her ongoing support and friendship. She's been welcomed into their circle with open arms, and I couldn't love them more for it.

My *consigliere* arches a brow and grins. I'm so glad he forgave me. To say Rico was pissed when he discovered everything I'd hidden from him is an understatement. He was frosty with me for weeks, and we only overcame it because I swore to never do it again. "If I recall it correctly, I said I never regretted putting a ring on Frankie's finger and knocking her up. Something you want to share, Maltese?"

"Nothing yet, but hopefully soon if I have my way. I promise you'll be the first to know after our families."

"I'm surprised you haven't knocked her up yet." He sips his beer.

Around us, everyone we know and love is enjoying our wedding reception after the emotional ceremony in the cathedral earlier today.

"I've wanted to, but it wasn't the right time."

"Of course." His expression switches from jovial to somber. "How is she doing now?"

"She's good." I grip the bottle in my hand tight, grinding my teeth and wishing I could resurrect Cesco Ferraro from the grave to make him suffer for what he did to my kitten. I don't think I'll ever stop feeling guilty for not protecting her from him. I promised her no one would ever hurt her again, and they did. Valentina refuses to let me blame myself, but I can't rid myself of these feelings no matter how many times she pleads with me to let the guilt go. "Therapy has helped her to work through everything, and she's in a much better place now." I sat in on several sessions with my wife, to offer moral support, and we had a few couples' sessions too.

"That's good. Now you can get on with the rest of your lives."

"That's the plan even if the situation in Florida is going to turn into full-scale war one of these days."

"That little shit really landed us in it," Massimo says, clearly hearing the tail end of the conversation as he materializes at my side.

"He did, but we'll find a way to come out the other side like we always do," Joshua says, joining our little circle.

Cesco believed he could take control of Florida using his gangland contacts and the cartel to oust us from the region and then dispose of the cartel so he could control the entire supply chain for the state. Never mind the cartel is the biggest and most powerful Mexican cartel and he was only a pup with delusions of grandeur. His plan was psychotic in the extreme, and he hurt a lot of innocent people.

Cesco had alluded to the cartel planning to kill me, so I didn't show to our meet. I was too busy taking care of my wife to leave New York anyway.

Thanks to Valentina's intel, we had the coordinates of all the warehouses the Ferraros were using to store drug supplies for the cartel. Before we could get to them, the cartel removed their product and burned the structures to the ground. What they—and we—didn't know is Cesco doctored the fentanyl, adding a chemical compound that reacted adversely in people with certain genetic predispositions, making the drug deadly for those individuals. Hundreds of innocents lost their lives, a lot of them kids, teens, and young adults. It horrified the nation and made global headlines, and it sickened us that any made man could do something so heinous.

The blame for the fentanyl tragedy squarely landed on the cartel's door because Cesco made sure all the drugs carried the cartel branding and that nothing traced back to *La Cosa Nostra*. The authorities might buy it, but the cartel knows exactly who set them up, and now they are looking for our heads on spikes.

We reached out, via an intermediary, in an effort to avoid a full-scale war, explaining it was the actions of someone who went rogue and we didn't condone it. We indicated our willingness to sit down and find a resolution, but they rebuked us. They don't care Cesco was acting alone and it wasn't sanctioned *mafioso* orders.

They want someone to pay, and that someone is us.

However, the authorities are all over this, which is advantageous for us. The public wants people locked up for the mass murders, and the government has pumped money into a covert campaign to capture the cartel leaders and get them behind bars.

The cartel had no choice but to lick their wounds and retreat to Mexico until the heat dies down.

It buys us some time, but they will come for us.

And we'll be ready.

"At least we have solid leadership now and Florida is a lot more settled," Ben says, joining us.

Gallo is a good man, and he's doing a fantastic job steadying the ship. The *soldati* respect him, and his underboss and *consigliere* appointments are solid. Gallo is working closely with us to safeguard the territory and prepare for battle. I'm traveling to Miami once a month to help lay the groundwork, and so far, we're making good progress.

"Cat will bust my balls if she hears us discussing business at your wedding," my best man says, handing me a fresh beer as I set my empty down on the table.

"She's right," Joshua says, frowning at something over my head. "This isn't the place or time."

Ben clinks his bottle against mine. "Marriage suits you, Maltese."

"Valentina suits me," I reply, waggling my brows. "It wouldn't have worked with anyone else. She grounds me, completes me."

A gagging sound at my back has me looking around in time to spot Sofia disappearing out the door of the ballroom with Rowan Mazzone's arm around her shoulders. Seconds later, Tullia bursts into tears and flees out the other door.

Fuck me.

Rowan is the younger man Sofia's been fucking? They've both kept that very quiet. I hope Sierra didn't see what I just saw. I don't think she'd be happy. Her eldest is a few months shy of twenty-one, and Sofia just turned twenty-nine. Not that she'll care much about the age difference. Rowan is an adult, capable of making his own choices. Sierra won't like it because Sofia has a love 'em and leave 'em reputation that is deserved. She won't like her son tangled up with my commitment-phobe sister. I make a move to go after my little sister, but Zumo claims my eyes from across the room, shaking his head and striding toward the door Tullia just escaped through.

"Super sperm." Caleb's words drag me back into the conversation in time to watch Joshua glower at his twin.

"Knock it off, or I'll knock you out," Joshua says through gritted teeth. "It wasn't funny the first time you said it, and it's not funny now."

Gia and Joshua had a little girl, Chiara Natalia Accardi, while Elisa and Caleb had a boy, Niccolo Alessandro Accardi. Caleb hasn't stopped winding his twin up about having super sperm because he produced an heir the first time.

"You need to educate yourself, Caleb," Gia says, looping her arm through her husband's as she joins him from the dance floor. The ladies have been dancing up a storm for the past hour. She wipes the back of her hand across her clammy brow before glaring at her brother-in-law. "Everyone knows women are the stronger sex, and it's Joshua who has the super sperm. You're just insulting yourself every time you spout that crap."

We all chuckle, and you won't find any of us disagreeing. No man here—Caleb included—believes women are the weaker sex. Not when our wives have each of us wrapped around their pinkies.

"Don Maltese, it's time to cut the cake," the wedding planner says, giving me a pointed look.

Handing my beer to Massimo, I waggle my brows and smirk. "Duty calls."

Epilogue Two
Valentina

"Happy, kitten?" Fiero asks, holding my hand over the large cake knife positioned on top of the bottom tier of our cake while our guests gather in front of us ready to take photos.

"Unbelievably so." Leaning back, I kiss him, and tons of flashes go off. "This is the best day of my life. I love you."

"Love you too, baby. You're so incredibly beautiful today. I can't believe you're mine."

I kiss him again even as I spy the wedding planner scowling in the background. Poor woman has been frazzled all day. I'll talk to Fiero about giving her a bonus because she's done an amazing job, and it's been a stress-free day for both of us.

We cut the cake to cheers from our friends and families, posing for a few more photos before accepting slices of the sumptuous lemon and vanilla cake Natalia insisted on making for our big day.

It's been a long time coming, but I'm glad we waited. Fiero was patient even though he wanted to do this way sooner, but I needed to focus on therapy, to process all my feelings from the things Dominic, Cruz, and Cesco had done to me and to come to terms with losing my baby. I needed time to grieve for my son and find a way to make peace with it.

For years, I compartmentalized my emotions. It was the only way I could cope. But they came crashing down around me in the aftermath of my kidnapping and assault, and I could no longer avoid dealing with them.

Fiero was so supportive. I couldn't have gotten through it without him. He was literally my rock, and I thank God every day for bringing him into my life. I'm living the dream now, and it's all thanks to the man with his arms around me, digging his hard-on into my back.

"Feel that, baby?" he purrs in my ear. "I need you."

"We have guests, and you fucked me in the car on the way here. You can wait another couple of hours." I say it, but he won't accept it. When it comes to me or sex with me, he's as unreasonable as he's always been. He'll get his way one way or another. I can't find it in me to protest. I love my husband just the way he is. I wouldn't want him to change a single thing. My sisters are all in love with him, hoping they find someone as amazing as Fiero when it's their turn to marry.

Thinking of the drive from the cathedral to here raises a smile to my lips. Fiero requested the privacy screen in the limo and then shoved his hands under the layers of my voluminous dress, pushing my underwear aside to impale me on his hard cock. It was hard and rough and everything I was craving. My pussy pulses in remembrance, my walls instantly soaking with a fresh wave of need.

I'm so hot for him and grateful for my compartmentalization skills that enable me to separate the things done to me against my will from my sex life with my husband. I never enjoyed sex until Fiero, which helped to keep them completely apart and ensure the trauma didn't affect my relationship with the man who is my everything.

"That was hours ago, kitten." He cops a cheeky feel of my ass through the dress. "You look like a princess in that dress. I've always wanted to defile a princess."

I snort out a laugh and swat his arm. "You're ridiculous and insatiable."

"Thought we'd already established that?" He arches a brow, and I stretch up and kiss him. Just because I can. Because I love him, and I love kissing him.

"We're leaving, Fiero," his mother says, forcing us to break our kiss and focus on them. "Your father is exhausted."

Roberto Maltese had a stroke four months ago that left him paralyzed and basically mute. He has problems speaking and understanding things going on around him. Fiero said it's an improvement and he didn't mind his father being here today because he can't spout any misogynistic shit. Right now, the retired don is dozing in his wheelchair, and it's hard to believe this fragile man was the tyrant who belittled my husband and tried to trample his free spirit.

"Thank you for coming," I say politely. I haven't worked out if Fiero's mother is just indifferent to me or if she doesn't like me. I've only met her a couple of times before today, and she's hard work. Cold and closed off. A little bitter too, if you ask me.

"We hope you're both very happy," she says, forcing a smile, before she pushes her husband away.

"It's a miracle my siblings and I are functioning humans with normal emotions and compassion for others," Fiero mutters, watching his parents leave. "We certainly didn't learn it from them."

"Maybe it was the things they didn't do that encouraged you all to become the opposite."

"Perhaps." Fiero plants a slew of feather-soft kisses up and down my neck while driving his cock against me and rubbing my ass. "Quickie upstairs in our suite now," he whispers in my ear.

"Valentina, come dance with me." My cousin Nina yanks me away from a grumbling Fiero, and he can do nothing as she drags me out onto the dance floor.

I blow him a kiss, giggling as he stomps off to rejoin his friends.

"This is the best wedding I've ever attended," Nina gushes, shimmying her hips and grinning as we join my siblings in a circle.

"I agree." My mom presses a kiss to my cheek. "It's been a wonderful day, and we're so happy for you, sweetie."

Fiero flew my family in four months ago after a session with my therapist where she suggested I needed to discuss everything with my parents. She believed I couldn't move on without confronting the hurt, resentment, and blame I felt toward them. Everyone stayed at our house in Long Island, and my husband took my sisters and brothers out for a couple of hours to give me privacy to talk with my parents.

It was an emotional afternoon. All of us broke down at one point. I haven't fully forgiven them, and I don't know if I ever will, but I understand it a little more. It wasn't deliberate or malicious. They thought Dominic would give me a good life.

Jacopo Pagano lied and made false representations to my parents, promising he'd ensure I was taken good care of. Before he died, he gave them fabricated reports of my marriage and my life in Miami, doctoring pictures and events to make it seem like I was happy. I hadn't told my siblings the truth of my situation because they were too young and I didn't want them worrying about me, and I refused to speak to my parents, so there was nothing to contradict what they'd been told.

I should have come clean, and they never should have forced me into an arranged marriage.

Taking What's Mine

My father broke apart when he discovered what Jacopo and Dominic had done to me that first night and for many other nights after. I know he feels huge guilt that won't ever go away.

It was a poignant reunion for all of us.

Since then, they have visited a couple of other times, and Fiero and I just bought a house in Detroit, ten minutes from my parents' house for future visits. I won't ever return permanently to Detroit. New York is my home now, but I want to catch up on lost time with my siblings, and it's easier for us to go to them.

We're still a work in progress, but I'm glad my parents were here today. Daddy gave me away, and it felt right.

Fiero chats with my dad and my older brother, keeping a watchful eye on me from the side of the dance floor as I dance with my mother, cousin, and the rest of my siblings, only stopping to throw the bouquet. I'm delighted when Tullia catches it, and it manages to put a smile back on her face. I'm not sure what's happened, but she disappeared for a while, returning with red-rimmed eyes and blotchy skin.

Nina comes with me when I need to pee, to help hold up my skirts. She's been the best bridesmaid, attentive and supportive all day.

As we are walking along the hallway, back toward the ball-room, I spot someone waiting for me. "You go on," I tell Nina. "I want to talk with Don DiPietro for a few minutes." My family knows about the baby I had with Cristian's older brother, but only my older siblings know the circumstances and they aren't privy to all the gory details. I don't want to give my sisters nightmares.

"You look beautiful, Valentina," Cristian says, keeping a few feet back from me on purpose, I'm guessing. "One of the most beautiful brides I've ever seen. Fiero is a lucky man."

"I think I'm the lucky one."

He smiles, gesturing toward an alcove tucked into the

window of the wedding venue. It's a private house on Long Island used solely for weddings. We rented the whole place including all the guest bungalows. My family and the bridal party are staying here tonight. "Could we talk for a few moments? I promise not to keep you from your groom for long."

"Of course." We haven't spoken at all since the baby shower last summer, but Fiero has spoken to Cristian and told him everything he needed to know.

We settle into opposite corners of the window seat, facing one another. "I'm so sorry for the things my brother did to you. I've been really upset since Fiero spoke with me."

"It's not your place to apologize for Cruz, Cristian. Though I appreciate the gesture, you have nothing to be sorry for. I apologize if I upset you or Elio that day at the shower. Seeing your gorgeous little boy made me think of the son I had to give away, and your resemblance to your brother sent me spiraling."

"I understand. I didn't know what I'd done to trigger you at the time, but it made sense when Fiero explained."

"I notice you didn't bring Elio today." Fiero and I discussed it, and I made sure his son was included on Cristian's invite, along with a plus one. "Was that for my benefit?"

"Mostly. I didn't want to upset you on your special day. He's also in the throes of the terrible twos, and I felt it was best to leave him with Isa."

"Your nanny?" I surmise.

He nods. "She's his biological aunt. On his mother's side," he adds. "The Da Rosa family weren't happy I wanted to adopt Elio. They wanted to adopt him too, but we reached an agreement, and part of it was Isa would help me to take care of him."

"Has it worked out?"

"For the most part, yes."

"I'm glad. He's a very handsome little boy."

"He's the best thing that's ever happened to me." His face

lights up as he smiles broadly, and looking at him now, I don't know how I ever thought he was the spitting image of his brother. Yes, they share similar features, but Cristian is nothing like Cruz. He's warm where his older brother was cold. Delightfully charismatic where Cruz was cruelly charming. Compassionate in place of Cruz's impassive nature.

"He is lucky to have you."

"I'm lucky to have him." The truth radiates on his face and resonates in his words.

Fiero told me Cristian's girlfriend, the woman he was hoping to marry, ditched him shortly after the adoption went through. It doesn't look like Cristian resents or regrets his decision even if it cost him the woman he planned to build a future with. If you ask me, he's better off without her anyway. *What woman walks away from a man she professes to love when he's made such a heartwarming sacrifice for his orphaned nephew?*

"At some point, I'd like to talk to you about those other women my brother impregnated."

"I'm not sure I'll be of much help, but reach out after we return from our honeymoon, and we can arrange to meet up."

"Thanks, Valentina." He pauses for a second, seemingly unsure if he can ask what he wants to ask.

"You can ask me."

"I don't want to pry or upset you, but I was wondering if you were planning to locate your baby and bring him home?"

Of course, he'd have a vested interest. My baby is his nephew and Elio's half-brother. "No," I quietly admit. "I wanted to at first, and Fiero was happy to support me whatever I wanted to do."

"He's a good man, and he'll make a great father."

"Yes, he is, and he will." I smile, rubbing at the little pain in my chest. I don't think I'll ever think of my firstborn son without a pain in my heart. "I can't be selfish," I admit. "My son has lived with his adopted parents for over a year. They love him, and he's theirs. I cannot take him from them. Legally, it wouldn't be possible, and I'm not kidnapping my child and putting his parents through that kind of hell. However, I still want to find him. To confirm Leandro is with good people. If he's not, that will change things."

"As it should. It's important to know he's being well cared for and loved." He trails a hand along his smooth jawline. "Will you make contact with the parents? Ask them for updates?"

Slowly, I shake my head. "I would love that but, given who his father was and the connections to *La Cosa Nostra*, I think it's safer not to talk to them. To keep him as removed from the *mafioso* as possible, at least for now."

"That's probably wise. I'd recommend having someone close by to keep an eye on him. My brother made a lot of enemies."

"Fiero already suggested the same thing, and we'll put that in motion as soon as we find him."

"Will the Camorra help?"

I nod. "Massimo and Bennett already spoke with them, and they agreed to locate him. Provided all is good, I think it's in everyone's best interests to leave things how they are, but I will contact him when he turns eighteen. I hope to form some kind of relationship with him then."

"You're a good person, Valentina. A selfless mother."

Tears stab my eyes, and Cristian reaches for me, hesitating at the last second. "Can I give you a hug?" he asks, and I nod. His arms are gentle as they fold around me. "In all the ways that count, you're my family, Valentina," he softly says as he hugs me. "I know you have Fiero, but if you ever need me, I'm only a phone call away. In time, you can meet Elio too, if you like?"

"Hands off my woman, DiPietro." Fiero's growl bounces off the walls of the alcove as he stalks toward us.

I roll my eyes as we break apart. "Ignore him. He's crazy."

Cristian grins. "We've all known that for years."

Fiero lifts me into his arms. "We've got an appointment with our suite. Catch you later, DiPietro."

"Fiero!" I thump on his chest. "Now everyone will know what we're up to!"

"Don't care, kitten." He slams his lips to mine as he strides along the hallway, his long legs eating up the distance to the stairs. "You okay?" His expression turns serious as he walks up the stairs with me in his arms.

My heart melts, and I wind my arms tighter around his neck. "I'm perfect. We had a good talk, and it helped. Cristian is a really nice guy."

Fiero grumbles again as he hits the landing, and I laugh. "You know I only have eyes for you. Everything I am and everything I have to give is yours and only yours."

"Fuck, I love you, Mrs. Maltese," he says, opening the door to our suite and stepping inside. "Even if this dress will be the death of me." He kicks the door closed with his foot before setting me down on the carpeted floor.

I spin around in my dress, loving how the chiffon layers fan out around me. There's a bunch of tulle under the chiffon, puffing out the lower part of the dress. If we'd gotten married in the summer, I'd never have been able to wear a dress like this in the heat, but it's perfect for a Saturday in mid-January.

The top part of the gown is a strapless, fitted corset style with a sweetheart neckline. The wide sash around my middle ties in an oversized bow that trails down the skirt a little. Diamante decorations, shaped like flowers, cover the dress from head to toe, sparkling and glittering under the old-world chandelier overhead.

"I might never take it off," I tease, still twirling around the room as he looks on in amusement. "I feel like a princess, and I never want this day to end."

Tears well in Fiero's eyes, and I slow down, concerned. "What's wrong, baby?"

"Absolutely nothing." He reels me into his arms, holding me tenderly and gazing down at me with so much love it blows my mind. "I'm so proud of you, kitten." He plants a sweet kiss on my lips. "You have been so strong, and I'm in awe of you."

"I couldn't have done it without you, Fiero." I cup his face. "You gave me strength on the days when it all felt insurmountable. You gave me a reason to get up out of bed each day. Your love lifted me up when I felt like crumbling to the floor."

"Are you good, baby?" His eyes probe mine. "Like really good?"

"Yes." I stretch up and kiss him. "I'm going to continue my therapy, but I've turned a corner, Fiero. I'm happier than I've ever been and ready to move forward in life with you."

Walking us backward, he presses me up against the wall. His blue eyes are earnest and full of emotion as he holds my hips and stares at me for a few intense beats. The vein in his neck is pulsing, and his heart beats frantically against my palm when I place my hand over his chest. I wait for him to say what he needs to say. The moment is thick with emotion, the atmosphere charged with our sizzling chemistry.

"I want to put a baby in you. Let me?"

I can barely speak over the messy ball of emotion clogging my throat. "Yes," I whisper, reaching up to cup his face. A giggle bursts free of my lips as tears shine in my eyes. "We are so in sync. I had my IUD removed earlier in the week, and I got a clean bill of health. I wanted it to be a surprise. A wedding gift of sorts. There is nothing standing in our way now. I know you're keen to start a family, and I'm on the same page. I want your babies, Don Maltese." Holding his stunned face in my hands, I kiss him fiercely. "I want lots of them."

"Hell yes." He sweeps me into his arms.

A delightful squeal falls from my lips as he tosses me on the bed and crawls over me. "Let's start right now."

Protecting What's Mine, Cristian DiPietro's story, is up next, coming in 2025. This is an age-gap, single dad, nanny-boss, forbidden, dark, stand-alone romance. Subscribe to my newsletter for all release information. Type this link into your browser: **https://bit.ly/SDRomanceNewsletter**

Start the *Mazzone Mafia* Series with *Condemned to Love*, a sister's ex, age-gap, secret baby/surprise pregnancy, second chance, dark, mafia stand-alone romance. Available now in ebook, paperback, hardcover and audio.

Her teen crush is now a ruthless killer and powerful mafia heir. Will one life-altering night unite or destroy them?

Bennett Mazzone grew up ignorant of the truth: he is the illegitimate son of the most powerful mafia boss in New York. Until it suited his father to drag him into a world where power, wealth, violence, and cruelty are the only currency.

Celebrating her twenty-first birthday in Sin City should be fun for Sierra Lawson, but events take a deadly turn when she ends up in a private club, surrounded by dangerous men who always get what they want.

And they want _her_.

Ben can't believe his ex's little sister is all grown up, stunningly beautiful, and close to being devoured by some of the most ruthless men he has ever known. The Vegas trip is about strengthening ties, but he won't allow his associates to ruin her perfection. Although it comes at a high price, saving Sierra is his only choice.

The memory of Ben's hands on her body is seared into Sierra's flesh for eternity. She doesn't regret that night. Not even when she discovers the guy she was crushing on as a teenager is a cold, calculating killer with dark impulses and lethal enemies who want him dead.

Understanding the risks, she walks away from the only man she will ever love, stowing her secrets securely in her heart. Until the truth becomes leverage and Sierra is drawn into a bloody war—a pawn in a vicious game she doesn't want to play.

As the web of deceit is finally revealed, Ben will stop at nothing to protect Sierra. Even if loving her makes him weak. In a world where women serve a sole purpose, and alliances mean the difference between life and death, can he fight for love and win?

CLAIM YOUR FREE EBOOK – ONLY AVAILABLE TO NEWSLETTER SUBSCRIBERS!

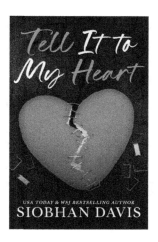

The boy who broke my heart is now the man who wants to mend it.

Jared was my everything until an ocean separated us and he abandoned me when I needed him most.

He forgot the promises he made.

Forgot the love he swore was eternal.

It was over before it began.

Now, he's a hot commodity, universally adored, and I'm the woman no one wants.

Pining for a boy who no longer exists is pathetic. Years pass, men come and go, but I cannot move on.

I didn't believe my fractured heart and broken soul could endure any more pain. Until Jared rocks up to the art gallery where I work, with his fiancée in tow, and I'm drowning again.

Seeing him brings everything to the surface, so I flee. Placing distance between us again, I'm determined to put him behind me once and for all.

Then he reappears at my door, begging me for another chance.

I know I should turn him away.

Try telling that to my heart.

———————

This angsty, new adult romance is a FREE full-length ebook, exclusively available to newsletter subscribers.

Type this link into your browser to claim your free copy:
https://bit.ly/TITMHFBB

OR

Scan this code to claim your free copy:

About the Author

Siobhan Davis™ is a *USA Today, Wall Street Journal*, and Amazon Top 5 bestselling romance author. **Siobhan** writes emotionally intense stories with swoon-worthy romance, complex characters, and tons of unexpected plot twists and turns that will have you flipping the pages beyond bedtime! She has sold over 2 million books, and her titles are translated into several languages.

Prior to becoming a full-time writer, Siobhan forged a successful corporate career in human resource management.

Siobhan currently lives with her husband in Cyprus while their two grown-up sons reside at the family home in Ireland.

You can connect with Siobhan in the following ways:

Website: www.siobhandavis.com
Facebook: AuthorSiobhanDavis
Instagram: @siobhandavisauthor
Tiktok: @siobhandavisauthor
Email: siobhan@siobhandavis.com

Books By Siobhan Davis

NEW ADULT ROMANCE

The One I Want Duet
Kennedy Boys Series
Rydeville Elite Series
All of Me Series
Forever Love Duet

NEW ADULT ROMANCE STAND-ALONES

Inseparable
Incognito
Still Falling for You
Holding on to Forever
Always Meant to Be
Tell It to My Heart
*Never Stopped Loving You**

REVERSE HAREM

Sainthood Series
Dirty Crazy Bad Duet
Surviving Amber Springs (stand-alone)
Alinthia Series

DARK MAFIA ROMANCE

Mazzone Mafia Series
Vengeance of a Mafia Queen (stand-alone)
The Accardi Twins
Taking What's Mine
Protecting What's Mine*

YA SCI-FI & PARANORMAL ROMANCE

Saven Series
*Broken World Series^*

---

*Coming 2025
^Previously the True Calling Series

www.siobhandavis.com

Printed in Great Britain
by Amazon

47448597R00229